AS GOD PLAYED HIS FIDDLE

BOBAN JOVANOVSKI

RIVER GROVE
BOOKS

Published by River Grove Books
Austin, TX
www.rivergrovebooks.com

Distributed by River Grove Books

Design and composition by Greenleaf Book Group
Cover design by Greenleaf Book Group

Publisher's Cataloging-in-Publication data is available.

Print ISBN: 978-1-966629-38-2

eBook ISBN: 978-1-966629-39-9

First Edition

To my mother

Preface

When I was twelve years old, I traveled from Detroit to spend the summer of 1980 visiting my grandmother, who lived in the village of Vratnica, in what was then Yugoslavia. One day, after attending a festival in another town, some friends and I were waiting for a bus to take us home. At the bus stop, we saw a man from our village. His name was Tome, and he was a hunchback. To look at Tome, you would swear he'd swung out of the pages of a Victor Hugo novel or sprang to life from the imagination of a Hollywood makeup artist. His body was so ghoulishly twisted, his ears so unnaturally large, his eyes so misshapen, what few teeth he had so rotted and crooked that he looked more monster than man. He made for such an inescapable figure—short, ungainly, and imperfect—that the villagers called him Tome Djudja (a bastardization of the word *midget*).

As we waited for the bus, I noticed Tome trying to put the head back on a doll. It was a flimsy figurine—made of thin plastic, with a painted-on face, and unconvincing brown tresses sprouting from its head. It was a doll that American girls would have tossed away long before it sullied their collection of Barbies. But in the austerity of Slavic village life—where money was scarce and spending it on toys was considered wasteful and bordered on sinfully indulgent—the doll might as well have come out of an FAO Schwarz catalog.

As I sat a few feet away, I watched Tome struggling with the doll and becoming distraught that he couldn't reattach the head. He looked up and asked in frustration if I could help. He gave me the doll, but unfortunately it was so cheaply made that trying to put the head back on was futile. When I told him that I couldn't get the head to stay on either, tears welled up in his eyes. He told me that he had promised a little girl he would bring her a doll, and he'd spent the only money he had on it. Now, he would have nothing to give her. I remember looking at him and being moved. Here was a man who seemed to be scarred by the hand of God Himself. A man who wasn't given even the most modest of blessings. Yet, he wasn't brought to tears out of self-pity or in anger, but from knowing he was going to disappoint a child. It was a moment of such genuine and unfiltered caring that it imprinted itself on me, and it made me feel ashamed. Ashamed for all the times I might have recoiled at the sight of him. Ashamed for ever having thought he was somehow lesser than me. Ashamed for not being a better person.

That was the inspirational seed that was planted what seems like a lifetime ago and eventually would grow into my novel—*As God Played His Fiddle.*

The main character, Ari, was inspired by Tome. However, this story doesn't take place on the hills and mountains of Yugoslavia but rather starts in Ottoman Turkey in the late nineteenth century and ends in America a generation later. Ari, a hunchback as well, is a poor and outcast Armenian living through a ruthless genocide. Like Tome, fate gave Ari no advantages. His struggles go beyond trying to survive the brutality of Ottoman Turkey. He must endure intense poverty, complete alienation, and his own self-loathing for falling short of being the man he so desperately wants to be—the man he needs to be.

Even though this story takes us on a journey of struggle and survival, in the end it's about salvation. However, Ari's salvation won't come from worshipping an idol on a crucifix, but from having the strength to sacrifice and the courage to care. Ari's redemption will come in giving others a gift. The gift of life to a child, and the gift of hope to that child's father. And in the end, he becomes the man he never thought possible.

I recall boarding the bus with Tome that day. I walked behind him as he held the doll's body in one hand and its head in another. I imagined the passengers looking at him and thinking, *What a savage this hideous creature must be, to find sport in dismembering a child's toy.* I learned then how deceitful our eyes can be.

Tome would die not long after that summer. I often wondered what he thought of his life when he passed away. In the end, I wish he looked at himself more as the man I saw that day than the monster his appearance would suggest. I hope he was happy, but I don't know. I do know that he gave someone a gift that day. It wasn't the gift he set out to give on that summer afternoon. It was the gift of inspiration.

And for that, I wish I could have told him thank you.

—Boban Jovanovski

Jephthah answered, "I and my people were engaged in a great struggle with the Ammonites, and although I called, you didn't save me out of their hands."

—Judges 12:2

Contents

Book I

1

The Waif

For most, the cemetery in the town of Van in Ottoman Turkey was a place to remember, to honor, and to grieve. For Ari, it was a place to wonder. Ari's first memory of the cemetery was when he was three years old. His mother took him there to light a candle on his grandfather's grave.

He remembered his mother kissing the tombstone and saying, "Your grandfather is buried here. He only had me, and I know he would have been proud to have a grandson. He would have loved you so much, Ari. Oh, how he would have loved you."

Ari recalled turning away from the grave, lest it had eyes. He feared that the eternal love his mother spoke of would be dashed if his grandfather could actually see him.

Now as an eleven-year-old Armenian, he often spent the fading years of the nineteenth century alone in that dirty and empty cemetery. Even at a young age, Ari knew how different he was from other children. He was a hunchback and noticed the unsettling way people initially looked at him. He had soft brown eyes, but while his right eye appeared normal, his left eye had a rounder shape and the eyelid could barely close over it.

He was small even for his age and was so thin that his crooked body looked like a series of knobby joints connecting a network of bones. His face was long and narrow and dominated by his large ears and nose. His dark black hair accented an appearance that looked more suited to a caricaturist's canvas than the towns and villages of the Ottoman Empire.

Besides looking different, the only other thing he knew with certainty was that he was poor. Poverty wasn't unique in Van. Many families made do off the strength of their backs and the concessions of their stomachs, but Ari was poor even among the poor. He had no money, no property, no one besides his mother to call family, and no place in any clan—be it Turkish or Armenian.

As he was sitting in front of his grandfather's grave, he pulled out a medal from his pocket. He fumbled with it, feeling its weight as he passed it from hand to hand. It was an unlikely item for an Armenian peasant to have. The Order of Osmanieh, which Ari was holding, was one of the most prestigious honors within the Ottoman Empire. Sultan Abdulaziz created the order in 1862, and it was awarded to Ottoman civil servants and military leaders for their outstanding service to the state.

As Ari handled the medal, he looked up at his grandfather's tombstone. It was an austere marker, just a simple stone cross with an inscription that read:

MARDIROS HOVHANNISYAN

1828–1884

"A NOBLE FATHER"

Ari had always considered the tombstone too modest for a man he had never met but whom he nonetheless regarded with great admiration and love, and whose medal he was holding. Ari's grandfather died prior to his birth, and the medal became an heirloom. His mother wrapped the medal in the swaddle of his birth blanket, and it had been with him ever since.

As Ari sat with his legs crossed, staring at the grave, a pigeon flew overhead. The distraction was enough for him to realize he had spent most of his day at the graveyard, and he decided to leave for the shores of Lake Van. He headed out of the cemetery, toward the northern hills that dropped directly onto the more secluded areas of the lake.

As he neared the lake, he breathed in the crisp air, wondering what it was like for his grandfather to have sailed the seas. His grandfather had been a merchant sailor in the town of Trabzon, a Black Sea port that lies on the historic Silk Road. Of all the stories his mother told him about his grandfather, Ari was captivated most by his adventures at sea.

He glimpsed the lake as the path he was on descended toward the shore. When the beach came into view, Ari saw a group of men. He fell back and hid behind an outcrop of rocks that jutted out in a semiarch from the side of the hill. No sooner than he did, he heard a blast echo from the beach. The sound startled Ari, and he felt his hands become wet and clammy.

He heard voices coming from the shore, some forty yards away. He calmed himself enough to peer through a sliver between the rocks and saw four men standing over a fifth, who had blood pouring from his head.

He looked closer and recognized one of the men, who had his hands tied behind his back, as a local Armenian leader. Another he knew to be a local Turkish official. Surrounding the Armenian were two men dressed in Hamidiye uniforms.

The Hamidiye were a light cavalry made of irregular Kurds, created by Sultan Abdul Hamid II to deal with rebellions and other threats to the eastern part of the empire.

The Turkish man seemed to be the one in charge. He was short and heavyset, with a thick mustache and wearing a black robe and a white turban.

"The Armenians are a scourge upon our great land," said the Turk to the Armenian. "They cleanse themselves in our waters, they fatten on the fruits of our soil, and they enrich themselves on our goodwill. But when you ask them, 'Is the empire great? Is the land that you live and rear your children in worthy of sacrifice? Is not Allah's mercy visited on you daily?' They say no!

"They speak of countrymen that live over mountains and beyond borders, and not the neighbor that extends a Turkish hand in brotherhood. They say they believe in God, but they are not humble before Allah. Instead, they mock His greatness with shiny baubles of a false religion."

"That's not so, Faruk," said the Armenian. "Our fight isn't with the Turks or the Ottomans, nor is our fight with Islam. Our struggle is with injustice. And in this we ask that all, be they Turkish, Kurdish, or Armenian, join in our struggle. For our fight is not fought with guns and swords, ours is fought with principles and truths."

"So, is it truth that you seek, Datev?" Faruk smirked. "What can you know of truth? You live in a land of Islam, yet you reject the Prophet and instead tell us a man is God. But I have not come here to deliver a sermon. Today, I've come to take payment for your treason to the empire. Allah will take His payment on your soul."

"If my blood is the price you seek, then you needn't delay any longer in collecting it," Datev said. "It would seem a small fee, as I'm neither a man of power nor distinction. I'll be forgotten soon enough, if I die here on this beach today or if I die as an old man in my own bed. But what you cannot kill is empathy, humanity, liberty—values that will haunt you no matter what just God you pray to. So, I beg you, my Turkish brother, don't spare your bullets. Grant me the honor to die today, while I still have those values surging in my veins and not as an empty old man atop a bed of doubt and regret."

One of the Kurds raised his gun and put it to the Armenian's temple, but Faruk motioned to him not to shoot.

"It's a reckless man that challenges the sultan's rule, and a foolish one that will not repent even before the Almighty," Faruk said. "I, too, am a man of ideals, and I believe in this great land, and my faith is in Allah, who will protect us from all threats to our empire. But you have your own mighty God. Is your faith in Him misplaced as well? If you pray to Him now, will he deliver you from death? As a pious man, I'll not deny you the chance to pray."

Datev straightened his posture, looked Faruk in the eyes, and shook his head. With that, the Kurd pulled the trigger. Ari's body shook with the gunfire, and he watched the man drop to the ground. Heart racing, he prayed he could remain undetected.

Faruk reached inside of his robe, then unfolded a letter-sized white sheet of paper. He looked at the letter briefly, then bent down and stuffed it in the shirt pocket of the murdered Armenian.

"Should we move the bodies?" one of the Kurds asked.

"No, leave them here," Faruk responded. "We're not too far from town. Someone will discover them soon enough. And if not, then we have prepared a feast for the wolves."

The men chuckled as they moved in Ari's direction. Ari looked around the rocks for a better hiding place until he saw a small opening at the base of the hill. Shielded by the rocks, he darted toward it and squeezed into the opening, scratching his back in the process. He found himself in a dark cave only about five feet deep. The only light came from the gap from which he entered, but otherwise he was engulfed in complete darkness.

"The Armenians are an infestation," Faruk said to the two Kurds as they walked. "A disease that seeks to make feeble our great empire and one that will not stop until all Turkish heads are bowed with shame."

"And how do we treat this disease?" asked one of the Kurds.

"The Armenian issue, as yet, has no answer. Wiser men than me are discussing it and planning on the proper course of action. It's our duty to carry out those actions, whatever they may be."

As the footsteps approached, Ari pulled as far back into the shadows of the cave as he could. He held his breath and waited. Within seconds, two of the men walked within a couple of yards of his hiding spot. He could see their legs from the opening of the cave. They stopped and looked back for their remaining companion. As Ari continued looking through the gap, a shadow fell on the opening. Ari tensed up and covered his mouth to keep from making a sound. He noticed that one of the Kurds had leaned against the boulders to shake sand from his boots. He could see the dramatic curved sheath that housed the Kurd's kilij sword swaying between the opening.

"Are we to remain in Van or are we to return to our post?" the Kurd asked.

"You shall stay here for the day. I have a meeting this evening," Faruk responded. "We'll see if there is any further assistance you can provide. Your horses should be well-rested and fed. You'll be able to return to your post by tomorrow evening."

As the men talked, Ari's body shifted inside the cave causing a rustling sound, and he heard Faruk tell the others to be quiet. Ari pressed himself against the wall of the cave. His heart beat faster, as he feared he had been detected. He saw the shadow begin to move and realized that the Kurd had bent down to look between the rocks. Ari pulled back deeper, flattening himself even more against the inside wall to avoid being seen.

"There's something inside the cave. I can hear it," one of the Kurds said.

"Whatever it is, kill it," Faruk instructed.

With the opening too small for the Kurd to enter, he took out his sword and began thrusting it in. He stabbed at different angles, each time getting closer and closer to Ari, who was moving inside the hollow, trying to anticipate the jabs and no longer worrying about the noise he was making. On the third thrust, Ari heard a shriek and saw something dart in front of him, through the opening, and past the three men.

"Only a cursed cat." Faruk laughed.

The Kurd remained at the opening, looking into the cave, trying to penetrate the darkness with his eyes. He gave another thrust of his sword, which hit the wall of the rock just two inches to the left of Ari, who remained frozen. Ari held his breath, awaiting another jab of the sword, but no more came. He then heard the man begin to move away.

After a few minutes, Ari peered through the hole and his eyes locked on the portion of the path he could see from his hiding spot. No one was there, nor could he hear any more footsteps. Several more minutes passed before he emerged from the cave.

When he came out, he scanned the entire area until his eyes fell on the bodies on the beach. He walked over and looked down at them. It wasn't the first time he'd looked at dead bodies, but this sight was not what he expected. Something about the men seemed odd to him. They looked peaceful. Their faces were clean and unmarked, with no hint of terror or anguish, even as they lay on a beach saturated with their own blood.

As he was standing over the bodies, Ari took out his medal and looked at it. He closed his fist around it and looked at the men again. For some reason, he didn't feel afraid any longer.

A cool breeze swept across the beach. Ari peeled his eyes from the men, looked up at the sun, and realized it was getting late. He knew his mother would be waiting for him at the center of town and she needed his help to walk the four miles to home. Ari walked in the opposite direction from the path the men left on and picked up another trail farther down the shoreline.

Once he safely got on the trail, he ran as fast as he could toward the center of town.

2

The Order of Osmanieh

The Order of Osmanieh was strikingly regal. The medal was a seven-pointed star coated in green enamel. There were two concentric circles within the star. The outer circle was a thinner band, also in green enamel, while the inner central circle was covered in red enamel. There was a design of a crescent at the bottom of the central circle and an inscription above the crescent that read *"Relying on the Assistance of Almighty God, Abdulaziz Khan, Sovereign of the Ottoman Empire."* The words on Ari's medal were all still legible even though there was a deep cut that ran across the red enamel. The back contained a circular gilt medallion bearing a trophy of arms and the date AH 699—the year the Ottoman Empire was founded.

It was only by chance that the medal in Ari's hands had found its way to his grandfather, Mardiros.

On the day that Ari's mother, Mariam, was born, Mardiros also became a widower, losing his wife to complications in childbirth. Nonetheless, he gave Mariam a happy childhood. Mardiros made a modest living by mining copper in the Turkish town of Diyarbakir, but his real love was the sea. When he was younger, he worked on merchant ships. Mardiros was part of a crew that would take cargo and sail west from Trabzon to the Bosporus Strait and then through the strait until they reached the Ottoman capital of Istanbul. The smell of the sea and the sense of freedom the open water gave him stayed dear to him until the day he died.

Mardiros left his job as a sailor shortly after Mariam was born, and he began working in the copper mines of Diyarbakir. The mines, although lacking the allure of the sea, gave him something more important—the ability to stay near his daughter. The love of the sea never left him, and in his spare time, he built a dinghy, which he would use to take Mariam and some of the town's children for rides on the Tigris River. These excursions made him popular among the children, who affectionately referred to him as Admiral Mardiros. One of Mariam's fondest memories was her father coming home after a long week of work with a jar of honey, which she would eat while they floated down the Tigris.

One spring afternoon, Mariam asked if she could spend the day with a friend. Mardiros agreed, and having free time, he decided to take his boat out on the river alone. As Mardiros guided his vessel down the Tigris, in what was an unusually strong current, he noticed a young boy playing in shallow waters near the shore.

"Help, someone! My son's in the river!" Mardiros heard a woman screaming from the riverbank.

He looked toward the shouts and realized the boy he had seen earlier had been swept into the river. The child didn't travel far before he was wedged in between some slippery boulders, which he clung to for his life. Two men began wading into the water to try to reach the boy, while another woman was holding the mother from entering the river.

"Hold on, darling! Hold on!" the boy's mother pleaded, even as the waters battered her son.

Mardiros noticed that neither of the men had the footing to reach the child. If the child wasn't rescued before being dislodged from the rocks, then the current would certainly pull him into deeper and more dangerous waters, making any chance of survival slim. Without hesitation, Mardiros maneuvered his boat to the shore just downriver of the boy. When he reached the shore, he swiftly exited his craft and tied a rope around a tree. He tied the other end around his waist and waded into the waters. Knowing he only had one chance to save the boy, he positioned himself in the boy's anticipated path and yelled for the child to let go. The child, still clinging to the rocks, couldn't hear him over the pounding waters and the desperate cries of his mother, who had begun entering the river herself.

Eventually, the boy's arms gave out, and the waters carried him downriver, farther away from shore. Mardiros waded out into the river as far as he could, stretching the slack of the rope to its extreme, while still struggling to maintain the footing he would need to absorb the impact and secure the boy. His heart sank as he realized that the rope wasn't going to afford him the length he needed to intercept the child. And then, as he pulled against the rope trying to stretch as far as he could, something miraculous happened. The current shifted violently and sent the boy within reach, and just as the child was about to pass him, Mardiros managed to grab hold of the boy's shirt and pull him in. Once Mardiros had the boy safely in his arms, he used the rope to pull himself and the child to shore. The boy, although frightened and shivering, was uninjured.

In the confusion of the rescue, Mardiros realized he had forgotten to secure his boat. He could only watch helplessly, on his knees, as the boat faded down the river, lost forever.

Screams shocked Mardiros out of his daze. The boy's mother was a middle-aged Turkish woman, and upon seeing that her son was safe, grabbed Mardiros's hand. Amid tears she kissed it, bowed, and thanked him for saving her son's life.

The next day, the boy's father, a military leader from Istanbul, came to see Mardiros at his home with a gift—the Order of Osmanieh.

"Please accept this as a symbol of my everlasting gratitude," he said to Mardiros as he presented the medal while standing on the dirt floor of Mardiros's modest kitchen. "The sultan bestowed this honor upon me for my humble service to the empire. I now place it in more worthy hands. May Allah always protect you and your family."

The man left with his family for Istanbul later that same day. Mardiros never saw him again, but the story grew into legend in Diyarbakir, and like most legends, it wasn't immune to embellishment. Scarcely a month would go by without a child in town asking Mardiros about the day he swam through the storm-battered waters of the Mediterranean to rescue the sultan's son. Or to describe the royal palace on the day he received his medal.

He would smile and tell them it was grand.

3

Hunger Comes upon You Like a Thief

Ari approached the town square and spotted his mother sitting in her customary spot—a stoop just off the main road. Visitors came into the town square from the south and would enter a dusty plaza with tightly packed buildings that formed a semicircle. During the day, there was a constant stream of people crisscrossing the circular plaza. The better-dressed men—Turks wearing decorative long robes, Armenians in Western suits—could be seen walking to and from the courthouse that sat on a hill on the north side of the plaza. Next to the courthouse stood a medical clinic that was operated by a doctor with a strange accent.

There was a post office tucked in the middle of a row of buildings on the right. Ari had considered the post office a magical portal run by wizards and warlocks ever since his mother told him that inside they could send messages to London simply by tapping buttons. Ari would take great measures to avoid the post office. If he had to pass in front of it, he would walk around its doors in a broad arch, lest the sorcery within run amok and sweep him off to some strange land. Directly across from the post office were a cluster of shops and administrative offices, and Mariam's stoop sat at the end of them.

At one time, Mariam had been a beautiful and vibrant woman, who would dive into the Tigris, seemingly mocking the river as she would swim effortlessly. But as she sat on the stoop now, it was clear that hard years had taken their toll on her. She could only walk with the help of a cane, a result of a shattered leg that was never set properly. Her health had deteriorated through a combination of poor nutrition and living conditions, and she had a deep scar on her neck that she would hide with a scarf.

Mariam's physical condition prevented her from working most jobs, so to make money, she would sit on the stoop with her threads and needles, hoping to find someone willing to pay for a small repair. It was mostly a fruitless endeavor. When she began her solicitations, she got by more on the goodwill of the town residents than any real demand for her services. Some people would occasionally drop coins on her lap as they passed by, while others would pay for her services even if they didn't have a real need.

Charity, however, had its limits. Sympathetic at first, townspeople soon grew wary, seeing their tokens had little effect on Mariam. She was still thin, she was still frail, she was still sick, and she was still poor. And, after a time, when they walked by and saw her sad condition, the sight only bred apathy.

Ari could see concern on his mother's face as he approached, and he thought that maybe she somehow knew what he'd just witnessed at the lake.

"Ari, I thought you'd be here an hour ago," his mother said in a voice that was barely above a whisper due to her damaged throat. "You gave me a fright. I thought the lake had swallowed you."

"I'm sorry. I wa-wa-was playing, and I fo-fo-forgot what time it wa-was," Ari stuttered.

"Were other children at the lake with you? What were you doing to be so late today?"

"Yes, th-th-there were a lot of kids from town. Almost everyone was th-th-there. We were throwing rocks at the cats, and we were playing games on the shore," answered Ari, his stuttering abating as he got deeper into the lie.

"I told you never to throw rocks at animals," she said angrily.

"I know."

"Please don't do it again."

"I won't. I promise."

His mother looked at him, and a smile slowly crept over her face.

"I have a surprise for you." She opened her hand and proudly showed him two five-lira coins. "I had some customers today. I was waiting for you to come before the market closed so we could buy some lavash and cheese."

Ari returned his mother's smile with a bigger one. Fresh lavash— Armenian flatbread—and cheese were a rare treat for them, and Ari viewed the promise of the modest meal as a virtual cornucopia.

Their nightly meal would usually consist of a stew of potatoes or beans, only because they were cheap and wouldn't spoil. However, they had run out of both, so the money Mariam made came just in time. The anticipation of the night's feast lifted his spirits, and for a minute he even forgot about the scene at the lake.

"Don't just stand there, Ari, help your mother get to her feet so we can make it to the market before they sell out of bread," said Mariam as she nudged him with her cane.

Ari offered his mother his shoulder, and she lifted herself off the stoop. Before they began to walk, he looked up at her and gave her a hug.

Mariam held her cane with one hand and put the other on Ari's shoulder, and they shuffled forward. It was getting late. The bustle of the town center was gone, and the last remaining people began making their way home. The market was a ten-minute walk, but for Ari and Mariam it was a much longer process. However, eventually they got into a rhythm and were making steady progress.

"Can I pay for the bread?" Ari asked.

"Yes, of course," replied his mother. "And when we get home, I'll make some tea, and we can eat and tell stories by the fire."

"Can you tell me about the time Grandfather's ship was attacked?" asked Ari, referring to an incident in which pirates boarded his grandfather's merchant ship. His mother smiled and gave him a nod.

The pair were about halfway to their destination when Ari heard footsteps approaching them from behind.

"Let us help you," said a deep voice as Ari and his mother rounded a corner and started walking down a descending road. Ari turned to see two Turkish men who looked to be in their twenties. Ari didn't recognize the two, and he tried to ignore them as they advanced on him and his mother.

"Allow us to carry your needles and help you along your way," one of the men said. Both were tall, had well-groomed handlebar mustaches, high cheek bones, and narrow dark eyes. They were each dressed in gray Western-style suits, including matching vests and bowties. To complete their identical attire, each wore a red fez—a flattop cylindrical Turkish headpiece—with a black tassel. They looked so much alike that Ari thought they could be brothers.

"Thank you, but my son and I can manage. We don't have too much farther to go," a startled Mariam said.

Ari looked around and saw that the streets were deserted. They were on the old and empty part of the road with only a line of crumbling houses on their right and a high retaining wall on their left. The only sound he could hear was the running water of an irrigation canal on the other side of the retaining wall.

"Yes, yes. Of course, of course, you have a fine son," the man said as he patted Ari on the hump of his back. "They say a mother's love for her son will outlast time, but sadly a son's love for his mother oftentimes falls to his ambition. Such is the nature of man. But this boy, no, this boy will never leave you.

"But we must insist. Would you have us retire for the evening with the knowledge that our hands idled while we watched a humble woman and her young son struggle down the road? We could not call ourselves good Muslims."

Before Mariam could utter another word, one of the men gently took her sewing kit while the other replaced Ari's shoulder with his arm, steadying Mariam and guiding her securely down the road.

"My name is Mahmut, and this is my friend Jabari. May I ask where you're heading this late afternoon?" said the man holding Mariam's arm.

"To the market," said Mariam nervously.

Such an act of kindness wasn't common, especially from someone Ari had never seen. Sensing his mother's nervousness, Ari felt more uneasy.

"Ah, the market," Mahmut said. "I'm afraid that if we continue on this path, any attempt to reach the proprietors before they conclude their day will be mere folly. Let us divert to a different route, one whose flat ground is more welcoming to tired feet."

"Thank you both," Mariam replied. "But we can see the market from here. I'm sure me and my son can make the final distance on our own. But I do thank you for your kindness."

"No, no, we insist," said Mahmut as he and his friend directed Mariam down a narrow and crooked road that branched off to the right.

It was a road Ari never ventured down, mostly because it led to the poorest Muslim section of the city. And even though the area was the ugliest and least desirable part of Van, its young inhabitants maintained a zealous watch over its borders. If its perimeter was breached even slightly by their Christian counterparts, the Muslim children would rally in defense of their ragged Jerusalem—protecting every dirty inch as if thwarting a crusade.

The prospect of getting a beating at the hands of a group of Turkish boys crossed Ari's mind and he hesitated as they stepped on the road. He began lagging and saw the men took little notice of him as they guided his mother along. Putting his fear aside, Ari quickened his pace until he was once again beside his mother and grabbed a fistful of Mariam's worn-thin cotton dress and held on tightly. He felt his mother's arm around his shoulder, and he looked up at her. He saw her looking at him, doing her best to hide her fear and reassure him. He was not as naive as he knew his mother thought he was. So, he tried to look reassured and hoped he was more convincing in fooling her than she was in fooling him.

They hadn't walked more than twenty paces down the new road when Jabari, who had been silent up to this point, stopped and said, "It's getting late, Mahmut, we have to leave."

"Ah yes," Mahmut replied. "In our haste to provide a modest

service to you and your son, I forgot that we had an appointment that we cannot miss. You will forgive us if we depart before we escort you to your destination."

"Of course, I thank you for your kindness," Mariam said.

"Gratitude, indeed, is a grand honor," Mahmut said. "There is no richer payment one person can give to another than gratitude. It humbles he whom it is bestowed upon, and leaves a man ashamed of receiving such a gift. For whom among men is truly worthy of gratitude? No, no, we cannot accept such an undeserving recompense."

And with that, the man bowed and turned to walk away. But after a few paces Mahmut turned back toward Mariam.

"But if you insist on payment, then we should not deny you your kind gesture, and we will accept something of lesser value," he said. "What of a few liras? Although gratitude feeds the soul, money feeds the stomach, and as of late I must regrettably admit that my friend and I have been attending to the former at the expense of the latter."

"I . . . I'm just a poor woman and have no money," said Mariam as she pulled Ari closer to her and clutched her fist to hide her coins.

"Such modesty, your virtues indeed seem to have no bounds," Mahmut said. "As we witnessed today, you are a gifted seamstress. You would be sewing clothes for the sultan had he any idea of your talents. But we will leave you to your modesty. Give us the money you earned today, and we will be on our way."

Just as Ari had feared, the magnanimity of the two men was a ruse, and it was now clear that they had come to rob his mother. His fear was soon confirmed when Jabari roughly pried open his mother's hand.

Ari's first instinct was to run, but he couldn't leave his mother, so he inched closer to her and buried his face into the abrasive fabric of her dirty sweater.

"Please, this is all the money we have," said Mariam as the man succeeded in opening her hand and taking the coins.

Ari buried his face deeper into his mother's side, clutching her even harder. Once they took the coins, the men tossed Mariam's sewing items on the ground, and the two thieves turned to walk away. In a desperate plea, Mariam grabbed Mahmut's arm. "Please, we have nothing to eat."

Mahmut stopped and looked down at Mariam, and without a word, struck her hard across the face—sending her and Ari crashing to the ground. Ari held his mother tighter and buried his face even deeper into her side, scared to the point of being incapacitated.

"If you lay your filthy hands on me again, it'll be more than your money that you'll lose, witch," said Mahmut.

Mahmut picked up Mariam's cane and stood over his two victims. He swung the cane, and it landed, with a deep thud, across Mariam's back. She instinctively covered Ari and raised her arm to defend as the second blow slammed against her forearm, causing her arm to go numb and fall to her side. No longer able to ward off the strikes with her arms, Mariam curled around Ari and absorbed four more blows on her shoulders and back without letting the wooden cane hit her son.

Mahmut stopped his assault, standing in silence as he listened to Mariam's whimpers of pain and Ari's muffled sobs. He gave his victims a final disgusted look, spat on them, and tossed the cane to the ground.

The two thieves pocketed their small booty and walked away, leaving Mariam and Ari helplessly clutching each other on the cold and empty dirt road.

4

Akhtamar Island

khtamar Island, lying nearly two miles off the south-east shoreline of Lake Van, got its name from an old Armenian legend. According to the story, an Armenian princess named Tamar lived on the island and fell in love with a commoner. Tamar's father disapproved of the relationship and forbade his daughter from seeing the boy. Against her father's wishes, Tamar and her young lover resolved to continue their relationship without her father's knowledge. The two devised a plan in which the boy would swim from the shore to the island each night, guided only by a light that Tamar secretly lit for him. Her father soon learned of the boy's nightly visits and was determined to put an end to them. One night, after Tamar lit her flame and waited for her lover to arrive, her father found the light and extinguished it. The boy, who had already begun swimming toward the island, found himself in the middle of the lake without a beacon to guide him. In the black of night, he no longer knew which direction to swim. The following day, his lifeless body washed ashore. When they turned the dead boy over and looked at his face, the words "*Akh*, Tamar" (Oh, Tamar) appeared frozen on his lips.

During his reign from 908 to 944 AD, the Armenian king Gagik I Artsruni chose the island as one of his residences. By the turn of the twentieth century, most of the king's structures were gone. What was left were monastic buildings and the Church of the Holy Cross. For more than seven centuries, Akhtamar Island was the location of the Armenian ecclesiastical primacy, and the Church of the Holy Cross was one of its most important shrines.

=====

Inside the Church of the Holy Cross, the serving Catholicos—the head of the Church—was deep in thought, sitting alone at one end of the building. Armenian clergymen filled the room, nervously conferring with one another, but none dared disturb their leader.

"Have we had word from Van?" asked the Catholicos as he broke his meditation.

The murmuring ceased, and all eyes turned to a single bishop, who was stationed at the doors of the church.

"Not yet, Your Holiness. We should expect their arrival momentarily," the bishop replied.

"Indeed. Alert me when they have arrived," said the Catholicos.

"I shall, Your Holiness."

=====

At the same time in another church within Van, Father Krikor Avedisian paced back and forth, awaiting the return of two Armenian civic leaders who had been scheduled to meet with an Ottoman official earlier that day. Father Krikor had served as the priest for thirty years, and never in that time had he been personally summoned by the Catholicos. But these were different times. The once-mighty Ottoman Empire was showing fissures. An empire that controlled the Middle East, annexed nearly all North Africa, and whose territory stretched into Europe as far as the Balkans was beginning to lose its grip on its perimeter. The Ottoman's recent defeats in the Russo-Turkish War, which occurred between 1877 and 1878, resulted in the empire conceding territories in the Balkans and the Caucasus.

The time had come for the Armenians to call for greater civil reform in a country in which they were long considered second-class citizens. To press the issue, Armenian religious and civic leaders had banded together to discuss how best to present their grievances to the central government. Father Krikor's mission was to gather the information from the meeting with the Ottoman official and then travel to Akhtamar Island and report to the Catholicos.

The church door opened, and an acolyte rushed toward Father Krikor.

"Very Reverend Father, no one has seen or heard from the two emissaries," the acolyte said. "We have volunteers looking for them now. I regrettably have nothing more to report."

"That is disturbing news," Father Krikor said. "They are four hours late, and I do not have the leisure to delay any further; I must leave for Akhtamar Island, immediately. Ready my carriage, and if you receive word in time, send a messenger to me on horseback. I will leave you a note. Please follow my instructions precisely in my absence."

"Yes, Very Reverend Father," said the acolyte.

After the acolyte left, Father Krikor sat at his desk to pen his instructions when he heard the church door open again. He eagerly looked up and was disappointed to see a local peasant woman and her child in the doorway. The woman was leaning on a cane and was steadied on the other side by her disfigured son. The woman crossed herself before entering the church.

"Very Reverend Father, I apologize for the intrusion, but may I speak with you briefly?" Mariam said.

"My dear Mariam, this is the house of the Lord and you need not apologize for any time you spend in the reverence of God," the priest said. "However, if it is my counsel you seek, then your visit is indeed ill timed. I have a pressing matter that requires my immediate attention. You will have to wait until my return if you wish to speak to me."

Father Krikor looked back down at his paper and resumed his writing.

Mariam shuffled a little closer to the priest.

"Please, Very Reverend Father," she said. "I have come with a simple and humble request. I have no food to feed my son, and I ask if the Church could spare some bread. I ask only enough for my son."

Father Krikor looked up again and put down his pen to focus on his two visitors and quietly studied them. He saw that Mariam looked even more feeble than usual, her voice was still weak, but her breathing was more labored. He looked at Ari, who appeared reluctant to follow his mother into the church.

"So, you have entered the house of God to beg, is that it, my child?" Father Krikor asked.

"Only to ask for His mercy," said Mariam.

Ari tightened his grip on his mother's arm and tried to nudge her away from the priest, but she resisted.

"We all seek His mercy. What of you, my son? Do you need God's mercy as well?"

Ari's only reply was to hide behind his mother. Father Krikor looked back at Mariam's dirty and bruised face.

"These are hard days, are they not, my child?" he asked.

"Only if you do not have God's grace," Mariam said.

"Indeed. God's grace should shine on all of us. However, we are entering into difficult days. Days that will not be measured by His grace to us, but by our service to Him. You have not been attending church, have you, my child?" Father Krikor asked.

"No, Very Reverend Father, I'm in poor health and don't have the strength I did as a girl."

"But you had the strength to come today in need of His mercy?"

Mariam remained silent and lowered her eyes to the floor. Father Krikor rose and approached her.

"I'm not naive to your struggles, Mariam," said Father Krikor as he lifted her chin with his hand. "You're a brave woman, and your strength can only come from the gift of true faith. I fear that in the coming years our people will face greater trials than even you have known, and your strength can be an example to us all. But no one will know of your strength if you hide it away. That is why I beg you to come to the Lord's house not to seek His mercy but to share His gift."

Just then the doors of the church burst open, and the acolyte came rushing in with another man.

"I have dire news," said the man. "We must speak immediately. In private."

Startled, Father Krikor turned away from Mariam to look at the man. He started walking to the front of the church when he stopped and turned to his acolyte.

"Please escort this woman and child out and give them what bread we have," Father Krikor said to the acolyte. "This good woman sewed some clothes for me, and in my failing memory, I forgot to pay. I promised her I would make reparations upon my return, but in the meantime she's graciously accepted a few morsels of food as a gesture of good faith."

"Yes, Very Reverend Father," the acolyte said.

Before Mariam could utter a word of gratitude, Father Krikor and the other man turned and walked to a corner of the church. The acolyte took Mariam's arm and led her slowly to the doors. As they were about to leave the church, Ari looked back at the two men, and he thought he heard, "We found them both dead by the lake." Ari watched as the man handed Father Krikor a piece of paper.

Ari saw Father Krikor read the paper and noticed his face turned ghostly pale, just as the acolyte closed the doors to the church.

5

Cowboys and Pirates

Ari and his mother slowly made their way home with a half loaf of bread and four hard-boiled eggs that they'd received from the church. The cooling night air gave little comfort to Mariam's battered body and tired legs. She struggled more with every step she took, and Ari found himself encouraging her and using what little strength he had to get her to their home.

Ari lived with his mother in an abandoned shed on the outer edge of town. The shed sat at the far end of a property used to raise livestock. The owner allowed them to live in the dilapidated structure under the condition that Mariam help tend to the cows and chickens—tasks that quickly fell to Ari.

Ari could feel his mother's legs trembling and hear her labored breathing as they neared their shed. He tried to steady her with one arm as he reached to open the door with the other. He guided her over the threshold and then to the bed. She sat on the bed and took a deep breath. The one-room shed was about eight feet long and six feet wide, and even at Ari's height, he could still jump up and touch the roof. The shed had room for one bed, which he and his mother shared. The bed was barely wide enough for both, so they would often sleep on opposite sides to maximize the space. They dug out a fire pit in the dirt floor of the shed. It was just inside and to the left of the door, and besides using it to cook, it was their only source of heat. There were four shelves, two on either side of the bed. One shelf had their kitchenware: a pot, a pan, two forks, two spoons, and a knife. The empty shelf underneath was where they kept their food.

On the other side was a shelf with neatly folded piles of clothes that belied the ragged condition of the garments. The shelf under that held a Bible.

As Mariam caught her breath on the bed, Ari started a fire in the pit, which was only a couple feet away from the bed.

"Are you okay, Momma?" said Ari as he sat next to Mariam to make sure she could feel the heat from the fire.

"Ari, I'm fine. Please bring the food here so you can eat, you must be hungry," said Mariam as her breathing began to steady.

"I'm not hungry. I had some grapes, and I ate them earlier," Ari lied.

"Who gave you grapes?"

"One of the boys at the lake. He had a lot and couldn't eat them all."

"That was nice of him, but you should eat some bread tonight. Bring the food here."

He brought over the bread and hard-boiled eggs to her. He unpeeled an egg and put it to his mother's mouth. Mariam grabbed his arm and pushed it away.

"No, Ari. Please, you eat. I'm an old woman. I don't need it. You only need to eat when you are young, so you can grow and be strong," Mariam said.

"I had grapes today. I can't eat anymore. My stomach is full. Please eat, Momma."

"You can always eat more. We have food. I wish it was more. I'm sorry, Ari," Mariam said.

Ari hugged his mother, and she turned and kissed his brow and rested her cheek on his head. Ari unpeeled another egg while his mother broke off pieces of bread for both, then they began to eat. There was an uneasy silence as they ate, and Ari looked at his mother, who was staring blankly into the fire.

"Can you tell me the story about Grandpa and the pirates?" asked Ari.

"I'm tired, Ari, maybe another time."

Ari nodded and stared at the fire himself. He could feel a knot form in his throat and his eyes begin to water. He looked away and wiped his eyes.

"Ari, would you really like to hear the story?" Mariam asked.

"Not if you're tired, Momma," Ari said.

"No, it went away, I'm not tired anymore. I'd like to tell it if you would like to hear it."

Ari looked up at his mother and nodded. Mariam covered the two of them with a blanket, and facing the fire, she retold him this story:

Pirates were pursuing his grandfather's merchant ship on the Black Sea. After desperately trying to outrun the bandits, it looked like their ship would be overtaken and boarding seemed inevitable. The young crew was frightened, and many had resigned themselves to a tragic fate. But one crew member stepped forward to rally his fellow seamen. He was an American from Texas named Wendell.

In his late forties, Wendell was the oldest member of the crew. Mardiros never knew how a cowboy from Texas ended up on a Turkish merchant ship, but it didn't matter—Wendell's Western wit and frontier personality made him a favorite among his fellow sailors. The Texan had a gift for lightening the mood with his humor and carefree attitude. When Wendell first stepped foot on the ship, he took one look at the Turkish captain's puffy and prematurely gray hair and nicknamed him Captain Cotton—a moniker that would stay with the captain until the day he stopped sailing.

The old Texan had become a mentor to Mardiros, and even though he was just a fellow deckhand, Mardiros said that when Wendell vowed to fight, the entire crew would have charged Alexander's phalanx with him.

"I'm from Texas, gundamit, and if we didn't give up the Alamo, we sure as hell ain't gonna give up this ship to a bunch of scallywags!" said Wendell.

Spurred on by this brash Texan, the crew resolved to fight. Mardiros said that the bravado of Wendell's words was no match for that of his actions. In the greatest act of bravery Mardiros ever saw, Wendell told the crew to hold back as he waited for the pirates to board and then launched himself off the top deck and landed on three of them, knocking one unconscious, slashing the throat of another, and then getting up and quickly killing the third before the pirate could retrieve his gun.

The rest of the crew rushed to the fight just as three more pirates boarded. The crew overcame the final three pirates, but *not before Wendell suffered a gunshot wound to the abdomen. In the end, all six pirates were killed, and the remaining bandits made a hasty retreat. Only one member of the merchant crew perished—Wendell.*

The crew buried Wendell out at sea with all his meager possessions except one—his Texas flag. The captain kept the flag and, as an everlasting tribute to the old cowboy, flew it high above the ship on every journey after.

"Do you know what the flag looked like?" asked Mariam, as she broke Ari out of his captivated trance.

"Ye-yes. I drew it," he replied.

"You did? Where did you draw it?"

Ari pointed at the Bible. Mariam gave him a quizzical stare.

"Bring it to me please."

Ari retrieved the Bible and meekly handed it to his mother. Ari saw her looking at him as he cast his eyes to his feet. He saw her open the book from the corner of his eye and examine his drawing of a flag with two horizontal bands and a vertical band with a star.

"It's perfect. Just like your grandfather described it to me," said Mariam as she ran her hand over the drawing.

Ari looked up at his mother and smiled.

Knowing it was time for bed, he brought in more firewood and got in bed with his mother. They lay in bed together, his mother's back to the wall while she hugged him close as he stared at the fire.

"I'm glad I told you the story again. I have more to tell you. Some you have already heard, but there are others that I haven't told you yet. So many others."

"Momma, you said I had a father, too." Ari said.

"Yes, of course," said Mariam, her voice becoming flat.

"Do you have stories of my father? Could you tell me one?"

"Another time, Ari. It is time for bed now, not stories."

"Just one story. You've never told me any about him."

"No, Ari. It's time to sleep."

Mariam turned over and lay with her back to Ari. He lay there silent as he watched the flames of the fire turn to embers. Eventually, he could hear his mother's steady breath and knew she was asleep. He got out of bed, careful not to wake his mother, and walked outside. He sat on the ground and then lay back and rested his head on a rock.

He looked up toward the heavens, staring at the countless stars in the night sky. He thought of how brilliant the stars appeared, how majestic, how peaceful. The night sky seemed at ease in its beauty—awash in silent pride of its own splendor. *What a grand domain the heavens make for the worthy*, he thought. But were there really gods that looked down on man from their heavenly perch? And if so, he couldn't help but think what they would make of him. What kingdom awaited the coward? What divinity embraced the weak? What saint patronized the useless?

These thoughts continued to run through his head as he fixated on the stars—for how long he didn't know. He simply stared toward the heavens until he fell under the spell of their gleaming lights and drifted off to sleep.

6

A Warning from Istanbul

The next morning, Father Krikor arrived at Akhtamar Island. Bishop Tovmas met him at the doors of the Church of the Holy Cross. Bishop Tovmas's diocese comprised the Van vilayet—an Ottoman administrative province— and Father Krikor's church fell under his auspices.

"Where have you been?" demanded Bishop Tovmas, not bothering with pleasantries. "His Holiness was expecting your arrival last night."

"My deepest apologies, Your Grace, but there were matters unforeseen and outside of my control that prevented me from arriving sooner," Father Krikor said.

"Well, quickly, we mustn't have His Holiness wait any longer," said Bishop Tovmas as he ushered Father Krikor into the church.

Even though Father Krikor had visited the Church of the Holy Cross before, he wasn't prepared for the sight that greeted him when he entered its doors on this occasion. Inside the church was a collection of nearly every Armenian religious leader within the empire. They were scattered around the church, all in conversations with their colleagues. However, the buzzing and chatter all ceased when Father Krikor walked in.

"Has he arrived?" asked a voice from the front of the church. The clergymen parted to give Father Krikor a view and a path to where the Catholicos was sitting in an oversized, gold-framed, red-felt chair. A gold cross loomed above the headrest of the chair, giving it the impression of a holy throne. Father Krikor approached the Catholicos, bowed, and kissed his hand.

"Your Holiness, I deeply apologize for my delay. Situations arose that prevented me from arriving any sooner," Father Krikor said.

"We can only thank God that you have made it to us safely. We owe you a great debt for your service to our people and our Church," the Catholicos said. "What is your report of the meeting with the government officials? What was their position on our grievances?"

"Your Holiness, I regrettably have little to report on the meeting. Our representatives never returned." Father Krikor paused. "They were murdered."

The congregation erupted in shock and anger.

"This is an outrage," said one of the patriarchs. "Is this how grievances are met by the Ottomans? This cannot be tolerated. We must demand justice for this crime, and the sultan himself must answer for this."

The agitated crowd followed the patriarch's lead, and calls for justice, retribution, and protest rang out from all corners of the church. Only the Catholicos remained silent and unmoved as he waited for the noise to settle. When it did, he spoke.

"Was there anything else?" the Catholicos asked Father Krikor.

"Yes, Your Holiness. When the bodies were discovered, this letter was found on one of the men," said Father Krikor as he handed a piece of paper to the Catholicos.

All went silent again as their eyes locked on the leader of the Church, who unfolded the piece of paper and read it silently. The letter read:

The empire has grown increasingly annoyed by the Armenians' malcontent and mischief. Our response to your destructive agenda is to deal with the traitorous Armenians with a firmer hand. We will give you a box on the ear, which will make you relinquish your revolutionary ambitions.

The bottom of the letter was marked with the sultan's seal.

The room remained silent as they waited for the head of the Church to speak, but he closed his eyes as if deep in thought. The silence seemed to stretch time to its extreme, and the moment grew heavier with each tacit second. Finally, a lone bishop broke the thickening silence.

"Your Holiness. What are we to do?"

"Pray," responded the Catholicos.

7

Burdens of Duty

Ari woke early the next morning. He headed to the shed to check on his mother, and saw she was still sleeping. He covered her with a blanket that had fallen to the floor and then went to tend to the animals. He first collected the eggs from the chicken coop, then milked the cows and carried the buckets of milk back to the main house of the property.

A childless, middle-aged couple, Razmig and Karun, owned the property that Ari and his mother lived on. The land, which was Razmig's inheritance as the only surviving child, had been in his family for generations. Toil and life were indistinguishable to Razmig. To live meant to work—neglect the latter and risk losing the former. There were always animals to feed, fields to plow, crops to harvest, wood to cut—all to have food on their table and a roof over their head. Razmig's disposition reflected this way of life. He was a tall, thin man, whose patience had, over the years, receded as fast as his hairline. He was a man of few words, had no humor for leisure, and no tolerance for charity.

When Ari and his mother first arrived in Van, they had little money, and the only shelter Mariam could afford was an old shed that Razmig agreed to rent to her. Razmig was planning to tear down the unneeded building as it had long outlived its usefulness and was close to collapsing on itself. But when Mariam approached him to inquire about a cheap place to rent, he offered her the shed. The negotiation was quick. Razmig told her she could take it or leave it. With no other choice, she agreed. It would be their only home in Van. The little money Mariam had soon ran out, and to remain in the shed, she agreed to help tend to the animals—an obligation that Ari eventually assumed.

Unlike her husband, Karun was a short, rotund woman, and always in a state of agitated anxiety. This condition was brought about by the belief that all the peoples in the world were united by a single nefarious conspiracy—the sole aim of which was to bring about her ruin through a coordinated system of cheating, swindling, and stealing. No action was exempt from this belief. A friendly greeting was simply a veiled attempt to breach her defenses and con her out of her money. An offer to help was a ploy to get closer to her possessions. A neighbor bearing gifts was laying a trap for a future payoff. Even a carpenter or blacksmith invoicing her for rendered services was just the culmination of their thieving plots.

Most of these tactics she would dismiss out of hand and shake her head in bemusement at their lack of sophistication. With others, the ones that called for her to pay someone, she would argue the price—amid insults and accusations—so unrelentingly that few left their dealings with her boasting even the smallest profit.

The reason she didn't have children had been a topic of minor debate among the locals. One camp argued that she was simply barren. Another side said she wanted to have children until she was told that they would require continued feeding and clothing, at which point she quickly put the idea to rest. The debate slowly faded as mounting evidence made it increasingly difficult to argue against the latter position.

It was Karun to whom Ari had to deliver the milk and eggs in the morning. Once he brought them to the kitchen, he was to stand there while Karun completed her inspection. She looked at each egg to make sure Ari didn't crack any on the way from the coop. She would then check the buckets to ensure that every drop of milk was delivered. It was never clear what mathematical formula she used to determine the precise volume of daily milk production. But whatever it was, the buckets Ari brought always came up short.

"This isn't all the milk! Did you spill some when you were carrying it?" Karun asked Ari.

He shook his head.

"Then you must have drank some." She grabbed Ari's forearm and squeezed it in an effort to measure his body-fat index.

When most grabbed Ari, they would feel the blunt angles and rigid resistance of bone. However, on this occasion, Karun's grasp must have isolated his body's few remaining fat cells.

"Look at this! You're getting fat! Are you drinking our milk? Don't lie to me, boy."

"No, I brought all the milk from the barn."

"Then why are you getting so fat? Do you think we'll house thieves? Where is that mother of yours? I will not tolerate this."

"She's not well. I'm sorry. I'll bring more milk next time," said

Ari, who knew better than to do anything other than stand at attention.

"She is always ill. Why I let you and that witch on my property, I'll never know. It's out of kindness. Do you understand? But I'll not let you take advantage of my kindness. I'll send both of you packing if I find that either of you stole from me. Now be on your way, you have work to do."

Ari nodded, turned, and went back to his chores.

=====

Father Krikor's stay at Akhtamar Island was brief. The clergymen had discussed their next course of action throughout the night. It was agreed that a more formal and direct grievance should be delivered to the sultan in Istanbul. When dawn broke, the Catholicos thanked Father Krikor for his report and told him that considering the circumstances, it was best that he returned to Van.

When Father Krikor returned to his church, a mob of Armenians greeted him. He pushed his way through the screaming crowd until he reached the stairs to the church. Father Krikor raised his hands to quiet the people.

"Please, please. I understand everyone's anger, but I ask everyone to be calm," Father Krikor said.

"How can we be calm after these murders? We demand that the Church do something about these injustices," screamed a voice among the crowd.

"I assure you that the Church is not taking this matter lightly. The Catholicos is meeting with other leaders and is formulating a response. In the meantime, I beg all of you for calm and patience."

The crowd erupted again, and a volley of angry questions and threats were hurled at Father Krikor from all directions.

"What type of response?"

"We should storm the courthouse!"

"How many more of us must be murdered and robbed?"

Father Krikor tried to quiet the crowd once more, but found he was having no success. Seeing that he couldn't calm the throng and fearing that if he stayed there longer it might incite a riot, he walked into the church. There was an initial surge from the crowd to get into the church, but the mob's path was barred by the acolyte and other church officials. Father Krikor stayed just inside of the church doors until he could hear the racket begin to subside and eventually dissipate completely.

Later that evening, Father Krikor sat at his desk inside the church, and sitting across from him was Taniel Martirosian— the man who had delivered the regrettable news about the murders. Taniel was a linguist and local businessman. He grew up with little interest in either politics or religion, but he was passionate about his Armenian heritage. Like other Armenians, Taniel took issue with government policies he felt were exploitive and unfair. Taking a greater interest in the Armenian cause brought Taniel within the inner circles of the Armenian leadership in Van—a place where religion and politics met. Soon, Father Krikor and Taniel had developed an unlikely friendship. One was a devoted Christian, the other an ardent atheist. Their respect for each other didn't come from a shared belief but, rather, from a mutual humanity.

"Have you thought about what you'll tell the congregation?" Taniel asked.

"I've thought about it a great deal," Father Krikor replied as he rubbed his forehead. "Has that helped me determine what to say? No."

"You should know that the local authorities have refused to

investigate the deaths. They consider the matter closed," said Taniel, tapping a pen on the desk.

"And what did they rule as the cause of death?"

"Bears."

"So, bears have started using guns," Father Krikor said. "God help us all."

"As you saw, the people are highly agitated. In your absence, I could only calm them with the promise that you and the Church will pursue justice. But I'm concerned that if swift action isn't taken, there may be more bloodshed."

"As am I."

"Krikor, I'd like to help in any way I can," said Taniel as he leaned over the desk. "But in times like these, no one looks to a merchant for answers, even if I had any to offer. This moment is a heavy one, and I don't wish to make it even more so for you. But the people will continue to look to you for guidance. You must be prepared for that. You must know what to do next."

"I understand this burden. I can only pray that the Lord can help a floundering shepherd find a path," Father Krikor replied. "As for what to do next, that part is clear. We have funerals to tend to."

8

Upon This Rock

Datev Tarpinian and Raffi Saraydarian were born two weeks apart. They grew up on the same street in Van, with only one house separating the two. Although not related, the two were inseparable growing up. Neither had a sibling. Datev's two older brothers had succumbed to illness as children, and Raffi was an only child. Each found more than friendship in the other; they found the brother that neither had.

It was a rare sight in Van to see one without the other. They were baptized on the same day. They would walk to and from school together. When they grew older, they went away to apprentice as printers together. They briefly separated when Datev went off to complete studies to become a lawyer, while Raffi finished his apprenticeship and married. They eventually returned to Van, where Datev and Raffi purchased a building to house their businesses jointly.

It was oddly fitting, then, that they would now be buried together.

Father Krikor decided that the funeral procession would not be short. He plotted the course to go through all the major areas of Van. The pallbearers all demanded that they carry the caskets the entire way, not setting them down or stopping until they brought the deceased to their final resting place.

Father Krikor led the procession, followed by the caskets that the pallbearers carried in parallel. The immediate family, dressed in black and carrying portraits of the deceased, walked closely behind the caskets. Datev was survived by only his mother. Raffi's parents accompanied his widow and newborn son. After the family members, it seemed as if the entire Armenian community came to escort the deceased, making the procession solemn and long.

It was not by accident that the procession passed many of the heavier Turkish-populated areas in Van. It was also not by coincidence that it passed directly in front of the local government building that housed the Turkish officials, including the *kaymakam*.

The government of the Ottoman Empire was based on one simple concept—a single just ruler. This supreme ruler was the sultan, whose job it was to ensure fairness and equity among his subjects. The divan, or imperial council, supported the sultan, and the viziers of the divan were the sultan's most powerful advisers, led by the Grand Vizier.

Branching further out from the central government were various levels of increasingly granular local rule. Van and its surrounding villages were part of an Ottoman Empire administrative division called a *kaza*, which was overseen by a kaymakam.

The kaymakam of Van was a short, heavyset man with a thick mustache named Faruk Yildirim. He was the man whom Datev and Raffi met with on the day of their deaths.

As the funeral procession passed the administrative offices,

Father Krikor noticed Faruk on the steps of the building, watching the mourners as they passed.

Faruk bowed his head in an ostensive show of respect. As Faruk and Father Krikor locked eyes, Faruk gave a slight nod to acknowledge the priest. Father Krikor turned his eyes away and continued his march.

Neither Ari nor his mother were in the funeral procession. Mariam was still recovering from the injuries she'd received days prior. Ari took advantage of his mother's need to sleep and snuck away to visit his grandfather's grave.

He was still at the gravesite when the funeral procession entered the cemetery. Surprised by the mass of people descending on the graveyard, Ari hid behind a tree and watched the mourners move past. The graves that awaited the bodies were next to each other and about fifty yards from his grandfather's. Ari had never seen so many people gathered in one place. His eyes went to the portraits the families were carrying, and he realized that these were the men he saw killed at the lake. Who were these men, he wondered. He only recognized them in passing. Otherwise, he knew nothing of them. What did they do to deserve such respect, such devotion, such love? Once again, he imagined them to be great men, and that was enough for him to want to watch the funerals, so he stayed.

The crowd gathered around as straps held the caskets over the graves. Due to the number of people, Father Krikor decided to address the mourners at the cemetery instead of the church. After a short prayer, Father Krikor folded his arms inside of his robe and turned to the crowd.

"I have been a priest for many years. Many of you have seen me grow from a young priest to an old one. I've presided over countless christenings, weddings, and funerals. But as a priest, you hope that the hands that held a boy's baptismal waters are not the same hands that cast dirt on his grave. A priest should not have to do that. A parent should not have to see that.

"But we find ourselves here to bury two men far sooner than we should. Two young men. Two brave men. Two good men. We mourn for Datev and Raffi. We mourn for them not only for the lives they had, but also for the ones that still awaited them.

"Datev has left his mother behind. Raffi is survived by a wife, a son, and his parents. To each of you, I tell you that you are right to grieve. The heart cannot be ignored. The pain of its wounds may lessen over time, but the scars will forever remain. They are there to remind us of our loss. But for the good man, the Lord tells us this loss is brief. For the just man, a kingdom awaits. And we will hurt no more. And we will wear the wounds of our hearts like badges. Just as our Savior bears the scars of his crucifixion.

"So, I say to the family again, that it is okay to grieve. But don't neglect to also celebrate your fortune.

"There once was a mighty king in the land to the west. His name was Croesus, and the land he ruled was called Lydia. Croesus's wealth was legendary. One day a wise man named Solon came to his palace. After Croesus had shown Solon his incredible wealth, he prepared a feast for his guest and asked Solon, who, in all his travels, was the most fortunate man he had known. Solon replied that it was Tellos the Athenian, who raised good and noble children and died a noble death assisting Athens in battle. Croesus then asked him who the second most fortunate man was, and Solon replied Cleobis and Biton—who not having oxen to pull their wagon, went under the yoke themselves and carried their mother to a religious festival. All the men applauded the brothers for their strength, and all the women commended their mother for having birthed such sons. The two brothers would die peacefully within the temple that very day.

"Confused, Croesus asked Solon how he could not be considered the most fortunate of men, given the vast wealth that Croesus had just shown him. To which Solon replied, 'My good Croesus, you appear to have incalculable wealth, and you hold rule over many people; but I cannot yet say that you are fortunate, not until I have learned that your life ended nobly.'

"Datev's and Raffi's lives ended nobly. And for that, they will always be the most fortunate among us. For that, their families will always be among our most blessed.

"But even noble deaths bring anger. I ask that you not give in to your anger. I ask that we, like Datev and Raffi, be noble as well. We will all come before God to be judged—good and evil men alike. Until then, I ask that you find strength in your faith, to believe in the Lord, and to remember what the Bible teaches us.

"In the book of Luke, we are told to 'love your enemies, do good to those who hate you, bless those who curse you, pray for those who mistreat you . . . If you love those who love you, what credit is that to you? For even sinners love those who love them. If you do good to those who do good to you, what credit is that to you? For even sinners do the same . . . But love your enemies and do good . . . and your reward will be great, and you will be sons of the Most High; for He Himself is kind to ungrateful and evil men. Be merciful, just as your Father is merciful.' Amen."

With that, Father Krikor nodded, and the gravediggers began filling the graves.

Ari noticed how Father Krikor's words seemed to wash over the throng like a soft wave. His voice drifting from their ears like a tide fading into the sea. Those gentle words seemingly bathing the suffering soul like ebbing waves cleansing a trodden beach in their tender retreat. For a moment, Ari felt this man of the cloth wielded real power.

Strangely, the biblical story of Peter came to Ari's mind. He remembered his mother telling him that when Peter proclaimed Jesus as Christ the Messiah, Jesus said to his disciple, "And I say also unto thee, that thou art Peter, and upon this rock I will build my church, and the gates of hell shall not prevail against it."

When his mother read him that passage, Ari always imagined a mighty stone foundation, rooted to the ground, with a majestic cathedral perched high. Now he felt foolish in his youthful naiveté. He knew the foundation the story spoke of was not a rock but something far more powerful. He wasn't wise enough to put a name to it, but he felt it, nonetheless. It was *hope*.

Once the graves were filled, Father Krikor sealed each side of the grave by drawing a cross in the ground.

"May the seal of the Lord remain unbroken on the grave of this servant of God until the Coming of Christ, who coming again, will renew it in glory to the Father and the Holy Spirit. Amen," said Father Krikor in concluding the service.

Ari stayed hidden behind the tree, watching as the crowd of people passed by the graves and then quietly headed out of the cemetery. The crowd quickly thinned until the only one remaining was a neighbor of the two deceased who stayed to clean up any debris. The neighbor left shortly after.

When he was once again alone, Ari came out from behind the tree and walked toward the burial spots. He picked up a pair of discarded red roses.

When he reached the graves, he paused to look at them. He then knelt and placed a flower on each one.

9

Seeds of Dissent

The church leaders remained on Akhtamar Island, where they were joined by contingents of Armenian civic leaders from throughout the empire. One of these leaders was Mihran Nazarbekian, who was not only the leader of the Sasun delegation but was also the head of the Social Democrat Hunchakian Party, also known as the Henchak Party. The party was founded in 1887 in Geneva, Switzerland, by a group of Russian Armenian Marxist college students. One of their primary objectives was to advance a revolutionary agenda within Ottoman Armenia. The group took an aggressive approach to realizing an Armenian state free of Ottoman rule. This approach was captured clearly within their manifesto, a line of which read: "Those who cannot attain freedom through revolutionary armed struggle are unworthy of it."

Less than a year prior, the Henchak Party had led an uprising and clashed with Ottoman forces in the Sasun region of the empire. The Ottomans turned back the rebellion, but in many ways the die was cast. Now, a year later, Mihran felt a renewed urgency to rally his fellow Armenians into action.

Everyone took their positions inside the church, with the religious leadership congregating on the left side, while the civic leaders took their seats on the right side. The Catholicos was sitting in his customary chair at the front of the church. Once everyone was gathered, Mihran stepped forward to address the assembly.

"It's fitting that we meet here today in this church," Mihran said. "This building stands as a symbol of our heritage, our history, our identity as a people. But we're faced with forces that would tear down the very foundation of our culture one stone slab at a time. Until what is left is an empty hole where an edifice once stood and fleeting stories of old men and women, who might still remember days when being an Armenian was more than a fanciful myth."

"We all share your concerns," said the Catholicos, who seemed unmoved. "But we must be cautious as well. The forces you speak of have shown that death is a weapon they are only too eager to wield. We must remember that our strength is in our unity and our faith."

An agitated murmur grew from the civic leaders. Mihran raised his hand to quiet the group.

"With all due respect, God is not there when the Hamidiye assault and kill our people, when they loot our villages," Mihran replied. "We cannot go before these wolves as helpless lambs. You teach that even Christ will one day return in battle. We must not be afraid to fight ourselves. To protect what is rightfully ours. To finally drive out the usurpers that have grown too comfortable in a land they have no right to, all the while consigning the Armenian to be a mere stranger in his own house. I fear if we do not meet this danger head on, then we will have signed our own death verdicts."

"Many of us still remember the bloodshed in Sasun, as I'm sure do you," the Catholicos said. "I ask that we be more prudent in pursuing the options that are before us. The world is watching as well, and they recognize the legitimacy of our concerns and are applying pressure from outside the empire."

The fidgeting from the civic leaders seemed to expand to the clergymen as well. A few of the bishops began shuffling their feet, and a handful of priests hung their heads.

"But the outside world has only offered words, which have not shielded us from the swords of Istanbul nor given us any relief as we're slowly taxed and robbed into poverty," said Mihran.

"That's the reason we meet here today. We all know the Great Powers have succeeded in having the sultan sign a treaty agreeing to reforms. It's true that these reforms have largely gone unheeded. It's now our time to force the sultan's hand more directly. We have agreed to send a delegation to Constantinople and present our grievances directly to the sultan and call for change and justice," the Catholicos replied.

"What justice can you truly expect?" asked Mihran. "We repeatedly suffer injuries at the hands of the empire and its agents and yet can't bear witness in its courts against our abusers. The Ottomans have been clear in demonstrating their belief that a Christian is half a man, and an Armenian not a man at all."

The contingent of civic leaders grew louder and bolder, shouting out individual incidents of Ottoman misconduct and injustices. The Catholicos waited for the shouts to die down and began speaking over the residual noise.

"The abuses of others should in no way define who we are. We will be judged only by our actions, our conviction to our principles, and our beliefs, and not by the injustices leveled upon our heads. We will be remembered by how we act in moments of crisis, moments of urgency. If we make decisions in haste or through blind emotion, we risk failing in the responsibility that is before us. We must understand that the legacy we will leave our children will be shaped by the actions and decisions we will make in the coming days."

Mihran clinched his jaw and made an aggressive move toward the Catholicos when Taniel grabbed his arm. He spun and gave Taniel an annoyed look, but Taniel held on to his arm and gave him a subtle nod to calm him. After he composed himself, Mihran turned back to the Catholicos.

"Your Holiness, we haven't come here to divide our people. We will all stand united in this. But when we speak of legacy, I can only pray that there will be children left to receive it," said Mihran as he finally tipped his head in reluctant acquiescence.

All fell silent, and the leader of the Diyarbakir contingent rose to speak.

"If the decision is to go before the sultan in Constantinople, then we must show a united front. I recommend we send a large delegation. One whose sheer numbers cannot be ignored. We have several people from Diyarbakir who will be traveling to Constantinople. Who here will be joining us?"

The speaker looked around the room. One by one, Armenian leaders from Kayseri, Malatya, Sivas, Van, Muş, Elazig, and all the other regions stood to be counted.

"It appears you have your delegation," the Catholicos said.

10

Matters of Friends and Foes

Ari attended school for only a week. He never forgot his first and his last day of school. He remembered how frightened he was on his first day, frightened how the other kids would react to his appearance and how he would be treated. He recalled how everyone stared at him when he first walked in. His teacher pointed to a seat next to a girl, and when he sat down, the girl got up and ran out of the room crying. The teacher ran after her while the other children laughed.

None of the children talked to him that week. During recess, he sat away from the rest and watched as they played. On his last day of school, he saw some of his classmates engaged in a race. They were three boys, all his age. They were known as the Mischief Makers because they were always together and were usually at the epicenter of any unruliness. Their names were Arman, Sako, and Vartan.

Arman was the loudest and most outgoing of the trio. Tall, thin, with dark hair and even darker eyes, Arman fancied himself the leader of the group, although no referendum on the matter had ever been conducted or considered. Sako was slightly shorter than Arman. He had curly brown hair and a round face that had already begun the process of sprouting a second chin to go with his slightly pudgy body.

And there was Vartan, who was the same height as Arman but more athletically built. Vartan was a handsome boy with arresting eyes that seemed to change from green to blue to gray through some mystical play of light. His eyes were so unusual, regardless of where they happened to fall on the color spectrum, that it was impossible for anyone to talk to him without feeling self-conscious for staring too deeply into them. Even Ari's mother, after seeing Vartan for the first time, called him the boy with the magic eyes.

"There is something about that boy, Ari," Mariam said. "The Lord doesn't give eyes like that by chance. There is a reason for them. For good or bad. You can be sure there is a reason."

Ari noticed that Arman seemed agitated as the trio stopped in front of him.

"Just because you beat me and Sako doesn't mean anything," said Arman to Vartan. "Why don't we have a relay race? If Sako and me run together, I bet we can beat you and anyone else in this school. You and me can run to that tree, and then Sako and whoever you pick will race back. Whoever comes back first wins."

"Okay, fine, then I'll find someone to run with me, and we'll race you after school," said Vartan, confidently.

"If you're so sure, why don't you let us pick your partner?"

"Okay, go ahead, pick someone," said Vartan.

"Him," said Arman, pointing at Ari.

By Arman's expression, it was clear he felt he had just cut off the chess board, cornering the king unwittingly, and was about to proclaim checkmate.

"Good," said Vartan as he walked up to Ari and patted the hump on his back. "That's exactly who I would have picked."

Ari remembered feeling pride surge through him. The fact that he was a pawn in this child's game of machismo was lost on him. The only thing that was important was that Vartan said he would have picked him. Out of everyone in the school, Vartan would have picked *him*. His anticipation grew through the day. Ari envisioned Vartan and him easily outdistancing their rivals. He thought of the adventures that awaited them throughout the school year. For the first time, he imagined what it would be like to have a friend.

Midway through the school day, Ari saw the teacher walk over to the door of their classroom. He looked toward the door and saw his mother standing there. The teacher motioned for Ari to come over and bring his belongings. Something in the look on his mother's face spoke to him. He knew at that moment that he was leaving the school and would never return. He was ashamed. For a moment, he had felt no different from the other children, but now they would know just how unlike them he was. For him, there would be no school, there would be no races, and there would be no friends.

———

Now, more than five years after that day, Ari, as usual, found himself at his grandfather's grave. He sat down in front of it, letting his mind drift as he stroked his medal. It was Ari's own form of meditation. When he was in this state, he didn't feel the cold or hear any sound. He was lost in his own mind, where anything was possible—even happiness.

Ari's thoughts were interrupted by a pigeon fluttering its wings as it landed on his grandfather's tombstone.

"Hello, Hoki. I didn't think I would see you. It's cold. I didn't bring you any seeds today. I'm sorry," Ari said.

Ari had barely finished his words when the bird flew away. Ari looked up as the pigeon soared overhead. As he continued looking up, he saw a stream of liquid arching over his head and landing on his grandfather's tombstone. He spun his head and saw that three boys had snuck up behind him, two of them laughing. The third had his pants down and was urinating on the grave.

"We didn't mean to bother you, I just had to pee really badly, and I couldn't hold it any longer," said Arman.

His two companions, Vartan and Sako, roared with laughter as he finished relieving himself and pulled up his pants.

Ari stood and, without looking at any of the boys, tried to walk away. Sako immediately blocked his path.

"Where are you going, you weirdo? Did anyone tell you that you could go?" Sako asked. "Arman just peed on your grandfather's grave. Are you going to let him do that?"

"I had to go badly." Arman laughed. "Now he's going to want to fight me just because you said that. Do you want to fight me?"

Ari tried to walk the other way, but this time Vartan blocked his way and pushed him back into Arman.

"That's it. I didn't want to fight, but you hit me first," said Arman as he pushed Ari.

Ari didn't respond or retaliate.

"Say something," said Arman as he began to lightly slap Ari on the face.

The slaps were meant more to get a reaction out of Ari than to inflict pain, but they had just the opposite effect. Ari was steadfast in not reacting to the slaps or lashing back—an action he was convinced would make his ordeal worse by an order of magnitude. And pain was indeed being inflicted. Not from the force of the slaps but from what they symbolized: disdain, weakness, cowardice.

Despite himself, he felt tears welling up, which only added to his shame. This boy had urinated on his grandfather's grave, and his only response was to try to cowardly walk away. Now he was being mercilessly slapped by the same boy, and again he was too frightened to stand up to him. The only thing left was for him to show them that he could endure whatever they doled out. But his weakness betrayed him even there, as his tears clearly signaled his resolve was fracturing. He hated himself even more for crying, for not being able to maintain his final and only line of defense.

"Oh, now you're crying. Fight back!" said Arman as he slapped Ari across the head with all his might.

The blow was so hard that it seemed to reverberate all the way down to Ari's feet. Ari tried to cry aloud, except no sound came from his lips. Ari's mouth was agape but seemed silently frozen in a pitiful expression of pain and helplessness. When his voice returned, he openly sobbed. He covered the side of his head that Arman had struck and, despite himself, gave Arman a pleading look.

The only response the boys had was to continue to laugh. Arman then lifted his leg and kicked Ari in the chest, pushing Ari to the ground. Ari continued to cry as he curled up, anticipating more blows.

"What's that?" asked Vartan as he noticed the medal Ari was holding.

Vartan stooped down and tried to take the medal from Ari's hand, but to his surprise, Ari wouldn't let it go. Vartan paused before redoubling his efforts to pry out the medal. Ari clutched it harder. Determined to get the medal, Vartan put his knee on Ari's neck to grind out the leverage he needed. Finally, he forced the medal out of Ari's hand.

"Where did you steal this from?" asked Vartan, with his knee still on Ari's neck.

Ari's only response was to lunge for the medal. But Vartan held it away from him and ground his knee into Ari's neck again.

"Where did you get this?" Vartan asked again.

"That's his grandfather's medal," Sako said.

"Is that true? Is this your grandfather's medal?" Vartan asked him.

Ari stopped struggling and nodded at Vartan.

"How did your grandfather get this medal? Is he some hero?" Vartan asked.

"Ye-yes," croaked out Ari.

"Ha, ha, ha. You're an idiot. You really think your grandfather was a hero? Do you think they make cheap and dirty graves like this for heroes? Are you that stupid? Your grandfather stole this medal. From now on this medal is mine," said Vartan as he lifted himself off Ari.

"He didn't steal it," screamed Ari as he got up and lunged for the medal again.

Vartan kept the medal out of reach and pushed Ari away. Ari slammed against his grandfather's tombstone before falling to the ground, scraping his forearm in the process.

"If you get up again, I'll give you a worse beating than Arman did," Vartan threatened.

Ari looked up at Vartan, whose typically bright eyes looked dark and menacing. Ari buried his face in the ground and sobbed again. This time he wasn't ashamed. The boys had taken the only thing he owned, the only thing he valued; there was nothing left for them to take. He no longer cared about protecting some false dignity behind a stoic facade, so he just lay there and wept.

"What are you gonna do with the medal?" Sako asked Vartan.

"I'm gonna keep it and tell everyone my grandfather was a hero." Vartan laughed.

The response got a chuckle out of the other two boys, who crowded around Vartan to admire the medal. With their prize in hand, the three boys now seemed to lose interest in Ari and walked away.

Ari lifted his head and watched them go. As they continued to walk away, Vartan glanced back at Ari and the two momentarily locked eyes.

Ari noticed Vartan slow down a little, allowing the other two boys to walk in front of him. Then inexplicably, Vartan turned and heaved the medal back toward Ari. It landed a few feet away. Ari desperately crawled over to the medal and clutched it to his chest. He didn't know why Vartan had thrown the medal back to him, and he didn't care; all that mattered was that he had it back.

With his head throbbing, Ari kept his eyes on the boys as they headed out of the cemetery. He felt an increasing sense of safety the farther away the boys walked, but just as calm settled in, Ari heard shrieks, screams, and cries coming from town. They were unlike any he had ever heard—they were loud, desperate, and chilling. He noticed that the other boys heard them as well and saw them begin to run in the direction of the sounds. All Ari could think of was his mother, and he ran toward the cries as well. Ari didn't know what was happening, but he felt it had to be something terrible.

And indeed, it was. The pogroms had begun.

11

The Pogroms

Weeks earlier, on October 1, 1895, a massive Armenian contingent had assembled in Istanbul to present their grievances to the central government. Approximately two thousand people gathered that day to present a reform package directly to the sultan. The reform package was designed to seek better treatment of Armenians and other Christian groups within the empire. The reforms called for greater representation, fairer rules of taxation, and equality in law.

Rather than viewing the assembled Armenians as suffering subjects, Sultan Hamid II saw them as agents of Christian Europe aiming to eviscerate the glory of the Ottoman Muslim state. He considered their cries of injustice as petulant tantrums of spoiled and thankless children.

Upon getting the reform package, the sultan was noted to have said, "This business will end in blood." He ordered his police units to disperse the gathered Armenians, and they did so through violence. What would ensue in the months to come would be a series of pogroms known as the Hamidian massacres.

These massacres, named after the sultan, began in Istanbul and spread to other Armenian-populated provinces. The killings were carried out by the Hamidiye, Ottoman forces, and even incited Muslim citizens. Some incidents occurred in 1894, but the killings grew in numbers and ferocity in late 1895 and through 1896. In the end, it is believed that anywhere from eighty thousand to three hundred thousand Armenians were killed during these pogroms.

———

Ari arrived in town just behind the other boys, and what he saw was worse than anything he could have imagined. Everywhere he looked he could see armed soldiers and Hamidiye indiscriminately killing Armenians, regardless of age or gender.

There were pockets of resistance, where some Armenian men fought back. In these cases, they would be overcome by greater numbers or their attackers would leave them and move to easier prey—the more defenseless children, women, and elderly.

To Ari's left, a soldier held a screaming Armenian woman by the hair. As the woman's young child clung to her leg, the soldier slit the woman's throat. To his right, a Muslim resident beat on a dead Armenian man's body, smashing his face with the blunt end of an axe. Everywhere Ari looked he saw men, women, and children run for their lives and lifeless bodies drop to the ground. The street beneath his feet had turned into a river of blood.

Ari's three tormentors from the cemetery had all run to hide. But the only thing Ari could think of was to somehow find his mother through all this violence and carnage. He feared that she might have fallen victim to the killings as well, but he refused to assume she was dead. He had to find her somehow and thought of how best to get to the stoop in the town square where he had left her.

He knew he couldn't walk directly to the center of town, as that would mean he would have to make his way through the most active part of the fighting and butchering. Instead, he carefully skirted the main streets, hiding behind wheelbarrows, trees, and even piles of manure, as he made his way. In this instance, his small frame and light body proved to be an advantage, as he needed little cover to shield himself from view. His steps were so light that he didn't have to worry about attracting someone's ear—although even the noise of a raging river would have been drowned out by the surrounding pandemonium. He slowly and stealthily made his way between the houses and through the streets until he could see the stoop his mother usually sat on.

His heart sank when he saw she wasn't there. Not far from the stoop, he saw dead bodies littering the ground. Fear and panic overcame him. He was certain that one of those bodies had to be his mother. He stayed hidden a few minutes more until it seemed as if the fighting and killing had moved farther away. As he inched his way to the stoop, he looked at each body. Most of the bodies were motionless, others gurgled and gasped for their last breaths. Waves of relief briefly washed over him when he didn't recognize his mother among them, but then an even greater panic began to set in. He searched more frantically, darting from body to body, almost forgetting about the danger he was putting himself in.

Instead of abandoning his search and trying to hide, he was drawn toward the brutality he could see moving down the street, feeling that it was the only place his mother could be. Just as he turned to run toward the butchery, he thought he heard his name. He stopped, then heard it again. He turned toward the sound and saw Mariam with her head sticking out of a cellar door only ten yards from the stoop she usually sat on. His dread turned into relief, and he dashed in her direction as she held the cellar door open for him. Once he entered the cellar, Mariam closed the door on top of them and slid a rod on the inside to lock it in place.

The cellar was used to store grain and wasn't very large, only dug about a yard into the ground, but it had enough room to hide Ari and his mother. They huddled together in silence and fear. Ari felt his mother holding him tightly, and he prayed that the nightmarish scene before them would be over soon.

The scene would eventually end in Van and other Armenian-populated towns where massacres occurred. But far from being the climax to merciless and senseless Armenian deaths, these pogroms would prove to only be a prelude.

12

The Sins of the Father

As a young boy, one of Ari's grandfather's chores was to herd the family sheep. The most challenging part of the job was overcoming the tiring monotony while the sheep grazed. On one of these instances, as Mardiros was sitting idly, he noticed a small bird pecking at something on the ground not far from him.

As he watched the bird, he picked up a rock and wondered if he could hit the bird with it. He decided to try, and to his surprise, the rock hit the bird on the head, and it dropped to the ground, motionless. Mardiros walked over to the bird to look at it and realized he had killed it.

Later that day, as the sheep continued to graze, Mardiros dozed off for a nap. In his sleep, he had a dream in which an old man came to him. The old man asked Mardiros why he'd killed the bird. Mardiros told him that he didn't know, he just felt like throwing a rock at it.

"That innocent creature was doing you no harm and yet you still killed it. For that, you will know my anger. For that you will see what I have in store for you," the old man said.

After Mardiros woke from his sleep, he herded the sheep home.

He recounted this story to his daughter many years later, and Mariam asked him if he believed that it was somehow the root of his misfortune.

"No, of course not. It was just a dream," he said.

But for some reason, he told his daughter about it. And on the day Mariam buried her father, it was the first thing that came to her thoughts.

═══

Ari and Mariam were among the lucky ones. They stayed hidden in the cellar while the pogrom raged deep into the night. When they could no longer hear any sound, they emerged and cautiously made their way home in the darkness of the early morning.

Karun and Razmig's property had the advantage of being on the outskirts of town and had been unmolested during the attacks. Like many Armenians, Karun and Razmig had barricaded themselves in their house.

Razmig peered through the window of his home, with a shotgun in hand to valiantly defend himself, his wife, and their property. When Mariam approached the house, she asked Razmig if she and Ari could hide inside the home as well, but he turned them away. With few options, Mariam and Ari went to their shed and locked themselves inside and hoped for the best. Days later, Father Krikor and other Church officials made their way to the property to inform everyone that it was safe to resume their lives.

The nightmare had ended.

13

Crime and Punishment

In the ten years since the pogrom, Mariam had only grown sicker and weaker. She was unable to walk more than a few yards before needing to rest. If she had to travel any real distance, she relied on Ari to transport her in a wheelbarrow. Age had deteriorated her eyesight, leaving her unable to sew any longer. However, she still insisted that Ari take her to the same stoop at the center of town with her needles and threads. She would then wait for Ari to leave and instead of soliciting work, she would simply beg for money.

Even though Ari was an adult, because of his deformities, he still looked like a child. His growth was stunted in his early teens, and his body remained unnaturally thin, making him look more like a prepubescent boy than a man in his early twenties.

His responsibilities back on the homestead continued to increase by the year, even though his incentive didn't. He now toiled nearly the entire day, taking over much of the physical labor from an aging Razmig. The rest of his time was spent caring for his mother. On the property, he did whatever was asked of him without complaint or debate. The constant threat of his mother and him being evicted was the only motivation he needed. Even though they lived in a rundown shed, it didn't leave them exposed to the elements or, more importantly, the contempt of their Turkish neighbors and the condescension of their Armenian ones.

Karun maintained a constant vigil over her property, looking for any evidence that Mariam and Ari were stealing from her. This proof would usually come in the form of food or items found on her impoverished tenants that weren't consistent with complete destitution.

On one occasion, Karun encountered Ari as he was leaving the market with a small block of cheese. She asked the proprietor if Ari had bought or stolen the cheese. The storekeeper told her that he had purchased it. Incensed, Karun rushed home to check the money she kept hidden in a jar. She quickly counted it only to discover it came out to the exact amount that she had stashed away earlier that morning. She counted it one more time and again came up with the same total.

Baffled at first, Karun suddenly smacked her forehead in realization. *What a fool I am*, she thought. It all made sense now. She realized she must have miscounted her money prior to putting it in the jar and the container had held more money than she thought. It was now clear that Ari and his mother exploited this miscalculation—sneaking into her house to help themselves to the unaccounted funds. How they knew the exact amount of the overage—so as to pull off the heist undetected—remained a pesky snag to the theory. But in the end, it was a minor detail—this had to be the only explanation.

Karun's rage built until her face turned a deep shade of red and her cheeks emitted a pulsing heat, which would have been felt by anyone daring to stand within a foot of her.

She immediately fetched her husband and explained that she had caught Ari and Mariam stealing from them. Brandishing an old broken-off broom handle, Razmig followed his wife as they went to confront the thieves.

"Do you consider me a fool?" asked Karun as they came upon Ari and Mariam outside their shed.

"What do you mean?" replied a confused Mariam.

"Don't play stupid with me, you treacherous wench. I don't have the patience for it. I saw Ari at the market today buying cheese. Cheese that he bought with money he stole from me!"

"I gave him the money for the cheese. We're poor, but we're not thieves. Ari wouldn't steal from any—"

"Shut your mouth, you cow! I will not stand here and be lied to after *my* money was stolen."

Karun turned to Ari. "Did you steal my money?"

"No," said Ari, shaking his head.

"Razmig," Karun called to her husband.

At his wife's signal, Razmig swung the broom handle, hitting Ari across his back. Ari's body stiffened, and he arched in pain from the blow.

"I'll ask you one more time. Did you steal my money?"

"No," Ari grunted out.

Again, Karun signaled to her husband. Razmig raised the broom handle and brought it down on Ari so hard that he crumpled to the ground.

"Please, Razmig, stop! We didn't steal any of your money. Karun, tell him to stop," Mariam pleaded.

Ari heard his mother's anguished pleas and didn't want to add to her agony with his cries of pain, so he bottled up what he could—letting out only dull grunts and groans with each blow.

Desperate, Mariam tried to get up and intervene, but her legs gave way, and she fell to the ground. Unmoved, Karun ignored Mariam and watched as her husband continued to beat Ari.

"Please, please stop! I'll give you what money we have if you please stop," Mariam said.

This offer caught Karun's attention, and she signaled to her husband to stop.

"Is it the money you stole from me?" asked Karun.

"No, no, we never stole anything, but if you stop, I'll give you the money I earned sewing today."

"All right then, give me the money," Karun said.

Mariam reached into her pocket and brought out a few coins.

"This doesn't look like all the money that was stolen, but it's a start," said Karun. "We will decide how you will repay the rest. But I'm warning you both, if I ever find that you stole from me again, I'll have you both thrown in jail."

And with that, Razmig and Karun turned and left.

Ari, neglecting his pain, lifted himself off the ground and went over to help his mother stand. He led her to a bench on the side of the shed so she could sit down. He hugged her quietly and tightly, not only to comfort her but, more importantly, so she couldn't see his face as he struggled to contain himself. He was a man now, and men weren't meant to cry. He stayed that way, with his chin resting on her shoulder, until he was sure he'd driven back the tears. But one determined tear fought its way out and rolled down his cheek. Ari gritted his teeth and silently cursed it.

It was the year of our Lord 1906. A time for the wicked. Yet another day to punish the innocent for their sins.

14

The Wayward Ball

Vartan could vividly remember the day he fell in love. He was twelve years old and was playing soccer on the playground outside of the school. A German missionary named Hans Breiner taught the sport to the Armenian boys. Hans brought much-needed medicine to Van, but he also had a passion for soccer and had donated soccer balls, shoes, and shorts to the school.

The sport was a much-needed diversion for the boys. Van was slowly recovering from the pogroms. In the year after the killings, loved ones were still being mourned, families still being rebuilt, and trust between Armenians and Turks still being sought. But on the soccer pitch, none of this mattered. Even if it was just for a moment, fear and pain could give way to laughter and joy.

As the boys were playing, two young Armenian girls sat together off to the side. At one point in the game, Vartan received the ball along the side and made a long run. As the last defender rushed to challenge him, Vartan unleashed a thunderous shot that ricocheted off the lunging defender's foot and hit one of the girls on the side of her face. All the boys stopped their game and stared at the girl, who covered her face as her friend hovered over her.

A terrible feeling came over Vartan. The pace of the shot was so hard that he was certain that the girl's face would be permanently maimed—or at the very least her nose broken or her teeth chipped. Concerned, he slowly made his way to the girl, who still had her face in her hands.

"Is she okay?" Vartan asked her friend.

"Why do you care? If you were so worried, you would have been more careful where you kicked the ball," spat out the victim's friend.

"I'm sorry, it was an accident. I wasn't trying to hit her with it," Vartan replied.

"Well, you did anyway, so now why don't you just leave us alone?" the girl said.

"I'm sorry. I just want to make sure she's okay."

The girl shot Vartan a final piercing look and turned her attention back to her friend.

"Are you okay, Anna? Can I see your face?"

Anna finally pulled back her hands, to reveal a slight reddish hue. Vartan was surprised to see that besides the blemish, she didn't appear wounded at all.

Anna turned toward Vartan as her friend continued to inspect her face. When she did, Vartan began studying her features. Her nose didn't look broken; in fact, it descended in a perfect slope to slightly upturned nostrils. Her teeth weren't chipped but rather, they were straight and as white as snow. He noticed how smooth her olive skin appeared, how full her lips were, how soft her long and thick black hair looked. And then when he looked at her brown eyes, they came to life, with a sparkle in them that made them appear to dance.

Anna was a classmate of Vartan's, and he had known her for years, but he had never seen her before like he did that day. Vartan started getting a strange feeling in the pit of his stomach and became overwhelmed with nerves. He walked away without saying another word, but he thought about that beautiful girl the rest of the day.

It took him nearly a year from that day to muster enough courage to talk to her again. His opportunity came one Wednesday before the start of school. As he was waiting for the school bell to ring, Vartan saw Anna leave her friends and walk to the hand-operated water pump that sat on the left end of the schoolyard. Sensing a chance to talk to her alone, Vartan followed Anna to the pump. Vartan approached her as she set her books down and began struggling with the heavy cast-iron lever.

"Let me help you," said Vartan as he took hold of the lever and began pumping it until a steady flow of water poured from the spout.

Vartan found he was so nervous he couldn't look at Anna, even though he could feel her staring at him, so he just concentrated on the water coming from the pump.

"Thank you, I just had to wash my hands."

Vartan continued looking down at the stream of water, his eyes drifting to Anna's hands when she began to wash them. He summoned enough courage to look up at her and was emboldened further when he saw she was too busy cleaning her hands to notice his gaze. He hadn't been this close to her since the day he struck her with the ball. There was a part of him that hoped what he saw on that day was some hallucination—that nothing could be so cruelly beautiful. But now, up close, he could see that it was no hallucination.

Anna looked up at him and his eyes immediately darted back down and away from her. He could see from the corner of his eyes that she was looking for something to dry her hands with. He took out a handkerchief and extended it to her.

"Thank you," said Anna as she took the handkerchief. She dried her hands with it and handed it back to Vartan. He took it and forced himself to look at her.

"I . . . I never apologized for hitting you with the ball," said Vartan as his knuckles whitened around the handkerchief. "I just wanted to tell you I'm sorry and I'm glad you weren't hurt."

"I wasn't hurt, I was just embarrassed. I know I must've looked silly," she said.

"No . . . no you didn't."

Vartan saw a shy smile on Anna's lips as she gathered her books. She held her books tightly to her chest as they stood there clumsily looking at each other.

"Well, I have to get back to my friends," she said.

Before Vartan could say anything, the school bell rang.

"Vartan! Come on, you son of a donkey! School's starting," Arman yelled from a distance.

Vartan looked toward Arman and then back to Anna. For nearly a year, Vartan had imagined what it would be like to talk to her. He had hoped that it would be easy to tell her how he felt, that such a beautiful moment would settle into its own elegance. After all, he was told that love is a wonderful thing, perhaps the most wonderful of all things. But he found there was no natural force to carry the moment; he would have to rely on himself.

"I have to go too, but I want you to know that one day I'm going to marry you," said Vartan as he turned and ran as fast as he could toward school.

That's how Vartan began his courtship of Anna. The next day he snuck into the classroom before the start of school and hid a piece of candy in Anna's desk. He did that unfailingly for an entire month, until one day he opened his desk and found a piece of chocolate shaped like a heart. He looked over at Anna, and she smiled at him. He smiled back.

It was tacit and wonderful. And he would never have a more magical exchange.

15

Bed of Opportunity

Vartan and Anna's relationship grew like a young colt—taking its first steps on trembling legs, weaned to maturity with care until its unbridled passion was bursting to be set free.

At first, Vartan and Anna would meet at the water pump before the start of school, under the pretense that they needed to quench their thirst. They would linger as long as they could and talk about small, childish things that seemed so important at that age. When they reached high school, Vartan would walk Anna home. Anna lost her parents and siblings during the pogroms and was taken in by her mother's brother and his family. Vartan was careful to walk her only as far as his uncle's street and would watch her as she walked the final hundred yards to her home.

Neither Vartan nor Anna came from wealth. As an orphan, Anna relied on the support of her uncle. Vartan's father, Krisdapor, was a laborer who would work odd jobs to make a living. When

Vartan reached high school, he felt he should start working to earn money in the hopes of marrying Anna after graduation. During his second year of high school, he asked his father if he could work with him. His father looked at him blankly and said no. It was a response that left no latitude for debate.

Undeterred, Vartan began going to local Armenian-run businesses to seek employment. He was turned down by everyone. There was one place left to try, a textile shop located in the town center. When he arrived, the store had already closed for the day. He sat down in front of the shop in frustration when he heard the clucking and clanking of a horse-drawn wagon approaching. The wagon stopped in front of the store and the driver stepped down and ran to the door of the shop.

"Damn it! He's already gone," the man said before looking over at Vartan. "Do you work here?"

"No," Vartan said.

"Do you know the owner of this shop?"

"I've never met him, but I recognize who he is."

"Good. I have a large delivery for him, and I have to leave it here. Can you make sure he gets it?" said the man, who without waiting for an answer, began unloading his wagon.

After he dropped off the delivery, the man jumped back on his wagon and sped off without thanking Vartan for his assumed assistance.

Vartan walked around the three large crates the man dropped off. They were nailed shut. He knew nothing was more enticing to a thief than something that required sealing. Even though he hadn't technically promised to look after the delivery, he knew that if he left the crates unattended, they stood little chance of being there when the shop opened in the morning. He decided to guard the merchandise and hoped that the shop owner would come before nightfall and rescue him from his inconvenient decency. When no one arrived, Vartan hunkered down and made a night of it—sleeping on the rigid crates. He was shaken awake just before dawn.

"I was expecting to find a shipment this morning, but not a young man in front of my store," said a perplexed Taniel Martirosian.

"I'm sorry, sir," said a groggy Vartan, rubbing his eyes and rolling off the crates and onto his feet. "I was here when they were delivered yesterday and didn't want anyone to steal them."

"So, you spent the entire night here?"

"Yes, sir."

"That is very kind of you. I don't know many people who would do that. I think I recognize you. Are you Krisdapor's son?"

"Yes, sir."

"Your father is a good man. He's always ready to help a neighbor. I'm sure he would be proud to see that quality has been passed down to his son."

Vartan looked down and gave a barely perceptible nod. He realized that the sun was coming up and that school would be starting soon.

"I have to get to school. Good morning, sir," said Vartan as he began to walk away.

"One thing before you go. Why were you at my store yesterday? Did you need something?" Taniel asked.

"I was looking for work, sir."

"Were you? Didn't anyone teach you not to look for work? You just might be unfortunate enough to find it. You should be looking for love instead," Taniel said.

"Love I have, money I don't."

"Then you're a lucky lad, indeed. Very well then, if you can't be talked out of it, I might have something for you. Come see me after school."

It took Vartan a second to recognize the offer. When he did, he ran over to Taniel and shook his hand enthusiastically.

"Thank you, sir. Thank you," said Vartan, who then turned and sprinted off to school.

16

The Laborer, the Merchant, and the Revolutionary

Vartan began working for Taniel immediately. At fifteen years old, Vartan started as a stock boy, then oversaw all the inventory. By the time he was twenty, Vartan had become Taniel's primary clerk and was helping manage the day-to-day operations.

One day, in his fifth year of employment, as Vartan was sweeping the floor, he heard the door open and saw a man walk into the store.

"Bonjour, Monsieur . . ." Vartan started, before realizing it was his father.

"Is Taniel in?" his father answered by way of greeting.

Krisdapor had always been a stern patriarch. Vartan couldn't recall his father ever hugging him, even as a child, but he remembered every harsh reprimand as if it were seared into his flesh. Vartan's greatest fear in life was disappointing his father. He was a man he loved and respected deeply. Someone he'd always looked up to, even if he would never fully understand him. They may not have had a close relationship, but, Vartan thought, perhaps they were never meant to.

"Ye-yes, he's in his office in the back. Do you want me to go get him?" Vartan asked.

Krisdapor ignored the question, walked past him, and headed to the back of the store. Vartan wasn't sure what he should do, so he awkwardly went back to work.

When Krisdapor opened the door to the spacious office, he found Taniel sitting at his large cedar desk and an unfamiliar man sitting across from him. On the wall, behind the desk, was a rendering of Father Ghevont Alishan's original design of the Armenian flag. The Catholic priest designed the flag in 1885 after a request by the Armenian Students Association of Paris, which wanted to use it for the funeral of the French writer Victor Hugo. The flag consisted of three broad horizontal strips of red, green, and white—from top to bottom, respectively.

The desk was covered with stacks of receipts and newspapers. A German copy of *Thus Spoke Zarathustra* by Friedrich Nietzsche sat on top of the pile of newspapers. Besides a couple of chairs in front of the desk and a coat rack, the only other piece of furniture was a Victrola—the cutting-edge talking machine that Taniel had imported from America. A box containing phonograph records of classical music sat on the floor next to the Victrola.

"Krisdapor, so happy you could make it," said Taniel as he and the other man rose. "This is the man that I wanted you to meet. Mihran Nazarbekian is the head of the Social Democrat Hunchakian Party."

The two walked back to the desk and each took a seat across from Taniel. When all three were seated, Mihran turned toward Krisdapor.

"Krisdapor, I won't insult you by explaining who I am or how dire a situation we find ourselves in," said Mihran, sitting on the edge of his chair. "You know our cause as well as any. What I've come here for is to ask for your help."

"What help could I possibly give to you? I'm a simple man, with no money or power to speak of," answered Krisdapor, sitting back in his chair.

"It's precisely who you are that makes you so valuable. People have grown tired of listening to the rhetoric of politicians and holy men. These men of lofty offices and revered titles have become distant from the common man. So distant, in fact, that they find their words can no longer reach them. And for good reason. Because the time for words has passed, and the time for action is upon us. That is why I come to you—because you are an honest man and those around you recognize that. You, unlike others, rightfully have merit in the eyes of your neighbors," said Mihran.

"I'm uneasy about our situation, as well. But I must admit I don't know of any course of action that I believe wouldn't incite those who would do us ill and worsen our situation," Krisdapor said.

"My friend," said Mihran, "I fear that the worst is still before us. We all remember the vile murders perpetrated upon us. We have all lost loved ones. But the bloodlust of the Ottomans will not be satisfied so long as there are any drops still pulsing in an Armenian vein. We cannot afford inaction. We have begun to arm ourselves and band together. We have camps throughout the countryside. We will not be taken unprepared again. But our numbers are few;

we need more men to join us in our fight. I have come to ask you to help us recruit more men willing to fight. Will you join us?"

Krisdapor appeared uncertain. He'd lost three of his four children during the pogroms, reducing his family to Vartan, his wife, and himself. And he'd also lost his brother and countless other relatives and friends. The fear that he might lose what remained of his family was all too real.

"If I were to join you, what would you need of me?" Krisdapor asked.

"As of now, nothing more than to identify and recruit men you believe would be willing to join us. You live and work with these men. You know them better than anyone, and they will trust you. Find others who are willing to fight for what they believe in. Who will fight for their fellow Armenians. Will you join us, Krisdapor?"

Krisdapor looked at Mihran and then over to Taniel and saw each man had fixed his gaze on him.

"My friends, I will admit you have caught me by surprise. I'm uncertain of what to do, and it's likely because I am uncertain of the life I have. I'm raising what is left of my family on a virtual powder keg that could be ignited on the whims of Istanbul. I know that is no way to live, even for a poor man like me. But more importantly it's no way to die. So yes, yes, I will join you."

17

Khosk-Kap

Vartan trembled as he and his father waited at the door of Anna's uncle's house. Armenian tradition called for the family of the groom to go to the bride's house to ask permission for her hand in marriage.

Having lost both of her parents during the pogrom, Anna's uncle was now the man whose consent was needed. Vartan was twenty-six years old now and had grown into an honest and hard-working man. He finally felt he had saved up enough money to be able to take care of Anna. He also felt it was time for Anna and him to begin a life of their own. Anna had already lost her entire family. Vartan's mother had succumbed to a long illness the previous year, leaving only him and his father.

The nervousness Vartan felt while waiting at the door was twofold. The first aspect was simply the anticipation of finally being with the object of his consuming love. The other was the uncertainty of how his father would represent him when asking for Anna's hand. Vartan believed that in the eyes of his father, he wasn't ready to be a husband, that he was unprepared to raise a family. He had known his father to be an honest and candid man, and that's what scared him. He had a real fear that when Anna's uncle asked why he should grant his permission, his father would say, "I can't think of a good reason; I wouldn't give it if she were my daughter either."

The door opened and Anna's aunt welcomed the pair into the main room. There, Anna's uncle invited the two men to sit down. Once they were seated at the table, Anna brought cups of tea for each man. Vartan couldn't believe how she could look more beautiful each time he saw her, but somehow, she did.

"Thank you for having us in your home, Margos, we hope we find you well," said Krisdapor, addressing Anna's uncle.

"It's always a pleasure to have your company. You always have a welcoming door in my home. But I must admit your visit has caught us all by surprise. To what do we owe the honor of your company?" said Margos, playing up the moment.

"The folly of the young, I'm afraid," responded Krisdapor.

"Ahhh yes," said Margos, shaking his head in feigned disapproval. "Youthful passion—the mother of all misguidance. Driven only by emotion with no measure of thought."

"I'm afraid so. My young son has gotten it into his head that he is ready to be a husband. To care for a wife and to raise a family."

There it is, thought Vartan. It was just as he had feared. The formality that everyone assured him would unfold was being systematically undermined by his own father. He felt himself sinking into his chair. What did he expect? His father was a man of integrity and principle. Of course he wouldn't endorse him in marriage. He hadn't yet proven to his father that he was a man, that he was ready to take care of a home. How could he have expected his father to portray him any differently? Vartan's shoulders slumped and his heart sank as he was sure that all was lost.

"Is this true? Do you think you're ready to be a husband? To be faithful, to care for, and to protect our Anna?" Margos addressed Vartan.

Had Margos ended his questions with the one inquiring about his readiness to be a husband, Vartan would have most likely echoed what he felt his father believed—and admittedly his own doubts—and he would have said no. But as the line of questioning continued—would he be faithful, would he care for Anna, would he protect Anna—to those he couldn't say no, even at the risk of contradicting his father.

"Yes," said Vartan as he sat up in his chair.

"This delusion appears to be even worse than we have feared, Krisdapor," said Margos as he smiled at Vartan's show of bravado. "I'm an old man, and I can't pretend to understand the thinking of a young mind. A mind that tells us that the reasoning of a lamb carries more truth than the wisdom of age. So, I will submit to your judgment, Krisdapor. We all know you as an honest man. Do you think I should give my permission in this matter?"

Vartan braced himself for the candid assessment he was sure was coming from his father; one that would most likely put an end to his amorous endeavor. He hung his head and prayed that it would be swift and not too severe. Krisdapor paused and then looked straight ahead at Margos.

"Vartan was my youngest son. He is now my only son," Krisdapor began. "We have all suffered and we have all endured pain. My family is no different. I've lost two boys and a daughter to the murders. When we lost our children, my wife was shattered, she was lost. As a man, I was taught that a husband and father was a pillar. The support that everyone relies on to keep a family standing even as the harshest winds assailed it. But in this matter, I found I was no pillar. I was just a broken man.

"My wife became sick. She wouldn't eat or drink. She was unable to sleep without waking in screams. Instead of caring for her, I was consumed by my own self-pity, my own anger, and my own struggle to cope from one bleak day to the next. But Vartan put aside his own pain and stayed at his mother's side. He awoke every morning to cut wood and make a fire, so that her skin would be warmed even if her heart couldn't be. Seeing her grow weaker, it was Vartan who cared for her. He cooked and coaxed her into eating, so that her stomach would be full even if her home wasn't. My wife, his mother, died last year of a broken heart. But she would not have survived the days after the tragedy if not for Vartan. The last few years of her life would have known no joy had it not been for Vartan's love. I don't know if I would be alive today if not for his strength.

"You ask me if he is deserving of your permission in this matter, and I say to you yes. Yes, he is. As a son, he has been a blessing. I have no doubt he will be a faithful husband and, God willing, a caring father. He has been a good boy. And he's the man that I wish I was."

Vartan turned to look at his father, who continued to stare straight ahead. He couldn't believe what he'd heard. He had a feeling he'd never experienced before, a feeling that can only come from a father's approval. He was moved and for a moment forgot the reason they were there. He wanted to embrace his father and tell him how much he loved him. But his father never turned to look at him. Instead, he fixed his gaze only on Margos.

"What can one say to that?" said Margos, who bowed his head and slowly massaged his brow. "The only thing left, it seems, is for me to give my permission. And that I will do gladly, along with my blessing."

Vartan turned toward Margos. "Thank you. I'll care for her and I'll protect her every day of my life."

Anna and her aunt were visible in the doorway of the other room. Vartan could see the two share an embrace before Anna's aunt tearfully pulled away and disappeared from view. Anna's youngest cousin, a seven-year-old girl, was pulling at Anna's dress. When Anna looked down, the girl began teasing her by bobbing her head and making kissing faces. A disembodied hand grabbed one of the girl's pigtails and pulled her out of the doorway.

And there stood Anna alone, as beautiful as he had ever seen her. Tears in her eyes and a smile on her face. Vartan wanted to rush to her and embrace her, but he knew there was one last thing he had to do.

He and the other two men raised their cups of tea and took their first sips.

18

A Day in White, a Call in Red

Vartan and Anna's wedding was held just a couple months after their betrothal. Father Krikor conducted the ceremony in front of a group of forty family and friends. After the ceremony, a three-man band, consisting of a drummer, a flutist, and an accordion player, led the wedding procession to Lake Van. A modest reception was set up on a plateau just above the shore of the lake. The bridal table sat on a platform a foot off the ground, and there were five tables that formed a semicircle in front of the bridal table.

On occasion, the wind would blow strong enough to lift sand from the beach and pelt guests trying to eat. When the wind took a break, the scorching sun stepped in and sucked sweat out of any exposed pore. The music couldn't always be heard over the wind and the sounds of the lake. And not all the food was as warm as it should have been. But somehow it all seemed perfect.

As the reception was winding down, Taniel approached Vartan as he chatted with some of his guests.

"I hate to interrupt you, Vartan, but the evening is getting late for an old man like me. Before I go, I was hoping you could spare a moment. I'd like to have a word with you."

"Certainly. Please excuse me," said Vartan to his guests. He followed Taniel to a secluded path.

"What a beautiful day this turned out to be, I'm glad I was here to see it," said Taniel as he stopped to speak.

"It means a lot to me that you're here," Vartan said.

"Vartan, you've done whatever I asked of you, and I've grown to love you as I would a son. And that's the reason I wanted to speak with you. I've seen you grow so much over the years. Grown into a man that we'd all hope to be. I brought you into my store to teach you a trade, and now I must admit there is nothing left for you to learn from me. So, I wanted to give you one final gift before I leave tonight," said Taniel as he handed over a set of keys to Vartan.

Vartan stared at the keys, confused.

"Those are the keys to my store. It's yours now. It's served me well, and I hope it'll do the same for you," Taniel said.

"I don't understand."

"Vartan, everything has its time. Every man has his calling. Mine is no longer as a merchant. The store is for those who are building a life. For the young and the hopeful."

"I still don't understand. You built that store. Why abandon it? What will you do?"

"I'm not abandoning it. I'm turning it over to someone worthier. As for what I'm going to do, I'll let your father explain that."

Vartan saw his father standing a few yards away.

"Vartan, I'll leave you with your father. I wish nothing but the best for you and Anna. May the sun always shine on your home," said Taniel as he shook Vartan's hand, then gave him a hug.

Taniel walked off and passed Krisdapor without saying another word. Krisdapor approached his son as Vartan watched Taniel leave.

"Father, I don't understand. Where's Taniel going? Why is he leaving?"

"He's leaving for a cause. As am I," Krisdapor said.

"What? What cause? Where are you going?" asked Vartan, even more confused.

"We live in a time of great uncertainty. As Armenians, we find ourselves in a sea of enemies. We have all seen what happens when these seas rise and lash out. I can no longer stand by and suffer these injuries, these injustices quietly. Taniel and I are leaving tonight. We have joined the Armenian Revolutionary Federation and have formed a resistance to respond to our abusers in the only language they know, the language of the sword. Unfortunately, it's not safe for either of us here, and we are needed out in the countryside to prepare for our fight."

"But you can't go! I still need you here. I'm not ready for the responsibility Taniel and you are asking me to face alone," said Vartan.

"My son, no one ever feels ready for the next chapter in their lives. I don't feel ready to leave, but I know I must. There's a greater calling that I must answer. I have few years left to devote to a cause greater than myself. As small a contribution as my life would be, it's all I have to offer our people. To the grandchildren that, with God's blessing, will one day see more hopeful times. But you are still my son, and I wouldn't leave if I didn't think you were ready."

"Let me go with you. I can talk to Anna. We can come with you. If you fight, I want to fight alongside you."

"No, no, my son. You have a more important responsibility. Taniel and I are fighting, and willing to die, so that our people have a future. But you have a life to build and children to have, and those children will have children. Otherwise, there will be no cause to fight for, and no one to leave a future to."

Vartan's mind raced. He no longer knew what to say. He just stood there looking at his father for what he began to feel could be the last time. He desperately tried to find something to say, words that would neatly resolve all the conflicts raging in his mind and heart. But he could find no words that would avail.

"You are a man now and—"

Vartan cut off his father's words by lunging and embracing him. It might have been the first time he hugged his father—he wasn't sure—but if this were to be the last time, he didn't want to let him go. It was an act of affection Krisdapor rarely shared with his son as he grew.

Krisdapor dug his fingers into Vartan's shoulders to break the embrace and straighten him up—to tell him he was a man, and men should be strong.

But oddly, he only held him tighter.

19

On the Sixth Day

It had been four years since Vartan's wedding day. In the intervening years, after taking over Taniel's textile store, he had become a respected and successful businessman in his own right. He hadn't seen or heard from his father since he'd left with Taniel. He didn't know if his father was dead or alive, but he knew he missed him greatly.

As he helped a female customer, a neighbor boy burst through the store's front door. "Vartan, it's Anna, she's having the baby!"

Vartan froze as he processed the news.

"Go," said the customer with a smile.

"Thank you, thank you," said Vartan, grasping the woman's hand. "My clerk will help you once he finishes with his other customers."

Vartan grabbed his hat and coat and ran to the door. Before he left, he turned toward the people in his store. "I'm going to be a father! I'm going to be a father!"

Everyone gave him a cheer, and he dashed out the door.

The clerk turned toward his own customer.

"I don't think I'll need anything today," said Karun. "You can go help the other people."

"Of course," said the clerk as he turned to assist the customer Vartan had been helping.

Once Karun was certain she was out of view, she took some of the fabrics, hid them under her coat, and walked out with everything she'd come to town to get.

=====

"How is she?" Vartan asked his neighbor, who was standing in the main room of his house.

"She's doing well, the midwife said she would let us know as soon as the baby arrived," the neighbor said.

Just then the sound of a baby crying came from Vartan's bedroom.

"I think it's here," said the neighbor with a smile.

Vartan squeezed his hat, crushing it, as he impatiently waited for someone to emerge from the bedroom. After a few minutes, the midwife came out and approached Vartan.

"Congratulations, you're the father of a healthy and beautiful baby girl," the midwife said.

"Can I go in and see her?" asked Vartan, anxiously.

"Of course, what daughter doesn't want her father? You've been waiting for her, now she is waiting for you," the midwife said.

Vartan cautiously approached the bedroom. He opened the door and saw Anna lying in their bed lovingly cradling their baby. She pulled her eyes away to look at Vartan.

"Vartan, she's beautiful. Come see your daughter," Anna said.

Vartan approached the bed and looked down at the baby, whose eyes were still unaccustomed to the light. She was indeed beautiful. As he gazed at the child, mesmerized, the love within him seemed to blossom like a flower until it reached an intense bloom, unlike anything he'd felt before.

"Can I hold her?" Vartan asked.

Anna handed the baby to Vartan, who gently took her into his arms. He ran a finger across her cheek, so that he could feel her skin. He put her forehead to his nose, so that he could smell her flesh. He rocked her tenderly, amazed how something so small could bring with it so large a joy.

Naming the child was easy. Both Vartan's and Anna's mother shared the same name. Now their granddaughter would have that name as well.

Her name would be Lena.

20

A Messenger at the Door

The first year of her life, Lena was seemingly always attached to her mother. No sooner would Anna set her down than the child would reach out her arms and cry. Although Anna would act frustrated by Lena's constant demands for her attention, she secretly adored it.

One evening, Anna sat at the table feeding Lena, while Vartan ate his dinner. Vartan made a funny face at his daughter, who laughed, which in turn caused her to spit out her food.

"Oh, Vartan, can you please stop? She hasn't eaten anything all day. And just when I get her to eat, you decide to tease her," Anna said.

"All I did is look at her," Vartan said.

Anna cast an annoyed glance to him and then turned her attention back to Lena. Vartan made the same face again, eliciting the same reaction from his daughter.

"Vartan, I told you to stop," said Anna, punching Vartan in the arm.

"I didn't do anything."

"Well, if you do it again, I'm going to scratch your eyes out."

Anna went back to feeding Lena. Vartan contemplated the risk of provoking his wife further. After brief consideration, he patted down prudence and made the face again. This one caused Lena to laugh uncontrollably.

"That's it," said Anna as she sprang from her chair.

Vartan jumped up at the sight of his enraged wife and made a rapid retreat—running to the front door with Anna in pursuit. Lena hopped in her baby chair and threw her arms up in encouragement. Whether the child's gesticulations were meant to urge her father in flight or to support her mother's violent ambitions could not be deciphered.

Vartan reached the door just as Anna grabbed hold of him. When the door opened both Vartan and Anna froze—there in the doorway stood Taniel.

"I went to great measures to ensure that my visit tonight would go unnoticed, but if you continue your chase outside, that may no longer be possible. May I enter?" Taniel said.

"Of course, of course. Please come in," said a confused and slightly embarrassed Vartan.

He hurried Taniel in and looked around cautiously before he closed the door. Vartan looked out each window to make sure no one else was outside and then drew all the curtains. When he walked back to the kitchen, he saw Anna holding Lena and Taniel playing with the child's hand.

"What a beautiful child, Vartan," said Taniel. "I had little doubt that you and Anna would have beautiful children. But this one is truly a gem."

"Thank you, Taniel," said Vartan. "It's good to see you after all this time. I wasn't sure if you'd ever return. What brings you to us today?"

"It's your father, Vartan. He's not well," said Taniel.

Vartan could feel his legs go weak, and he slumped into a chair. Taniel pulled up a chair next to him.

"What happened to him? Where is he?" Vartan asked.

"These last years have been hard ones on your father. He never told you, but he was ill even before he left. His condition has gotten worse, and I fear he only has a few days left. Right now, he is in one of our camps. It's a three-day march from here," Taniel said.

"I want to go to him."

"That's why I'm here. Your father forbade me to come. He didn't want me to risk bringing you to him. The Ottomans are actively trying to root us out, and they seem to be closing in on us by the day. But I couldn't have your father die only among colleagues and friends without his son's knowledge. I owe it to you. I owe it to him."

"Taniel, you know the debt I feel I owe you. I'm now more indebted to you than ever. I thank you for your friendship, and for your discretion."

"You might wish to reserve your gratitude. It's not without guilt that I come here today. Not only have I gone against the wishes of a dying man and a friend, but if you are to come, you must do so now—tonight. And it will mean leaving your wife and child. For how long, I cannot promise you. We will try to return you as soon as we can. But situations change daily; they become more deadly. And I can't guarantee that we'll find your father alive even if you decide to come. I'll understand if you wish to stay. If I find him alive when I return, I won't tell him that I was ever here. But as I said, I felt I owed it to you."

All Vartan could do was put his head in his hands, grappling with what to do.

"Vartan, I know how difficult this is," Taniel continued. "But I'm afraid we don't have the luxury of time. If you're to come, we must leave tonight. If you stay, I'll understand, and I hope you will not think ill of me for coming here this evening and putting you in this dilemma."

"Vartan," said Anna.

Vartan looked up.

"You have to go."

"But how can I leave you and Lena? I may be leaving you with wolves at the door."

"We'll be okay. Wolves can be fought off or hidden from, but your father cannot wait. What I wouldn't have given to have had a chance to see my father one more time before he died. To tell him I loved him. To hold his hand while there was still life in it. I couldn't call myself a good wife if I denied you that. You must go, not despite Lena and me but because of us."

"Thank you, Anna. When do we leave, Taniel?" Vartan said.

"As soon as we can," Taniel replied.

Vartan immediately began preparations. He gave Anna instructions to pass to his clerks who would tend to the store while he was gone. Anna made Taniel a plate to eat while Vartan got ready. She then prepared food for the men to take with them.

While Vartan was packing his essentials, Lena fell asleep and Anna tucked her in for the night. It was close to midnight when Taniel and Vartan were finally ready to depart.

"I'll come back as soon as I possibly can," Vartan said to Anna. "Please be careful. If anything happened to you and Lena, I don't know what I'd do."

"Don't worry about us; go to your father. We will be waiting for you when you come back," Anna said.

"I love you," said Vartan as he embraced Anna and kissed her.

"We love you too. Please be safe," Anna said.

Vartan turned to leave and halted, realizing he hadn't said good-bye to his daughter. He walked back to the bedroom, where he gazed at Lena as she slept. He took her hand, squeezed it, then put her hand to his lips and kissed it softly.

Then he set her hand down and left.

21

The Golden Crucifix

Vartan and Taniel traveled almost exclusively by night. They followed the North Star toward the mountains of Karasu. By the third night, they began climbing over the foothills of the mountains. As they reached the top of one hill, the ground plateaued and they headed east for another mile before they began to descend. They reached the bottom as dawn was breaking, and Vartan could see they were in a concealed valley. The hills rose high on all sides, but in front of them, Vartan could see a narrow passage cutting through the hills.

As they approached the passage, Taniel put his arm out to stop Vartan from walking ahead. He put his finger to his lips.

Taniel announced loudly, "We have traveled from Eden, covered by the waters of Lake Van."

A few seconds later, two guards, dressed in all black with bullet belts around their waists and crisscrossing their chest, emerged from either side of the passage with rifles aimed at Taniel and Vartan.

"Come forward," said one of the riflemen.

Taniel and Vartan slowly approached the man until he could make out their features.

"Taniel, it's you. Welcome back," the rifleman said. "Who is with you?"

"This is Vartan, Krisdapor's son. How is Krisdapor doing?"

"Not well. He rarely awakens, and we fear that he may pass any day."

"Take me to him," Vartan blurted out.

The men stepped aside to let Taniel and Vartan pass. The pair traveled for another fifteen minutes until the passage opened into a wide valley. Vartan could see tents set in a circle in the middle of the valley. At the center, two men were warming stew and cooking meat over an open fire.

The sounds of rocks sliding on steel could be heard from all corners of the camp, as the men were sharpening their swords. There was the brief greeting when one of the men recognized Taniel, but other than that Vartan couldn't make out any sounds of conversation.

Taniel led Vartan into one of the larger tents, where Vartan saw his father lying unconscious and another man watching over him.

"Hagop, this is Vartan, he's Krisdapor's only son," said Taniel. "He's traveled here to be with him. How's he doing?"

"He hasn't passed. We're doing what we can to keep the fever down, but his last minutes are near," said Hagop as he turned to Vartan. "It's good that you came. Your father is a noble man. He deserves the dignity to have his son here. Now, I'll leave you two. Taniel knows where to find me if needed."

Vartan approached the cot and peered down at his father. He was considerably thinner than when he last saw him and remarkably older in appearance. Vartan took his father's hand. As a child, he had felt the chastising sting of that hand many times. As he held it now, it was far thinner and weaker than he recalled. He laid his father's limp hand on his left palm, and with his other hand, Vartan began stroking it as if the warmth of his caress would bring some life back to it.

"Father, it's me, Vartan. I have come to . . ."

The final words would never be uttered, as Vartan dropped his head to his father's chest and wept.

Vartan maintained a vigil over the next four days, taking over responsibility for his father's care, trying to make him as comfortable as he possibly could as he waited for the inevitable.

Late at night on the fourth day, Vartan sat next to his father's bed, fighting the urge to sleep. He was startled to attention when he heard someone calling his name.

"Vartan, is that you?" his father feebly called out.

Vartan looked over to see his father's eyes open and staring directly at him.

"Yes, yes, it's me, Father. I've come to see you." Vartan approached his bed and grabbed hold of his hand.

"I never thought I would see you again, my son. It does my eyes good. How is Anna?"

"Anna is well. We have a daughter; she was born a year ago. Her name is Lena."

"Lena, ahh yes, a beautiful name. A beautiful name," said Krisdapor. "Vartan, there is a small pouch in my coat. Can you please get it?"

Vartan went to retrieve the pouch. His father motioned for him to open it. Vartan shook out the contents, and a golden necklace with a crucifix spilled into his hand.

"Your mother bought that on the day you were born. She wanted us to give it to your first child. I was hoping to be able to put it around my grandchild's neck myself. Could you please do it for me?"

"Yes, she'll love it," Vartan said.

"Thank you. It's good to see you, my son. It truly is. But I must rest now."

Vartan desperately wanted to continue talking to his father. He felt as if he had so many more things to tell him, but he remained tongue-tied as he watched his father drifting out of consciousness.

"I love you," blurted out Vartan, hoping his father heard him.

If he did or not, Vartan would never know. His father would be dead by morning.

The following day, Vartan helped bury his father in the camp. It wasn't the usual drawn-out ceremony he was accustomed to, but rather simple and quick. The grave had been dug weeks in advance. After a few men praised Krisdapor for his bravery, commitment, and friendship, the body was placed inside a crate and lowered into the grave.

As the men huddled over the burial site in prayer, they heard urgent footsteps and turned to see a messenger running into camp. He was dirty, disheveled, and covered in sweat.

"Van is under attack," he blurted out.

22

The Siege of Van

In the spring of 1915, Javdet Bey, the governor of the Van vilayet, had requested that the city provide four thousand Armenian men to be conscripted into the Ottoman Army. The local Armenian leadership was immediately suspicious, fearing that the aim was to render the Armenian population defenseless and vulnerable. The local Armenian leadership instead proposed to give five hundred men and offered to pay exemptions for the rest. This counteroffer was rejected. The local Ottoman officials then accused the Armenians of rebellion, and Bey issued an ominous warning.

"If the rebels fire a single shot, I shall kill every Christian man, woman, and every child up to here," said Bey, pointing to his knee.

Shortly after Bey issued his warning, two Armenian men coming to the aid of an Armenian woman were shot and killed by Ottoman soldiers. This incident set off what would be known as the Siege of Van, in which the outnumbered Armenians desperately defended the city's Christian residents against Ottoman forces.

———

The siege was now in its third day, and Christian residents huddled in the city's Armenian quarter, some three hundred yards from the city's outer stone walls. The men had dug trenches behind the fortified walls. They burrowed holes in the walls just big enough to fit the barrel of their rifles, and they made their stand. There weren't enough rifles to arm all the men, so those without guns made do with whatever weapon they could find.

As the men guarded the perimeter, the women, children, and elderly sought refuge as far back from the fighting as they could. Mariam's health continued to decline, and Ari stayed with his mother, along with the other women and children within the Armenian quarter. Those who had houses within the quarter opened their homes to take in as many people as they could, but there wasn't enough room to take in everyone and many were left to prop up a lean-to or another simple form of shelter in the makeshift camp. The Armenians had stockpiled their supplies, and food was being rationed carefully. While the men occupied themselves with the defense of the city, a few of the women undertook the responsibility to watch over and distribute the rations.

Mariam slumped against the wall of a crumbled home, hacking and coughing. With the ongoing battle and the overall fight for survival, few had the luxury to concern themselves with an old peasant woman, so Ari knew that his mother's survival was left to him. He carefully wrapped a blanket around her and left his mother's side to get in line for their rations. After a ten-minute wait, Ari reached the front of the line.

"Do you need food for just yourself?" asked a woman handing out the rations.

"For me and my mother," said Ari, pointing to Mariam against a far wall.

"You're a fine boy to look after your mother," replied the woman, mistaking Ari for an adolescent.

"He's no boy! He's a man, and he should be out there fighting and not here hiding among women and children like a coward," said a woman behind Ari.

He spun around to see Karun—brows furrowed and ears glowing—in her natural state of anger and indignation.

"Are you going to take food from children, from women, and from our poor elderly to fatten your stomach? Are you going to bask in the sun while the sons of other mothers, the husbands of other wives, and the fathers of other children risk their lives to protect you?" said Karun as she cast a venomous glare at Ari.

Everyone in the ration line turned around toward Karun and Ari as he lowered his eyes to the ground.

"Don't give this man any food. He seeks to live off the sacrifice of others, instead of fighting alongside men like my husband, who is old and sick. He is a healthy man, and yet he disguises himself as a child and cowardly hides himself away," Karun said.

Everyone seemed to look at Ari for a reply, but none came.

Ari had spent his life learning that he was entitled to nothing. He now felt like a beggar, in line for food rations that he and his mother hadn't contributed to, and behind a line of defense he wasn't helping to protect. He wanted to walk away and hide from all the disdainful eyes boring into him, but he knew if he did, his mother would have nothing to eat. His concern for his mother overrode the indignity brought about by Karun, and he stayed in line even though his mind could offer no words in his defense. He slowly turned back to the woman handing out the rations with a look of guilt that also contained a plea for mercy.

"We are all Armenians, and we all have to care for our own," said the woman as she handed Ari two ration bags.

Ari took the bags with trembling hands. He wanted to thank the woman, but his shame still wouldn't allow him to speak, so he just nodded to her and turned to walk away.

"Go have your feast like the coward you are," Karun hissed. "May God curse you for your gluttony and wickedness."

Ari tried to ignore her as best he could and continued walking toward his mother, who was far enough away that she hadn't heard Karun's tirade.

Ari sat next to his mother and opened her ration bag. He took out the bread, pepper, and cheese and gave them to his mother.

"Please eat with me, Ari," said Mariam when she noticed he hadn't opened his bag of food.

"I will," he said.

He sat down a few feet away. He turned his back to his mother, his face in the direction of the setting sun. He reached into his bag and brought it to his mouth. He continued in this way, with his back to his mother, until Mariam had finished her food and the sounds of fighting had dissipated.

After sundown, Ari made a bed for his mother on the ground using blankets and old rags. Once he laid her down, he watched over her until she fell asleep. Before he lay down to sleep himself, he took his bag of rations and put it under his mother's blanket.

The bag would be there for her when she woke in the morning—without a single crumb missing.

23

A Fateful March

The camp stirred to action after hearing news of Van's plight. The courier was told to continue north to try to reach the Russian Army in the Caucasus and ask for help. The remaining men packed provisions for their march to Van in the hopes of arriving there before the city fell.

Nervous energy rippled throughout the camp. For Vartan, the news was far more personal, and he was gripped by guilt.

It was approaching dusk when the forty-two men of the camp finally set out for Van, marching shoulder to shoulder in lines of two. Vartan had arrived as a civilian son coming to see his dying father. Now he found himself leaving as a member of this ragtag band of fighters.

Vartan marched alongside Taniel near the back of the line. Taniel had given Vartan a rifle and instructed him to not break ranks or make any hasty moves that might compromise the unit.

"The messenger said the Armenians are holding up well, and

that the women and children are protected," said Taniel as he marched alongside Vartan. "I'm sure Anna and Lena are safe for now. We'll make haste and arrive as soon as we can."

"I can only pray. I don't know what I'll do if anything happens to them," said Vartan as he stared ahead.

An hour into their march, the men were about to enter a mountain pass when Taniel sensed something wasn't right. They'd passed the sentry positions and hadn't seen any guards.

"Wait, wait," Taniel called out to the men in front who had entered the pass.

The men at the front stopped and looked back. But before Taniel could say another word, gunfire rang out. The bullets rained down from both sides of the Armenians, mowing down the men at the front first and then working their way back, dropping the men like dominoes.

"It's an ambush! Everyone, fall back," Taniel cried.

But for most, the warning came too late. The well-planned and orchestrated attack had systematically gunned down most of the unit. Only the handful of Armenians in the back of the lines were able to take cover and survive the initial onslaught. But the offensive from the unseen enemy was unrelenting.

Vartan could hear bullets whizzing all around him—one even grazed his ear, leaving a lingering buzz as he ran for cover and dove behind the safety of a mound with Taniel. They were now pitched in at the base of a slope that rose and fanned out toward the mountain pass in front of them. They still couldn't see any of their assailants, but it was clear that the ambush was coming from the sloping forest above and in front of them. From behind the mound, they saw more of their companions gunned down as they ran for cover.

"Have you been hit?" Taniel asked Vartan.

"I don't think so," Vartan replied.

Taniel peeked his head out and surveyed the situation. With no more exposed Armenian men, the shooting stopped. The enemy still hadn't shown themselves.

Suddenly there was more gunfire, but Taniel could see that this time the shooting came from their side and was directed at Ottoman soldiers to the right of their position. The gunfire was returned by the enemy, who quickly killed the two men firing. Taniel and Vartan looked out again and could make out a flank of Ottoman soldiers slowly advancing on them from the right. They were joined by another group of soldiers on the left, pinching in the last remaining Armenians. Vartan knew that the enemy would soon be directly above them on both sides and the cover the mound was providing would be compromised. The initial attack was so ferocious and efficient that he estimated there couldn't be more than a handful of the forty-two men still alive.

Another volley of gunfire erupted, and three more Armenians were killed. Taniel and Vartan heard someone say, "We have two of them here." Taniel peered out from behind the mound and could see Ottoman soldiers leading a pair of captured Armenian militiamen at gunpoint.

"You, behind the mound there," called out the Ottoman leader. "We know there are two of you. You're the only ones left. All your friends have been killed or captured. You can put down your weapons and surrender now and live, or you'll die here today. We'll happily accommodate whichever choice you make."

"Taniel, we'll wait here until nightfall and get away in the darkness," Vartan whispered.

"No, they know our position. They have us surrounded. If we try to escape, they'll kill us."

"Then we'll fight them back. We have guns as well."

"Vartan, I won't allow you to die here today. A dead man is of no use to anyone, least of all his wife and child. The only thing left to do is surrender and live through this day. As long as you're alive, you still have a chance."

"No, we must try. They'll kill us anyway."

"Give me your rifle, Vartan," said Taniel as he grabbed Vartan's weapon.

The two men looked at each other as Vartan tried to pull his rifle away. Taniel held it even tighter. Vartan's eyes turned dark as he yanked the rifle free of Taniel's grasp and then raised it as if he was going to strike Taniel with the butt of the firearm.

"Please, son," Taniel pleaded.

Vartan continued to glare at Taniel with his darkened eyes, but then he slowly dropped his head, his shoulders heaving as he tried to suppress sobs of frustration.

"I know, son. Let's get through this day. Give me your rifle," Taniel said.

Vartan released his hold on the rifle. Taniel took both their rifles and tossed them over the mound. Taniel put his hands in the air, stood, and emerged from behind the mound.

He looked over to Vartan, who stood and did the same.

24

The Armenian Solution

At the same time the siege on Van was taking place, the Ottoman government's final solution to the Armenian issue was already underway. The first phase saw the Ottomans round up and deport Armenian intellectuals from Istanbul to Ankara. Most of these intellectuals would ultimately be executed. Shortly afterward, the Ottomans began an extensive campaign, which called for the imprisonment and murder of able-bodied Armenian men within Ottoman Turkey. This left the Armenians defenseless and paved the way for the final and most heartless part of the extermination—the death marches.

The forced deportation of women, children, and elderly from the Anatolian peninsula to the Syrian Desert would litter the land with Armenian corpses. The deportees were denied food and water as they were mercilessly herded to a destination they were never meant to reach. The only thing that grew out of these death marches was desperation. And as a sickening byproduct, newborns were abandoned, the neglected elderly died quickly, and aimless orphans were being created by the second. In the end, it is estimated that anywhere from 800,000 to 1.5 million Armenians would lose their lives.

———

The Armenian resistance in Van held off the Ottoman forces for nearly a month, at which point the Russian Army arrived and pushed back the Turks. The fighting continued for two more months until the city was secured. However, the Russian forces weren't faring as well in skirmishes with the Turkish army to the north, and the Russians decided to evacuate their combat forces from Van to assist on other fronts. Without the protection of the Russian Army, the Armenians knew that remaining in Van would mean death. The Armenians began leaving the city in waves, seeking to reach the safety of Russian territories through the northern passages.

Feeling the urgency, most Armenians abandoned their possessions to preserve their lives. However, Karun couldn't bear the thought of leaving anything of hers behind. Just before taking shelter within the Armenian quarter, Karun had been diligent in packing her possessions in two wagons. The first wagon carried their essentials, including food. The second wagon held most of her valuables. They had driven the first wagon to the Armenian quarter with the understanding that Razmig would go back for the second wagon. However, the fighting had begun just as they reached the Armenian quarter, cutting them off from the rest of the city. The defense of Van wasn't without its casualties, and her husband had been one of them—taking a bullet through his left eye, killing him instantly. Now, for the first time, Karun found herself alone and at a disadvantage, no longer having the strength of a man to rely on.

As she mulled over her options for retrieving the second wagon, she spotted Ari helping his mother climb into their wheelbarrow. Karun waited until Ari walked to collect his and his mother's few belongings.

"Ari, my good boy. May I have a word with you?" said Karun.

It was a tone Ari rarely heard from Karun. Her soft and tender voice troubled him far more than if she'd addressed him in her more familiar bellicosity. As she approached him, he remained silent.

"Ari, God never blessed me with any children, but I have always considered you as a son," said Karun.

Ari didn't say a word.

"Razmig, God rest his soul, gave his life to protect you. He loved you like a son as well. Your poor mother will be little help to you on this journey. We have a long road ahead of us and we will need each other. I have a wagon and good horses back at my home. If you can go and bring them here, then the two of you can travel much easier."

"They told us not to leave. The house is to the south. They said we could only leave to the east," Ari said.

"Ari, those words are coming from the mouths of thieves. They want all of us to leave behind what we have spent our whole lives working for so that they can go through and steal at their leisure. The fighting has stopped, and the roads to the south are safe, especially for a man young and strong like you."

Ari didn't say a word and instead turned around and collected their last few blankets. Items in hand, he started walking toward his mother.

Karun grabbed his arm. "Ari, don't you see I'm trying to help you? Your mother is sick. She will be nothing more than a burden to you. If you get my other wagon, with all the supplies, you will give her a better chance to survive."

"I can't leave my mother, and we want to go with the next group out."

"And how do you think you'll make it without a wagon to go in? The wagon I have here is already filled, I don't have room for anyone. Ari, the only way you can help your mother is to get my other wagon. Once you bring it, we'll all be able to reach Russia safely. Without it, you and your mother won't have much of a chance. You won't be able to push her in that wheelbarrow the whole way."

Ari looked over at his mother, who was coughing as she sat cramped in their old wheelbarrow.

"Where's the wagon?" Ari asked.

"Just behind our house. It should still be there, but you must leave now before someone gets their hands on it," said Karun, her face beaming.

"Okay, I'll do it. But please watch my mother until I come back. And if I don't make it back in time, you have to take her in the wagon you have," Ari said.

"Of course, my boy, I wouldn't think of ever leaving her behind."

Ari walked over to his mother and told her he needed to get something before they left. He told her he might be awhile, but he promised to be back as soon as he could.

He left the quarter and made his way to Karun's home. He was so used to sneaking around Van unnoticed that he found that he wasn't afraid of leaving the relative safety of the Armenian quarter. His only fear was that he wouldn't be able to make it back with the wagon before the last group of Armenians left.

He made it to the house within a half hour. When he reached the home, it was unusually quiet. It seemed no one had come to plunder the home. Ari walked to the back and saw the wagon just as Karun had said. The horses were hitched to it, which he found odd. He approached the wagon and looked inside. It was empty. He couldn't understand why it wasn't filled with supplies like she said.

Not wanting to waste any more time, he climbed onto the wagon and whipped the reins above the horses. The horses lunged forward, but the wagon barely moved. Ari looked down to see a wooden board wedged between the spokes of the wheels, preventing the cart from moving. He climbed down and began to remove the board. He managed to get it out after a brief struggle. When he started climbing back onto the wagon, he felt something cold and hard pressed against the back of his head and heard the click of a trigger.

"It looks like we've caught a thief," said a Turkish voice.

25

The Horse Thief

Ari was led to Karun's house by two Ottoman soldiers wearing identical military green jackets, slacks, and peaked caps. One of the soldiers roughly pushed Ari forward with the blunt end of a rifle, causing Ari to stumble as he was ushered into the house. The soldiers marched him into the kitchen, where three other military men were sitting at the kitchen table eating.

"Sir, we found this creature outside trying to steal our wagon," said the lead soldier to the man at the end of the table.

"Is that so? Bring him over to me. Let me take a look at him," said an older, heavyset man, who was wearing a long coat with a red collar.

Ari was pushed forward until he was standing in front of the man, who turned his chair to get a closer look at him. Ari cast his eyes to the ground but could still feel the man's eyes as he surveyed him.

"I'm Erkan Mustafa Cengiz. These two men are my *miralays*," said the man motioning to the other men at the table. "What do they call you?"

"Ari."

"Ari. I'm here by the orders of the sultan to put an end to this traitorous rebellion," Mustafa said. "And although I consider myself a man of restraint, I'm finding I have little patience for traitors and thieves. Both are born from selfishness and deserve whatever punishment awaits them. But by the looks of it, it seems God has already punished you. Why do you look like this?"

"I don't know," said Ari as he tried to compose himself and calm his shaking legs.

"Is that why you have resorted to thievery, because of how you look? Do you think that gives you a right to take what doesn't belong to you? Do you think that'll make you a better person?"

"No, sir. I didn't come to steal. I was sent by the woman who owns the horses and wagon. She asked me to bring them to her," said Ari with his eyes still fixed on the floor.

"She did, did she? This was a house of a traitorous Armenian, who are killing innocent Turks as we speak. Those horses, this house, and everything else here is now the property of the empire. So, tell me again that you have not come here to steal?"

This time Ari remained silent.

"How old are you, boy?" Mustafa said.

"I'm thirty-one," Ari replied.

"Thirty-one? Why you look like nothing more than a child. Lift your head up and let me look in your eyes," said Mustafa as he leaned in and stared into Ari's eyes. "I thought you were a liar in addition to being a thief, but your eyes have age to them. It's a shame, I would have been inclined toward leniency if you were just a boy. But you're a man, you should know better."

Mustafa sat back in his chair, resting his interlocked hands on his overstuffed abdomen, and continued to stare at Ari.

"Search him. Let's see if there is anything else he might've stolen," Mustafa ordered.

The two soldiers who brought Ari in began patting him down and going through his pockets. One of the soldiers pulled out his medal and set it on the kitchen table.

All three of the men at the table sat up in surprise when they saw the medal in front of them. Mustafa looked at both of his companions, and each had the same look of disbelief on their faces.

"You're an Armenian. Is that right?" said Mustafa, addressing Ari.

"Yes."

"Where did you get this medal?"

"It was my grandfather's medal."

"Your grandfather? An Armenian? I'm warning you to be careful of what you say next. This is the Order of Osmanieh, this honor is not meant for Armenian hands. How did your grandfather get this medal?"

"My mother told me that a Turkish man gave it to him for saving his son," Ari said.

"She did, did she? And how did your grandfather save the man's son?"

"A boy fell into the Tigris, and my grandfather was there and pulled him out of the water," Ari replied.

"So, your grandfather waded in the shallows to make sure a child didn't get wet. What bravery. And for that he receives one of our empire's greatest honors," said Mustafa. "Do you take me for a fool, boy?"

"No, sir," Ari replied.

"What do you make of this story, Hamza?" said Mustafa to one of his miralays.

"I think the only thing left to determine is if this creature simply stole the medal or if he killed its rightful owner in the process," said Hamza, his thin and long face etched with contempt.

"And what of you, Ihsan?" said Mustafa, turning to the other man, who was about the same age as Mustafa but slightly built and wearing round spectacles.

"I don't know what to make of it, honestly," said Ihsan. "It would seem unlikely. But it would be interesting if it were true. And who would we be to question what a man does with the honors that are bestowed upon him?"

"Indeed, but we know that it's not true. No man who deserves an honor like the Order of Osmanieh would let it be sullied by Armenian hands," Mustafa said. "Chain him up for the time being. I'm leaving for Istanbul in the morning. I'll see this thief hanged for his crimes, which I believe includes murder, and I'll return this medal to the sultan myself."

"Please, sir. I didn't steal the medal," said Ari as he dropped to his knees and clutched his hands together. "What I told you is the truth. But you can have the medal, just please let me go. My mother is waiting for me. If I don't get back to her, there is no one to look after her. I beg you, sir."

"Stand up, you cretin. No amount of begging is going to save you from justice. You'll be hanged. I'll make sure of it," spat out Mustafa. "Now take this beast away from me, and if he makes another sound, beat him until he knows how to keep his lying tongue quiet."

"Yes, sir," said one of the two soldiers as he dragged Ari away.

Mustafa picked up the medal and examined it, running his

fingers over the cut of its surface. He then turned to his two companions.

"The filthy beast didn't even have the decency to treat this medal with the honor it deserved. Look how damaged it is. I'm traveling for Istanbul tomorrow. I'm taking the wagon and the horses with me. The rest I'll leave here. I want to have a presence on the perimeter until everything in Van is settled. I'll have one of you stay behind in my absence, but I do need the other to come with me."

"Let me come, sir," offered Ihsan.

"It will be a long journey, so I was hoping for Hamza, as he is a little younger." Mustafa laughed. "But at our age, we should have enough stories to fill the time."

"Thank you, sir," Ihsan said.

26

A Faithful Witness

Chained by the waist to a tree, Ari pulled against his restraints in a futile attempt to get away. It was well past midnight, and he couldn't hear any of the soldiers, so he became more aggressive in trying to get loose of the chains. But as hard as he tried, his efforts had no effect on the restraints.

He stopped to catch his breath and heard something rustling behind him. He remained still and looked around. He heard the striking of a match and saw the light from a lamp about thirty yards behind him. He saw a figure of a man walking toward him, but his face was obscured by the light. The man walked up to him, knelt, and moved the lamp from in front of his face. When he did, Ari recognized it was the bespectacled man he'd seen at the kitchen table. Ari instinctively pulled away.

"Don't be frightened. It's Ari, correct?" he asked.

Ari nodded.

"I'm Ihsan. I came here to make sure you're okay. I brought you some water. Are you thirsty?" he said.

Ari licked his blistered lips and nodded.

"Here drink. And please relax, I'm not here to harm you," said Ihsan as he took a ladle of water from his bucket and put it to Ari's lips. "Drink, son. I hope you haven't been treated too harshly."

Ari drank five ladles of water before he felt his thirst was quenched enough to speak.

"Sir, I'm sorry I came here for the horses and wagon. I didn't mean to try to steal them. I thought I was getting them for the lady who owns them. You have to believe me. I beg you, sir, not for me and my life. I beg you for my mother. She is ill. No one is there to look after her, even tonight. I have to make sure she is okay. Please, sir, I beg you. My mother won't live long if I don't go back to her," Ari pleaded.

"I'm sorry for your mother, son. I really am. I don't know if there is much I can do. But I don't believe you to be a thief. I hope you know that," Ihsan said.

"Then please unlock these chains and let me go," Ari said.

"I don't have the keys to the chains, and I don't know how far you would get even if I could unlock them. The perimeter of this property is being guarded. I'll let you know that you didn't just sneak in here. You were allowed to enter. They could have easily shot you if they wanted to. They'll shoot you now if you try to leave. No, you'll leave with me and Mustafa for Istanbul tomorrow. That is your best chance to survive," Ihsan said.

"But what about my mother, sir?"

"I'm sorry, son, I can do nothing for her."

Ihsan brought another ladle of water to Ari's lips. Ari turned away. Ihsan paused and put the ladle back into the bucket.

"Is the story you told about the medal true?" Ihsan asked.

"It is, sir. I wouldn't lie about that," answered Ari.

"You said it was the Tigris. Where did your grandfather live?"

"Diyarbakir."

"Diyarbakir," repeated Ihsan as he rubbed his chin in thought. "Do you know the name of the man who gave him the medal?"

"No, sir. My mother never told me."

"Did your mother tell you if there was anyone else who witnessed what happened?"

"Yes, she said the boy's mother tried to go into the river herself to save him, but others held her back. And there was no one else there to grab the boy once he let go of the rocks, except for my grandfather."

There was a long silence as Ihsan stared at Ari with an emotionless expression.

"I'm going to leave this water here with you. Drink as much as you can and please get some rest. We will be leaving for Istanbul early in the morning," said Ihsan as he got up and started to walk away.

"But, sir, what about my mother?" Ari called out after him.

Ihsan stopped and turned back to Ari. He raised the lamp up, this time to illuminate his face.

"There is nothing I can do for her. I'm sorry. May Allah have mercy on her."

27

The Hearts of Men

Ari was woken early in the morning by a kick to the thigh. He saw two soldiers standing over him and noticed he was unchained from the tree.

"Get up, the erkan is waiting for you," spat out one of the soldiers.

The soldiers led him around the property to Karun's wagon, where Mustafa, Ihsan, and Hamza were waiting, and had Ari climb onto the back of the wagon. They handcuffed him to one of the sideboards and handed the keys to Mustafa, who, along with Ihsan, climbed onto the front of the wagon.

"We're going to take this wagon to our station on the other side of Van. We'll leave the horses and wagon for our men there, for them to use as they need," said Mustafa to Hamza. "They have transportation waiting for us at the station. Carry on here as we have discussed. I'll send word once I arrive in Istanbul."

With that, Mustafa motioned to Ihsan, who was holding the reins, and the two officers, along with their Armenian prisoner, headed out.

Twenty minutes into their trip, the outline of Van came into view. Ari pulled at his handcuffs and the wooden board they were attached to. He became so desperate that the sounds of him struggling could be heard over the snorting of the horses and the clanking of the wagon.

"Keep it down back there, you Armenian bastard!" yelled out Mustafa. "This wagon is unpleasant enough without having to hear you back there."

"Sir, I beg you, please let me go see my mother. She'll die without me. She has no one else. Please, sir," pleaded Ari.

"The only place you're going is the gallows, now shut up," responded Mustafa as he lashed out behind him and struck Ari in the head with his fist.

"Mustafa, that's not necessary. He is our prisoner. The courts will deal with him when we arrive in Istanbul. In the meantime, he is under our protection," Ihsan said.

"What did you say to me?" Mustafa asked.

"Nothing, sir. I was suggesting that we just have more patience with the hunchback."

"Your suggestions were neither solicited nor wanted. And let me be clear, this is my prisoner, and as the commanding officer, his treatment falls to my discretion. Understood?"

"Yes, sir," said Ihsan, avoiding Mustafa's piercing glance.

After a prolonged silence Mustafa spoke. "Ihsan, I know it has been hard for you. When we were at the academy together, no one would have thought I would rise to a higher rank than you, considering who your father was. You were the one marked for greatness. My father was a drunk. He was an embarrassment. You don't think I knew what everyone thought of me? Do you know what it's like to have to earn everything yourself? No, of course you don't. Your father could snap his fingers and they would move you to the front of the line. Yet, through all the doubting eyes and the stinging words, I was the one who persevered and rose to the position I have now," Mustafa said.

"We were all proud of you, Mustafa. Everyone at the academy. You earned everything you received, no one ever doubted that."

"Do you know what my father told me when I graduated from the academy?"

"No, I don't."

"He told me he was proud to have a son like me. Can you believe that? That bastard had the audacity to call me his son. And you know what I did? I spat in his face, and I told him to get out of my sight. That I was an officer now. Not the son of some drunken, spineless peasant."

"I'm sorry, Mustafa."

"Sorry? I don't want your sympathy. Who are you to show me sympathy? Let me ask you, my friend, since we are being candid. Do you think your father was proud of you? Do you think if he were alive today, he would be proud seeing a son of his being a subordinate to the progeny of a drunkard?"

"My father always respected you."

"I believe he did," said Mustafa as he nodded his head. "But the question is, did he respect *you*?"

Ihsan didn't answer as they continued their journey in silence. Ten minutes later, they came across a stream.

"Pull over here. We can let the horses drink. I have to relieve myself," Mustafa said.

Ihsan pulled the wagon over to the stream and loosened the horses' harness, and they began drinking from the stream. Mustafa walked to some nearby shrubs to relieve himself. After a few minutes, Mustafa returned to see Ihsan standing in front of the wagon, twirling the medal in his hand as he was examining it.

"What are you doing? I thought you would have had the horses harnessed back up by now. We don't have time to waste," Mustafa said.

"I was just thinking. We're going through a lot of trouble for a small medal like this. Do we really need to burden the courts? Why don't we let the hunchback go?" Ihsan said.

"That isn't some small medal as you like to put it. And the hunchback has no right to it. He could have only come by it unlawfully. He will be made an example of. I'll see to it. And I thought I made it clear that I'm not interested in what you think we should do. Now harness the horses and let's be on our way," ordered Mustafa as he began to walk toward the front of the wagon.

"Not before you give me the keys to the hunchback's handcuffs," said Ihsan as he drew his sword and blocked Mustafa's path.

"Ihsan, are you mad? Get out of my way and do as I say, or I will see to it that you're court-martialed for this outrage."

"As I said, not before you give me the keys. Neither you nor I are going anywhere until we set the hunchback free."

"Oh, I see what's happening. I hurt your feelings, did I? And now you're trying to prove, what? That you are some brave, noble man? What are you going to do with that sword? Kill me?"

"If I have to."

"You've lost your mind. Have you ever killed anyone?"

"No, and I'd rather you not be my first, but the hunchback must be set free. Give me the keys and I'll let him go. Then I'll set my sword down, and you can take me to Istanbul as your prisoner and I'll confess to everything."

Ari observed the confrontation from the back of the wagon when Mustafa cast an angry glance his way, which caused Ari to pull back.

"Put down your sword, you fool, and get back on the wagon!" said Mustafa as he began to advance on Ihsan. "I'm the one giving orders here; I will not be dictated to. I'll see the hunchback hanged, just before I see you hanged. Now get out of my way."

"Don't test me on this, Mustafa. Give me the keys," said Ihsan calmly.

Mustafa ignored the plea. He walked directly toward Ihsan, who raised his sword. Mustafa stopped when he felt the sword pressing against his stomach. The two men locked eyes, each testing the other's resolve. Mustafa was the first to break the stalemate as he went to slap the blade of the sword away, but he wasn't able to, as Ihsan plunged the blade into his commander's abdomen. Mustafa's expression changed from anger to disbelief as he grasped the blade of the sword with his hands, cutting them in the process. Mustafa looked down at the blood gushing from his wound, then back up at Ihsan.

"Why?" uttered Mustafa before his eyes rolled back and he crumpled to the ground.

Ihsan pulled the blade out of Mustafa and tossed it to the ground. He went through Mustafa's pockets until he found the keys. He climbed onto the back of the wagon and unlocked Ari's handcuffs.

"Son, take these horses and this wagon and head to Van. That is all I can do for you," said Ihsan as he jumped back down and started harnessing the horses back to the wagon.

"Sir, why would you do this for me? They will hang you for this," said a confused Ari.

"I know they will. I knew that before I did it. But I'll tell you why, Ari. It was a lovely story you told about your grandfather and the boy he saved. A lovely story. But I knew the story already. I was there that day. You see, that boy was me," Ihsan said.

Ari looked at Ihsan with shock and incredulity, blinking his eyes in disbelief. To him, it was as if a character in some familiar fairytale had come to life.

"I-I . . ." stammered Ari.

"It's okay, Ari. There is no reason to say anything. And if it's gratitude you want to express, please save it for the worthy. This act was simply one of duty. I wish I could do more, but whatever influence and power I had is gone now. We're living in deadly times. I don't know if you will be alive in a day's time, a week's time, or a year's time. Only God knows, and I believe He will protect you. But you must go now, quickly," Ihsan said.

"But what will you do?"

"My fate is sealed, Ari. Don't worry about me. My end will come on my own terms. Go now, hopefully you can find your mother."

Ihsan helped Ari climb onto the front of the wagon. He gave him the reins. He then reached into his pocket and brought out the medal.

"This belongs to you, Ari. My father cherished this medal, and I felt guilty that he gave it away because of me. I told him that on his deathbed. He told me how proud he was of the medal and how he loved it, but that he loved me more. He said his only regret is that he should have taught me how to swim. And then we laughed. That's how I said goodbye to him. I couldn't ask for more," said Ihsan as he handed the medal to Ari.

A nostalgic smile crept over Ihsan's face as the two men shared a moment of silence. Then Ihsan slapped the rear of one of the horses, which sent the wagon on its way.

Ihsan watched as the wagon sped away. When he couldn't see it any longer, he walked over to his fallen colleague. He looked at the body and saw Mustafa's face was frozen in shock—eyes open, mouth agape. The blood had all but run out of his body.

Ihsan picked up his sword, placed it to his own stomach, and fell to the ground, impaling himself with it.

28

The Silent Earthquake

As Ari drove the wagon toward Van, he couldn't rid himself of a growing fear. Unlike before, when he had only himself to hide, now he had the impossible task of making it back to the Armenian quarter with a clumsy and loud wagon. He briefly considered abandoning the wagon but then thought of his mother and how much they needed it. So, he decided to continue.

Instead of taking a direct route and entering the city from the south, Ari determined it was safer to stay on the country roads and travel around the city and enter from the north. This gave him the best chance of avoiding danger, as most of the Ottoman forces were concentrated to the south and the west. He urged the horses on, knowing he had to make up time.

He was on the road just shy of an hour before he entered the Armenian quarter.

"God bless you, my good boy," said Karun when she saw Ari

riding up with the wagon. "When you didn't come back last night, I thought all was lost. But deep down I knew you could do it."

She peered in the back of the wagon, and her eyes darkened. "Where's everything? What did you do with all my things?"

"There was nothing in the wagon. It was empty when I arrived," said Ari angrily. "Where is my mother?"

"Nonsense, I loaded it myself. This wagon should have been filled."

"Soldiers were there, and they took everything. Tell me where my mother is," Ari demanded.

"Your mother is exactly where you left her. And you should have snuck everything back onto the wagon before you left. You most likely divided things among you and those soldiers. I should have never trusted you," Karun said.

"I didn't take a thing. I brought the horses and wagon just as you asked," Ari said tersely. "I'm getting my mother, and we have to leave. Stay here with the wagon while I bring her. They told us everyone had to leave by yesterday; I hope it's not too late."

Ari grabbed the two canisters of water that were in the wagon and rushed toward the wall of the building where he had left his mother the day before. Once Ari had receded from view, Karun called out to another man.

"Do you still need a wagon? I have a wagon and two good horses to sell. They'll get you and your family to safety."

After a brief inspection, the man agreed to purchase the wagon and horses. He piled his wife and four children aboard, took the reins, and drove off.

Meanwhile, Ari rushed to find his mother. When he turned a corner, he saw her lying on the ground. Her eyes were closed and she wasn't moving. He bent down and shook her, and still no movement. He could see her lips were chapped and blistered.

"Momma," said Ari as he shook her harder.

Mariam responded by flickering her eyes open.

"Ari. Is that you? Thank the Lord. I thought something happened to you when you didn't return," said Mariam in her feeble voice.

"I'm sorry, Momma, but I had to go on an errand. I thought I'd be back sooner, but I won't leave you again. Drink some water, you look thirsty," said Ari as he opened one of the canisters and placed it to Mariam's lips.

Ari watched her drink and saw some vigor come back into her.

"I got a wagon and horses for us. It'll be easier to travel now," Ari said.

"Horses? A wagon? How'd you get a wagon?"

"Karun had two and left one back at her house. She said if I got it for her, we could ride in it."

"She did?" asked Mariam, suspiciously.

"Yes, but we must go now," said Ari as he helped his mother back into the wheelbarrow and pushed her forward.

Ari transported his mother as fast as he could to the spot he had left the horses and wagon. He turned the corner to the main road expecting to see Karun waiting with the wagon, but there was nothing there.

"Ari, no one's here," Mariam whispered.

As Ari fought a rising panic, he looked around but couldn't see or hear anyone. He lifted the wheelbarrow and started frantically pushing his mother forward again. It seemed as if they were the only two people left in the city. About fifty yards away, he saw the back of a man dressed in black talking to a woman holding a child. Ari guided the wheelbarrow in their direction. It was only when he got closer that he noticed the man was Father Krikor.

"Anna, you have to leave immediately. The last group has already left," Father Krikor said to the woman.

"I had to go back and get Lena's things and we got separated from the group. I can't find the group now and they have all the horses. Can I leave with you?" Anna asked.

"My child, it's too late for me. I must stay behind to make sure everyone gets out safely, but you and your child must get out now," finished Father Krikor just before hearing rumbling behind him.

"Ari, Mariam . . . what are you still doing here?" Father Krikor asked, the shock apparent on his face.

"We were going to leave, but I didn't know which way the group went," Ari said.

Before Father Krikor could reply, his acolyte came rushing toward the group.

"Father, the Ottomans have cut off our exit to the north, and they have entered the quarter," he said.

Almost instantly, a flood of Ottoman soldiers descended on the small group, their rifles drawn. Out from behind the line of soldiers emerged a short, fat man with a heavy mustache, wearing a white turban and a gray robe—it was the kaymakam of Van.

"Father Krikor, my apologies. I thought we would find murderous rebels and not holy men and harmless women and children," said the kaymakam as he motioned for the men to lower the rifles.

"Hello, Faruk," Father Krikor said.

"It appears we came just in time. We have been told that an earthquake of disastrous magnitude is set to hit Van. The orders are to evacuate all our residents. There is a convoy of evacuees to the north. They are heading west and eventually to the south where it's safe. A few of these soldiers will escort these women and children to meet up with the convoy. I'll ask you and your young assistant to stay behind. There is business we must attend to. You understand, don't you?" Faruk said.

"I understand, only too well," Father Krikor said. "Anna, Mariam, please go with these soldiers. And, Faruk, may I remind you that these are women and children. I ask that you please give them the consideration they deserve."

"Of course," replied a smirking Faruk.

With that, a pair of soldiers escorted Father Krikor and his acolyte away from the group.

"Follow us," ordered another pair of soldiers, to the remaining group. Ari lifted the wheelbarrow and stoically pushed it forward while Anna clutched Lena closely. For nearly an hour they walked, no one speaking a word until they came upon a line of refugees. The soldiers waited until they saw a gendarme on horseback at the end of the procession. When he reached the soldiers, they had a brief conversation, and the soldiers left. The gendarme looked over the motley crew that he'd just inherited.

"Okay, time for us to take you to your new home. Start following the others," he ordered.

29

An Unholy Exodus

Two Turkish gendarmes on horseback bracketed the convoy of Armenians—one at the front and one at the rear. In between the two was a quarter-mile-long line of Armenian deportees.

Of the two gendarmes, the rear one was far more menacing. The gendarmes were dressed alike. They wore dark, high-collared military jackets with a row of buttons running from the abdomen to the base of the neck. Slightly loose-fitting slacks and leather boots made for ease of horsemanship, and black fez hats topped off their ensemble. But whereas the front gendarme was stern yet disciplined, his rear counterpart was more impulsive and unpredictable.

Ari had the added burden of pushing his mother along in the wheelbarrow. This caused them to drop to the back of the procession, but he was cautious not to fall too far behind. A day into the march and he'd already seen how the gendarmes dealt with anyone not keeping pace. The day prior, while struggling up steep hills, Ari watched a fellow refugee helping her rapidly weakening elderly mother. The two began to lag until the mother had to stop and rest. The rear gendarme told the pair to keep walking. Neither moved. The gendarme pulled out his gun and shot the two point-blank.

Ari was not a strong man, but a life of struggle had taught him how to persevere. He learned it wasn't his lack of strength he had to overcome, or the pangs of hunger that had to be conquered, but rather the limitations of his own mind. If he allowed it, the mind would tell him how ill-suited he was, it would compel him to stop, it would demand nourishment for his body. But he found that his mind was not his master. It could be ignored. Its discretion be damned. He learned to control this mental nuisance, with all its meddling rationality, and force his mind to focus on simple things that he could lose himself in—like the cream-colored swirls in the buttons of his mother's sweater. And when properly occupied, properly caged, the mind no longer held an alliance to blistering feet and begging lungs.

The trek north brought them to the eastern tributary of the Euphrates. The caravan then turned west, following the flow of the river, which they could see below them. The forced march was taking its toll on the Armenians, many of whom were old and feeble. Ari began to see more and more bodies littering the ground. Most were motionless, others he could hear panting out their final breaths.

As they continued walking, Ari passed a mother crying over the body of her young son. The child was frothing at the mouth but was otherwise still.

"Please help me. Please help my son," the woman pleaded to anyone passing by.

But no one stopped. No one even looked her way. Help would finally come from the gendarme, who ended the mother's grieving by cutting her throat.

Ari and his mother were last in line, just in front of the rear gendarme. It was getting late, and Ari knew they would soon be stopping the march for the day. Suddenly the gendarme rode past them and farther up the line of Armenians. He slowed his horse until he was alongside a woman in line.

The rear gendarme was a short man, and despite inserting padding in the soles of his boots and a habit of raising onto his toes when speaking, he fell far short of the six-foot stature he boasted of having. However, what he lacked in height, he made up in girth. He was so wide across the shoulders and hips that his body took on a boxy shape. He was not a handsome man, and impolite company might even go so far as to call him ugly. He had an oversized, aquiline nose with gaping nostrils that flared when he tried to suppress a persistent facial tick. A jagged scar ran from the left corner of his mouth to his cheekbone. His right eye had lost its pigment, and his two front teeth were chipped in the middle, creating a near perfect triangular gap. During idle times, he had a habit of sucking air through the opening—letting out a lazy hiss not unlike a lurking asp. Despite all that, he had an air of vanity and would have most likely scoffed at the suggestion that the fairer sex didn't swoon at the sight of him.

He could always be seen holding a *jambiya* dagger. He had the curved knife out so much that he adapted it as an extended appendage—using it to scratch his back, to pick his teeth, and to smooth his mustache.

"You with the child, what's your name?" said the rear gendarme, hissing in air as he waited for a reply.

The woman ignored him.

"I said, you with the child. The pretty one. What's your name? Don't be impolite."

Seemingly afraid to anger the gendarme, the woman slowed and looked over at him.

"My name is Anna," she said.

"Anna. A lovely name. I am Ozan," he replied. "Is that your daughter?"

Anna's only response was to nod as she instinctively clutched Lena tighter and continued walking.

"This has been a hard road. You and your daughter look in need of some water. Here, take this," said Ozan as he extended a canister of water to Anna.

"Thank you," said Anna as she accepted the canister and put it to Lena's lips.

The sight of Lena quenching her thirst invigorated Anna a little. Even though she was also thirsty, she was conscious of leaving some water in the canister, so as not to return it to the gendarme empty. She pulled the canister from Lena's lips and went to hand it back to Ozan.

"No, you finish it off. You need it more than I do," he said to Anna.

"Thank you again," said Anna as she took her turn.

"We're going to stop for the night. And it would be a great honor and pleasure for me if you would grace me with your company."

"I thank you for your kindness, but I must stay with my daughter. She's young, and I fear this journey has weakened her a great deal."

"I insist. I would make a better friend than I would an enemy to you and your daughter."

Anna had already witnessed the gendarme's ruthlessness along this road. Despite his ostensive act of kindness, she could easily see through Ozan's veiled threat. And more than anything, she had Lena to consider. Despite her misgivings, whatever advantage she could give her daughter to survive through this ordeal, she felt she had to. Reluctantly, she fell back with Ozan. A few minutes later, the caravan stopped for the night.

Anna watched as Ozan prepped a tent in front of a line of trees. The tent was designed to sleep one man, and simple enough to erect and take down in minutes. Still cradling Lena in her arms, Anna sat down about twenty yards from Ozan and directly across from Mariam.

"What a beautiful child," said Mariam, who was sitting on the ground propped against the wheelbarrow.

It was the first genuinely kind word Anna had heard since they joined the caravan. Her maternal pride made her feel normal for a moment.

"Thank you, she's my angel," replied Anna, as she locked eyes on her daughter.

"What's her name?" Mariam asked.

"Her name is Lena."

"That's a beautiful name for a beautiful child. How old is she?"

"Just over a year. My hope is that her father, Vartan, is back for her second birthday. I want to make a cake for her."

"Vartan, the shop owner? You must be his wife."

"Yes."

"He's the one with the magic eyes. I've never seen eyes like that," Mariam said.

The women heard Ozan approaching and stopped their conversation. Dagger in hand, Ozan stopped in front of Anna. He scratched the back of his ear with his blade and looked over the area and noted the clusters of people scattered on the plain. Most people set up for the night farther up the trail. The only ones close to his tent were this sickly old lady and her disfigured son.

"I'd like for you to join me in my tent. You can leave your daughter here," said Ozan. It was more a demand than a request.

Anna looked around, frightened and confused. Anna looked back at Mariam, who was the only person who seemed interested in her plight. No words were exchanged between the women, but there was an understanding, nonetheless. Mariam simply nodded. Anna walked over to Mariam and handed Lena to her.

"Thank you," said Anna as she ran her hand through her daughter's dark hair.

Anna turned and followed Ozan to his tent. He motioned to Anna to enter. Ozan began taking off his uniform as he watched Anna crawl inside the tent. Once he undressed to his undergarments, he followed Anna into the tent as well. He lay down next to Anna and snuggled against her body, his foul breath filling Anna's nostrils. She tried to repress the fear and disgust, but as he ran his hand across her cheek, she instinctively recoiled.

"Shhhh, it's okay. It's lonely on this journey. We're both human, both in need of company. You're a beautiful woman," Ozan said.

Anna didn't resist, she just lay still and looked up at the roof of the tent, stifling her cries and desperately fighting back tears. Outside the tent, dusk was falling, and all seemed still. The calm was disturbed only by the muffled sounds of rape.

"I remember when you were this small," said Mariam to Ari, who was busy clearing a space on the ground for him and his mother to sleep.

Ari nodded and continued his work.

"You were a beautiful baby as well. You fussed more than this little angel . . . you didn't have enough to eat," said Mariam.

Mariam continued talking to Ari about anything and as loud as her feeble voice would allow. The conversation was meant less to reminisce and more to protect some of Anna's modesty. An hour later, Anna returned for Lena. Anna found she couldn't look at Mariam. But when Mariam handed Lena to her mother, Mariam grabbed Anna's hand.

"It's okay, my child. We'll be here for you and your daughter. It's difficult, but I want you to know you have a friend," Mariam told her.

Anna looked up briefly at Mariam, tried to force a smile, and gave a slight nod of acknowledgment before walking off with her daughter.

Each subsequent day, Ozan had Anna walk alongside him at the rear. When night fell, Ozan would again have Anna come to his tent, and Mariam would watch Lena. After a couple of days, Ozan insisted that Anna stay with him throughout the night, leaving Mariam and Ari to care for Lena until morning.

Even though Mariam's health was faltering by the day, when she would hold and play with Lena, she seemed to get some life back in her. Ari watched her holding and playing with the child, and even giving her some of the little food they had. He asked his mother to be careful about giving the child their food as they would soon not have any for themselves. Mariam said she would but continued feeding Lena anyway.

On the fifth day of their march, Ozan awoke to find Anna gone. Walking outside, he saw the other gendarme, who was usually camped at the head of the group. His partner was adjusting his belt and gave Ozan a slight nod as he passed by. Ozan looked in the direction his companion had come from and saw Anna standing up from behind a row of shrubs and buttoning her blouse. With downcast eyes, she walked over to retrieve her daughter from Mariam. Moments later, the caravan began to move.

At first, Ozan rode silently beside Anna and Lena. Anna could feel his eyes burning into her, but she was too frightened to look at him.

"So, is that it, my little nymph? I've been sleeping with a filthy whore."

Anna didn't answer; instead, she kept her head down and continued walking. Ozan dismounted, approached Anna, and yanked her arm, roughly pulling her out of the line of refugees. He forced her to look at him.

"Why!?" Ozan demanded.

"He made me," said Anna, trying to hide her face.

"You're lying!"

Ozan slapped Anna hard across the face, causing her to stumble back and fall to the ground with Lena on top of her.

"Please, sir," pleaded Anna as she clutched a crying Lena to her chest.

"Please? Now you want mercy? After all that I've done for you, and you betray me. I can't stand the sight of you. You're vile and filthy. I want you out of my sight," said Ozan as he spat on Anna.

Ozan turned away and walked back to his mount. Anna slowly rose and tried to quiet the child. She walked back toward the group, wanting to return to the others as quickly as she could, hoping to get in line farther away from Ozan. She was too busy calming Lena to see Ozan take out his gun behind her. Anna would never hear him fire it. The bullet tore through her head with little effort, and her body crumpled to the ground once more, but this time she would not rise.

Ari and Mariam were closest at the back of the line, and Mariam witnessed the murder.

She heard Lena's cries grow louder as the toddler crawled over to her mother and pushed her, urging the lifeless body to move. Ari turned and saw the scene but tried to ignore it and continued pushing his mother along.

"Ari, stop! We can't leave the child. Please get her. She'll die if we leave her," said Mariam as she grabbed his arm.

Ari acted as if he didn't hear his mother and continued walking. Mariam tugged his arm again.

"Please, Ari," Mariam begged.

Ari looked at his mother and saw the pleading in her eyes. He could see how desperately his mother wanted to help this child. Maybe it was because no one ever helped them. Maybe it was because, for once, here was someone they could help. Whatever the reason, he could see it was important to Mariam to save this child, and what was important to his mother still mattered to him. Ari slowly set down the wheelbarrow, turned, and began walking toward Lena. Ozan saw him approaching and immediately rode in front of Ari, barring the path with his horse. He took out his gun and pointed it at Ari's head.

"If you take one more step, I will kill you as well. Get back in line," Ozan said.

Ari looked over at the still-crying child. Realizing there was nothing he could do, he reluctantly turned around, walked back to his mother, lifted the wheelbarrow, and pushed it forward. This time, Mariam didn't utter a word but continued to gaze helplessly back at the child tugging at her mother's body. Ari fixed his eyes forward. There was nothing he could do. He had to stay alive. He had to take care of his mother. He had to catch up with the rest of the group. He had to think of simple things, he told himself—simple things.

But the child's cries would not allow him to.

———

With a horde of Turkish citizens looking on, the executioners tightened the nooses around Father Krikor's and his acolyte's neck. After an expedited trial, their sentences were to be carried out. In a show of transparency, and in the spirit of justice, a judge read the government's case to the crowd. The two men remained still while the judge recited the litany of crimes they were convicted of—top of which was treason. Father Krikor looked calm and emotionless, but his acolyte was visibly shaking.

"Very Reverend Father, I'm ashamed to say I'm afraid," the acolyte whispered.

"There is no need to be ashamed. I am afraid as well," Father Krikor said. "But you above all have nothing to fear. You have been a selfless servant to the Lord. God is merciful and He will always have a place for you in His house. The deeds man chooses to punish, God will choose to reward. Your soul is pure, and your heart true. You have given much for your brothers. The Church, this world, could ask nothing more of you."

"Then what is it that you fear, Father?"

"I fear that I haven't done enough."

The trap doors opened, the rigid rope stopped their fall with a jolting snap, and the two men hung lifeless.

30

The Good Shepherd

The convoy continued its journey until slightly before dusk. Just as the sun was setting, the skies opened, and heavy rain poured down on the deportees. The gendarmes were forced to stop the line as everyone scrambled to find cover.

Ari wheeled his mother off to the side of the path. What few trees there were in the area were quickly encircled by Armenians, and the two gendarmes pitched their tents nearby. Seeing no shelter, Ari set down the wheelbarrow about ten yards from a group of Armenians that were clustered under a tree. The gendarmes were another twenty yards away, already in their tents. Ari found four branches, stuck them into the softening ground, then tied a blanket to them to cover him and his mother from the rain.

Once the two of them were under the blanket, Mariam grabbed Ari's arm. "Ari, I'm going to ask you to do something that you won't like or understand, but you have to promise me you'll do it."

"What is it?" asked Ari.

"Ari, please go find the child and get away from here. If you leave now, you can still save her. You can still save yourself. In this rain and this dark, no one will see or hear you. But you must go now," Mariam said.

"I'm not going to leave you," said Ari, looking away from his mother.

Mariam gently touched his chin and pulled his face toward her so that she could look into his eyes.

"Ari, they're not leading us to a new home, they're leading us to death."

"Then I'll die with you," said Ari, gritting his teeth.

"Please, Ari, don't be foolish, I'm an old woman. When death comes to collect its dues, the old pay so that the young need not. You're still young and strong enough to escape and save yourself."

"I will not leave without you. If I must die with you, I will. If I must die for you, I will as well."

Mariam's body stiffened after Ari's last comment, and she looked away from him.

"No," she said softly. "Too many have already died for me. I will not allow my son to be counted among them. Please tell me you would not be so cruel as to do that."

"You told me grandfather loved you and that he was a good man. You may have never said it, but I know you would want me to be like him. So how can you ask me to leave you, when you know he wouldn't do that?" said Ari as he dug in his resolve. "I may not be like him, brave and unafraid. I'm scared, but I'm more scared of being without you."

With her eyes glistening, Mariam lifted her head and looked at Ari.

"Your grandfather was a brave man, but don't confuse that with a lack of fear. He was as frightened as you are now, as frightened as I am. You cannot be brave if at first you aren't afraid. He acted bravely in the face of fear. And it's his example that I'm following now when I tell you to go. I, too, am scared for you to go, scared knowing I'll never see you again, but I know that is the only way you will live. Please do not deny me that. I wasn't able to protect you as a child like your grandfather protected me. I wasn't able to give you the happiness he gave me. For that, I'm sorry. But my life will soon end on this road. There is nothing you can do to prevent that. If you are by my side when it does, I will die in misery knowing I couldn't protect you even with my last breaths. If you leave, I will die in peace, knowing that you will live. Please do not deny me that. That is the only thing left for me to give you."

"No!" exclaimed Ari with growing frustration.

"Ari, you must. We will be reunited one day in the Lord's house. My journey is ending, my son, and yours has yet to begin. So please do as your grandfather did and be brave. Have the courage to leave me and the strength to find the child. Take her with you to Trabzon and find your grandfather's old ship. Ask for Captain Cotton and tell him you are Mardiros's grandson. He will help you."

"Don't ask me to leave you," said Ari, clenching his jaw in anger and frustration.

"You must, you must. If not for me, if not for yourself, please give this child a chance to live. She may have lost her mother, but her father could still be alive. Bring her to him. Just as your grandfather brought the boy to his family. You can still save this child and give her to her father. If you truly love me, be brave—please go."

"No, I can't," said Ari as he hugged his mother. "I'm not strong enough. I would be no use to the child."

Mariam hugged him back, then broke their embrace.

"Ari, I may not have been able to give you much. I wish I could have given you a happier life. But I know you're strong. I've seen it. Because of me, you grew up far sooner than you should have. But you could not have endured as you did without strength. I know you are brave. I see in you what I saw in my father. Bravery comes from sacrifice, and I've seen you sacrifice quietly. I ask you to please sacrifice again, be brave again, go find the child and save her. It would be what your grandfather would do."

Mariam sensed the fracture in Ari's resolve, and felt the time was now for her to make her final plea.

"Ari, I tried to protect you when you were younger. There were things I didn't think you should hear—stories of my life, stories of your father. You asked, and I kept them from you. I did so out of love. I did so to protect you. I thought when the time came, I would tell you this story. I would sit with you and answer all your questions. I know now I will not have that chance. So please take this," said Mariam as she handed Ari an envelope.

Ari instinctively took the envelope without looking at it and absently put it in the pocket of his trousers.

"I have kept this letter for a long time. This letter will explain everything that I have been ashamed to tell you. Everything I should have told you. But please know that I have received no greater gift than you as a son. You filled my life with love, with pride. So please take this and go. I want you to run and whatever you do, don't turn back. Please run until you find the child. By doing so, you will give me a final gift. You will allow me to be as your grandfather was—a good shepherd."

Mariam pushed Ari away. "Go!"

In tears, Ari stood from under the blanket, bolted through the rain, down the embankment, and toward the River Euphrates. No sound could be heard above the heavy rain and thundering sky. Ari wouldn't have known if one of the gendarmes was pursuing him or shooting at him, and he wouldn't have cared. He did just as his mother had told him—he ran without looking back.

Mariam watched him run, praying that he wouldn't turn around. In the darkness and rain, Ari faded out of his mother's view quickly.

It's said that the shepherd lives for the flock. But Mariam was the Good Shepherd, and the Good Shepherd dies for their sheep.

31

The Unfaithful Euphrates

As Ari ran blindly along the river's embankment, he could hear the thundering waters even over the rain. For a second, the Euphrates felt like a chance companion as they ran alongside each other—each trying to escape something. Ari began to slow as he gave in to fatigue. He panted for breath, and his heart seemed ready to break the confines of his chest with every hammering beat. Ari fell to his knees as he tried to catch his breath, and he found he could no longer escape his thoughts.

Ari looked toward the Euphrates and felt an odd kinship with the old river. Like him, the Euphrates had abandoned its mother—showing neither care nor regret as it raced away from the loving spring that gave it life. He noticed the Euphrates grew strong and immodest in flight and wondered how its waters could swell with pride in the face of its infidelity. *What impatient quest was it on?* he thought. Is it the seductive glory of the sea that it's chasing? Or is it trying to escape the haunting specter of its own essence? If it's glory that it seeks, then will it be there at its journey's end? And if so, at what cost? Will the salty mouth of the great sea welcome it with the same loving affection as the humble spring, in whose pure womb it was cradled, or will it swallow its waters without care? If the river was running from itself, then he felt its odyssey was in vain. The Euphrates, in all its timeless wisdom, should know that as long as its waters run, the river will forever remain a river—it cannot escape itself.

Ari turned back toward the direction he'd come from. He started walking back, but after a few yards, he stopped and dropped to his knees. His mother tried to convince him that he was doing a brave and noble thing, but he felt the only brave one was his mother. She was willing to sacrifice her life in exchange for a child she barely knew, and she trusted him to make sure her sacrifice was not in vain. He willed himself to rise and this time began walking with purpose toward the direction in which he last saw the child, struggling to keep the thoughts of his mother out of his mind.

Ari plodded along the uneven ground of the river's embankment. After a couple of miles, he felt it was safe to climb back up and try to find any sign of the trail they'd been on. He battled the muddy embankment but was finally able to climb up to the flat ground overlooking the Euphrates. He glanced around but couldn't find any trace of the trail through the darkness and rain. He started for the east, scanning for any landmark that would tell him he was on the right path.

He walked for about a half hour, and as his eyes grew more accustomed to the dark and the rain began to let up, he could see more of his surroundings and was finally able to pick up the trail. He began to see finer details, and he noticed something odd on the ground ahead. He cautiously approached and realized it was the body of an old woman and then saw another dead body a few yards away. It was a sickening trail of crumbs that he hoped would lead him to the child.

A little while later he started feeling the cold more. His concern for the child started to grow as he felt she couldn't stay alive for long exposed to these harsh elements. He felt a greater urgency and for the next several hours stumbled over body after body. Finally, on an open plain, he arrived at a familiar-looking corpse.

First, he noticed the way the body was positioned completely straight and parallel to the trail, with one arm frozen as if cradling something. Then it was the way the body was attired. It had the dress of a younger woman. And finally, when he reached the body, he could see a pool of caked blood underneath the head.

He carefully peered down at the face and saw that it was Anna. Even now, he noticed how striking Anna was and how unfair it all seemed. Anna was a woman who had every right to live, and yet her life was taken while he remained alive. Anna was beautiful, she was young, and she was needed. With that thought, he was immediately shaken from his trance. *Her daughter*, he thought. Ari realized the child was not there. He began looking around the area where the body lay, but there was no sign of the child.

As if to mock him, the rain fell harder as Ari frantically searched the perimeter of the body in greater and greater circles. He walked nearly one hundred yards in each direction, calling out her name desperately, and still found no trace of the child. Where could she have gone? Did someone else find her and carry her off? Was she in the belly of some beast? A sickening feeling came over him. *It was all for nothing*, he thought. Instead of staying with his mother to give her whatever comfort he could, he'd abandoned her to a lonely death for nothing.

Disconsolate, Ari made his way back to Anna's body. He willed his challenged mind to come up with some course of action but couldn't think of anything. Rain fell on him harder, and the sky flashed with lightning, followed by a prodigious thunderclap that shook him to his core. He turned his head skyward, awaiting another angry outburst from the heavens, but none came. Even still, he felt he should try to take cover. As he rose, he looked back down at Anna one last time. As he did, a slight movement near Anna's chest caught Ari's attention. He looked more carefully and saw another barely perceptible heave of Anna's chest. He focused on her thick shawl and carefully peeled it back. As he did, he saw a little hand with a fistful of Anna's dress. He peeled back the shawl farther and saw Lena's face pressed against her mother's bosom. The child was curled up and clinging to her mother as she slept.

With the rain now falling on her uncovered face, Lena stirred from her sleep and fluttered her eyes open and briefly looked at Ari. Seemingly unfazed by Ari's presence, Lena unclenched the fabric of her mother's dress and crawled on top of Anna to gaze at her mother's face. This time, Lena didn't tug at Anna's body, nor did she cry for her mother to rise. She just looked down at her mother with an unusual calm. And then, after what seemed like minutes, Lena turned toward Ari and reached her arms up to him.

Ari responded by picking up the child. Once in his arms, she rested her head on his shoulder and hugged his neck. He recognized something in the way the child was holding on to him. It reminded him of the way he would cling to his mother's leg when he was young—longing for his mother's protective embrace. And when it would come, he would feel safe. Without thinking, he softly brushed the back of the child's head with his hand.

"You're not alone," he whispered in the child's ear. "Your father will come looking for you one day. I'll keep you safe till then."

More lightning bolts lit up the sky, followed by thunder. Ari removed Anna's shawl and wrapped it around Lena. A sack that Anna had been carrying was lying next to her. He looked inside and saw clothes and a modest store of food. He picked it up, closed the strings, and slung it over his shoulder.

Ari began walking toward the foothills that he knew were a mile to the north, hoping to find a cave or any other cover from the rain. When he reached the hills, he stumbled across a shallow recess, about three yards deep and two yards high—it was nothing more than a notch in the rocks at the base of a hill. However, it was enough space to get them out of the rain. He entered, sat as far back as he could, and leaned against the rocks with Lena on his lap. He looked at her and noticed the child had fallen asleep again. He bent his knees to better cradle her in his lap and then opened Anna's sack. He rummaged through it and pulled out some clothes for Lena, as well as a blanket. He carefully removed Lena's wet clothes and dressed her in drier ones. He then took the blanket and covered her as she slept on his lap.

Once the child was comfortable, Ari noticed how cold his hands had become. They had turned a bloodless white, and he could feel them begin to numb. He didn't have anything to make a fire, so he put his hands inside his trousers to try to warm them, and he felt something in one of the pockets. It was the envelope from his mother. He'd almost forgotten about it. Lightning flashed across the sky long enough for him to read the words "To my son Ari" on the front. Before he could process the words completely, an explosion of thunder seemed to shake the rocks around him.

The sound startled him, and he realized again that his mother was out there alone. He thought of how frail she had become, and he didn't fool himself into believing that she would live long past this night.

He crumpled the envelope and fought against his own self-loathing, against the desire to bring on his death by his own hand. If he were alone, it would have been a losing battle—he would have welcomed death like others welcomed sleep. But he wasn't alone. He looked down at the child sleeping on his lap, and he felt even more inadequate. He longed to be the man his grandfather was, but he was far from it. He was lost, weak, and frightened, but he was all this child had.

As Ari fought with himself, the lightning and thunder continued their pas de deux, each taking its turn until their dance built to its climax. And then, as if the heavens could no longer suppress their rage, they unchained their lightning and thunder in frightening synchronization. Now the flashes and blasts seemed to come all at once, and they engulfed him, making him feel that God's fury was set upon him. *But what was the reason for God's anger?* he thought. Haven't enough souls been collected on this day? Beautiful, faithful, and pure souls. What more could He want? God surely had no need for him. So why had the heavens become so petulant? Was it because of the child? Was the day's harvest meant to include Lena? Did God's greed extend to the innocent?

As the skies raged on, Ari leaned over Lena to shield her as she slept on his lap. He put the envelope back in his pocket and buried his head in his knees to try to shut out nature's wrath.

The child was in his hands now, and he vowed that not even God would take her.

32

The Journey to Salvation

Ari awoke early the next morning with Lena still sleeping on his lap. Ever so carefully, he laid her on the ground and wrapped her as snugly as he could in the blanket. Then, he decided to take inventory of everything they had.

Besides the clothes for Lena, Anna's sack contained a few pieces of dried meat, three apples, some bread, matches, and a knife. He also had his own water flask, which was full.

He stood and walked out into the morning. The sun rising in the east let him know roughly the direction he had to go to reach Trabzon. He looked toward the north, to its unwelcoming, sparse terrain and imposing mountains in the distance. The magnitude of their situation, of what lay before them, briefly washed over him, but he quickly dashed it from his mind.

Ari saw a meandering stream about twenty yards from their shelter. He walked over to it and splashed water on his face. As he finished, he heard Lena crying. When he got back to the shelter, he found Lena sitting up and alternating between coughing and crying.

When the child saw him, she smiled and ran over and reached her arms up to him. It was a reception he was not accustomed to getting.

"Up, up," Lena said.

"Don't be frightened. I didn't leave you," said Ari as he lifted the girl. "You must be hungry, let's get you something to eat."

Ari sat down with Lena on his lap, cut up one of the apples, and began feeding her. After a few bites, he gave Lena some of the water to drink. Lena seemed more thirsty than hungry and drank nearly half their supply of water.

Ari wrapped her in the blanket again as Lena finished eating. When she was done, Ari packed their supplies, lifted Lena in his arms, and walked toward the Euphrates to see if there was any way to cross the river.

When he reached a perch that overlooked the river, he was overwhelmed with how vast the Euphrates was and realized how great an obstacle they had before them.

The rain from the previous night had swelled the river and increased its current, making it more perilous to cross. He looked down the gentle slope that descended to the river, across its waters, and along the bank and could see no easy way to cross. With no option, he headed upstream, hoping that the river would present a safer opportunity to cross. Aside from a few fits of coughing, Lena remained relatively silent. He found his arms tired faster than expected when he was carrying her, so he would set her down on flatter ground to walk beside him. Lena would only walk a few hundred feet before stopping and reaching her arms for Ari to carry her again. This exercise was repeated three or four times until Ari became frustrated.

"We aren't going to make it to Trabzon this way, Lena," said Ari as he refused to pick her up. "You're going to have to walk more on your own."

Lena looked up at him and when he wouldn't pick her up, she grabbed fistfuls of his trousers and tried scaling up his body.

"No, you are going to have to walk," said Ari, detaching the child and walking away.

Instead of following him, Lena plopped on the ground. Ari walked a few more yards and turned back to look at her.

"Well, come on. What are you waiting for?" asked Ari as the child remained unmoving.

"No," the child said.

The battle of wills was underway, but Ari knew that if Lena was going to survive, she would have to find strength of her own. The impasse lasted for a few minutes more before Ari began to walk away again. This time Lena jumped up, yelled no again, and ran after him. She reached him, grabbed a handful of his trousers, and held on to him as she walked alongside.

As morning turned to afternoon, the sun's rays became warmer, and the damp ground started drying. Ari was thankful for the relative warmth the sun brought, and he also noticed the river seemed to calm a little. However, they had been walking the entire morning and he felt that they were no closer to crossing the river than when they started.

A couple more hours of walking and Lena began to cry again. Ari found a soft spot at the base of the embankment and took out some of the dried meat. He broke off little pieces and fed them to Lena, who devoured them. He felt hungry himself and took out an apple and shared it with Lena.

After a brief rest, Ari rose and gathered his supplies, when something caught his eye farther up the embankment among some bushes. Ari hoisted Lena into his arms and made his way to the bushes and found what appeared to be the remains of an old crate. Most of the pieces had splintered into small fragments. However, the base seemed to be intact. He set Lena down, dragged the crate to the river, placed it in the water, and saw that it floated.

He realized she could ride the crate across the river as he swam behind it—steering it.

It would be a challenge, but the current had subsided enough to convince him that it would be possible. He sat Lena next to the bag and pulled the crate into the river with him. The child cried out when he set her down, and she reached for him.

"Don't worry, Lena, I'm not going to leave you. See, I'm coming too," said Ari, and he waded into the cold waters.

With Ari gripping the crate, Lena lay down, inched over to him, and grabbed ahold of one of his fingers, squeezing it tightly in her small fist. The two were face to face, and Ari noticed how scared the child looked, so he did his best to look calm.

As they began to float, Ari found himself smiling as he looked at the child. He started imagining his grandfather guiding his boat down the Tigris, with a young Mariam gleefully riding along.

After a few more moments, he could see the opposite bank approaching. His focus on the shore prevented him from noticing the small rapids downstream. They weren't much as far as rapids go, really nothing more than a minor agitation. But with Ari distracted, the little turbulence was enough to wrestle the crate from his grip.

He lunged for the crate, but the waters had carried it just out of reach. In a panic, he began to swim after it frantically. He saw Lena crawl to the edge of the crate and cry out to him.

"Don't move, Lena! Stay where you are!" he screamed.

The crate drifted slightly toward shore, then lodged itself against a set of boulders peeking above the waterline. Ari redoubled his efforts, watching as Lena inched herself closer to the edge. Struggling to cut through the current, Ari made his way to the crate and immediately pushed Lena safely to the middle. He then nudged it off the rocks and swam the remaining distance to the shore. When he finally reached the bank, he lifted Lena off the crate and grabbed their supplies, then pushed the crate out into the water with a disgusted kick.

All he could feel was Lena's warm breath on his neck as she buried her face and hugged him tightly.

33

The Turkish Bull

For the next two days, Ari and Lena walked without interruption, not encountering a soul. Well into the afternoon on their third day, they reached a small mountain range. Ari climbed to the top to survey the land on the other side before nightfall.

When they reached the peak, he scanned the plains and saw a single farmhouse with livestock below. He thought he could see pigs, chickens, cows, and sheep. He spotted a barn and a chicken coop a safe distance from the farmhouse. At that moment, he came up with a plan, but he wanted to wait until it was completely dark.

Ari found a small depression, about twelve feet in diameter and two feet deep. It was surrounded by trees and rocks. It made an ideal place for a camp, so he built a fire, took out their last food supplies, and shared a comfortable meal with Lena. He reached into his pocket and took out his medal, along with the letter his mother gave him. He thought back to the moment his mother handed the letter to him. She said it would tell him everything he had ever wanted to know, all the things she never told him, things about his father. Of all the stories he had yet to hear, that was the one he most wanted to know. He now had all the answers in his hand.

He went to open the letter but was distracted when a spark from the fire glinted off the medal that he had set down in front of him. He turned his attention to it and became oddly transfixed. He didn't know why he'd kept it all these years. The medal had long since lost the magic it held when he was a child. If anything, it was a burden—not symbolizing who he was but rather a reminder of what he was not.

Lena picked up the medal. Ari's first impulse was to take it back, but he noticed she was playing with it like a toy. He enjoyed watching her playing, and the slight distraction was enough for him to put the letter away for another day. She tossed the medal on the ground and dug it in the dirt. Ari smiled at how differently she treated the medal than he did when he was young.

"Careful," he said. "That belonged to a great man."

"Daddy?" said Lena.

"No, it's not your father's," said Ari, with a hint of disgust. He caught himself as Lena peered at him with what seemed like a confused look.

"That medal is not your father's," said Ari as he composed himself and softly looked at her. "But your father is a good man. You'll see when he comes for you. He'll come for you one day. I promise. Do you know if it wasn't for your father, I wouldn't have that medal now? Do you want to hear the story?"

Ari wasn't sure if the child understood anything he was saying, but he saw her smile and he took that as affirmation. Ari took the medal from Lena, held it up to her face, and leaned in.

"One day, I was coming home from school, and three Turkish boys surrounded me. They heard that I had this medal, and they wanted it for themselves. I told them that my grandfather won that medal, and he told me I should always protect it, so I refused to give it to them," said Ari as he got up and began to circle the fire to reenact the event.

"One tried to sneak up behind me, but I saw him and spun and struck him in the face. Then another rushed me from one side, and another from the other side. I was able to punch and kick each attacker as they approached," continued Ari as he spun and struck at the air to demonstrate the action of the story.

Lena seemed more entertained by Ari's performance than anything else, giggling each time he added his dramatic flair.

"And just when I thought I was going to get away, I felt a heavy blow land on my head," said Ari as he interlocked his hands over his head and brought them down like a hammer. "I was knocked to the ground and looked up and saw their leader. He was an enormous boy, we called him the Turkish Bull, and everyone was frightened of him. With one hand, the Turkish Bull lifted me off the ground by my belt. He lifted me over his head and then threw me twenty feet in the air. When I hit the ground, the medal rolled out of my pocket. The Turkish Bull picked it up. I found I was too hurt to move, and I thought the medal was lost forever.

"But then Vartan, your father, who had been watching high in a tree, jumped down in front of the Turkish Bull. The Bull snarled at him, thinking that Vartan would be afraid like everyone else and run away. But no, not Vartan, not your father.

"Vartan told him that he could give the medal back to me and leave peacefully or if not, there would be blood. The Turkish Bull told him to come get it if he dared. Your father calmly approached and stood in front of the Bull. Vartan then opened his fist and blew sand into the Bull's eyes. This made the Bull mad, and he charged your father. But your father had speed on his side, and the Bull couldn't catch him. 'I'm over here,' Vartan said as the Bull blindly lunged in all directions trying to catch your father. When he heard your father taunting him, the Bull charged as fast as he could toward Vartan's voice. And just as he was going to ram into him with all his might, Vartan stepped aside, and the Bull ran into an oak tree. The Bull dropped to the ground, bleeding from the head. Vartan took the medal from his hand, walked over, and handed it to me. He told me that you don't have to be the biggest or strongest to win a fight. Just the smartest. Everyone heard what your father did, and no one ever tried to take this medal after that."

Lena was still laughing as Ari sat next to her. He put her on his lap and reached for the last piece of bread they had. He smiled and put the final morsel in her mouth.

"Did you know your father gave me some chocolate once? Chocolate is very tasty. I'm sure when he sees you again, he will buy you lots of chocolate."

"Daddy?" Lena said.

"Yes, your daddy. He'll buy you lots of chocolate."

A few hours later, as Lena was sleeping, Ari walked over to the ridge that oversaw the farmhouse. Under the light of the full moon, Ari saw the residence was dark and silent. He lifted the still sleeping child in his arms and started descending the mountainside.

About thirty minutes later, they reached the perimeter of the farmhouse property, and he set the sleeping child on the ground next to the chicken coop. He entered the building and began searching for eggs. He found some immediately and placed them in his bag, wrapping the eggs in the extra clothes to keep from breaking them. His fishing for eggs soon stirred the hens, who clucked in agitation. Fearful that the noise would wake the farmhouse residents, Ari abandoned looking for more eggs and instead grabbed a chicken and stuffed the flailing fowl in his sack. He rushed out of the coop, collected Lena, and hustled across the moonlit plains.

Once he felt he was a safe distance away, he stopped to listen and heard only silence.

———

Alone on a deserted trail, a young Turkish boy struggled to haul a sack of grain on his back. To settle a barter, his father had instructed him to take the grain to a butcher, who lived twelve miles away. Just shy of his eleventh birthday, the boy needed to set the sack down to rest frequently.

Halfway through his journey, he saw a wheelbarrow on the path ahead of him, and he lugged the sack toward it. When he approached the wheelbarrow, he saw that it wasn't empty. At first, he thought there was just a pile of clothes in it, but when he got nearer, he saw it was the body of an old woman. The flies hovering around her opened mouth and the stench of her body made it clear that she was dead.

He looked at her for a moment, his young mind wondering why she had chosen such an empty place to die. He imagined she was most likely delivering something herself and had stopped to rest in the wheelbarrow and simply passed away as she slept.

The boy scanned the area, making sure no one else was around, and set down his sack of grain. He grabbed both handles of the wheelbarrow and tilted it to the side, dumping the dead woman on the ground. He put his sack of grain in the wheelbarrow and began pushing it forward.

And he thought he might just make it home in time for supper.

34

The Legend of Melik Sasuni

Vartan landed roughly in the dark cell, beaten, bleeding, and emaciated. Vartan's crime had been getting dirt on one of the guard's shoes while digging a ditch. For that, he had to be punished. It wasn't the first beating he had received at the hands of his captors, and he knew that the only way it would be his last was if he didn't live past the day.

For more than a year, fortune had been playing a maddening game with Vartan and Taniel, who were among the few who survived the ambush. They were taken into custody, and after a quick trial, they were sentenced to be executed. However, as the day of their execution approached, a request for prison laborers came down from the Ottoman Army.

Ottoman forces were spread thin, and to lessen the army's burden, the military instituted the use of labor battalions. To augment these battalions, prisoners were added to their ranks. The labor battalions would be used to build roads, repair bridges, and dig trenches. No one within these battalions was treated well, but the harshest treatment was reserved for the prisoners.

Vartan and Taniel were worked to the point of exhaustion, given only leftover scraps for food and a small ration of water. When the day's work was done, they were locked in the closest filthy cell the guards could find. In the absence of a cell, they were chained, uncovered, to a tree. If the labor didn't kill them, then an executioner's bullet ultimately would. Either way, neither was expected to live to see freedom.

"Are you all right, Vartan?" said Taniel as he tried to get Vartan to sit up. Taniel and the other prisoners had already been locked in the cell for the night, while Vartan was held back to receive his beating.

As Taniel helped Vartan sit up, one of the other prisoners came over to assist. The two men propped Vartan against the cinder-block wall on the left side of the cell. Once Vartan was in place, the other prisoner—a shaggy, fidgety man—turned to Taniel to get his attention, but Taniel was too concerned for Vartan to notice. With his nervous tics becoming more pronounced, the prisoner leaned his bobbing head close to Taniel's ear.

"Did you hear about Melik Sasuni? Did you hear what he did?" whispered the prisoner to Taniel. "He walked off the line and grabbed food from the guard's hand and sat down to eat it in front of him. And you know what the guard did? Nothing! They're afraid of him. That's why they won't let us see him. They're afraid of Melik Sasuni."

Taniel turned to face the prisoner, whose twitching upper lip couldn't disguise his sly smile.

"They say he sits in his cell whistling Armenian songs," continued the prisoner. "But what he's really doing is planning. He's waiting for his moment, and then he'll kill the guards and free us.

They tried to break him, but they know they can't. They're afraid of him. Melik Sasuni, oh bless you, Melik Sasuni. Oh, what songs they'll sing of you! Shhhhhhh, don't let the guards hear us."

Taniel didn't say a word. He watched as the prisoner slithered across the cell to clandestinely share his news with the other captives.

It wasn't clear when Melik Sasuni had joined the labor ranks. No one had actually seen him, but his exploits grew daily among the prisoners. He was rumored to be an Armenian aristocrat from Russia. His love and commitment to his fellow Armenians was so great that he was said to have defied his father and given up his vast inheritance to come to the aid of his people. It was believed that he led extensive campaigns throughout the Anatolian peninsula, saving countless Armenians and causing the Ottoman Empire no small measure of grief. The Ottoman government grew so frustrated with his mischief that they placed the empire's largest bounty on his head. However, no one could catch him until Melik walked up to the Ottoman Army one day and surrendered.

As the story went, the Ottomans were afraid that killing Melik would make him a martyr and galvanize the Armenians further, so the government opted instead to place him in a labor camp. That, according to everyone, is what Melik wanted. By being arrested, he had outwitted the Ottomans again. He had now infiltrated enemy lines, placing him closer to a ready-made army of prisoners, who were all waiting for him to set his plan in motion. When he did, they would be ready, they would be free, and the Ottomans would have no chance.

Ignoring the hushed yet gleeful chatter on the other side of the cell, Taniel tried to give Vartan some of his water. Vartan clutched his ribs and pushed the water away.

"I'm okay, just give me a second," said Vartan as he slowed his breathing.

Vartan held the crucifix hanging around his neck. It was the same one that his father had given him on his deathbed, and oddly it was left with him even after being processed during his arrest.

The two men sat in silence until Vartan felt well enough to speak. He finally unclenched the crucifix, put it to his lips, and kissed it. Taniel looked away.

"Taniel, I look at you like another father, but sometimes I can't help but pity you," Vartan said.

"Why is that?" Taniel asked.

"You don't believe in God."

"I never said that."

"But you didn't attend church, and more than once I've heard you doubt our faith—doubt God's word."

"That's all true. It's the teaching of man that I doubt. That's all. Priests and popes who try to teach us something they don't understand themselves."

"That's why we're taught to have faith. Without it, you'll never find God," Vartan said.

"Perhaps," said Taniel as he took off Vartan's shirt.

Taniel could see the fresh welts of a whip on Vartan's back and chest. There were open wounds where the whip had cut into thin skin. Taniel ripped a piece of his undershirt off, wetted it with water, and began cleaning Vartan's wounds.

Vartan winced as a sharp pain shot through his ribs when Taniel touched them. He slowed his breathing again and waited for the pain to subside.

"Can I ask you where you get your strength from?" Vartan asked.

"I didn't know I had any. Not enough to consider, anyway."

"You've been in this prison as long as I have. We've broken our hands and backs out there every day, and you've never complained or looked for mercy."

"If I thought it would help, I would've done so long ago."

"Well, my strength comes from God. I must believe that He has a plan for me. For us. That He will protect my family. That I'll see them again one day. That I'll embrace my wife again. That I'll once again hold my daughter's hand. That's what keeps me going."

"I know."

"Is believing in God so bad? Where's the harm in it? I only see goodness in it," Vartan said.

"I don't think it's bad. Many people get their strength from it. And it's not so much that I don't believe in God, it's that I don't know what God is," Taniel said.

"The Church tells us what God is. He's the Holy Father, the creator. Everything we see before us is made by His hand."

"That may be true. There could be a creative force at work, but it would be so unlike God as we conceive Him that it would be a completely different thing altogether. But I know why you believe as you do. And I want you to keep believing. Never mind what this foolish old man thinks."

As they finished talking, another prisoner crawled over to them from across the cell.

"Did you hear what Melik Sasuni did?" he began.

35

The Third Man

Ari shuffled his feet as he carried Lena in his arms. It was the fourteenth day of their journey, and he was lost. He had continued to walk north only because that was the direction to Trabzon, where his mother had told him to go. Besides that, he had no further plan on how to get there, nor any real understanding of how much longer their journey would take. What he did know was that everything was different now, as the fact that he would never see his mother had fully set in. He was on a dark road and knew that, even though he was holding this child, for the first time in his life, he was alone. The strength to endure, which he had relied on all his life, seemed to have abandoned him.

Fatigue had long since set in and fogged his mind as he struggled forward aimlessly, willing his legs to move in what was becoming a losing battle. He had killed and cooked the chicken long ago. And since the farmhouse, the land had become more barren and resources scarcer. With nothing to catch or steal, what little food they had ran out a couple of days prior, and a gnawing hunger seemed to grow within him by the second. Each night seemed to grow colder, and his tired arms and legs intensified their revolt with each labored movement.

Even though he had not fed her for days, Lena scarcely made a sound any longer. She just clung to Ari, digging her tiny fingers into the fabric of his shirt. It was as if she could feel Ari's arms weakening and knew the only thing between her and falling to the frozen ground beneath was the strength of her grip.

Ari's mind cleared enough to realize night had fallen and they should stop, but he had neglected to look for a safe shelter and now, as the night grew darker, finding a suitable place would be nearly impossible. He tried to push himself forward, hoping that they would happen upon some cover from the increasing cold, but Ari found it harder to move with each step, and he stumbled along a path he could no longer see.

A few minutes later, his legs finally gave out, and he slumped down to the ground—letting go of Lena as he did. He no longer wanted to hold her, he no longer wanted to move, even if he could.

As Ari lay curled on the ground, he could feel the cold set into his bones, and he shivered uncontrollably. Lena crawled over to him and put her face next to his, grabbing his shoulder and trying to shake him.

"Up, up," she begged.

Ari could barely see Lena through the haze that clouded his eyes, which he struggled to keep open.

His mouth was parched from thirst, he was cold, and he was exhausted. He knew he couldn't do anything about the first two, but the third, for the third he had an easy remedy. *Just close your eyes*, he told himself. *Let sleep give you the rest you desire. Let it envelop you with its warmth. It may even bring dreams of sweet nectar with it. Surely the shivering will stop if I could only sleep.*

The only thing preventing him from sleeping was Lena's warm breath that he could feel on his face as she kept up her incessant babbling. It reminded him that he was not alone, but he no longer had the strength and energy to care for the child. *Maybe she will sleep too*, he thought.

He felt his eyes closing, and before they shut, he glanced at Lena once more. Perhaps it was to try to tell her that he was sorry she had the misfortune to be with someone as weak as him; perhaps it was to simply see one last face before he closed his eyes for good. But when he glanced at her, he noticed her brown eyes now appeared white and translucent. He realized the child was no longer looking at him, nor was she making any sound. Instead, she had her head turned upward, staring at something else with her bizarre eyes. Ari mustered enough strength to turn his head in the direction of her gaze. When he did, he saw a tall, thin man staring down at them.

Something about the man's presence startled his senses. The haze in Ari's eyes and mind began to clear. The man didn't say a word, and Ari felt as if the man gazed down at him not with curiosity or sympathy, but with disappointment. Ari suddenly felt ashamed that this man was seeing him lying on the ground, giving in to his weakness so willingly.

Ari noted that his own feebleness was in contrast with this stranger's strength. The man seemed unaffected by the cold or the violent gusts that swept around them. Ari desperately wanted to stand, to try to hide from this stranger the pitiful man he was, but he found he could barely move his limbs. Ari tried to push himself up, but his arms gave way, and he fell back down again. Ari hung his head. When Ari looked up at the man again, he saw the man walking away. He only traveled ten yards or so before he stopped and looked back at Ari. Ari felt a slight vigor reenter his body, enough so that he could once again command his limbs. *I must get up*, he thought. *I must show this man that I can get up.*

With a great struggle, Ari finally rose. He was still cold and tired, but now he felt a desperate and powerful need to move, to follow this man. He lifted Lena in his arms once again. Lena remained silent and continued staring at this strange man as Ari carried her toward him.

When Ari reached the man, the stranger turned away once again. Ari didn't want him to leave them. Whoever he was, Ari felt he could help them. Ari followed the man, slowly gaining strength as he tried to keep pace. After a few minutes, Ari walked alongside this mysterious man, matching him stride for stride.

Ari walked this way for nearly an hour, and the man never spoke a word. In that time, Lena never turned her eyes away from the stranger, but Ari was still ashamed to look at the man's face. Ari felt this was a great man. A man who didn't need charity, a man who didn't need pity, a man who had no use for weakness. It was as if Ari could feel the man's strength by walking next to him—a strength that seemed to enter his body until he no longer felt fatigue or cold.

Another hour into their journey and Ari felt more comfortable in this man's presence, comfortable enough to turn and study him. Ari noted the man was tall, broad-shouldered, and thin. Ari didn't think the man had a coat on, but for some reason he couldn't be sure. However, he could clearly see that the man was wearing a hat, which was pulled low on his forehead. The hat cast a dark shadow on the man's face, making it impossible for Ari to see any of the man's features. But even though he couldn't see the man's face, Ari somehow knew his expression was somber.

Suddenly the man stopped. Ari stopped as well, awaiting the man's next action, but the stranger remained silent and fixed his gaze straight ahead. Ari felt confused and unsure what to do. He looked straight ahead as well and in front of them was a two-story barn.

Before Ari walked into the shelter, he turned back to the man to express his gratitude, but the man had disappeared. He looked toward Lena, who had never turned her eyes away from the man, and noticed she was now looking at the barn as well.

Ari once again felt the cold in his bones, and his arms and legs seemed to grow heavier. The warmth of the barn beckoned to him, and he stumbled into the building. Careful not to wake the cows, he climbed the stairs to the second floor and lay down on the stacks of hay.

He managed to cover himself with their lone blanket and could feel the cold slowly receding. He curled himself around Lena to keep her as warm as possible and closed his eyes. Before he fell asleep, his mind went back to that strange man one last time.

What a peculiar dream to have, he thought. *Especially when you're awake.*

36

For Love of the Beautiful Game

"Wake up!"

Ari felt a sharp pain stab his side, and he woke to see a man standing over him with a rifle. The man appeared to be a farmer. His dirty face, unkempt hair, and matted beard gave the impression that he had already been at toil for some time that morning. The farmer had deep creases around his eyes, but otherwise he looked to be no older than his early thirties. Both his cracked and calloused hands were holding the rifle high, with the stock of the weapon pointed toward Ari.

"What is this? Have you come here to steal?" accused the man as he turned the rifle around and pointed the barrel at Ari's face.

Ari was too startled to speak, so he simply shook his head. The commotion woke Lena, who hugged Ari and began to cry.

"No? Then why are you on my property?" the man demanded.

"W-w-we needed a place to sleep," Ari stuttered.

"A place to sleep? Honest men sleep in their own beds. It's only thieves and evil men who come unwelcomed into another man's home. Which are you?"

"Neither," said Ari over Lena's cries.

"Keep the child quiet," said the man as he thrust the rifle at the two of them.

Ari clutched Lena closer and tried to soothe the child with his trembling arms.

"So, if you are neither, then how did you come to spend the night in my barn?"

"W-w-we were cold and found th-th-the barn."

"The cold was most likely a penance for your crimes. An honest man does not wait until the cover of night to sneak into another's home. You are either a thief or a criminal running from your past crimes. Are you an Armenian?"

Ari's silence gave the man the answer he needed.

"As I thought. Get up, you dog. And if the child continues crying, I'll shoot both of you here."

Ari quickly rose. He covered Lena's mouth, shushing her softly, as the man marched them toward the farmhouse.

As they approached the house, Ari noticed a couple of young boys, no older than eight or nine, chasing each other in front of the home. When the boys saw Ari and Lena, they dashed into the house. A couple moments later an old man exited the home, followed by two women—one older and the other younger. The old man had a full beard and was wearing a tight white turban and a baggy shirt and pants, and was using a walking stick.

"Samed, what is this?" the old man asked.

"I found this hunchback in our barn, Father. He's an Armenian trying to hide from the authorities, or else he was plotting to do us ill."

The old man walked closer to Ari, whose eyes were cast down to the ground.

"Are you an Armenian? It's okay, my son. My name is Ibrahim, and you are in my home. I promise that no harm will come to you in my home. In return, I only ask that you be truthful."

Ari looked up and nodded.

"I see. Please come in," said Ibrahim.

"Father, shouldn't we notify the authorities?" Samed said.

"Right now, this man and the child are guests in our home," said Ibrahim as he turned to his wife and daughter-in-law. "Our guests look like they are hungry, please get them something to eat."

Ibrahim led Ari inside the house, and they sat at a bare wooden table in the main room, Ari holding Lena in his lap. The younger woman set bread and jellies in front of Ari, followed by hot tea and warm milk for Lena. A few seconds later, the older woman brought a large bowl of porridge. Upon seeing the food, Lena reached for it, but Ari pulled her back toward him.

"Please eat, we can talk after you have finished," Ibrahim said.

With the little encouragement, Ari took the cup of warm milk and put it to Lena's lips. The child instantly began drinking it. Ari grabbed a spoon and scooped out some of the porridge. It still took some effort to swallow, but once it went down, he found that it became easier to eat. Soon he was alternating spoons of porridge between Lena and himself. The child was even hungrier than him, and she swallowed each spoonful eagerly.

Ibrahim remained silent throughout, and when Ari and Lena had finished, he motioned to his wife to bring more milk and tea. She did so and set them down in front of Ari and Lena. With their hunger satisfied, Ari held a cup of milk to Lena's lips and let the child leisurely drink.

"I hope you had enough to eat," Ibrahim said.

"Yes, thank you."

"May I ask, where is it that you come from?"

Ari remained silent.

"It's okay, my son. You are among friends," Ibrahim said.

Ari wasn't bright enough to be able to consider all the ramifications, nor did he have enough guile to manipulate his way out of a predicament. But what he did know was that if this man and his son wanted to do him harm, there was little he could do about it.

"Van," said Ari.

"Van? You're quite a distance from home," Ibrahim said.

"Father, if he is from Van, then that confirms what I've been telling you. This man is most likely a murderous rebel running from the law. We must turn him in to the authorities at once," Samed said.

Ibrahim waved his son to be silent.

"Were you among the people who were evacuated? The resettlements?"

Ari nodded.

"Then how is it that you are here and not with the rest of your people?"

Ari looked down at Lena, who was still drinking from the cup of milk.

"This child lost her mother and she was left on the trail. I went back to get her."

"Who is this child to you?"

"She is no one."

"Then why did you go back to save her?"

"Because she had no one else."

"Father, I must have a word with you," said Samed as he motioned for Ibrahim to follow him.

Ibrahim rose and walked with his son to the front door of the house. Samed still held his rifle firmly.

"Father, it's clear what we must do. The man admitted that he left the resettlement lines. By law, he is a criminal and we must do our duty and bring him to the authorities or settle the matter ourselves," said Samed as he raised his rifle.

"And what has this man done to you to believe that justice will be served by his death?"

"Father, surely you can't be naive enough not to realize what is going on. The Armenians have rebelled against us. Their traitorous actions are causing the downfall of our empire and have cost countless Turkish people their lives. We will be traitors ourselves if we don't turn this man over to the authorities."

"Who is being naive, my son? Many just men have suffered and have been punished for the deeds of others. If an Armenian does evil things, if he breaks the law, then let that Armenian be punished and not the innocent Armenian. As proud as we are to be Turkish, to be Muslim, we can't be so proud as to be led down the path of the unrighteous.

"It may be true that an Armenian has done bad things, has broken laws, but so, too, has the Turkish man. It may be true that the Christian has sinned and done evil deeds, but so, too, has the Muslim. We live in a time of fighting, but we have forgotten what we are fighting for. We are only too eager to pick up our guns and kill our neighbors in the name of duty. We do this by dressing up good and evil until we can no longer recognize either. And we fool ourselves into believing that we are doing good when we are causing another to suffer. That it is peace we are seeking at the end of our swords. That is not the way of the good man. So, I ask you to do as the good man would do and lay down your arms, so that you may stand up and fight."

"Then if we're not going to turn this man over to the law, what are we to do with him? He cannot stay here. We will be hanged alongside him," said Samed.

Ibrahim thought for a moment, then went over to a small desk next to the front door and wrote something down on a piece of paper. When he finished, he put the letter in an envelope. He called his two grandsons over and informed them where, exactly, they were to deliver it.

Hans Breiner had run the medical clinic in Van for twenty-five years, but his first love was soccer.

Growing up in Germany, he would practice kicking the ball against the side of his house. At twelve, he was kicking the ball with such force that the dust from the roof of their two-story home would fly off with every thundering strike. On more than one occasion, the impact of his kicks would startle his mother who was cooking inside the home, causing her to drop their evening's dinner on the floor.

"Hans, I am going to make you eat that ball!" screamed his mother, who would run to the yard with every intention to make good on her threat, only to find her son and his potential meal gone.

By the time he was a teenager, coaches had begun taking notice, and he was invited to try out for a club team. During one scrimmage, he was tackled from behind. His cleats stuck in the soil, and he blew out his right knee. It took him six months to be able to walk on the leg again and another year after that before he could run. But he was never able to move around the pitch as he had before. His once powerful strikes no longer inspired awe.

Seeing a change in their son, Hans's parents reached out to a local doctor and family friend to ask if he would speak to him.

The doctor showed up at their house and asked Hans if they could take a walk. They walked to a park and sat down to watch some young children playing soccer. He pointed to one of the boys on defense. He asked Hans what he thought about the boy's ability and asked him to be candid in assessing the boy's talent.

Hans watched the slightly pudgy boy, who desperately tried to defend another player, only to be dribbled around repeatedly. He saw him trying to kick the ball to a teammate, only to see the poorly struck ball go out of bounds. He observed as the uncoordinated boy picked himself up time and time again as he stumbled from one end of the pitch to the other.

"He's not very good," Hans said.

"No, no he isn't." The doctor laughed. "But do you think he loves this game any less than you do?"

Before he answered, Hans studied the boy as the play moved away from him. He noticed the boy clapping when a teammate made a good run, pumping his fist to acknowledge every save, and jumping in elation when his side scored a goal.

Hans shook his head.

"If you let it, the beautiful game will love you no matter how well or poorly you play it. No matter how young or old you are. That boy was a patient of mine. He had been sick with the fever, sicker than I've ever seen a child. I treated him for six months and I began to lose hope. To lift his spirits, I asked him what he would do when he got better, never believing he would see his next birthday. He told me he would like to learn to play soccer, and he asked me if I would teach him. As you can see, I'm a better doctor than a trainer. But it gives him joy to play. And it gives me something even greater to watch him."

With that, the doctor excused himself. He took out a whistle from his pocket and blew it. The children stopped their scrimmage and formed a line. At that moment, Hans stopped feeling sorry for himself. That day everything changed. The doctor would become a mentor to Hans, and he would follow him into the medical field. He decided to become a missionary, but his mission wasn't to convert religious followers. His mission was to bring medicines to children in need and share with them the love of the beautiful game that was rekindled for him on that day.

When he arrived in Van, he taught soccer to Christians and Muslims alike. He would watch Turkish boys play alongside Armenian boys for days on end in a youthful brotherhood—simply sharing with each other the joys of sport.

For that reason, it was particularly hard for Hans to witness the bloodshed in Van firsthand. He protested the treatment of the Armenians directly to the local Turkish officials but was told it was a matter of state. He wrote letters to the German embassy; however, not wishing to strain the two countries' relationship, his government didn't intervene.

He did his best to pressure the local Van authorities, who soon became tired of his persistent interference and had him relocated to an enclave of Muslim villages to the north.

He was working in a clinic, giving vaccines to some local children, when two boys walked in. They approached one of the nurses, and she pointed to Hans.

One of the boys walked over and handed him an envelope. Hans opened it and scanned the letter inside. He jerked his head up.

"Take me to your home," he said.

37

Code Word: Bethlehem

Hans arrived at Ibrahim's home as fast as he could. He was met by Samed in the front yard. Samed went in and brought his father out.

"It's good to see you, my friend," Ibrahim said. "I'm glad you could come on such short notice."

"Yes, of course. Your letter said you had a friend from Van in your home. I assumed you meant it was an Armenian."

"It is. He's a hunchback, and he has a child with him. They looked to be lost and in need of help. I don't have to tell you the climate we live in. Our villages are under scrutiny because of the number of Armenian refugees trying to escape the resettlement lines. If they're found they'll be arrested—and worse, as you know," Ibrahim said.

"I thank you for your discretion," Hans said. "Could you please take me to him?"

Ibrahim walked Hans into the home, where Ari still sat with

Lena at the table. When Hans heard it was a hunchback, he knew it could only be one person, even though he couldn't remember his name. Hans did remember giving him vaccines when he was young, mostly because of the challenge it was to find a meaty spot on his body. Besides that, he rarely saw him among the other children and would only see him occasionally in town with his mother.

"Hello . . . Mariam's son, right? I lived in Van as well. Do you remember me?" Hans asked.

Ari nodded. Ari remembered him as the man with the odd accent who gave him a shot in his arm. He remembered that the shot hurt, even though the man told him it wouldn't.

"I knew your mother, but I'm sorry, I can't recall your name."

"Ari."

"Ari, yes that's it," said Hans as he became more serious. "Ari, I've come here to help you. Ibrahim is a good man. He would like to help you as well. So, you don't have to be afraid. We must know how you escaped the deportation lines. We have to know if you're in any immediate danger."

"I left a while ago. It was at night, when it was raining."

"Did anyone see you leave?"

Ari shook his head.

"So, you don't believe anyone's following you?"

Ari shook his head again.

"Was your mother with you?"

Ari's eyes welled up with tears, and his lip trembled as he looked away. The reaction told Hans everything he needed to know.

"Who is this child?" asked Hans.

"Vartan's daughter," Ari said.

"Vartan and Anna?" asked Hans, who knew the couple well but only saw the child when she was first born. "Is Anna still alive?"

Ari shook his head.

"She was shot on the road. And the child was left with her body. My mother told me to go back to get her, so I . . ." A sob ripped through Ari before he could finish his sentence.

Hans rose and put his hand on Ari's back, and Ari buried his face into Hans's side to try to hide his tears.

"It's okay, son. I understand," said Hans as he rubbed Ari's back.

After Ari got control of his emotions again, Hans sat back down.

"Ari, even though no one is following you, it's not safe for you to stay here and it's not safe for Ibrahim to have you in his home. I can only help so much, as I'm being closely watched by the authorities. It'll be a challenge, but we must get you out of the country. Is there anyone you know of who can help?"

"My mother told me to go to Trabzon. To find my grandfather's old ship, and that the captain would help me."

"Trabzon? That's a two-week journey. Do you think he could make it there safely?" Hans asked Ibrahim.

"It would be difficult," admitted Ibrahim. "But we could give him enough supplies. He would just have to be cautious on the road—but he made it this far, so perhaps he has a chance. It might be the best chance he has."

"If you make it to the ship, do you think the captain could take you to Greece?" Hans asked Ari.

Ari nodded.

Hans grabbed his briefcase and took out some papers. He began filling out some forms and then stopped and looked up at Ari.

"Ari, I'll not be able to protect you, but I might be able to protect the child. I could take her to an orphanage, at least she'll be safe there. The journey to Trabzon will be dangerous, and traveling with a child will make it more perilous for you. Both of you might have a better chance if you leave her behind," Hans said.

Ari gripped Lena harder, and he shook his head.

"No, I promised my mother that I would keep her safe until Vartan came for her. I'm not leaving without her," Ari said.

"Ari, how do we know if Vartan is still alive?"

"He's alive—I know it. And I know he'll come for his daughter. If she goes to an orphanage, he'll never find her. Or someone else will take her and never give her to him. I'll watch her until he comes."

Hans looked at Ibrahim, who silently nodded.

"Very well," Hans said.

Hans went back to filling out the forms. He took out a piece of paper and wrote a letter, then put all the papers in an envelope and handed it to Ari.

"Ari, this is important, so please listen to me. When you get to Trabzon, tell the captain to take you to Athens. When you reach the port, you must go to the American embassy. When you get there, give them these papers. They will take you to America, where it's safe. That is all I can do for you, Ari," Hans said.

"America? Then you must tell Vartan that Lena is in America and that I'll watch her. Tell him we'll wait until he comes. Tell him I'll keep her safe," said Ari.

Hans was moved by Ari's faith and naiveté. As unlikely as it was, Ari needed to believe that Vartan was still alive—that he would be able to reunite him with his daughter. It was a hope that Hans could not bear to take from him.

Hans nodded. He took out another envelope, addressed it, and put a blank piece of paper inside.

"When you get to the embassy, please write this word on this piece of paper and ask them to mail it. When I see it in your handwriting, I'll know you're safe," said Hans as he scribbled down a word and showed it to him.

Ibrahim instructed his wife and daughter-in-law to prepare a place for Ari and Lena to sleep. The following morning, Hans came by with a gift for Ari. It was a German Army–issued backpack. Ibrahim had his wife and daughter-in-law fill the backpack with food and supplies. Hans then fitted it on Ari's back and showed him how to tighten the straps.

When Ari was ready to leave, Hans wished him good luck and asked him if he remembered the word he was to write down when he reached the American embassy.

"Bethlehem," Ari said.

38

Trabzon

Trabzon was founded by Milesian traders in 756 BC. Situated on the Black Sea, Trabzon's location gave it access to Persia to the east, the Caucasus to the north, and Europe to the west, and it quickly became a major trading post. The city changed hands many times throughout its history, and in 1461 the city was ultimately surrendered to Sultan Mehmed II and absorbed into the Ottoman Empire.

In ancient times, Trabzon's prominence as a trading post was buoyed by its location on the Silk Road—a network of routes that got its name for the lucrative trade of Chinese silk conducted on it.

Emerging from a hilltop clearing, Ari was overcome with awe and reverence when he saw Trabzon's harbor beneath him and the vast sea that it was connected to. To him, the city, its ships, and its waters were all part of some unattainable mythology—they were the heroic settings of his grandfather. It was the Troy of Achilles, the Ithaca of Odysseus, and it was all lying before him in living color.

It had been a tenuous two-week journey. Ari had been fortunate to avoid any serious dangers, but negotiating the northern mountains had taken its toll on him physically. Both his feet were bleeding from blisters, his shoulders were burning from the straps of the backpack that were cutting into him, and his back appeared even more bent than usual. Now with his destination beneath them, he exhaled and sat down to allow his body to heal.

He and Lena still had some of Ibrahim's provisions, so he decided to sit and enjoy a meal together from their perch above the city.

Feeding Lena dry fruits and cheeses, he marveled at how mature she was, and how much she seemed to understand, given she was still six months shy of her second birthday. Since they'd left Ibrahim's, whenever he motioned to her to be silent to avoid danger, the child wouldn't make a sound. When he fed her smaller portions to ensure that their food would last, the child ate them without so much as a fuss. Necessity had forced him to grow over this last month; perhaps it had done the same to the child.

Ari looked over the city again. He reached into the pocket of his shirt and brought out his medal. In his youth, the medal had been a source of pride and wonder, but in his adult hands it became a piercing reminder of something he could never live up to. The medal was meant for the hero. And he knew the hero doesn't abandon the helpless. The hero doesn't hide in the shadows. The hero isn't crippled by fear and doubt. He closed his hand around the medal and squeezed it until its edges dug into his dry calluses and his palm began to bleed.

After finishing a meal, Ari picked his way down the mountain, traversing the narrow path that was hidden by the thick forest. When he and Lena reached the bottom, he stayed hidden within the tree line and observed the harbor, some thousand yards in front of him. He could see men coming and going to the docks. They seemed foreign to him. Not only in the way they looked but in the way they carried themselves—purposeful, unabashed, and unencumbered.

He saw some men as black as crows, others with blond hair as long as a woman's, still others with slanted eyes. He didn't know people could look so different. Out of the corner of his eye, he saw a brigade of Ottoman soldiers riding on horseback. Frightened, he pulled himself and Lena deeper into the shadows of the forest and waited until dusk. With the activity of the harbor dying down, Ari entered the city. He immediately made his way to the docks. He studied the flags of each of the forty or so ships, looking for one particular flag. It was the one that he'd drawn in the Bible based on his mother's description. A red, white, and blue flag with a single star on it—the flag of Texas.

He walked the length of the harbor, but not a single flag resembled the one his mother described. He walked back inside the tree line with Lena to spend the night in the forest. He came back to the dock the next day looking for the flag, to no avail. He spent a week repeating the exercise before he began thinking that the ship may no longer exist.

After a while, he learned enough of the city to be able to situate himself in areas that allowed him to observe its nuances and traffic patterns. This enabled him to get in and out of the city without so much as raising an eyebrow, and he noticed the sailors barely paid attention to him. Trabzon was a port of commerce, and few had time to concern themselves with a hunchback and a peasant child.

One day, as he carried Lena on the docks, he heard some commotion behind him. He turned to spot armed Turkish militiamen herding a group of people to a decrepit ship. Ari ducked behind some empty barrels just as the line of people passed him. The group was made up mostly of women and children. They had shackles on their hands. He was close enough to hear some of the children crying out to their mothers, and he realized that they were Armenian. Hidden from view, he watched as they were crammed aboard. The ship then set sail and headed out to sea. Of all the ships he had seen on the docks, he thought that one looked the least seaworthy, with its splintered wood and torn sail. He watched the ship sail toward the horizon and witnessed it capsize into the Black Sea.

Days passed, and Ari felt continuing to search the docks was futile and that he was putting Lena and himself at unnecessary risk, so he decided to go back up the mountain, to the clearing from which he first saw the city. He made a camp consisting of a small tent that he made from a blanket and branches, and dug a small fire pit. He had a view of the harbor, and he spent his days awaiting a new ship to arrive. When one did, he would make his way down to check its flags, only to return disappointed, repeatedly. He scavenged for food and was even able to make snares to catch small game. His mother taught him how to make the traps when he was young, and it was one of the ways he and his mother were able to feed themselves. Snaring prey required patience and time, both of which he now had. However, he wasn't sure how long they would be able to stay there before their safety would come into question.

A little more than three weeks after arriving at Trabzon, Ari noticed a ship on the horizon. Like the others that came before, he watched it sail into the U-shaped harbor and noted that it pulled into the second to last spot of the near docks. With little hope, he set out on his routine to check the ship's flags. When he reached the ship, all he could see were three limp flags, but then a strong wind snapped them to attention. As he fixed his eyes on one of the flags, an odd sensation bubbled up in the pit of his stomach. He locked his eyes on the flag until he was sure it wasn't his imagination.

Flying above the 125-foot ship was a red, white, and blue flag with a lone star—just as his mother described.

39

Joseph and the Well

Captain Yusuf had one superstition when he pulled his ship into Trabzon; he would never look toward the hills in the distance and the abandoned well at their base. The well was one of the persistent memories he still had of a childhood he yearned to forget.

Yusuf had no memory of his parents other than being told they were dead. His father was an elderly patriarch, and his mother was his father's third wife. Yusuf and his brother, Ayman, two years his senior, were raised in a remote village by their adult half brother and his family. Even at a young age, the two boys were put to work and had to endure the wrath of their ill-tempered older brother. They suffered brutal physical abuse that grew in intensity as they got older. Yusuf didn't speak his first word until he was nearly four years old, by which time his half brother had gotten into the habit of calling him the Idiot.

The two young boys often went to bed hungry. Yusuf could recall lying in bed with Ayman, and his brother telling him not to worry. He promised that one day he would take him away from that place, that one day they would be happy. That day never came for his brother.

One morning, Yusuf awoke to find he had wet the bed. He woke his brother to tell him. Fearing that his younger brother would be beaten, Ayman exchanged clothes with him. When their half brother discovered the wet bed, Ayman told him that he had done it. Enraged, their half brother grabbed a broken-off axe handle and, with Yusuf watching, beat Ayman with it until he no longer moved. His half brother stripped the clothes off the body, took it to the woods, and buried it. Yusuf was only eight years old.

That night, when everyone went to bed, Yusuf snuck out of the house, picked a direction, and began to walk. He didn't know how long he was out in the wilderness, but he recalled sleeping in the forest so often that it started to feel like home—that the trees were the walls to his room and the starry sky its ceiling. Then one day, as he was walking, a town appeared before him. It was unlike any town he had seen. It had ships, it had water, and it had energy.

He was too frightened to venture into town, so he sat down by an abandoned well and watched the ships coming in and going out. He saw the sailors and imagined what it would be like to be one. The sailors looked so assured, so purposeful, and yet so free. For weeks, he slept next to the well, with his back against its sturdy outer wall. He came to feel safe next to the well and would only leave it to scavenge for a few morsels to eat.

One day a sailor took notice of the boy next to the well and thought it was odd that the boy spent his entire day barely moving from it. The sailor set out to sea, but when he returned three weeks later, he saw the boy was still at the well. Curious, the sailor made his way to the well. As he approached, the boy stared at him with an apprehensive look.

"Hello, I wanted to take a break and eat my lunch. Do you mind if I share a seat with you for a bit?" the sailor asked.

The boy didn't respond, and the sailor sat next to him on the well. He opened a bag and took out some fruits. He unpeeled an orange as the boy quietly looked on.

"Well, it seems I've brought more food than I can eat. Would you care to have some fruit? I'm afraid it would go to waste otherwise," said the sailor as he handed the boy some of his oranges.

The boy timidly took the slices and put one to his mouth.

"My name is Mardiros. And you?"

The boy didn't know how to respond. He had been called the Idiot for so long that it became the only name he knew.

"I don't know," the boy said.

"Do you have a home or a family?" asked Mardiros, who knew the answer even before he asked the question.

The boy shook his head.

"Ah, so that could only mean one thing. You're an adventurer. Only adventurers are so unfettered," said Mardiros.

The categorization surprised the boy. Adventurers were strong and intrepid. Did this man really think him a person of that ilk? The boy had an unfamiliar feeling wash over him—a feeling that could have been mistaken for pride—and he found himself hoping that this man wouldn't see past his unintended facade.

"Do you see that ship there?" said Mardiros, pointing to a white vessel in the harbor. "I work on that ship, and the captain has room for one more sailor. I know adventurers love the sea as much as anyone. Would you be interested in joining our crew? I could talk to the captain for you."

The boy smiled broadly and nodded.

"Very good, but there's just one thing. Working on a ship is difficult and the captain won't hire anyone who isn't strong enough to do the work. So, I must ask: Are you a strong lad?"

"Yes," said the boy.

"Can you make a muscle, so I can see?"

The boy stood and flexed his bicep as hard as he could, hoping that his thin arm would somehow impress Mardiros enough to earn his endorsement. Mardiros squeezed the boy's bicep and recoiled in feigned shock.

"Oh yes, you are certainly strong enough."

The boy's smile grew even larger, and he and Mardiros made their way to the ship.

At first, the boy was simply the ship's mascot, but he never stopped trying to help in any way he could—fearing that if he didn't show his usefulness, the captain would kick him out. The captain, a middle-aged man named Ediz, quickly grew to appreciate the boy's sincere efforts, and took a liking to him, even naming him Yusuf (Joseph). The captain had four children, all daughters, and eventually decided to adopt Yusuf and groom him as his successor.

When he grew older, he asked his adopted father why he had decided to name him Yusuf. The old captain reached into his desk, brought out his Quran, and slid it across the desk to him.

"Because you came to me from a well," his father said.

Yusuf was a far cry from the child he was when he first stepped onto the ship. His hair had thinned and receded. What remained was a semi-wreath of gray follicles neatly wrapped around his head.

Decades on the sea had given his skin a dark, leathery look that made him appear even older than he was. The cartilage in both of his knees had worn so thin that his bones would painfully rub together, forcing him to use a cane when he walked. However, his overall health was buoyed by a life that didn't allow enough leisure to get fat, and he maintained a fit weight even now.

As Captain Yusuf walked off the gangplank, he noticed a hunchback staring at his ship so intensely he seemed oblivious to the child pulling at his leg. There was something odd about the way the hunchback was looking at his ship, and when Yusuf reached the end of the dock, he turned back and saw Ari still staring at the ship. Yusuf grabbed his son Muhammad's arm.

"Look at that hunchback," Yusuf said to his son. "Why do you suppose he's looking at our ship that way?"

"I don't know," said Muhammad, after observing Ari. "That does seem strange. I'd say he's a thief, but if that's the case, he's a foolish one. We don't have much worth stealing, and what we do would need stronger hands than his to carry."

"Strange, indeed, but we can't afford any mischief. Go see what he wants and send him on his way before he can do anything."

Muhammad left his father's side and walked back toward the ship. Yusuf saw Ari startle when Muhammad addressed him. After a few minutes, Muhammad firmly pointed the hunchback away from the ship, and the hunchback scooped up the child and scurried away.

Muhammad made certain they were gone before walking back to his father.

"What did the hunchback want?" Yusuf asked his son.

"He was talking nonsense," Muhammad said. "Something about looking for a ship his grandfather sailed on, and he thought it was our ship. When I asked him why he wanted to find the ship, he said that his grandfather was a friend of the captain, and he wanted to speak to him. He looked too nervous to be telling the truth, so I told him I would take him to the captain, all he had to do was tell me the captain's name. He came up with a ridiculous name that made it clear he was lying, so I told him to get off the dock immediately or I'd call the authorities."

At that moment, Yusuf picked up Ari with his eyes and tracked him as he carried Lena farther away from the harbor. His eyes were still on Ari as he passed in front of the well.

"What was the name of the captain the hunchback gave you?" Yusuf asked his son.

"Captain Cotton."

40

Captain Cotton

Captain Cotton! The words jolted Yusuf like a lightning bolt.

Yusuf hadn't heard that name for what seemed like a lifetime. It was the name the crew called his adopted father when Yusuf first came aboard the ship. His father always felt the name was undignified, but he allowed his crew to use it only because it was given to him by a man who sacrificed his life for the ship.

When Yusuf was ready to take over the operations of the boat and hire his own crew, his father had one request.

"Can you make sure no one ever calls me Captain Cotton? I never cared for that name," the old captain said.

Even though Yusuf felt the moniker was fitting for all the right reasons, he smiled, nodded, and agreed. Out of respect for his father, Yusuf never used the name again, not even telling his son that it was his grandfather's old nickname.

When he heard it now, the blood seemed to rush from his face, making even his dark complexion appear pale.

"Go get the hunchback and bring him to me immediately," Yusuf said to his son.

Muhammad knew better than to question his father when he took a firm tone, and he rushed toward Ari, hoping to reach him before he disappeared into the forest.

＝

"Hey! Boy! Stop! I must talk to you," yelled Muhammad when he was within about fifty yards of Ari. It had been a hard chase for Muhammad, first running through a crowd of sailors, then scaling a six-foot-high fence, and finally up a steep incline in the hopes of cutting off Ari before he reached the woods. He saw Ari stop in front of the opening to the forest.

Ari turned his head, but instead of waiting for Muhammed, Ari quickened his pace and disappeared with Lena into the woods. Muhammad followed them into the forest, still hollering at them to stop. As he ran up the path, he could see no sign of the pair. They couldn't have stayed on the path for this distance without him having run them down, so he stopped to listen.

"Please, boy. The captain would like to speak with you. I'll take you to him. Please come out."

Still no response.

Muhammad scanned every visible area of the forest but again saw no sign of the two. With no other option, Muhammad followed the trail back out of the forest, disappointed in himself that he would fail his father.

He was only a few yards away from exiting the forest when he noticed some shrubs rustle to his left. They were large enough to hide the hunchback and child, so he pushed them aside. Ari's fear-filled eyes stared back as he huddled himself around Lena.

Muhammad extended his hand. "Come, the captain would like to see you."

Ari clutched Lena tighter and didn't move.

"There is no need for fear. We are far from prying eyes. If I wanted to harm you, there wouldn't be a more suitable place to do it. I've come to help," said Muhammed, still holding out his hand.

Ari slowly took his hand, and Muhammad helped him to his feet.

———

Yusuf, who hadn't moved from the dock, watched his son lead the pair to him. When they reached him, Yusuf quietly looked at Ari, noting he looked frightened before addressing him.

"I'm Yusuf, and this is my son, Muhammad," he said. "I'm the captain of the ship you were speaking to my son about."

Ari nodded but otherwise remained silent, his eyes fixed on the ground.

"How do you know of Captain Cotton?"

Ari shrugged.

"You came here looking for someone, but that man is no longer alive. I'm the captain of the ship now, so if there's anything I can do for you, you'll have to speak to me. Captain Cotton was my father. I must ask—how do you know of him?"

Ari raised his eyes from the ground. "My grandfather sailed with him."

"That must have been a long time ago."

"It was."

"And what's your name?"

"Ari."

"And the child?"

"Lena."

"And where did you come from? And why is it that you've come seeking my father?"

Ari, trembling slightly, found himself tongue-tied.

"There's no reason to be frightened, son. Are you Armenian?"

Ari nodded.

"I see," said Yusuf. "My father had many Armenians, Kurds, and Greeks who worked on his ship. If you're fearful that I harbor some ill will toward your people, you need not be. The sea knows only one nationality, one race—that of sailor. So please tell me why you came looking for my father."

"We traveled from Van to ask if he or you would take us to Greece. But I don't have any money to offer."

"To Greece?!" said Yusuf as he looked over to Muhammad, who was subtly shaking his head. "I know what you're asking, and I know why you're asking it. I would be placing the lives of my crew at risk if I were to do that. So, I don't know how I could agree to it."

Ari gave a slight nod.

"I can have Muhammad bring some food for you and the child if you're hungry, but I'm afraid I can't do much more," Yusuf said.

"Thank you," said Ari, shoulders slumping even more.

Yusuf motioned to his son to go back to the ship to get Ari and Lena some food, then turned back to Ari.

"So, was it your grandfather who told you about Captain Cotton? Is your grandfather still alive?"

"It was my mother who told me about him. My grandfather is dead."

"I see. Do you know when he worked on this ship?"

Ari shook his head.

"So how did you know which ship was ours?"

"From the flag."

"From the flag? Which flag is that?"

"The one with the large star on it."

"And how did you know to look for that one in particular?"

"My mother told me my grandfather was on the ship when the pirates attacked, and the flag belonged to a man who was killed."

"Your grandfather was there that day?" said Yusuf, whose eyes suddenly grew wide.

"Yes."

"And what was your grandfather's name?"

"Mardiros."

"Mardiros," repeated Yusuf, as if the name had whisked him away to another place and time.

"Father," said Muhammad as he approached the captain, who hadn't heard his son's footsteps. "I've brought the food."

Yusuf grabbed his son's arm.

"Please take this man and the child to our ship."

"What? Why?"

"Do as I say and do it immediately."

Ari stared at the captain, his eyes flooding with emotion. He wasn't sure why the captain changed his mind, but he was over-come with relief.

"Thank you, Captain," Ari said.

———

Muhammad was confused, but his father and captain gave him an order, so he told Ari to follow him to the ship. Muhammad tried to make sense of his father's peculiar attitude and the urgency in which he wanted Ari and the child on the ship.

As he walked away, Muhammad turned to look back at his father and saw the captain rooted in place, observing them strangely as they made their way to the ship. Muhammad helped Ari and Lena board the vessel. Instead of climbing aboard himself, he snuck behind a mast and peeked his head around to look at the old captain again. When he did, he saw his father do something he had never seen him do before.

He saw the old captain fall to his knees and begin to cry.

41

Stands Still in Esperance

With Ari and Lena occupied with a meal of leftover rice and meat, Muhammad went to see his father. When he entered the wheelhouse, he caught his father rifling through some papers and writing something down on a notepad.

"Father, I'm not sure what we're to do with the hunchback and the child," Muhammad said in a low voice.

"I'm taking them to Greece," Yusuf replied.

"Father, I don't understand. You know the risk, not only to you and this ship but to our crew as well."

"That's why I'll take them myself."

"Father, you can't take this ship all the way to Greece alone. You know that better than anyone."

"I know it will be difficult, but not impossible. I'll leave in the morning, and I'll need some supplies. Take this and make sure the supplies are here by the morning," said Yusuf, handing his son a piece of paper.

"Father, this doesn't make any sense. Why are you risking your life for this hunchback? I don't know what he told you, but how do you know you can trust him? He's certainly desperate and will say anything to get your help."

"I don't expect you to understand, but no harm will come to the hunchback and child if there is anything I can do to prevent it."

"Then I'm coming with you."

"No, you'll stay here. Now, get me those supplies."

"Father, please."

"You have your orders. Now go!"

Muhammad reluctantly took the sheet of paper and exited. He was determined not to let his father sail without him, and decided he'd take up the matter with his father when he returned.

Yusuf waited until he was certain his son had left the dock and then went down to the kitchen.

"Have you ever sailed before?" Yusuf asked Ari, who was still sitting at the table holding Lena.

"No," Ari replied.

"I want you to know that I'm going to take you to Greece, but I can't take my crew with me. It'll be difficult, but with your help, we can get the ship there. Are you willing to help me?"

"Yes."

"Good. How old are you?"

"Thirty-one."

"Thirty-one!?" exclaimed Yusuf. His initial thought was that Ari was trying to hide his youth for some reason. But then Yusuf looked more closely and saw the marks of time on his skin, a slightly receded hairline, and the unmistakable look of age in his eyes. After a minute or so, it was no longer difficult to see Ari as a man and not the boy he assumed him to be.

"I'm sorry, I thought you were younger."

Ari nodded.

"If we're to leave, we must do so immediately. I'll teach you what you need to do once we're at sea. Now, I need you to untie the ship from the dock. Can you do that?"

"Yes," Ari said.

Yusuf had Ari set Lena down in his sleeping quarters and then took him outside. Ari barely had enough strength to lift the thick ropes, but he was able to untie the boat and toss the rope on the ship, just as Yusuf had instructed. He jumped back on the ship before it moved off the dock.

Ari watched the dock recede, and for the first time he felt that perhaps he had a real chance to save Lena, that he might keep her alive long enough for Vartan to come for her. A wiser man would have known how foolish an undertaking it was, but on this day, he still had hope.

Ari reached into his pocket, pulled out his grandfather's medal, and put it to his lips.

═══

Captain Yusuf wasn't the only one who had noticed Ari staring at the ship. One of the ship's deckhands, a young Kurd who had been part of the crew for only a few months, also found Ari's gaze curious. However, as a junior member of the crew, he felt it wasn't his place to say anything, and he ignored it.

Standing behind some crates, he watched as his captain and Muhammad spoke in low tones about the hunchback looking at their ship. He'd heard the hunchback tell the captain that he was

Armenian and ultimately saw the captain instruct his son to take the pair to their ship.

The deckhand's brother had been a Hamidiye cavalryman until he died in an Armenian uprising. Not having anything to do, the deckhand found a place at the end of the dock and hid behind a cart to have a cigarette—a habit not accepted by most Muslims. He took a sheet of paper out of one of his pockets and unfolded it. He had picked up the sheet from the police post the last time he was in town. It was a posting of wanted fugitives within the empire. His eyes went to one line in particular, which read: *Armenian man, thirty-one years of age, formerly of Van. Wanted for the murders of two Ottoman officers. Identifiable features: HUNCHBACK.*

He lit a cigarette and thought about what he'd just heard when he saw Muhammad leave the boat and walk to town. A few minutes later, he noticed activity on the ship. He looked closely and saw the hunchback untying the ship and then jumping back on board. As the ship sailed away, the deckhand walked back down the dock to watch.

After it had sailed out of sight, the deckhand turned and walked to a single-story, brick building at the center of town. The structure jutted out from the surrounding buildings and was lit by two lamps on either side of the main door. He entered and approached a uniformed man sitting at a desk.

"I have a crime to report," the deckhand said.

42

The Hand of God

Ari took quickly to life at sea, even though Captain Yusuf hadn't understated how difficult it would be. Ari found himself constantly running from one end of the vessel to the other—adjusting the sails, inspecting mechanisms he knew nothing about, making repairs to a gasket or lever that he prayed would work.

The ship had been rigged with an engine a few years earlier, but when they came across favorable winds, the captain used sails to conserve fuel.

Ari didn't know how many days they had been on the ship, but the weather had been calm, so their voyage had been uneventful.

"What do you need me to do next, Captain?" Ari asked one day after he'd completed all his tasks. He stood at the entrance to the captain's wheelhouse waiting for a reply.

"Nothing for now. The seas are calm. We're making good time. Have a seat and rest for a bit," Yusuf said.

Lena, who was playing with some marbles on the floor, abandoned her game when she saw Ari, smiled, and rushed to him with her arms raised.

"Ah-we, Ah-we," said Lena enthusiastically.

"Hello, princess," said a smiling Ari as he picked her up and sat in the chair across from the captain. Ari felt her hugging his neck tightly. He smoothed the back of Lena's head as she rested it on his shoulder.

"You mean a lot to that child, Ari," said Yusuf as he observed them.

"I think she's just tired," Ari said.

"It's not hard to see that you're Mardiros's grandson." Yusuf smiled. "You're a lot like him, Ari. People were drawn to your grandfather because they could sense what was in his heart. The child knows what's in your heart, even at her age; believe me when I tell you that."

"Did you know my grandfather?" Ari asked.

"Yes, yes. I knew him. I was a young boy when I met your grandfather. What I'm teaching you, he taught me. So, in a way, you're learning from him. It's a shame that situations aren't different; you would have made a fine sailor just like your grandfather," Yusuf said.

The thought of that warmed Ari, and he nodded in acknowledgment as the two men enjoyed a moment of silence. As Ari stared out, he noted how vast, peaceful, and brilliant the sea was, and it wasn't hard to imagine why his grandfather loved it.

"I'm sorry about what happened to your grandfather," said Yusuf, breaking the silence. "Death awaits us all, but no one deserved to die like he did. No greater crime has ever been committed."

Ari remained silent. Of all the stories his mother had told him about his grandfather, she never related how he'd died. He just assumed he'd passed away as most old people do—peacefully in their beds. He was ashamed to tell Yusuf that he didn't know this part of the story, so he forced himself to nod again.

"You know, one of my favorite stories about your grandfather happened when I was about fourteen. We sailed to Naples. It was my first visit to Italy. Your grandfather was still on the crew then. After we unloaded our cargo, another young deckhand and I wanted to see the city. My father, knowing we were young and likely to get into trouble, asked your grandfather to go with us.

"After an afternoon of walking the streets and taking in the culture, we headed back to the ship when two men approached us. One of them took out a knife and demanded we hand him our money. It was the biggest knife I'd ever seen," said Yusuf, holding his hands almost two feet apart to illustrate the size of the blade.

Ari blinked his eyes in genuine awe of the terror a weapon that size would inspire.

"My friend and I froze in fear," Yusuf continued. "The scoundrel with the knife told me to approach him. As I took a step toward them, Mardiros grabbed me and told me to stay where I was. The thief told me to come at once or they would kill all three of us."

"What did you do?" asked Ari.

"I didn't do anything, but I'll never forget this," said Yusuf, shaking his head. "Your grandfather, as calm as the sea ahead, walked right up to the thief and said, 'If you are going to kill anyone, then you can start with me, but first you have to aim at the heart.' And he pressed his chest against the blade. The thief, no doubt as shocked as we were, just stood there holding his knife to your grandfather's chest. 'To kill someone, you have to thrust. The knife won't do it itself,' Mardiros said. When he said that, you could see all the courage drain from the thief's eyes. 'You're crazy,' the man yelled. And then the pair of them turned and ran off.

"Relieved, we told your grandfather that he was either extremely brave or extremely stupid. 'I'm certainly not brave, and I hope I'm not stupid,' he said. So, we asked him why he was so reckless. And he said, 'When you've been to as many ports as I have, you meet lots of different people. You can always tell the dangerous ones, the ones who could take a life without a thought. Their eyes betray them. The men just now would have a hard time killing a chicken if they were starving.' We asked him what if he had been wrong. And he said, 'In that case, they would have left with a broken knife,' and he lifted his shirt to show us a vest made of chain mail. We laughed all the way back to the ship."

Ari smiled at the thought. He never tired of listening to stories about his grandfather. Hearing Yusuf tell the story, he felt like a child again. For a man who had no place, no fraternity, he oddly felt like he belonged there on that ship, there with this captain.

"How did my grandfather get the chain mail?" Ari asked.

"How did he, indeed? That story is even more remarkable, but we will save that for another time." The captain laughed.

Yusuf jolted up in his chair and grabbed his marine binoculars and peered out toward the sea. Ari strained to see what the captain was looking at. He watched as a speck danced on the water and grew larger and larger on the horizon. He saw it was moving in their direction. As the speck—now clearly a ship—got closer, Yusuf strained to make out the letters on the side. After a few minutes, Yusuf could finally see the letters. He paused and then peered into his binoculars at the letters again to make sure, and he could see the words form as clear as day. There, on the ship's starboard side, were painted the words Το χέρι του Θεού.

The captain paled as he set down his binoculars. Ari waited for an explanation, but Yusuf didn't say a word.

"Captain, what is that?" asked Ari, nervously pointing to the ship.

"That's *The Hand of God.*"

43

A Final Voyage

As the ship sailed closer, Captain Yusuf idled his vessel and watched as the other ship's crew dropped a three-man skiff into the water.

Το χέρι του Θεού (*The Hand of God*) was a Greek merchant ship. Its captain, Nikos Pavlou, had been a friend of Captain Yusuf's since the two took over the ships of their respective fathers decades earlier. They'd met in the ports of Istanbul, which was the most easterly point Captain Nikos would sail his ship.

As Europe had plunged into World War I, Turkey had aligned itself with Germany and the other Central Powers; however, Greece had remained neutral. Even so, seeing a Greek ship this far into the Black Sea was not only unexpected but extremely dangerous as well. Captain Nikos would never venture this far past Istanbul even during peaceful times. Yusuf knew that for him to do so in a time of war required a purpose.

"Nikos, this is unexpected," said Yusuf as he helped the men board the ship. "What are you doing here?"

"I have an urgent matter to discuss. Can we talk privately?" Nikos replied.

"Certainly, let's go to the wheelhouse. Ari, can you please see if these men need anything to eat or drink?" said Yusuf.

Ari nodded and led the men back to the galley.

The two captains made their way to the wheelhouse. Yusuf closed the door behind them.

"I received a telegram from your son. I know what you're doing—"

"So that's it? Well, if you've come here to stop me, that was foolish, you put yourself in danger for nothing," said Yusuf, cutting off his friend.

"Do you know the hunchback is wanted by the law?" Nikos asked.

"For what? Being an Armenian?"

"No. For murder. They say he killed two Ottoman officers. They want him brought back and hanged."

"Murder," exclaimed Yusuf with a slight chuckle. "Did you see the hunchback? Do you really think he could kill two military officers? I've sailed with him the whole way here. Even if he was able to, Ari wouldn't kill anyone."

"Everyone could kill for the right reason," Nikos said.

"Well, then if he did, he had a good reason to. I'd say that doesn't make him a criminal. So, as I said, if you have come to stop me, you wasted a trip."

"Yusuf. We've been friends for a long time. That's the only reason your son reached out to me, because he trusted me. I had to tell you about the situation you are in with the hunchback and what's at stake. The authorities are waiting. They're going to seize your ship and everyone on it when you reach Istanbul. You'll never make it through the straits."

Yusuf slumped in his chair and rubbed his brow in thought.

"Then what am I to do?" he said.

"Abandon this ship here. I can take you and the hunchback on our ship. We won't port in Istanbul. We'll continue directly to Athens."

"If they've mobilized as you say, then what if you're stopped at the straits?"

"If we're boarded, then I can claim the hunchback and child as our own. They can't prove it's the same hunchback. They know you well at the ports. We'll hide you on the ship."

"I can't let you do that. I'm still captain of this ship, and I'll stay with my ship. I'll sail to Istanbul alone. They'll be looking for this ship, and it'll give you a better chance to get by unmolested, as they'll be occupied with me."

"Yusuf don't be foolish, that's suicide. I knew the risk when I came here to help you. The risk is mine and mine alone."

"No, you might be risking your life and that of your crew, but if I go on your ship, I'll be risking the life of the Armenian. I won't do that."

"Please, Yusuf, you don't stand a chance."

Yusuf gave a weary grin as he looked at his friend.

"No, I have chosen my path. But I ask you to please take the hunchback and the child with you, and if you still have any friendship for me, promise me that you will take them safely to Athens. And please send word when you have arrived."

"You have my promise," Nikos said.

"Thank you. I've always treasured your friendship. I want you to know that," said Yusuf as the two men shared an embrace.

When Yusuf explained the situation to Ari, Ari was reluctant at first and asked Yusuf if they could stay with him instead and risk getting through the straits.

"Ari, if I believed there was even the slightest chance that we would make it, I would keep you on this ship, so that I would know you made it safely out. But they know this ship well. The straits are narrow. We are certain to be boarded. And if we are, then I won't be able to protect you or the child," Yusuf said.

Ari was torn, but he had grown to trust Yusuf's judgment. Ari packed up what few possessions he and Lena had and made his way to the skiff. The two deckhands accompanying Captain Nikos boarded the skiff first, followed by their captain. Ari handed them his bags and lowered Lena into the arms of one of the seamen. Before he climbed down himself, he turned to Yusuf.

"I want to thank you again for helping Lena and me," said Ari above the sharp sounds of waves slapping against the idling ship.

"Please, there is no reason to thank me, I regret I couldn't do more. May Allah always protect you," said Yusuf as he extended his hand.

Ari awkwardly nodded and shook Yusuf's hand. He turned toward the skiff, only to turn back to Yusuf again.

"This child is all I have now. I've tried to convince myself that it was an honorable thing to leave my mother so I could save Lena. But maybe I did it because I was simply afraid to die. Maybe my mother knew that and, out of love, she gave me a reason to act cowardly. Remember when you said I was a lot like my grandfather? In truth, I'm not, but I want to be," Ari said.

"As do I," Yusuf replied.

44

The Privilege of Death

As soon as Captain Yusuf entered the straits, two port-authority vessels bracketed his ship and escorted it to the dock, where an armed party of six men came aboard. The leader signaled to four of the men to search the boat, while he headed to the wheelhouse with the remaining armed man.

"Hello, Haydar," said Yusuf, who was still sitting in his captain's chair and didn't look up from his logbook even as the men entered.

Haydar was the head of the port authority, and the two men had known each other for years. Haydar massaged the end of his pointy beard, as a man would when he is choosing words or when no words could be found.

"Yusuf, there are some serious allegations against you. I have to know who else is on this ship," Haydar said.

"As you can see, it's only me," said Yusuf as he put down his pencil, closed his logbook, and looked up.

"This is not the time to be coy. Did you sail all the way here by yourself simply for the joy of it?"

"Would that be so odd?"

Just then one of the men searching the ship barged in.

"Sir, we checked the entire ship—there's no one else aboard," the man said.

"Where is he?" Haydar asked Yusuf.

"I don't know what you're talking about. As the man said, there is no one else on board."

"Yusuf, this is a serious matter. They'll have you tried and hanged. I still have some influence, and I can help you, but only if you allow me to. You must tell me where the hunchback is."

"I'm the only one on this ship."

Haydar looked at Yusuf, wanting to desperately grab ahold of him and shake some sense into him. But he had known Yusuf for too long and knew when this old captain dug his heels in, a tsunami couldn't uproot him.

The muscles of Haydar's jaw tensed, and he lowered his head.

"Take him away," Haydar said to his men.

A pair of deputies took Yusuf to the police station. Over the next two days, he was interrogated but refused to give the authorities any information. They told him that he could avoid a trial and a potentially harsh sentence if he cooperated, but he remained silent. Seeing no alternative, the government put him on trial. It would be a short one. After the judge read the charges, which included harboring a fugitive, and asked for his plea, Yusuf responded with a single word.

"Guilty."

A week later, on the eve of Yusuf's sentencing, Muhammad came to visit his father in his jail cell. The jailer opened the cell and let Muhammad enter. He sat next to his father on a wooden bench against the back wall of the cell.

"Have you heard word from Athens?" Yusuf asked his son in a hushed tone.

"Not yet, but I'm sure Captain Nikos will send word as soon as possible," Muhammad said.

Yusuf nodded.

"Father," Muhammad began, "you have many friends here, no one wants to see you punished for this. Most understand that it was simply an act of mercy that you helped the hunchback. But if you go to court tomorrow, they'll sentence you to death. You'll have given them no options. But you don't have to be there. Our friends have spoken to the guards, they'll leave a key just outside your cell. All you have to do is wait until midnight, take the key, unlock the door, and walk out. We have a ship ready for you. They'll simply say that you escaped," Muhammad said.

"No, I'm staying here," Yusuf said.

"Father, I don't understand. It's as if some madness has overtaken you. This is a dire matter. You must think clearly."

"It's with a clear mind that I choose to stay. A just man doesn't run from the consequences of his choices. Whatever fate awaits me tomorrow, I'll welcome it. I'll accept it without guilt or regret."

"Father, please reconsider. If not for yourself, for me."

Yusuf stared at his son. It took all the strength he had not to embrace Muhammad and weep at the thought of never sharing another voyage with him. But he was a father, and a father's duty isn't always easy, his love not always meant to be tender.

"One day you will understand," Yusuf said. "You're a man now. A good, strong man. You're a better sailor than me. I hope that one day you look back on this moment not with sadness but with pride. That for once your father, with his head raised, had the courage to do for another what others have done for him."

"Father, please don't do this. You don't deserve to be punished. If you leave, you'll save the court from itself. It will not have to bear the shame of its injustice," said Muhammad, squeezing his father's left hand desperately.

Yusuf felt his son's grasp. He clasped his right hand atop his son's and rubbed it warmly. He turned his head and looked down at the dirt floor of the cell.

"I've not always been brave. And I haven't lived a life free of guilt. For that, I'm ashamed. For that, my head hangs with regret. In the end, a man must face himself. When night falls on his days, the good man will blow his candle out on a life well-lived. For the rest of us, it will be a time for amends," he said.

Yusuf paused and took a deep breath. He put his hand on his son's knee but kept his eyes fixed to the floor.

"I never told you this, but I had a brother once," said Yusuf, his voice growing heavier. "He would have been your uncle. I wish you could have known him. For love, he died as a child. That is how I will always remember him—a beautiful and brave child. I wish I could see him again. I hope he could forgive me. How I've prayed for that. But that's not in my hands any longer. The only thing I have left is to show that I've carried a part of him with me. To prove that his life was not in vain. To show that the frightened, stupid boy he loved, loved him as well. Perhaps then, in some small way, I would feel worthy to call myself his brother."

Yusuf's bowed head prevented his son from seeing a tear fall on the dirt floor. Before Muhammad could respond, a guard rapped on the door and told Muhammad it was time to leave. Unable to contain his emotions and not having the strength to hug his father, Muhammad ran out of the cell in tears. The guard closed the cell door behind him and set a towel just outside the cell. Yusuf glanced at the towel and then at the guard. The guard gave him a slight nod, and Yusuf understood that under the towel were the keys to the cell. Yusuf leaned his head back against the wall and closed his eyes.

The next morning, the guards found Yusuf where they'd left him. They shackled his hands in front of him and escorted him from the cell to the courthouse. They passed by Muhammad, who was waiting at the courthouse door. Muhammad asked the guards if he could have a final word with his father. The guards agreed.

Muhammad embraced his father and kissed his cheek.

"Word is that the skies are clear in Athens," said Muhammad as he broke his embrace.

Yusuf looked at his son to make sure he understood what he'd just heard. Muhammad nodded.

"Thank you, my son. Thank you," said Yusuf as he gently touched his son's cheek with the back of his shackled hands.

Muhammad stepped aside, and the guards took Yusuf into the courtroom. There was a larger crowd than usual for such an early sentencing, but the room was somber. Yusuf remained standing at the front of the bench while the judge entered and took his seat.

The judge began by reciting the charges and reaffirming that the court accepted Yusuf's guilty plea. With the formalities out of the way, it was time for the judge to hand down the sentence. And it was a sentence that everyone had feared—death by hanging.

"Yusuf, would you like to say some final words?" the judge asked.

For the first time that day, Yusuf showed emotion. His chin trembled, and his eyes glistened with tears. Yusuf's friends and family, who had only known him as a strong and stoic man, found it hard to watch. His voice crackled when he tried to speak, but he cleared his throat and began again, this time in a clear, strong voice.

"I'm not a courageous man, and I'm not ashamed to say I rose from a sleepless night frightened," Yusuf began. "However, it wasn't the knowledge that this court serves its justice with a heavy hand that I feared. I neither asked for nor expected any leniency as you prepared my sentence. No, what I feared most is having spent my life questioning my faith in God, even as I fell to my knees daily to pray.

"I haven't had an easy life, and perhaps that's why I had more doubt than most in God's greatness. But now I stand before you no longer uncertain of it. Allah has taken mercy on this old and unworthy man. He has reached His hand out and given me this day.

"Many years ago, a stranger took pity on a poor and frightened boy. What others looked upon with disdain, he chose to look at with compassion. That day, the stranger placed an immense burden upon me. A debt too great for a desperate child to ever repay. A debt I believed had long expired. But I was wrong, and a herald was sent to collect. And to my surprise, the price was set low. You see, to die for that debt—to give this old life for it—would not be punishment, but a privilege."

Yusuf was hanged the following day.

<hr>

Hans Breiner sat in his office at the end of his workday. The mail had been dropped off that morning, but a busy schedule didn't allow him to go through the letters until he finished his work. Most of the mail contained polite, or not so polite, rejections to his requests for additional funding or his urgent pleas for more medicine.

As he rifled through the mail in frustration, his own handwriting on the front of an envelope, postmarked from Athens, seized his attention. He tore open the envelope and saw the letter inside contained just one word. He read the word silently and then repeated it aloud.

"Bethlehem."

Book II

45

O Fortuna

One year after receiving the letter, Hans didn't know much more about the fate of Ari and Lena, as wartime communications had become more challenging. However, he did get word from the US embassy that the manifest of a ship called *The New Horizon* showed that Ari and Lena were aboard and that the pair made it to America. Beyond that, he knew nothing more. He hadn't received word from his contacts as to where Ari had settled, and no one could confirm that Ari made it to Boston. Given the communications situation, Hans felt he knew as much as he was going to.

Winter passed, and an unnaturally hot spring had thawed the land. At the end of May, Hans learned an Armenian labor battalion was building a road through the area and that the men working looked ill-treated. Hans met with senior military leaders and requested that he be allowed to examine the men and provide any needed medicine or treatment.

"Of course. After all, we are not inhuman," the military leader said.

When Hans arrived at the work site with two nurses, he wasn't prepared for what they saw. The shirtless men were clearly suffering from malnutrition and laboring in the hot sun. The bodies of the hundred or so men were riddled with open wounds and lesions. Hans felt the rage build within him as he stood next to the colonel in charge.

"These men are being mistreated," Hans spat out. "What you are doing here is torture and not work."

"Doctor, be mindful of your place. We've granted you permission to enter a site of a military operation, but don't test my tolerance. You're here to provide medicine, not to tell me how to run my battalion," the colonel said.

"You won't have a battalion much longer if these men aren't adequately fed. How do you expect them to work in the condition they're in?"

"As I said, how I run my battalion is no concern of yours, so I suggest you do what you came here to, or you can leave and let us get back to work."

"Then I ask, if not for the sake of these men, then for the sake of the work you need done, please give these men more food. It'll be best for everyone," said Hans, trying to appeal to the colonel's rationality.

"Very well, I'll see what I can do."

Hans left the colonel and made his way to the lines of men. The labor area stretched for nearly half a mile, and with the guards patrolling the perimeter, they let Hans tend to the men unescorted.

None of the workers took notice of Hans or the nurses, not even looking up as he approached. He could only get a man's attention if he stood in front of him and addressed him directly. He explained to each man who he was and why he was there. He would pull a worker aside, examine him, and then instruct one of the nurses what treatment, if any, to administer. He continued in this manner, examining one man after another until he came upon another shaggy-haired and bearded laborer. This man, although thin like the others, appeared sturdier—swinging his sledgehammer with one smooth motion after another. Hans noticed that the man didn't seem bothered by the insects flying around an open wound he had on his left shoulder. The man remained focused on his task and didn't look up even as Hans stood directly in front of him.

"Son, please stop working if you can. I'm a doctor, and I've been given permission to enter the site. I'd like to take a few minutes to examine you," Hans said.

The man didn't respond. Instead, he turned away and continued breaking rocks with his hammer.

"Please, son, this will only take a minute," said Hans as he gently took the man's arm.

The man ceased working and slowly raised his eyes to Hans. Hans couldn't help but notice the odd look in the laborer's eyes. The man's mouth fell agape, and his eyes widened. At first, Hans thought that perhaps the man was suffering from the early stages of mental illness. But then the man spoke.

"Hans?" the laborer said.

Startled, Hans studied him more closely. Even though he could sense some familiarity, Hans didn't recognize him.

"Hans, it's me, Vartan."

Hans looked into Vartan's eyes, those peculiar eyes that had always been so colorful and bright. The eyes looking back at him were gray and far duller than he recalled. He looked deeper, and there in some recess of the iris a light seemed to flicker, and the gray began to look bluer, until the eyes became familiar once more.

"My Lord, Vartan, is that really you?" Hans said.

"Yes, yes, it's me."

"Are you okay? I know they aren't treating you well, but are you suffering from anything that I can help you with?"

"Only with a longing heart. Have you heard word from Van? Do you know if my family is safe?"

"Yes, I have news," said Hans, with some hesitation. "I know your daughter has survived and has been taken to America for her safety."

"America?" said Vartan, confused by the news. "What about Anna? Is Anna with her?"

Hans paused as he looked into Vartan's desperate eyes, uncertain what to say.

"Anna didn't make it, Vartan. I'm sorry. She died on the deportation lines," he finally said.

Vartan's body stiffened, and his jaw muscles tightened, protruding like large marbles from his wasted face. Hans noticed Vartan's reaction and held back the urge to speak.

"How did Lena get to America, who is she there with?" asked Vartan, either pushing the pain of Anna's death from his mind or refusing to accept it.

"I had papers that gave her refugee status. Ari, the hunchback, has her and they made it to Greece, and from there they traveled to America. I know they made it there safely, and they were supposed to be taken to Boston, but that is all I know."

"Ari?" said Vartan, even more confused.

"Vartan, you must know that young man sacrificed much to save your daughter. Lena was left behind with Anna's body. Ari left his own mother to die so that he could go back and save her. He had me promise to find you and tell you that he'll keep her safe until you come for her. A promise I can now keep through no effort of mine," Hans said.

"Hans, I have to get out of here. I have to find my daughter. She is all I have. Is there anything you can do? I beg you, if you have any mercy, please help me," Vartan said.

"Vartan, they've been watching me since I left Van. The authorities know where my sympathies lie. They aren't naive to my desire to help your people, and they're suspicious of all my actions. I'm not sure what I can do."

"Is there anything you can think of that could help?"

"I may be able to convince them to have you transported to my clinic so that I can give you additional treatment, but I'm certain that they'll have you escorted by a guard, and once you reach the clinic, there is little we can do. The villages are overrun by soldiers. You would just be killed if you tried to escape once at the clinic."

"Could you do that?"

"I could try. I'm sure they'll refuse a request to see multiple prisoners, but I think I can convince them to have them send me just one. But what will you do once you reach the clinic? How will you get yourself out of the village without getting killed?"

"Don't worry about that. I'll either be free or dead long before I reach the village."

Months earlier, Ari and Lena boarded the passenger ship *The New Horizon* and embarked for America. At first, the large ship was frightening and confusing, but a day or two into their journey,

Ari learned where to go for food, what compartment they were to sleep in, and most importantly, how to best avoid the many odd-speaking people on the ship.

While eating with Lena in the dining hall one day, Ari was approached by a man. The stranger was a short man, attired in a three-piece tweed suit, a bowler hat, two-tone oxford shoes, and a pocket watch clipped to a gold chain. He had a head full of wavy black hair that was parted on the side.

"Please forgive me, but I overheard you speaking to the child," said the man in perfect Armenian. "Are you Armenian? My mother was Armenian, and I spoke it with her growing up. Do you mind if I join you?"

"You can have a seat," said Ari, cautious but grateful to finally hear something he understood.

"Terrible developments," said the man shaking his head. "I assume that you're one of the affected Armenians. I'm sure you're thankful to get away while you still can."

Ari nodded and instinctively hugged Lena, who was sitting on his lap, tighter.

"My name is Sinclair Spencer Scott," the man said. "Or if you like, Scott Sinclair Spencer, or even Spencer Scott Sinclair, or a multitude of other variations. That's the beauty of having three first and last names, you can be someone different every day. But my friends call me Spence. And you?"

"Ari."

"Ari, well it's a pleasure to meet you, Ari. And is the beautiful angel with you your sister? Or maybe your daughter?"

"No. I'm just bringing her to America, until her father comes."

"Very noble of you, very noble indeed. The climate for Armenians is a dangerous one these days. America is the perfect place for the two of you," said Spence as he took out a pipe, filled it with tobacco, and lighted it for an after-dinner smoke.

"Ari, you will have to forgive my candor. America is a great country, and it's ripe with opportunities. But I'm afraid some aren't as tolerant to those a little different. I think you might have difficulty finding work in America because of your condition. But, Ari, you don't have to be afraid or ashamed. I believe your appearance is your greatest asset. I have clients who are looking for people like you. You'll be able to make money and take care of this child while waiting for her father. I just want you to think about it. If you're interested, I'm here every evening at six. Come see me if you would like to talk. In the meantime, I'll leave you to your dinner. Good evening, Ari," said Spence as he stood and extended his hand.

Ari shook his hand.

46

No One Greater Love Than This

Vartan and Taniel sat at the far end of the cell, away from the other prisoners. Inexplicably, the meager nightly ration of food that was slipped under the cell door on individual rusted plates had been doubled, making the prisoners feel like they were enjoying a feast.

"This is Melik Sasuni's doing," said one of the prisoners on the other side of the cell. "He's making sure we're fed and strong. That must mean the day is nearing. We must be ready. Bless you, Melik Sasuni. We won't fail you. We'll be ready."

Vartan gave the prisoner a vacant look before turning to Taniel.

"Taniel, did you see Hans today? Were you able to talk to him?" Vartan asked.

"I was. It pained me to learn about Anna. I'm sorry," Taniel responded.

Vartan clenched his teeth to drive out the maddening truth and try to convince himself that it was all a mistake and that his wife was still alive.

"Did he tell you about our plan?" Vartan continued.

"He told me he would try to get you out of the camp and bring you to the village."

"Yes, I'll escape along the road, and then I'll come back to get you."

Taniel shot him a look of genuine anger.

"Don't be stupid, Vartan! If you escape, I'll kill you myself if you come back here."

"I'm not leaving you here. If I can overcome the guard on the road, then I might be able to free you."

"Don't let some stupid notion of loyalty cloud your judgment. There are only dead men in this cell. All of us. If one of us is fortunate enough to save his life, then you owe it to the rest not to waste it on dead men. You know where your path lies, it lies with your daughter, not here."

"Taniel, I can't . . ."

"You'll do the only thing you must. Now I'll not discuss this any further. The matter is settled," Taniel said.

But the look in Vartan's eyes told him it wasn't settled.

The next day, the men went back to labor. The sun bore down again, but the guards gave the prisoners more water, invigorating the workers. It seemed that the German doctor had been right—a little extra food and water and everyone was happier, and the work improved.

The doctor had expressed particular concern for one of the prisoners. He feared that the prisoner might have contracted a contagious disease, and if not treated, the disease could spread to the other inmates, and perhaps even to the guards and the soldiers.

The colonel approached the lead guard and pointed to Vartan. Though on the far side of the work site, Vartan was clearly visible as he labored to level ground in preparation for laying a railroad that would be used to move army supplies from the north to the south.

"Please have that man taken to the clinic in the village at the end of the day. He may be sick, and the doctor has asked that he treat him before he infects us all," the colonel said.

"Yes, Colonel," the guard said.

Taniel was working only a few feet away and overheard the conversation. It would be today, then, that Vartan's fate would be decided one way or another. As the day passed, Taniel continued working. When it was time to call an end to the work, one of the guards yelled to Vartan, who was bound ankle-to-ankle with another prisoner by a six-foot chain. The two men walked toward the guards.

As Vartan approached, he and Taniel locked eyes. Taniel lowered his shovel and made the sign of the cross toward Vartan. Then, Taniel gave out a yell and charged the guards, swinging his shovel at them.

Vartan froze in shock as he saw one of the guards draw his gun and shoot Taniel in the head.

"Taniel!" cried out Vartan. He lurched toward Taniel's body, but his fellow prisoner grabbed his waist.

"Calm yourself and don't be rash. There's nothing you can do," the prisoner said. "Melik Sasuni will avenge this for us. This will not go unpunished."

Vartan gave up struggling and looked over at Taniel's motionless body.

"You, come over here now," the guard called to Vartan.

"Be calm, my brother. Be calm. We must see what they want," said the prisoner as he nudged Vartan toward the guards.

"Taniel's given me no one to come back for," said Vartan numbly. "He either thought very highly or very little of me."

Vartan shuffled over to the guards, who unchained Vartan from the other prisoners and then rechained his hands in front of him.

With a rough push, the barrel-chested guard led Vartan away. One of the bigger men, the guard was known throughout the battalion as one of the more ruthless overseers. He climbed on his black horse and instructed Vartan to walk alongside him. When first arriving to the area, the battalion had passed the village, so Vartan knew it would take roughly an hour to walk there. With dusk approaching, the guard prodded Vartan to quicken his pace.

They reached the outer pastures of the village, and Vartan knew if he was going to make his move, it had to be now. The chains securing Vartan's wrists had nearly three feet of slack.

Vartan ran a finger up and down the chains that secured his wrists until he found a link with a jagged edge. He bent the chain on either side of the jagged link and tightened his fist around it. In one violent motion, he thrust the sharp, jagged chain into the horse, driving it as deeply as he could into its hindquarters. The steed bucked, and Vartan grabbed the back of the guard's jacket and yanked him to the ground as the horse surged forward.

When the guard crashed to the ground, Vartan seized the moment to jump on him and wrap his chain around the man's neck. The guard grabbed at the chain to relieve the pressure around his throat, but the chain was already too deep.

"You Armenian dog," the guard choked out as he clawed at Vartan's face and eyes.

Vartan turned his face to protect his eyes but kept the pressure around the guard's thick neck. The guard bucked his hips and was able to roll the smaller Vartan off him but still couldn't get the chain from around his neck. The guard started desperately raining blows down on Vartan's face. The first one smashed into his nose, breaking it and causing blood to gush from his nostrils. Still, Vartan kept applying the pressure on the chain. Another blow hit Vartan's forehead, another one his jaw, a third his eye socket. Vartan felt each blow, and each brought him closer to unconsciousness, but he was determined not to release the tension of the chain. Despite his resolution, Vartan felt his arms tiring, and he realized his muscles lacked the energy to keep the pressure going for much longer. In one final, desperate attempt, Vartan marshaled the last of his remaining strength to pull the chain even tighter.

Vartan heard the guard gasp and felt the weight of his limp body fall on top of him. Vartan rolled the guard off, crouched on top of him, and put a foot on the chain to increase the pressure until he was sure the guard was dead.

Vartan took the key that was clamped to the guard's belt and unchained his hands, then collected the guard's possessions—his clothes, his gun, his sword, his water, his food, and finally his horse. He climbed onto the horse and was about to ride away when he paused. He turned the horse toward the direction of the prison camp. He pinched his fingers and crossed himself.

He turned the horse northward and raced off.

47

The Man of Many Names

Ari watched Lena playing with a book on the floor of a lounge just down the hall from their ship cabin. The lounge area wasn't very spacious, just enough room for a traditional button-tufted white sofa against one wall and two matching chairs against the opposite wall. Next to the sofa, tucked snuggly into a corner, was a single-person desk that passengers would use to write letters or postcards. Traffic through the lounge was usually heavy, as it was situated between a hall of passenger cabins on one end and the ship's main promenade on the other. However, on this evening, Ari noted that barely anyone was around. He understood that they would reach America by noon the next day and most passengers were in their cabins preparing for the arrival. With Lena unable to sleep, Ari didn't have that luxury, so he took her to the lounge, hoping the child would exhaust herself enough to finally get some rest.

Thinking that flipping the pages of a picture book wouldn't tire Lena enough, Ari stood up and started making animal growls, lumbering toward Lena. "The bear is going to get the princess," rumbled Ari.

It was a game the two had played before, and the second Lena heard the growl, she got up and started running around the lounge, alternating between screams and laughter. "Roarrrrrrrrr," continued Ari as he pretended that he couldn't catch Lena.

Lena jumped on the couch and laughed as Ari approached her, trying to sink into the cushions to keep away. When Ari finally reached her, he started to tickle her, causing Lena to laugh even harder.

"Ah, it warms my heart to hear the laughter of a child," said a voice behind them.

Ari jolted around and saw Spence lighting his pipe and sitting on one of the chairs across from them.

"I'm sorry, sir. I should have known better than to make her laugh and disturb others," said Ari as he sat on the sofa and tried to hush Lena.

"No need to apologize; as you can see, there doesn't seem to be anyone else awake. I'm glad I saw you again, Ari. Did you consider my offer?" Spence asked.

"I can't go and work, sir. I'm going to Boston. That's where Lena's father will come looking for her. I don't think it'll take him long to come," Ari said.

"I see. And where are you going to stay in Boston? Do you have a place to live?" Spence asked.

Ari looked away and shrugged his shoulders.

"Ari, you're going to have to forgive my candor again, but you don't appear to be a rich man. America is very different from what you're used to. If you don't have money in America, then you can't eat. If you're really trying to do what's best for this child and be able to reunite her with her father, then you can't do that without money."

"But I have to go to Boston," Ari said.

"Well, that is the beautiful part of my offer. You'll be in Boston and in Philadelphia and Washington and in New York. You'll be part of a traveling show. Just little skits, you won't have to do much. They will give you small parts. And the company is like a family—they will open their arms to you. I'll be there as well. We'll take care of you and the child, and when we get to Boston, we'll find her father. I know many Armenians in the Boston area. It would be easy to reunite them. I promise you."

"It will be?" said a wide-eyed Ari.

"Yes, of course. The Armenians are a close community in Boston. Everyone knows each other. I have many friends there. I just have to put out the word. If her father is there and looking for her, it'll be a small matter to reunite them," Spence reassured.

Ari looked at Lena and realized she had fallen asleep on the couch. He noticed how fat and healthy her cheeks had become since their time on the ship. He turned back to Spence.

"What do I have to do?" Ari asked.

"Just meet me here tomorrow morning. And I'll take care of everything."

The next day, the ship docked and Ari, holding Lena by the hand, met Spence at the lounge. The three left the ship together. When Ari walked outside, he was frozen in awe at the towering buildings in front of him.

"That's New York, Ari," Spence said. "The greatest city in the world. Remember everything is possible in New York."

"What is that?" said Ari as he pointed at the enormous statue in the harbor.

"That's the Statue of Liberty. She was put there to greet people like you. People who need a chance. She's saying, welcome home, Ari."

With Spence's help, Ari and Lena were ushered through customs and immigration faster than normal. They then took a barge to Hoboken, New Jersey. Ari couldn't take his eyes off the skyline of the city that stood like man-made mountains. Once they reached Hoboken, Spence hailed a cab, and the trio were taken to an industrial area that was littered with empty shipping containers and marked by crisscrossing railroad tracks.

After being dropped off in front of a large warehouse, Spence led Ari and Lena to the back and knocked on a rusty metal door with a dirty sign that read Muldoon's Traveling Theater and Sideshow. A thin, frizzly-haired woman answered.

"Hi, Lucy, is Eddie in?" asked Spence.

"He's in his office," said the woman as she stepped aside and eyeballed Ari and Lena as they walked past her.

The three made their way to a glassed-in office at the back of the warehouse. The man in the office looked up from his desk and enthusiastically waved to Spence to come in.

"It's good to see you, Eddie. Based on our last conversation, I think I found someone who would work for what you need," said Spence, motioning to Ari.

Eddie walked around his desk to get a better look at Ari. He examined Ari from head to toe, even walking around him to see if the hump on his back was authentic.

"I don't know how you did it, Spence. But he's exactly what I've been looking for," said Eddie.

48

Muldoon's Traveling Show

Edward Muldoon started his traveling company when he was in his midtwenties. By the time he was thirty, he'd grown the company into a profitable business, employing more than forty showmen, crewmen, and actors until he had the misfortune of falling in love. The object of his affection was a fresh-faced, red-haired Jewish girl whom he plucked from behind the counter of her father's Pittsburgh convenience store. Smitten with her at first sight, Edward convinced her that despite her stained, raggedy apron and the line of impatient customers she was serving, she was really a glamorous actress in need of a break, and he was there to give it to her.

Having never acted, nor even considered it, the lazy seventeen-year-old was nonetheless impressed that Edward had so easily identified the vast potential she knew lay within her. She ran off with him that same day, leaving a note to her parents explaining that she planned on marrying a gentile and becoming a famous actress. She received a reply, via telegram, nearly a year later, when her father wrote, "You are no longer my daughter, and I forbid you to carry my name."

By that time, it didn't matter; she had taken the stage name of Trudy Sapphire and Edward had thrust her in his feature slot at the expense of his other performers. Edward's decision had predictable consequences, as Trudy's lackluster performances resulted in thinning crowds and greater performer attrition. Now the once thriving company had only five employees, carried a crushing debt, and was on the verge of insolvency.

Trudy was sitting in front of her vanity and brushing her hair in their Manhattan apartment when Edward walked behind her.

"Close your eyes, my beauty, I have something for you," said Edward as he looked at her in the mirror.

"Oh, what is it, Eddie? You know how much I love gifts," Trudy replied.

"I know, darling. And I think you'll love this. Now close your eyes and don't open them until I tell you to," said Edward as he watched her shut her eyes. He then placed a diamond necklace around her neck. "Okay, you can open them."

Trudy opened her eyes and gasped.

"Oh, Eddie, it's beautiful," said Trudy, looking at it in awe. "Is this the one that I wanted from Tiffany?"

"Yes, the very one."

"I was hoping that I would get it for my birthday or some other celebration. But I'm so happy you got it for me now. I've wanted this for so long. I was beginning to think I would never get it. I love you, Eddie," said Trudy as she stood up and threw her arms around Edward's neck, kissing both of his cheeks.

"Nonsense, whatever my darling wants, I'll make sure she has it. This apartment, diamonds, jewels. Whatever it is, I just want you to be happy. But there is another reason I bought it for you today. It's to celebrate," Edward said.

"To celebrate? What are we celebrating?"

"We are celebrating you!"

"Me? Well, what did I do, Eddie?"

"It's not what you did, it's what you're going to do. You're going to be a star. Your career is going to take off now."

"You always say that, Eddie," she said with an annoyed pout. "We have been together for seven years, and you told me I would be on Broadway by now or acting in one of those moving picture shows. I'm a better actress then any of those harlots, but I seem to be stuck in the mud."

"I know, I know. But this time is different, my darling."

"How is it different this time, Eddie? What's different?"

"Darling, I've been in show business my whole life. My father was a great composer and had gone on to do great things. The Muldoon name is like currency in London. And my mother was hailed as a treasure in Buenos Aires, with people lining up for blocks to listen to her sing. I'm telling you this because there is a formula to success. You need talent, that's true, but more importantly you need timing and the right showcase. Well, we've always known you had the talent, and the timing is right, so that leaves us with the showcase. And now we finally have that!" Edward said.

"What showcase, Eddie?"

"Darling, I have been toiling on a play. It's my best work so far. It's an adaptation of Victor Hugo's *Hunchback of Notre Dame*, but I have set it here in New York. It's now finished. Of course, you will play the part of Esmerelda—the stunning, sensuous gypsy girl.

Oh, the crowd will love you. They won't be able to take their eyes off you. I just needed one final piece. The one element that will give it the authenticity that will separate it from any other version. We have a real hunchback!" said Edward, outlining a curve with his hand for emphasis.

"A hunchback? Wherever did you find a hunchback, Eddie?"

"Spence found him. How he did it, I don't know. He's a master of those things. But you should see the hunchback, darling. He's hideous! It'll make your beauty shine all the more by contrast. We couldn't have picked a better hunchback. Your time is now. I promise you!"

"I hope so, Eddie. I'm tired of working these small shows when other actresses are living in the spotlight. I have more talent in my little finger than most of them have in their entire bodies, and I have to read about them in the newspapers. It's almost too much to take, Eddie."

"I know, I know, darling, but that is all about to change. I promise you, there is no way this play will not propel you to the top. Broadway should be preparing the marquees as we speak."

"I hope so, Eddie. I'm ready," she said.

Trudy threw her arms around Edward again and hugged him. He buried his face in her hair and breathed in her scent, the intoxicating aroma floating through his nose and into his brain like some dizzying opiate. He wanted to stay lost in the embrace, but he gathered enough strength to break it slightly, so he could look at her.

"I hope you are ready for something else as well, darling," said Edward as he reached into his pocket and brought out a small jewelry box and opened it to display a diamond ring.

"Oh, Eddie, we already talked about this," said Trudy as she turned her back to him. "I told you that I don't want to marry until I have started my career properly. Right now, that is the important thing."

"I know, darling, but is it so bad to have someone love you so much that he can't wait to make you his bride? And this is my mother's ring. It's blessed with success. It'll give you luck," said Eddie, turning her toward him by her hips so he could look at her again.

"We had a deal and you agreed to it. No weddings until after I've made it, Eddie. A married actress isn't as glamorous. It'll hurt my chances."

"I just don't want to lose you, darling. That is all. It would kill me if I lost you," said Eddie, his shoulders slumped, his eyes cast to the floor.

Trudy lifted his chin with her finger so she could look into his eyes.

"Then make me a star, Eddie," she said. "That's all you have to do. Make me a star."

49

A New Tenement

After meeting with Edward, Spence led Ari, who was carrying Lena in his arms, back outside to a fenced-in, trash-filled lot in the rear of the warehouse. The lot contained stripped cars, piles of tires, tin signs of all sizes, and ceramic theater props, among various other discarded items.

They meandered through the junkyard until they reached a dirty trailer. Spence struggled with the door before violently pulling it open.

"Come on in, Ari. This is where you'll stay," said Spence as he extended his arm to usher Ari up the stairs.

Ari walked up the stairs and into a cramped trailer filled with piles of papers, old costumes, and an assortment of boxes.

"Don't mind the mess, Ari. We'll have it cleaned up for you. But for now, there is plenty of room for you and Lena. There's a bed in the back, and we'll bring whatever else you need to you," Spence said.

Just then a woman appeared in the doorway. It was the same frizzle-haired woman that let them into the warehouse.

"Eddie said you needed me, Spence," she said.

"Yes, yes. This is Ari. He'll be acting in Eddie's new show. He and this child will be staying here. He doesn't speak English, so just ensure when you and the rest of the crew are eating to bring him supper as well," Spence said.

"Certainly. Whenever it is that we eat, of course," the woman smirked.

Turning back to Ari, Spence addressed him in Armenian.

"Ari, this is Lucy Dithers. She will get you whatever it is you need when I'm not around. She stays just over there," said Spence, pointing to another trailer across the junkyard.

"Where will you be?" Ari asked.

"I have an apartment in the city. I do come here as often as I can, but don't worry, Lucy will take care of you. Right now, I want you to get some rest. Edward wants to work you into the act as soon as possible, and we have a show next week. I think you'll be great, Ari. I really do," Spence said.

"Could we get something to eat? Lena hasn't eaten all day, and I know she's hungry," Ari asked.

"Of course," said Spence before turning to Lucy. "Can you get Ari and the child something to eat right now?"

"Sure, I think we have something left over," said Lucy, who walked to her trailer.

"So, what do you think, Ari?"

"It's fine. I just want to make sure we can make it to Boston, and you can talk to the Armenians there," Ari said.

"In due time, in due time. Right now, let's get you settled in and working. Everything else will take care of itself," Spence replied.

"Take a look around. You have a nook with a table right here. A sofa on this side and of course the bed in the back. Water you'll have to get from the hose out in the main yard. And there is an outhouse in the back as well. If you need a bath, there is a tub in the warehouse. You'll have to coordinate that with Lucy, so they have enough hot water."

Just then Lucy reappeared with a bowl of potato stew and a piece of bread.

"Dinner is served," she said.

Spence took the bowl and bread from her, pushed a few newspapers off the table, and placed the food on it.

"Ari, why don't you eat and get some rest. Tomorrow is when work begins, and we can talk then. You're going to be marvelous!" said Spence as he walked to the stairs.

Spence closed the door behind him. Ari, with Lena on his lap, sat down at the table, scooped up a spoonful of stew and swallowed it as Lena eagerly awaited her turn. The stew was cold. The next spoonful he gave to Lena, who swallowed it hungrily.

It was their first meal on American soil. The first in their new home. The meal was fine, he thought, he just wished it weren't so cold.

50

The Crimson-Haired Esmerelda

"What in God's name is that?" exclaimed Trudy, sitting in her makeup chair and pointing at a long, black wig that Lucy was holding.

"It's your wig for the show," replied Lucy.

"There's no way I'm going to wear that hideous thing. I'll just have you do my hair as usual," Trudy responded.

"But Esmerelda has dark hair. No one ever heard of a red-haired gypsy girl."

"I'm the star of this show, and you'll do my hair like you usually do," snapped Trudy. "My audience adores my hair. I'm not going to hide it under that repulsive thing. Now get to work, we only have a couple hours before we go on."

"Yes, ma'am," said Lucy, sardonically.

After brushing and styling Trudy's hair, and then doing her makeup, Lucy walked out to the back of the makeshift stage, where she searched out the two stagehands. She found them ready-ing the curtain. Both were large men. The taller man was just over six feet, with an athletic build. His muscles peaked even under his clothes, and his rolled-up sleeves displayed thick forearms. He had tattoos running on the inside of each forearm, with the Latin words *Cadere Angelum* (Fallen Angel) etched on his left forearm and *Vindicta Mea Est* (Vengeance is Mine) on his right.

His companion was a couple inches shorter, but wider and heavier. He was a hairy man, from his moppy black mane and unkempt beard, to the coarse chest hair that was blooming out of his half-buttoned flannel shirt.

"Is everything ready, Sal? We don't have much time left," said Lucy to the taller of the two stagehands.

"Yep, everything should be a go. Me and Butch just waitin' for the signal so we can draw the curtains," said Sal as he motioned over to his scruffy cohort. "Is her highness ready?"

"As ready as she'll ever be. I'll tell you what I wouldn't give to have ten minutes alone with that pompous succubus. I'd rearrange that pretty face she thinks she has," spat out Lucy.

"Easy, that's the boss's girl. If he says we have to take care of her, then that's what we got to do," Sal said.

"Is that so? And what has Eddie ever done for you or Butch?" Lucy asked.

"He's kept us out of the penitentiary. That's what he's done. If it weren't for him and Spence, me and Butch would still be rottin' away in there. And more importantly, he's kept us out, which ain't no small feat considering we ain't completely weened ourselves off the stuff that got us in there in the first place," Sal said.

"Well, he ain't done much for me. Least not like he has for that tomato-headed tramp," Lucy said.

The comment got a snicker out of Butch, exposing a picket-fence smile.

"What are you laughing at, you toothless orangutan?" she lashed out at Butch.

"You callin' anyone a tramp. Seeing as the only reason Eddie has you around is so's you can spread them legs for a couple nickels. As Spence says, your bottom up helps the bottom line." Butch laughed.

"Least my price is negotiated upfront. Men know what it'll cost 'em. No hidden fees like that pasty-face wench has. Eddie has no clue what she'll ring him up for next, just that he's got to keep paying," Lucy said.

"So, you're an honest tramp? There is something to that. No doubt," interjected Sal just before he noticed Eddie signaling over to him. "There's our cue. Let's draw the curtains, Butch."

The two men pulled the ropes, and the stage opened to a crowd of roughly twenty people, mixed between adults and children. The stage was set up on the end of a county fairground, with constant sounds of bells, whistles, visitor chatter, and even pigs oinking in the background.

Trudy, dressed in a classical gypsy outfit with her red tresses flowing over her shoulders, sauntered onto the stage and began the first of many soliloquys. These soliloquys, all accompanied by dramatic arm movements and pained expressions, contained all the exposition, inner dialogue, and scene setting needed to condense the classic novel into a half-hour show. This made Edward's magnum opus equal parts *Hunchback of Notre Dame* and *Hamlet*, while being performed within the constraints of a vignette.

The highlight of the show was when Sal and Butch, both dressed as French peasants, tied Ari to a pole on the stage. The two men then walked through the crowd with buckets of rotten fruit, handing them to the spectators. By way of demonstration, Sal heaved an apple at Ari, hitting him in the head. A shocked Ari started yelling unintelligibly, pulling at his restraints, while the crowd laughed. With Sal's and Butch's encouragement, the rest of the crowd started throwing fruit at Ari, with the children in the audience being the most zealous participants. The crowd was in hysterics the more Ari struggled to free himself and avoid the onslaught.

Lena was sitting in between Spence and Edward in the audience and upon seeing Ari's assault, started crying and jumped off her chair and ran toward the stage.

"Ah-we, Ah-we," the child screamed.

"Get the kid, Spence, she's going to ruin the show," Edward barked.

Spence rushed after Lena, grabbing her just before she got to the stairs of the stage. She was still crying and calling out for Ari, so Spence put his hand over her mouth and carried her behind the stage and out of sight.

Trudy, observing offstage, noticed the excitement of the crowd and felt the time was right to enter for her climactic scene. She stepped on stage with a commanding posture and thrust her palm out toward the crowd.

"Stop. This is a man and not some animal. Leave him be," commanded Trudy.

Her directive was met by a tomato to her forehead, thrown by a freckled-face boy in the front row. She wiped the splatter from her head, doing her best not to lose her composure.

"Cease, I say," she yelled louder while motioning to Sal and Butch to collect any unlaunched fruit from the hands of the audience.

Once certain she was safe from the risk of flying produce, she turned to Ari, who was covered with the rotten fruit. She knelt in front of him.

"My good man. You need not have any fear, I'm here to free you. No harm will come to you while you're under my protection," said Trudy before turning back to the crowd and giving them a melancholy look.

The curtains fell and the audience applauded. Trudy took a deep breath and looked up to see Edward, who came in from the side of the stage, rushing toward her.

"That was marvelous, darling! You were spectacular! Listen to the crowd," said Edward as the spattering claps faded.

"Do you think so, Eddie? I think it was one of my best performances," Trudy said. "Did you see how much the crowd loved me?"

"They were captivated by you. This is your showcase, darling. There is nowhere to go from here but Broadway!"

The two continued their enthusiastic conversation, rife with unabashed compliments, as they walked off the stage to Trudy's dressing room.

They took no notice of Ari, who had slumped down the pole, still tied up and sitting in the juices of the fruit he was painted with.

Ari was no longer struggling. He had struggled for too long.

51

The Sputtering Syndicate

Two months after the debut of Trudy's showcase act, Edward's traveling show was no closer to being in the black, and Trudy was no nearer to her acting dream than before.

Edward called an emergency meeting with his crew at the warehouse office. He, Spence, Sal, and Butch sat around the desk. Edward pored over a ledger, massaging his temple with an anxious look on his face.

"We owe, we owe, we owe! That's all I see here! The show hasn't made any money for a year now, but all of you haven't helped either. Spence, you're supposed to be managing all the business outside of the show, but you don't have enough coming in. Why has the numbers racket dried up?" Edward asked.

"There's a lot more competition now. The Jews are killing us. They're running numbers all over the city. They have number runners at every synagogue, bar mitzvah, and corned beef joint in New York City. They're putting the rest of us out of business," Spence said.

"Well, if you don't have the numbers, what else do you have?" Edward asked.

"I'm working on a few things. I think I'll have some things coming in. Just takes a little time," Spence said.

"Well, I don't have any goddamn time!" Edward snapped. "What about you two buffoons?"

"It's been light. I lifted a few watches and a little bit of cash. Butch stole a case of liquor," responded Sal. "We turned it all over to Spence, but it wasn't much. Folks have gotten better at keeping an eye on their things when they're out and about. It's not as easy as it used to be. The opportunities just ain't there."

"Or maybe you two have gotten lazy at your trade. I don't keep you around for your brains. If you ain't making any money, I might as well call your parole officer and have you two sent back to prison," Edward said. "The only one making any money in this outfit is Lucy."

"Well, sir, there's always money in pussy. And she always has it on her, so there's not much chance of her missing an opportunity," Sal said.

"I don't think you're funny, Sal," Edward shot. "Why don't you and the mongoloid go and figure out how to make some real money. I want to talk to Spence alone."

Edward watched as the two men got up and left the office. He pulled a bottle of brandy from his drawer and poured a glass for him and Spence.

"It's too early for me to drink," said Spence as Edward went to hand him the glass.

"Oh, drink it for Pete's sake," Edward said. "I have something to tell you, and if there was ever a time for drinking, it's now."

"Fine, then. What's it that you need to tell me?" said Spence, taking the drink.

Edward answered by downing the glass of brandy in one gulp and pouring another with shaking hands.

"I think this could be it, Spence," he said.

"What could be it?"

"The end."

"The end of what?"

"The end of this," said Edward, throwing his hands up and looking around the room. "The end of this company. The end of the life I've been trying to build. The end of me. I think I'm going to lose Trudy. I've failed her. I know she doesn't love me. I'm no fool. Now that the money is gone, there's no reason for her to stay."

"Eddie, you're being too dramatic. We've had bumps in the road before, and we always come out ahead. And giving up isn't like you. We'll turn this around," Spence assured.

"No, it's different this time, Spence. I'm going to lose the apartment. I owe too much, there is no way I can keep it. If I lose the apartment, then I will lose Trudy. I won't be able to hide it from her anymore. She'll see me for who I am," said Edward, pacing the office and gulping down the second glass of brandy.

"How much do you owe?"

"Almost a thousand dollars."

"Jesus, Eddie!" exclaimed Spence. "I told you not to get on the hook for an apartment that expensive."

"I know, I know, but I did. And I have to pay the whole thing or they're throwing us out. There's no way I can come up with that money in a month. Things are already strained with Trudy; the apartment will be the last straw. Once I lose that, she's gone. And I might be as well. I don't know what to do, Spence."

Spence took a generous swig of the brandy and started rubbing his forehead in thought. He looked over at Edward, who was still pacing.

"There might be a way," Spence said.

"What way?"

"Our next show is in Bethlehem, Pennsylvania. I have been corresponding with a couple from Richmond. The husband comes from money. I've been talking to them about a problem they're having and maybe helping them with it."

"What problem?"

"The wife can't have children," Spence said. "And it's messed her head up something terribly. She's started acting odd, and no one will let her adopt because they don't think she's fit to be a mother. The husband loves his wife, and it's killing him to see her that miserable. He's afraid she won't be able to shake it. He reached out to me because he heard I can fix things. He thinks that her having a child might be the only thing that could make a difference."

"And how are you going to help them with that?" asked Edward as he sat back down.

"The hunchback I brought isn't alone, he has that child. It's not even his kid. And he can't take care of her even if it was. I can send a telegram to the couple I'm talking about. They can meet us in Bethlehem, and we can sell the kid to them. It's perfect, there aren't any real records of the child. So, no chance of it ever coming back to us. I just have to get the forged adoption papers drawn up, which shouldn't take me long."

"How much are they willing to pay?"

"We were talking eight hundred dollars, but I think I can get a thousand."

"Can you really get a grand for the kid?" said Edward, his eyes widening.

"Absolutely. That's how desperate this guy is."

"What about the hunchback?"

"What about him?" Spence said. "The way I see it is that we're done with him. The act we brought him in for isn't making any money. I say we sell the kid and bury the hunchback in Bethlehem. Fuck him! What do you think?"

Edward pursed his lips and scratched his head. He grabbed the bottle of brandy and topped off Spence's glass and poured another one for himself. He lifted his glass to Spence.

"I think you're a goddamn genius, Spence," he said.

52

The Gift of the Fallen Magi

Ari sat in the last row of the train car, with Lena resting her head on his lap as she slept. He ran his hand over her matted hair, noticing how thin she had become and how dirty her dress was.

He looked to the front of the car and saw Trudy, immaculately dressed and fanning herself as Lucy brought her tea. Spence was sitting in the row behind her, reading a newspaper. The remaining members of the company—Edward, Sal, and Butch—had gone ahead to Pennsylvania to set up for the show.

Ari lifted Lena's head off his lap and laid her gently across the chair. In the three months he'd been in America and part of Muldoon's Traveling Show, Ari had few opportunities to speak with Spence. He was rarely at the warehouse, and when Ari did run into him at the show, Spence would always be too busy to engage in anything more than a courtesy greeting. When Ari tried to voice a concern, Spence would assure him that he would look into it and provide a suitable solution. Since no one else in the company spoke Armenian and since he still had no understanding of English, except for *please* and *thank you*, he was left to his own devices.

"Excuse me, Spence, can I talk to you?" said Ari as he walked over.

Spence peered over his newspaper, then folded it up and set it down on the chair next to him.

"Certainly, Ari. Have a seat and let me know what's on your mind," said Spence as he extended his hand to offer the seat across from him.

"Well, we've been in America for a while now, and I really want to go to Boston. I think by this time, Lena's father has come, and I'm sure he's looking for her. I want to get her to him a soon as I can," Ari said.

"Of course, I understand. Well, the good news is that Boston is our next stop. It'll be the last stop of our tour. What an ideal place to end. Once the show is over, it won't take us long to unite her with her father. I've already reached out to my contacts in Boston, and they are working on finding her father. And you'll be done acting in the show, so you can do whatever you choose," Spence said.

"No more having things thrown at me?"

"Yes, no more of that. As you know, acting is not always easy, and I think you handled your role exceptionally. Not everyone could have done what you did. You should be proud."

"I'm not worried about me. I'm worried about Lena. I don't think she's well. She has been coughing a lot and doesn't have an appetite. She is thinner than I have ever seen her. That is why I want to get her to Boston as soon as we can," Ari explained.

"She'll be fine, children are resilient. Once the show is over, everything will be better for her and you."

"I just want her to be well. I don't care what happens to me. You might think I'm upset that people throw fruit at me. That somehow it hurts me, but it doesn't," said Ari, looking down at his shuffling feet. "I've never had anything, including dignity. So, what's there to hurt? I've seen worse. I've felt worse. I know I'm not something someone could love. I left the only person who loved me on an empty road to die alone. That's what I've done. That's who I really am. Even uglier than I appear. But Lena is different. She's special and she comes from a beautiful place. Don't think otherwise just because she's with me."

"Ari, I would never think that. We think the world of Lena. Both of your stories will end well," Spence said.

"She's barely had a bath since we arrived. And she has no clean clothes to wear. I know you said I have money from the work. Can I use it to buy her some clothes?"

"Well, I have a surprise for you, then," said Spence as he reached under his seat and pulled out a suitcase. He opened it and pulled out a yellow dress with a flowery white collar. "I bought this dress for Lena. We want her to look like a young lady. We'll have Lucy give her a bath at the hotel Edward and Trudy are staying at. She'll look like a new girl."

"It's beautiful. Thank you, Spence."

"It's my pleasure. Now just relax and enjoy the train ride. We should be there shortly."

"Thank you again, Spence. It'll be good to see her in something clean and nice," said Ari as he shook Spence's hand and then began making his way back to Lena.

When he reached his seat, Lena was still sleeping. He sat down next to her and gently picked her head up and rested it back on his lap. He absently smoothed her hair with his hand again as he looked out of the window and saw a sign coming into view. He knew it was a welcome sign like he had seen when entering the other cities and towns they had traveled to. But unlike the others, this sign had a word he recognized. He couldn't pull his eyes off the word as it grew larger with every churn of the train's wheels. And just as the welcome sign passed his window, he mouthed the town's familiar name.

"Bethlehem."

53

Within the Serpent's Lair

The weeklong show was over, and Edward sent Trudy and Lucy back home on the train. He told Trudy that the rest of the crew had to stay back to take care of some business. He then packed the rest of the crew in their Model T pickup truck and headed out of town.

Spence was driving, Edward was in the cabin with him, and Lena was in between the two. She wore her new yellow dress, which was two sizes too big. No one had bothered to iron the dress's considerable wrinkles out, leaving her looking disheveled, even with the colorful ribbons in her hair.

Ari, Sal, and Butch loaded themselves onto the flatbed for the ride. During the trip, Lena would stand on the seat, turning around to slap the rear window until Ari looked at her. He would make a face at her, and she would smile over her persistent coughs. If he ever dared look away, she would pound on the glass until she got Ari's attention again. Ari thought her eyes looked tired, and he had a sudden urge to hold her. He slid over to the window. Lena's tiny hand was pressed on the glass, and he placed his hand against hers.

When they reached the outskirts, Spence pulled the pickup over to the side of the road. It was a secluded country road, with the trees of a thick forest rising on all sides, and the road bending out of view from the city.

The three men in the back jumped down off the flatbed, while Spence and Edward climbed out of the cabin. Lena followed and weakly walked toward Ari.

"Up, Ah-we, up," said Lena, asking Ari to lift her.

"I wasn't far, Lena," said Ari, as he caressed her head. "I'll never be far from you."

Spence leaned his back on the front of the car, filled his pipe, and lighted it. He took a deep puff as he looked at the empty road to the south. Edward motioned Sal and Butch over.

"We're going to wait here for the couple to come," said Edward to the two. "As you know, there was a neighborhood a mile back. While we're waiting, I need you two to go back there and see if there are any homes you might be able to lift something from. I don't trust this deal completely, and the more money we can make on this trip the better."

"Sure, Eddie. Me and Butch already cased the houses yesterday. There are a couple of promising ones. We should be able to make a score and be back in no time," Sal responded.

"You're going to take the hunchback with you," Edward said.

"Why, Eddie? He don't understand a word we're saying. All he's going to do is slow us down. Plus, he sticks out like a sore thumb," Sal protested.

"Oh, and you think you two neanderthals pass as unassuming citizens? Why do you think we picked this time of day? By the time you get there, it should start getting dark. People should be clear of the streets and less chance of anyone seeing you."

"But we don't need the hunchback. Me and Butch can handle it. Let him stay here," Sal said.

"No, I need him out of here. Him staying will complicate the deal. I can't risk this deal going south. Plus, we're done with him, I don't want him coming back."

"Then what do you want us to do with him?" Sal asked.

"You know what to do with him. Bring whatever loot you get and make sure he doesn't come back here. Got it?"

"Got it, Eddie. We definitely got it," said Sal with a sly smile.

"Good. I have to go talk to Spence," said Eddie as he made his way to his fixer.

Edward approached Spence, who was still puffing on his pipe.

"It's all set. Go talk to the hunchback and tell him to go with Sal and Butch. Make up some story. You're good at that," Edward said.

"Not a problem at all. I better do it quickly before our customers get here," Spence said.

Spence took a final puff of his pipe, emptied it, wiped it clean, and put it away in the inside pocket of his suitcoat. He walked over to Ari, who was sitting with Lena on the grass just off the road.

"Ari, we have to wait here for the promotors to come with our payment. It's going to be enough money for our Boston trip and enough left over to get you on your feet when we get there," Spence explained. "While we're waiting, Sal and Butch are going to go help a widow move a few things into her house. They're too big and heavy for her to move, and there is no one to help her. She doesn't live too far from here. We need you to go with them. They could use the help."

"But what about Lena? She doesn't seem well," said Ari as a lethargic Lena began coughing.

"Edward and I will watch her. You shouldn't be long. If the three of you go, you'll be done in half an hour's time."

Ari stood up and lifted Lena to her feet. He knelt in front of her and took her face in his hands.

"Lena, my child, I'm going to leave for a little bit. Don't worry, Spence will watch you while I'm gone. I promise I'll be right back," said Ari as he kissed her forehead.

Lena lunged toward Ari to hug him, but he held her off. Spence grabbed her arm and tried to pull her toward him, but Lena resisted.

"Go with Spence, Lena," encouraged Ari as he pulled away from her.

"Ah-we, come, Ah-we, come," babbled Lena as she reached out to him again.

This time, Spence scooped her up in his arms and began to walk back to the truck with her. She looked back, still calling Ari's name and extending her arms to him. Ari forced himself to turn and walk to Sal and Butch.

"Let's go, freak. I hope you don't mess anything up," said Sal, even though he knew Ari didn't understand him.

The three began making their way back to town. After walking on the main road for a couple of minutes, they picked up a side road that cut through the forest. They stayed on the dirt road until the trees thinned and they reached a street full of houses. It was the first of many streets lined with colonial homes. They stayed at the edge of the forest and listened. The only thing they could hear were the sounds of children playing stick ball.

"Hey, there's the house," said Butch, pointing to a red-brick, two-story home. "Looks like the curtains are still drawn. The automobile still ain't there. It looked like they were leaving for a trip yesterday. I say we walk around and hit it if all's clear."

"Okay, you stay with the freak. I'll check it out and let you know if that's the one. Try to stay out of sight until I get back," Sal said.

Sal started walking toward the house, while Butch motioned for Ari to stay back. Butch led Ari into the forest and the two waited. A few minutes later, Sal came back.

"It's all clear. No one's home. Plus, I know how to get in. They have a cellar window that ain't locked. It's not too big, but I think the freak is small enough to climb through and get us in," Sal explained.

"So, the freak might be helpful after all," Butch said.

Butch motioned to Ari to follow them, and the three made their way to the red-brick colonial. Sal led them to a twenty-inch-high, two-foot-wide window at the rear of the house. Sal lifted the unlocked window upward. Butch pointed to Ari to climb through, while making an unlocking motion and pointing to the side door. By the sign language, it was clear to Ari what was being asked of him, and he hesitated.

"Get in there, freak. We ain't got all day," said an impatient Butch as he pushed Ari toward the window.

Ari stumbled forward. Facing away from the house, he reluctantly flattened himself on the ground in front of the window and began sliding his feet through. He got his legs through, then continued to push his way until he got to his hump and became wedged and couldn't go farther without resistance. He felt the frame of the window scraping his back as he tried to inch his way farther inside the cellar. Ari's progress was too slow for Sal, who put his foot on Ari's shoulder and started pushing him through the uncooperating opening.

"Get in there," said Sal as he gave a final shove with his foot and Ari fell to the floor of the cellar.

Butch peered into the window at Ari and again made the unlocking motion with his hand and pointed in the direction of the side door. Ari picked himself up from the musty cellar floor and felt his way around until his eyes got acclimated to the dark. He stumbled across a stairway and made his way up. The door at the top of the stairway opened into a kitchen, and the house's side door was just off to the left. Ari unlocked the door, and Sal and Butch rushed past him.

Ari stood in silence as the other two began ransacking the home. He looked around the home and noticed toys, schoolbooks, and portraits of a young family. Ari stayed rooted in the kitchen as his two companions piled as many objects as possible into a pair of oversized bags.

"Did you find any cash?" Sal asked.

"No, but I got some good jewelry and some china," Butch replied. "We better get outta here."

"Yeah, just one last thing to do before we leave," said Sal as he looked over at Ari. "Eddie said to take care of the freak."

"Well then hurry up and get it done so we can get out of here."

"Oh, I'm going to enjoy this," said Sal as he walked over to Ari and looked down at him. "It's a good day isn't it, freak? It's going to be for me, but maybe not for you."

Ari stared blankly up at Sal. The muscular stagehand with a gleam in his eyes took hold of Ari's neck and began to squeeze. He lifted Ari off the ground and held him as Ari clawed at his hands and flailed his legs. Sal then slammed him against the kitchen wall and put just enough pressure on Ari's throat to slowly feel the strength ooze out of him.

"Come on, get it over with, Sal. Snap his neck so we can get outta here," Butch urged.

"Let me enjoy this a little, Butch. It's been a while. I always liked watching their eyes when they're dying. That's the deal. No point in it if you can't watch the soul leaving," said Sal, intoxicated by the moment.

Ari tried to claw at Sal's eyes, but his arms were too short to reach his assailant's face. Sal increased the pressure on Ari's throat, and Ari's eyes began to roll to the back of his head.

"Well, I'm lugging this stuff out. I'll meet you up the road," said Butch as he headed for the side door.

As Butch reached the doorway, an earsplitting explosion tore through the air, sending him hurtling back into the house like a ragdoll. He hit the floor hard, blood pouring out of his chest.

"What the hell?!" shouted Sal, his eyes wide as he stared at his fallen partner. Panic surged through him, but it quickly turned to fury when he spotted the gleaming barrel of a shotgun poking through the side door.

Without a second thought, Sal dropped Ari and lunged toward the doorway—just as an elderly man, weathered but resolute, stepped inside. Sal's hands clamped down on the scalding hot barrel, ignoring the pain as he wrenched the weapon free. The shotgun clattered to the ground as the two men grappled in a savage struggle.

"The police are on their way, you filthy crooks!" the old man spat, his voice shaking with a mix of fear and determination. "I saw you from next door! I won't let you get away with this in our town!"

But Sal wasn't listening. His eyes burned with murderous intent. "You should've stayed out of this, old man," he snarled, pinning him to the floor. "Now you're gonna pay the price."

As the old man struggled to get Sal off him, Ari staggered to his feet, clutching his throat. He watched in horror as Sal's hand shot out, grabbing a kitchen knife from the counter. The blade flashed in the dim light as Sal plunged it into the old man's chest again and again, the sound of flesh tearing filling the room.

Ari's instincts kicked in, and he bolted for the side door, his heart pounding in his ears. He barely evaded Sal's grasp as he made it out into the night air.

"Get back here, you freak!" Sal roared, abandoning the dying man to give chase.

Ari's legs pumped furiously, but terror clouded his vision, and he didn't see the rake until it was too late. He stumbled across it, crashing to the ground. Sal was nearly upon him, when another deafening blast shattered the night. Sal crumpled to the ground mid-stride, lifeless.

Ari spun around to see the old man standing in the doorway, his body riddled with knife wounds, blood staining his clothes. He held the shotgun with trembling hands, barely able to keep it steady. With a final burst of defiance, he leveled the gun at Ari.

But the old man's strength failed him. He collapsed before he could pull the trigger, the shotgun slipping from his fingers and landing with a dull thud on the ground. Silence fell over the scene as Ari stared, breathless, at the old man.

Ari got up and ran as fast as he could to the forest. Once he was safely within the tree line, he stopped to catch his breath and for the first time heard the commotion of an awakened and confused town.

Ari now knew that his time in America had been spent in a lair of thieves. A base and ignoble band. But the two men he saw gunned down were nothing more than the body of the snake. The head of the serpent was still back with the pickup truck.

And Lena was within reach of its venomous fangs.

54

The Child Wallace

"Where are they?" said Edward as he paced in front of the pickup truck. "We don't have much time. I don't trust those two behemoths to get the job done fast. For all we know, they might have the whole town chasing 'em out. So, I want to get out of here as fast as we can."

"They'll be here. By the sounds of the telegram, the husband was eager to get the deal done," said Spence as he set a droopy-eyed Lena inside the cabin of the truck.

"With the way my luck's going, he'll probably have a change of heart and we'll be stuck with the kid."

Just then, the two heard the unmistakable sound of a shotgun blast coming from town. Both men turned their suddenly ashen faces toward the sound. They remained frozen as they began to hear the faint sounds of the distant town coming to life.

"Jesus, Spence. I don't like this. I don't think we can wait any longer. We have to get out of here."

"Wait, I think that's them coming right now," said Spence, pointing to a black sedan coming into view on the undulating road.

Both men stood in front of the pickup truck, which was still parked on the side of the road, and watched as the sedan came closer and pulled to a stop in front of them. The driver of the sedan was a light-haired man, who appeared to be in his late twenties, and sitting next to him was a blonde woman, about the same age, who was absently staring forward.

The man got out of the car. He was wearing a brown pleated tweed jacket, black slacks, and brown loafers.

"Mr. Wallace, I presume?" asked Spence, trying to put aside his anxiety.

"Yes, and you must be Mr. Sinclair," replied the man, as he extended his hand.

"Indeed, I am," said Spence as he shook his hand. "This is my colleague, Edward Muldoon. Eddie, this is Cyrus Wallace, the young man I was telling you about."

"Nice to meet you, Mr. Muldoon," said a fidgety Cyrus as he shook hands with Edward. "My wife, Cassidy, is in the sedan. She doesn't fair well outside of the home, so if you gentlemen won't mind, I would like to get on with our business."

"Of course, of course," replied Spence. "The child is resting in the truck. We'll bring her out in a minute. The price is what we negotiated. Nothing has changed there."

"Yes, the price is fine. I just want to make certain that my wife takes to the child. As I said, if she doesn't want the child for any reason, then the deal is off," said Cyrus as he noticed Edward rubbing his hands and rocking nervously.

"There'll be no risk of that," replied Spence as he glanced over at an increasingly agitated Edward. "The child is a beauty. She isn't a newborn as you preferred, but we talked about that already. She is young enough to only know you and your wife as her parents. Here, let me bring her out."

Cyrus followed Spence as he walked around to the driver's side door. Spence opened the door and stirred the sleeping child until she awoke.

"Come, darling, there is someone here who wants to meet you," said Spence as he brought a sniffling Lena out and stood her in front of Cyrus, who knelt to get a better look at Lena.

"How are you, darling?" said Cyrus as he touched her cheek with the back of his hand, causing Lena to recoil and hide behind Spence.

"She's a little shy," said Spence. "Come, Lena, this is your new daddy. He and your mommy will take care of you."

"Are you sure she's all right?"

"Yes, of course. The poor girl has been an orphan her whole life. We had to take her in just so she would have a place to stay and something to eat. But the road is no place for a child. She needs something stable and normal. Unfortunately, the road is all she has known, so she just has to get used to normal," Spence said.

Cyrus extended his hand to Lena, who continued to hide behind Spence. The fixer pulled Lena from behind him and took her hand and placed it in Cyrus's palm.

"It's okay, honey, I just want you to meet someone," said Cyrus as he took out a handkerchief and wiped Lena's dripping nose as she began to cough, exposing a wheezing in her chest. "It seems she's not well. Has she been sick for a long time?"

"Only just in the last couple of days. That's why I say the road is not a place for a child. She needs to be someplace safer and warmer, otherwise we would never think of parting with her. We've all grown so attached to her. But knowing she'll be in a wonderful home will give us all peace of mind," Spence said.

"Of course," said Cyrus.

Cyrus, still holding Lena's hand, walked the listless child to the passenger side of his car. He rapped on the window and shook his wife out of her hypnotic stare. She rolled down the window and locked eyes with her husband with an intense glare.

"Yes?" she said.

"Darling, there is someone I would like you to meet. It's a young girl in need of a home," said Cyrus as he nodded toward Lena.

Cassidy's eyes drifted to the child. As she looked at Lena, her blank stare returned. Eyes still fixed on Lena, Cassidy tilted her head in one robotic motion but didn't say a word.

"Darling, are you okay?" asked Cyrus as he looked at his unresponsive wife.

"Why, Cyrus, is this Charlotte?" said Cassidy as a smile formed on her otherwise inanimate countenance. "Why, yes, it is! Charlotte, darling, where have you been? We have been worried sick about you."

Cassidy climbed out of the sedan, knelt in front of Lena, and grabbed the child's shoulders to get a better look at her.

"Charlotte, what on earth are you wearing?" said Cassidy as she looked at Lena's wrinkled and ill-fitting dress. "This isn't how a proper young lady should dress. I thought I taught you better than that."

Lena's only response was a fit of coughing to go with her running nose.

"Cyrus, give me your handkerchief, Charlotte seems to be ill. We must get her home quickly."

"Certainly, darling," said Cyrus as he handed his wife his handkerchief.

Cassidy wiped Lena's nose roughly, causing the child to give out a cry.

"Hush, darling, we are going home now," said Cassidy as she lifted Lena in her arms and carried her to the sedan.

Lena began crying louder and struggled as Cassidy opened the door of the sedan, climbed in, and sat Lena on her lap. When she closed the door, Lena cried even more frantically. The three men could see Cassidy struggling with the child as Lena squirmed on her lap and pounded on the window with her hands.

"Here, come with me so we can finish up with the business," said Spence, eager to pull Cyrus away from the disquieting scene lest apprehension begin to sprout.

With Edward following, Spence led Cyrus behind the pickup truck.

"Do you have the money?" exclaimed Edward when the three were out of sight from Cassidy and Lena.

"Certainly," said Cyrus, casting Edward a scrutinizing look. "Are you sure everything is okay with the child? She seems incredibly frightened."

"Of course, of course. A little excitement is to be expected in someone so young," interjected Spence. "She just has to get used to you and your wife. She was no different when we took her in, but she quickly got attached to us. And it seems like your wife has taken to the child already, which is the important thing."

"You're right," said Cyrus. "You have to understand it's all just so unsettling. I've never done anything like this before, and I want to make sure it's the right thing for everyone. Most especially the child."

"I can assure you it is," Spence said. "We love the child and want what's best for her. And it will give us all peace of mind that she will be with such loving people and in a healthy home. The sooner we can finish up with business, the sooner you and your wife can get her acclimated to her new family."

"Spence is right, we have to get on with it," said Edward, trying to urge the moment along.

"Indeed," replied Cyrus as he cast a sharp look toward Edward. "A deal is a deal, and I think it's better that we conclude our business."

With that, Cyrus reached into the inside pocket of his jacket and pulled out a roll of twenty-dollar bills. Eddie's eyes immediately lit up at the sight of the cash. Cyrus started peeling off one bill at a time and counting the money in the process.

"A thousand," said Cyrus when he was finished counting.

Just as he was going to hand the money over to Spence, the three men heard a bloodcurdling scream.

"That's Cassidy!" yelled Cyrus, still clutching the money as he instinctively darted toward his sedan.

55

Theater for the Gods

As Cyrus rounded the pickup truck, he was faced with an alarming scene. His wife was in the passenger seat of their sedan, door open, screaming as she grasped her bleeding right forearm. A few yards away, a hunchback was holding the young girl who had been on his wife's lap.

"That creature ripped Charlotte from my arms," screamed Cassidy. "Get her back, Cy! You have to get her back!"

Spence and Edward came running behind Cyrus, and the fixer immediately jumped into action.

"I'll deal with this," said Spence to Cyrus. "Go tend to your wife. We'll get the child."

Cyrus hesitated, as his first impulse was to do as his wife instructed, and from his belief that the child was in danger from this deranged mutant. But as the scene settled into clearer focus, he noticed the child was clinging to the hunchback, her arms wrapped around his neck as he held her in his arms protectively.

"Cy, please get Charlotte before that monster does something to her! He already bit me to get to her. She's not safe," Cassidy pleaded.

"Mr. Wallace, go calm your wife. And don't be alarmed. I'll deal with this. This is a misunderstanding. That's all it is," said Spence, grabbing Cyrus by the arm and urging him toward his wife.

Cyrus turned away, then looked back at the hunchback, who was running his hand over the back of the child's head—rocking her gently in his arms. He then walked to his hysterical wife and tried to calm her as he checked her wound.

Spence and Edward made their way closer to Ari.

"Ari, what's the meaning of this? How could you assault that woman?" said Spence in Armenian.

"You lied to me, Spence," spat out Ari. "I'm not stupid. I trusted you and you lied to me. You and your friends are a bunch of thieves. May God damn you, Spence! I told you I don't care what happens to me, but I won't let you do anything to Lena."

"You don't know what you're talking about, Ari. No one is going to do anything to Lena. This couple are business partners of ours, and the wife was simply watching Lena while we were finishing up a deal."

"Just like the way those two animals you sent me with were going to help an old lady at her house. You sent us to rob the house. Don't worry, your two friends are dead now. They were shot for their crimes."

"I-I never trusted those men," stammered Spence, trying to hide his growing anxiety. "Believe me, Ari. Let's not let those two rogues cloud your judgment. Put Lena down so that we can talk. Eddie can watch her, while you and I come to a better understanding. You're not thinking clearly, Ari."

"She's not leaving my arms. I saw how scared she was in the car with that crazy woman. You and your friends aren't ever going to lay a hand on her again. Now go! I have my things from the truck. We don't need you!" yelled Ari.

"What's he saying, Spence? Get the damn kid already," interjected Edward.

"Give me a minute, Eddie. He doesn't want to let her go. I'm dealing with it," replied Spence.

Just then Cyrus walked up.

"Gentlemen. My wife has bites on her arm. I must get her to a doctor before it gets infected. This was obviously a mistake. The deal is off. I don't know who this man is and what he is to this child, but I won't be a party to it," said a disgusted Cyrus as he turned to walk away.

"Mr. Wallace. Please give me just a minute. I'll get this manner resolved, and you and your wife can be on your away," begged Spence as he raced after Cyrus.

As Spence was pleading with Cyrus to keep the deal alive, Edward turned his attention to Ari and Lena.

"I don't know what Spence has been saying to you, but you're giving us that kid," said Edward, who lunged to grab Lena, trying to pull her out of Ari's arms. Lena screamed and hugged Ari's neck tighter.

Ari clung desperately to Lena, twisting with all his strength until Edward's grip slipped. As he pulled Lena away, Ari made a frantic dash to escape, but Edward's hand latched onto the back of his shirt, yanking him to a halt.

Trapped in Edward's grasp, Ari set Lena down and gave her a desperate shove toward the forest. "Run, Lena! Hide! I'll find you. Just get away from these men!"

Lena hesitated, her eyes wide with fear as she watched the fierce struggle unfold before her. Edward tossed Ari aside and lunged for the little girl, his face twisted in a sinister snarl. But before he could reach her, Ari sprang back up, diving low and slamming into Edward's legs with all his might.

Edward hit the ground hard, inches from Lena, who stumbled back as his clawing hands lashed out in her direction. Ari climbed onto Edward's back, grappling to keep him pinned down, his heart pounding with desperation. "Run, Lena! Go now!" he shouted.

This time, Lena turned and bolted toward the forest, her small figure quickly swallowed by the shadows of the trees, leaving Ari to face Edward alone.

Edward bucked the smaller man off his back and ended up on top of him. He punched Ari in the face and split his left brow open. Just as he was about to land another blow, he saw the Wallace sedan speed by him. Spence came running immediately after.

"Eddie, we gotta get out of here. I can hear sirens from town. If what the hunchback told me is true, then Sal and Butch are dead and they are probably coming for us," Spence said.

"Where's the kid?" said Edward as he kept Ari pinned beneath him.

"How should I know? She was here with you when I was dealing with Wallace."

"Did you get the money?"

"No, he jumped into the car before I could get to him and wouldn't listen to anything I had to say. He's gone, and we gotta split, too, before it's too late."

"Damn it! This freak ruined everything. We had the money in our hands. I almost had my life back," said Edward as he grabbed

Ari's shoulders and slammed his head into the ground with each phrase.

"Let him go. There's nothing we can do about it now. We gotta get out of here!" said Spence as he tried to pull Edward off Ari.

"I'll let him go all right," said Edward as he slammed Ari one last time and climbed off him.

"Hurry! Let's go, Eddie. It's getting dark, and we gotta make our way out," urged Spence as he tried to pull Edward toward their truck.

Ari slowly lifted himself, legs wobbly, head spinning, and a defiant smirk slowly forming on his lips.

Edward yanked his arm free from Spence's grasp. He pulled out a switch blade, opened it, and lunged at Ari—stabbing him in the chest. Blood spurted out, and Ari slumped to his knees.

"Eddie! For Pete's sake, we gotta go," yelled Spence as the sounds of sirens became louder.

This time, Edward followed Spence to their truck and the pair climbed in and sped off as fast as they could.

"Lena," Ari whispered as he struggled to get up. Clutching his chest, he forced himself toward the forest. Blood was still pouring from his wound, and he felt weaker with each step. He noticed how dark and cold it was. He was able to make it into the forest and walked another thirty feet before his legs gave out.

"Lena," he called in a feeble, barely audible voice.

He rolled onto his back and tried to listen for the child as the last of his remaining strength faded away.

As Ari fought against his closing eyes, he locked in on the darkening sky he could see through an opening in the canopy of trees. The heavens suddenly looked familiar to him, as beautiful as they did in Van. He realized the gods truly have no limits; there is no place to escape their gaze. They built their thrones to look, without obstruction, on the naked Earth below.

He thought they must take great pride in their creation to demand such a view. And what a drama man has given them. But is the story of man a tragedy or comedy? Do the gods lounge together—fattening on ambrosia, drowning their sensibilities in mead—and laugh at man's pain and suffering? Do they stand and applaud his cruelty?

After all this time, how have they not grown tired of it?

56

Şeytan'ın Haydut

For nearly a year after his escape, Vartan lived as a highwayman—robbing and killing whatever Turkish person he could find.

He initially planned to travel to Russia through the north passages, but it had proved to be a hazardous and near impossible journey.

Military blockades cut off nearly all the roads to the north. So, Vartan had to take to the countryside, finding little-used paths or crossing over virgin Turkish terrain. Instead of hunting for food or scavenging for resources, he killed for them. There was a Hamidiye infantryman, who stopped to rest his horse next to a stream. While the man brushed his horse as it drank, Vartan stole behind him and drove a sword through the man's kidney. He took the man's food and money, as well as his rifle and knife. After that, he killed a pair of Ottoman soldiers—shooting them from a hillside perch as they rode. There was a farmer after that, two pilgrims, a glass merchant, and a fisherman bringing his catch to market. Hopelessness and anger had consumed him, and his only outlet was death.

The Turks in the area began to fear this unknown terror and named him *Şeytan'ın Haydut* (Satan's Bandit). The locals even banded together to mount an unsuccessful campaign to capture him. Soon, he became part of the region's lore. Parents would warn their children that Şeytan'ın Haydut would come for them if they didn't behave. They said he had eyes that burned with white flames and warned that if any unfaithful Muslim looked into those eyes, they would become blind.

Hate had found its way into Vartan's heart, and he had come to feed off the killing, and because of it, he might have lingered in the Turkish countryside for longer than he needed. He didn't look at himself as a blind murderer or a thief, but rather a fighter avenging his people, slaying the enemy whenever he could. Causing them a small measure of pain and suffering for the great amount his people had to endure seemed morally righteous. Even if only for a second, vengeance did indeed taste sweet—addictingly so. And he wanted to savor it just for a little longer.

One day, as he hid in a ditch along a deserted path, he noticed a Turkish woman carrying a tattered mesh sack, accompanied by a young girl who looked to be about seven years old. The woman struggled down the road, bent by the weight of the sack slung over her shoulder. Vartan waited for them to approach, then emerged from his hiding place and cut the pair off. The dark scarf wrapped around the bottom of his face and his leathery skin made his bright eyes seem to glow by contrast. Gun drawn, he ordered the woman to open her sack.

The girl, visibly shaking, clung to her mother's side. Trembling herself, the woman nonetheless tried to calm her daughter as she set the sack on the ground and opened it. Inside was a treasure of assorted silver and gold cups, plates, and coins. Vartan couldn't believe that such a fortune could be transported by only a woman and a young girl. It seemed too good to be true, and Vartan quickly scanned the area, convinced it was a trap.

"Why are you out here alone with all these treasures?" Vartan asked the woman when no one else appeared.

The woman didn't say a word, but Vartan heard the girl ask her mother, "Is that Şeytan'ın Haydut? Is he going to kill us?"

"Şeytan'ın Haydut? The only devils in this land are Turkish. But yes, if a Turk calls me Şeytan'ın Haydut, then it's an honor. It means they accept their crimes and know that their sins won't go unpunished. But for now, I want to know why you have all this gold."

The girl buried her face in her mother's side while her mother kept her arms around her.

"Please, sir, she is just a child. She didn't know any better. What you have in your hands is my husband's inheritance. Please take it and spare us," said the woman, her voice quivering.

"His inheritance? Then why isn't he out here carrying it? What kind of man sends his wife and daughter to carry his fortune and leaves them to the mercy of another man's greed?"

"My husband was a soldier, and we learned two months ago that he was killed in battle. His father was ill and passed away a month after, and we were told if we didn't come to take our inheritance within the month, it would be divided among the other brothers. It's just my daughter and me now. We're poor, and we have no other money, so we had to go."

Vartan closed the bag, slung it over his shoulder, and told the pair to begin walking. As mother and daughter clutched each other, Vartan marched them to a large patch of tall grass a few hundred yards off the road.

"Go," ordered Vartan as he jabbed his gun into the mother's ribs when she hesitated to enter the towering grass.

The three trampled through the tall meadow until they reached a circular clearing. Vartan then ordered the pair to kneel on the ground, and he carefully walked behind them. He massaged his pistol and quietly surveyed them. He realized he had never killed a woman, or a child, before. But these were the wife and progeny of an Ottoman soldier—a murderer—so it shouldn't be too hard.

He considered which order to kill them. Was it crueler to kill the child first or the mother? And did he want to be cruel? He raised his gun and pointed it at the mother, and then the child, and then back to the mother. He oscillated back and forth a few more times until he finally settled on the child when he realized it would increase the mother's suffering. He took a step forward and put his finger on the trigger when he heard the child speak in a barely audible tone.

"Have I been a good Muslim, Momma? When the day of judgment comes, will I go to paradise? Will I see my father there?" the girl asked.

"Yes, you have been a true gift, and Allah is just. He will take mercy on you," her mother said.

Something awakened in Vartan at that moment, and he suddenly saw the scene in front of him differently. No longer were the two the vile consort and offspring of an enemy. Instead, he saw a frightened mother and a helpless girl yearning for her father. Humanity fought its way back into his soul, and he could see that love and suffering was not exclusive to the Armenian, nor to the Christian. He thought of his daughter, lost out there in a strange world, longing for her father's love and protection. He felt the hatred drain out of his body, only to be replaced with guilt and shame. He realized he had become that which he detested. His place wasn't here, terrorizing the innocent, it was thousands of miles away searching for his daughter.

"Get up," he told the mother and daughter.

The two did as they were told. Vartan put the gun in his belt and led the pair out of the meadow and onto the path. He handed the woman her sack. He then squatted down so he could be eye level with the girl. He placed his hand gently on the girl's cheek.

"You needn't fear Şeytan'ın Haydut any longer, my child. That man is no more," he said.

57

The King of America

Ari's eyes flickered open. He had no idea how long he'd been unconscious, but the sun was peeking over the horizon, so he knew morning was approaching. *Lena,* he thought.

The weight of a tiny body sleeping on his chest caused his panic to subside. It was replaced by a stab of pain. He carefully set Lena on the ground to examine his wound.

He lifted his shirt and saw only a flesh wound. While still open, the wound had stopped bleeding—the pressure of his hand and Lena lying on top of the wound was enough to stanch the flow of blood. He realized his grandfather's medal inside the front pocket of his shirt had deflected the blade enough that it only caused a superficial injury.

He reached into his backpack, pulled out another old shirt, and used it to bandage his wound. With the sun coming up, Ari became frightened that the men would come back for Lena.

What he thought would be a land of salvation had turned out to be another hell—fraught with dangers, occupied by even more vicious demons. He had no money, but that wasn't what frightened him most. What he feared most was how close he'd come to losing Lena.

The only place that seemed safe was the forest they were in. As Ari carried Lena deeper into the forest, she stirred and intuitively hugged Ari's neck. It was autumn and the mornings were cold. The forest provided some shelter from the cold, but not nearly enough. He found three trees in a close cluster and decided to make a camp in the middle of them. He set Lena down and began to collect fallen branches. The forest was so thick, he had little trouble finding everything he needed to construct a tepee-style enclosure by leaning the branches against each other and then filling the gaps with smaller branches and leaves.

While he did so, Lena wobbled over to him, shivering, and hooked onto his leg. Ari used a stick and his hands to quickly dig a small pit. He rushed to collect some twigs, leaves, and branches, and used his matches to light a fire. After a few minutes, Lena stopped shaking. He tried to feed her with the little food that remained, but the child refused to eat.

He spent the entire day barely moving from the fire—leaving it only to collect more wood to fuel the blaze. When night came, Ari settled just inside his wooden tepee and bundled himself and Lena in a blanket, curling himself around her, facing the fire that was a few feet away, as they drifted off to sleep.

At some point in the night, the fire went out, and when Ari woke, Lena was shivering. He noticed her looking unnaturally pale, and he felt her forehead. It was warm to the touch, but he didn't think it was anything to be alarmed by. He quickly made another fire. He didn't want to risk the child getting sicker, so he made a mental note to make sure that she ate something that day. He also felt that she needed constant warmth and decided that if he couldn't find better shelter, he would stay awake the whole night to ensure that their fire didn't go out.

As the morning passed, the weather showed them mercy and warmed to a pleasant autumn day. He heated some water in a bowl, added breadcrumbs to it and coaxed Lena into eating the modest meal. After Lena had eaten, Ari decided to try to get his bearings and explore the forest. He hadn't paid enough attention when they'd entered the forest and was now unsure which direction the town lay in. He picked up Lena, who seemed a little more invigorated and alert, and began walking. After fifteen minutes, they stumbled upon a trail. Thankful for more level ground, he picked up the path.

Ari was on the trail for another ten minutes when he heard a strange sound. He stopped walking and perked his ears to pick it up better. As he did, he could hear the faint sound of music. He walked toward the music and could now hear the beautiful sounds of violins, their wafting calls beckoning to him like a Siren's song.

He quickened his pace until he came to the end of the trail, which opened onto a large estate. He hid behind a cluster of trees and peeked his head out. And there in front of him he saw what looked like a fairytale.

About fifty yards away, a Jacobean-style mansion rose three stories above the ground. To its left was a horse stable, and to its right was a thirty-foot-wide stage with an orchestra and a choir of teenaged boys. There were about a hundred people sitting at tables of eight to ten around the stage. To Ari, the vast grounds looked more like a palace than a home, and he imagined that he must have stumbled upon the residence of the king of this strange land. He found himself hoping that he was a good and just king.

He briefly looked down at Lena, who seemed as mesmerized as him. He glanced toward the stage and noticed one of the boys in the choir step forward. As the violins faded to accompaniment, the boy began to sing these beautiful and unintelligible words:

> *Nid wy'n gofyn bywyd moethus,*
> *Aur y byd na'I berlau mân:*
> *Gofyn wyf am galon hapus,*
> *Calon onest, calon lân.*
> *Calon lân yn llawn daioni,*
> *Tecach yw na'r lili dlos:*
> *Dim ond calon lân all ganu*
> *Canu'r dydd a chanu'r nos.*

Ari was hypnotized by the boy's voice as the rest of the choir stepped forward and joined in the singing. The choir's collective voices carried the notes forward in an undulating wave that seemed to stir the resting leaves above Ari's head, as the song continued:

> *Pe dymunwn olud bydol,*
> *Hedyn buan ganddo sydd;*
> *Golud calon lân, rinweddol,*
> *Yn dwyn bythol elw fydd.*
> *Calon lân yn llawn daioni,*
> *Tecach yw na'r lili dlos:*
> *Dim ond calon lân all ganu*
> *Canu'r dydd a chanu'r nos.*

The choir slowly built to its crescendo with each verse, until its voices sent forth a soaring movement that Ari felt vibrating in his chest and perforating his skin as the song reached its climax:

Hwyr a bore fy nymuniad
Gwyd I'r nef ar adain cân
Ar I Dduw, er mwyn fy Ngheidwad,
Roddi I mi galon lân.
Calon lân yn llawn daioni,
Tecach yw na'r lili dlos:
Dim ond calon lân all ganu
Canu'r dydd a chanu'r nos.

When the song ended, the crowd rose and applauded, which shook Ari out of his reverie. He looked at the tables full of food and thought that perhaps he had stumbled upon the king's wedding day or a coronation.

Lena seemed just as captivated by the sight, and Ari felt her try to squirm out of his arms toward the scene, causing Ari to pull her closer to him. Not having any better way to pass their time, the two sat in the forest and observed. *How wonderful it must be to be the king,* he thought. To be adored, to be feared. To want for nothing, to fear no one. The king was a far different man than he was.

Try as he might, Ari couldn't make out who the king was. No one wore a crown, and the king's throne must still be in the palace. The festivities soon wound down, and as the guests took their leave, they all approached a pair of men at the center table. One was an older middle-aged man, tall, thin with a strong posture and a full head of salt-and-pepper hair. The other looked to be in his early thirties, about the same height as the older man, but a heftier physique and with a full complement of black hair. Ari noticed the guests paid special attention to the older man. *That must be the king*, Ari thought. What a peculiar king, to go about without his regalia. He may have disguised himself as one of his subjects, but he couldn't hide from the homage everyone paid him.

Feeling it was time to go, Ari headed back to where they'd camped the night before, making sure to note how to get back to the king's palace. Even though the day had been warmer and Lena was no longer shivering, the child still had her wheezing cough. When they reached camp, Ari built another fire. When night fell, Ari watched over the fire and made sure Lena stayed warm. The next morning, Lena became more lethargic. He didn't have anything for her to eat, and she slept most of the day.

Ari could feel the cold and knew that winter was coming, and they would have to find shelter soon if they were to survive. He recalled seeing farms on the train ride to Bethlehem. Perhaps, just as he had done in Van, he could somehow convince the owner of the farm to let him and the child stay in a barn or shed in return for working on the farm. If he took the trail in the opposite direction, Ari was confident it would lead him to town. From there he would try to find one of the farms. It wouldn't be a final solution, but it would keep Lena safe until Vartan came for her. Ari knew Vartan would come soon.

Satisfied with his new solution, Ari set off with Lena in search of a farm, but after several minutes, the trail ended at a swampy lake. Confused, Ari searched for another path but could find none. He heard the low rumbling of thunder and looked up at an overcast sky. Suddenly the heavens let loose, and Ari dashed into the forest with Lena in a vain attempt to escape the downpour. Within seconds, despite standing under a towering tree, they were soaked.

Ari felt Lena begin to shiver again. This time there would be no fire to take away the cold, so Ari huddled with her as best he could, cursing his ineptitude and carelessness once again.

Ari and Lena spent the night in misery. Lena shivered and coughed the entire night. Ari could feel her fever radiating hotter and hotter with every passing hour. Ari had developed a cough as well, but his concern for Lena caused him to barely take notice of it. The next morning, Lena was listless. She lay limp, her only movements being a slight turn of her head or fluttering eyelids. It was too damp to make a fire, so Ari wrapped her in the only blanket they had to keep her warm. He found his way back to their camp and put dry clothes on Lena. Then he made a fire to get some warmth into her. He noticed she would continuously drift in and out of sleep the whole day.

As the sun went down, the temperature dropped further, and the winds began to blow, amplifying the cold. Ari noticed Lena was completely unresponsive. He started nudging her and prodding her.

"Lena, wake up, my child," he pleaded. "Please, Lena, you must wake up. I promise I'll bring you chocolate. Your father is coming, my darling. You'll be safe with him; you just have to wake up."

But the child didn't move. He hugged her tightly next to him as he sat on the ground and rocked her back and forth. He could feel the heat from her fever, so he knew she was still alive. But he didn't think she would be able to survive long in those conditions, and he had no answers.

"I'm sorry, my child, I've done this to you, and you must never forgive me. I don't deserve your forgiveness," said Ari as he choked back tears.

Ari then looked up to the sky.

"Do you see this, mother? Do you see what I've done to this child? You said I could save her, but I didn't. How could these cursed hands bring anything but suffering and pain? I was never the boy you thought I was. I could never be a man worthy of something as beautiful as this," he said as he raised Lena up to the sky. "You made me love this child, and now look what I've done."

Ari lowered Lena until he was cradling her again and looked at the motionless child, then he snapped his head up and looked toward the palace.

Maybe the king is merciful, he thought.

58

Ashes of a Phoenix

It was rumored that Stetson had once been a child, although no evidence had ever been produced to that effect. If the rumors were true, then any vestiges of childhood had long since vanished, leaving a dour man who seemed to feed on obligation and revel in dispassion. His personality was reflected in his posture, which was straighter than a carpenter's level and never wavered off the y axis. In his role as a butler, when dealing with anyone other than his employer and guests, Stetson had only two moods—indifferent and forbidding. Smiles he treated like contagions and had thankfully developed an immunity to them. Laughter, a more advanced form of the disease, he had likewise eradicated, apparently by way of an undisclosed inoculation.

He had devoted his life to serving, to looking after the affairs of another. His duty was to manage the home of Myron Shackleton, a colonial Brit, and he ran the household with the discipline and precision of a military regiment. Following his master's wishes, a breakfast of eggs, ham, cheese, bread, and an assortment of jellies was to be served each morning at 8:07. Lunch was taken in the study at precisely fifteen minutes past noon. There was some latitude for dinner, due to the variance of his master's evening plans, but the staff had to be ready to serve the multi-course meal between seven-thirty and eight-thirty p.m.

Stetson managed a staff of seven that included a cook, two housekeeping women, a maintenance man, a stable man, a groundskeeper, and a young woman who served as an assistant to the household staff.

Myron Shackleton's family moved from Wales to Trinidad and Tobago to make their fortune in the sugarcane industry. As a young butler with a promising future, Stetson followed the Shackletons west. The Shackleton empire steadily expanded into South America and stretched into the East Indies. It grew to include the cultivation of rubber and the growing and distribution of cocoa beans.

Three weeks after Myron's second birthday, their family home in Trinidad and Tobago went up in flames. Stetson had pulled a sleeping Myron from his crib—the child still clutching a brown teddy bear—and out of the house to safety. After setting Myron down a safe distance away, he rushed back to the fire. When he tried to reenter the home to search for Myron's parents, the front entrance collapsed, barring his way. He ran around the perimeter of the house, desperately trying to find a way in, but the inferno offered no openings. When Stetson bravely ignored the fire and tried to force his way through, he was repeatedly turned back by the flames, which lashed out with the ferocity of a lioness guarding her prey.

Crestfallen and badly burned, Stetson went back to the spot where he had set Myron down and lifted the child in his arms.

He recalled seeing Myron hugging his teddy bear and looking at the blaze as if he were watching a fireworks display—not realizing what he had just lost.

Stetson sustained burns to both his hands and forearms, leaving scars that stayed with him the rest of his life. But he would carry more than traces of burns from that day. A guilt-ridden heart for not being able to save his master and lady—for failing to serve them and Myron—beat agonizingly in his chest from that moment forward.

Myron was left with only one living relative, his father's younger brother, Endicott Shackleton. Unlike his older sibling, Endicott was an indifferent millionaire. He was an explorer and adventurer who preferred the riches of discovery over the wealth of business.

When the tragedy occurred, Endicott was deep in the Amazon seeking the fabled city of gold—El Dorado. He wouldn't emerge from the Amazon for two more years, by which time most felt he had perished.

In that time, Stetson, as Myron's sole guardian, had overseen the family empire with the care of a custodian. He moved to Pennsylvania and raised Myron the only way he knew, not as a parent, but as a servant. Myron was the master of the house, regardless of his age. His needs were to be met, his wishes to be followed. No sooner did Myron learn to read and write, than Stetson began to involve him in every decision relative to the family business and his wealth. By the time he was twelve, a precocious Myron had begun making his own decisions, with Stetson only as an adviser and executor.

Stetson would never marry and would never take a salary, a fact that Myron would only discover on the day his lifelong servant died. Myron never bothered to discuss compensation with

Stetson. In his mind, Stetson looked after the affairs of the house, which included his pay. Stetson had complete access to a substantial account specifically for the operations of the household. It was the one area that Myron left entirely to Stetson. The servant would only use what monies were needed. He lived in the mansion, he had food to eat, and he saw that he was dressed according to his station. Anything more were luxuries he neither needed nor desired.

When Endicott found out about the death of his brother and sister-in-law, he rushed to the States to seek out his nephew. But Endicott was just as challenged in raising a child as Stetson was. The only playgrounds Endicott knew were in the blinding sands of the Sahara, the stifling humidity of the Amazon, and the burning cold of the Arctic—environs that were not suited for the delicate constitution of a child. And the pull of exploration was still too strong for Endicott to abandon. It was decided that Stetson would continue to look after the child, with Endicott returning as often as he could to check on his nephew. Despite their limited time together, Myron grew to respect his uncle deeply. As a teenager, Myron even accompanied him to Patagonia in search of the giants Magellan was said to have encountered on his circumnavigation of the globe. But in the end, Myron was more his father's son than his uncle's nephew. He was a businessman, and his adventures were to be found in boardrooms and his explorations in the marketplace.

Myron was in his early thirties now, an imposing figure at just over six feet tall. He had a hefty physique, but he wasn't so much fat as he was well fed. In business, he had grown into an exceptional entrepreneur and was comfortable in, and proud of, the fortune he was given and had enlarged. If wealth was a game, then it was a game he had mastered. In this game, he felt he had few peers, and among his peers, there were even fewer who deserved his respect. One man he deeply respected was his uncle Endicott, who remained the only man whose approval he still sought.

"Will there be anything else, Master?" asked Stetson as he finished serving tea to Myron and Endicott.

"No, Stetson, thank you. Just ensure that Uncle Endicott's room is ready for him. Even great explorers need the comforts of a warm bed at times," said Myron, puffing on a Cuban cigar as he relaxed in his oversized chair.

"You make too much of a fuss over an old man like me, my boy. In the future, I'll have to arrive unannounced so we can avoid all this pomp and circumstance," said Endicott as he lit a pipe and sat back into a recliner opposite his nephew.

"Did you not enjoy your little homecoming the other day? You come to Pennsylvania so infrequently that when news of your visit circulated, we had so many people wishing to see you that we felt better to make a grand event of it."

"It was lovely, but fit for a hero and not me. But I did quite enjoy the music."

"Good, I thought you might," said Myron. "So, dear Uncle, what adventurous stories are you going to spellbind me with this evening?"

"What stories could I possibly tell you that wouldn't come off as the ramblings of a mad man?" replied Endicott. "I envy you, my good boy. A life of commerce has few mysteries. Its treasures are all clear to see and within reach. What can be said of a man who digs for myths and risks life in search of legends—knowing neither where to find them nor what they will look like if find them he did?"

"Is Atlantis proving to be elusive, dear Uncle?"

"As elusive and vexing as an unrequited temptress."

Uncle and nephew continued their conversation into the evening. The howling wind that battered the windows provided a fitting backdrop for Endicott's tales of explorations.

The same wind, however, was mercilessly tormenting the unfortunate who found themselves outside of those mansion walls on that cold and bitter night.

═══

As he carried Lena through the forest, Ari put his hand on her forehead, and his palm felt as if it were hovering over an open fire. Her fever was getting worse. Ari shook her, but she didn't respond. He put his ear to the child's chest and didn't hear anything, nor could he feel any heartbeat. He stopped and unwrapped Lena's blanket and put his ear to her chest again, but again—nothing.

"Please, Lord, please, Lord. Take me and not the child, please take me and not this child," he begged as he continued listening for a heartbeat.

And then he thought he felt a beat coming from her chest. He felt it again and heard a steady, faint heartbeat. *Alive, she's still alive!* But now he had to get her help, and the only place he knew to go was the king's palace. The king might mistake him for a beggar and run him off, but if he was a good king, he wouldn't turn away a dying child. *He must take her; he must help her.*

He started wrapping the blanket around her and stopped. He reached into his pocket and took out his medal. His hands had soiled it long enough. He never felt worthy to hold it, feeling it was meant for better men, and now he felt less deserving of it than ever. But this child was different. Her mother had been killed in front of her, and she clung to her, willing to bravely accept the same fate. Due to no fault of hers, the child's life had been cruelly placed in his hands. It should have been a death sentence long ago, but the child had persevered, despite him. It was a testament to her spirit that she fought for her life even now, even as he had no way to help her. The medal was meant for someone like her and not him.

He put the medal in her blanket, wrapped the coarse wool around her, and rushed through the forest.

59

Among the Bulrushes

Virginia wrapped a shawl around herself as she walked out the door, bracing herself against the biting wind. She bowed her head and watched as the wind assailed the nearby forest, forcing the trees to bow to its might as it swept through like a conquering army.

It was November and night came early. As an only child, she would normally be home with her parents for the evening, but Stetson had requested her to come to the mansion this night to relieve the cook, who had fallen ill. Virginia didn't mind—she was only nineteen and knew she was fortunate to be working for such a wealthy and powerful man.

Her father had been a farmer. When she was eleven years old, he fell from the roof of their barn and became paralyzed from the waist down. Her father was never able to work again, and the mounting medical bills crippled the family financially, forcing her parents to sell most of their property. The only thing they could keep was the house in which she was born. But with her father unable to work and her mother needing to provide constant care, their home, too, was soon in jeopardy of being lost. She remembered hearing her mother crying one evening when her parents thought she was sleeping in her room. It was a cry of hopelessness that only comes when the wolf is at your door.

The next morning, she awoke, put on the newest old dress she had, and, without telling her parents, set out to find work. The only place she could think to go was the mansion whose roof she would see above the tree line when she and her father rode their buggy to town. She set out on the nearly five-mile walk with nothing but hope. When she arrived at the mansion, she nervously rang the doorbell.

"May I help you, young lady?" asked the slender, humorless man who answered the door.

"Yes, sir. My name is Virginia Hoffman. I've come to inquire if you're in need of help on your estate. My parents used to own a farm, so I'm used to hard work, and I'm a fast learner."

Stetson was distrustful by nature, and in his role as young Myron's guardian and keeper of the family fortune, he found that to be a useful and necessary trait. His defenses never rested, not even at the sight of a young girl at the door.

"How old are you, young lady?"

"Twelve, sir."

"Indeed. Although I admire the ambition in one so young, I am afraid we are fully staffed. I do wish you well on your pursuit," said Stetson as he made a motion to close the door.

"Please, sir, would you reconsider?" said Virginia as she thrust her forearm against the door. "I'll work without wages for a week, doing whatever it is you need. If you're not happy with me, I'll go and never bother you again. But please, sir, I'm an honest girl, and I've been raised by honest parents. I only ask you to give me a chance to prove that I can be of service."

The plea did little to sway Stetson, who was set to give the girl a firmer rejection, when something stopped him. It could have been the attempt at pride he saw in the girl's upturned chin, which was meant to hide the self-doubt and desperation churning within her. It could have been her naiveté in believing the worn-out fabric of her raggedy dress could be masked by the careful pressing she gave it that morning. Or it could have been the look in her eyes that made him feel that this girl had come to his door out of necessity. He told her to return at five a.m. the following day—believing a girl so young would never rise so early. She was back at his door at four-thirty the next morning.

Stetson was determined not to make it easy on her. He had her begin by helping the housekeepers with washing and ironing the laundry—a task that took most of the morning. When she had finished, he immediately instructed her to help the cook prepare lunch. Once lunch was over, she had to clean the kitchen, even scrubbing the floor. In the afternoon, he sent her off to the stables to help groom the horses. When she had finished that, he told her that they needed firewood—even though their stockpile of wood could last for months—and told her to go to the back of the property and chop wood. Stetson half expected her to beg out of the backbreaking work, but instead she spent two hours filling an empty wagon with firewood. When she was done, she approached Stetson in the kitchen and asked him if there was anything else he needed done.

"No, I believe your work has been satisfactory. You may leave for the day, and if you return tomorrow, we shall have more work for you to do," said Stetson flatly.

"Thank you, sir. I'll be here early," said Virginia as she turned to leave.

Stetson observed her as she walked past the kitchen table and the baloney sandwich that he had asked the cook to prepare for her.

"Young Virginia, Guy made that sandwich for you. Didn't you care for it?" he asked.

"Thank you, sir. But it's just that I don't have any money to pay for it. I'm sorry if it'll go to waste."

"So, you didn't eat anything the entire day?"

"No, sir, but I wasn't particularly hungry."

"Virginia, I will only tell you this once. Master Shackleton is a gentleman, and this is his home. While in his home, if offered food or drink it is done so with the principles of a gentleman. To suggest that they are offered with an expectation of payment is an insult."

"I meant no harm, sir," said Virginia as she cast her eyes to the ground.

"Very well, please take the sandwich with you."

"Thank you, sir," said Virginia as she picked up the sandwich.

Virginia returned the next day, and Stetson told her that as long as she exhibited the same work ethic, she would have a job.

Three months into her employment, she approached Stetson to tell him that she would have to resign. When Stetson asked the reason, she told him that the bank was foreclosing on their home, and they would have to leave their property.

Stetson wished her well. "You have been a fine worker. I am sure that you will find suitable employment no matter where you and your family settle. Good luck to you, young Virginia."

The next day, the man from the bank arrived early at the Hoffman's residence. Virginia watched from her room as the man spoke to her parents, then she heard her mother scream with excitement. She peeked her head into the main room and saw her mother hugging the man from the bank. The man walked over to her father, shook his hand, and left.

"Virginia, it's a miracle. We don't have to leave! This is our home for good now," her mother exclaimed.

Virginia was confused. Her mother explained that someone had come to the bank that morning and settled all their debt. It took a few minutes before Virginia fully understood what her mother was telling her. After spending most of the day unpacking and resettling into the home they never left, Virginia headed to the mansion, feeling that their benefactor could only be one person. Virginia never spoke to Myron Shackleton in all the time she worked for him, but he was the only person she knew wealthy enough to pay off a debt that large.

"Young Virginia, I am surprised to see you here," said Stetson when he greeted her at the door. "I believed you to have left with your family."

"Sir, I didn't think I would be here either, but an amazing thing happened. A man, who I can never repay, settled my parents' debt this morning. We own the home now. We don't have to leave. Do you think it was Mr. Shackleton who done it?"

"Well, young lady, that was an incredibly fortunate turn of events, but I can assure you that it was most definitely not Master Shackleton."

"Who, then?"

"That is a mystery indeed. But good fortune, just as bad fortune, comes when we least expect it. We must accept both when they do. I assume you would like your job back."

"I would, sir."

"Very well, then. Martha needs assistance in the laundry."

On this night, Virginia had set out later than she had planned, and the wind slowed her journey further. On most days, she would take the more familiar and safer path around the forest to get to work. However, to get some relief from the wind, and to make up for her late start, she decided to take a more direct route by cutting through the woods.

Even though the trees blocked out most of the moon's light, her eyes eventually adjusted to the darkness, and she made good progress. When she saw the lights of the mansion between the trees, she felt a sense of relief. Just a few more turns, a slight climb, and she would be out of the forest and on the grounds of the estate. Virginia quickened her pace, then stopped dead in her tracks.

To her left, about twenty feet down the trail, a small hunched-over figure blocked her path. She tried to turn and run but found she couldn't move her legs. She wanted to scream but the muscles in her throat had locked up and wouldn't let any sound escape. She was forced to stand there and look at this unknown creature, who she was certain was some carnivorous animal out on its nightly hunt. The creature remained still as well, and in the darkness, she couldn't make out any of its features at first. But as she slowed her breathing and focused on it, she could see the features of a man, which only frightened her more, and she felt her heart begin to race faster. He looked dark, dirty, and disheveled, as if he'd crawled up from a pit in the earth. He stayed hunched over, and she could see an unnatural hump on his back.

She could finally feel her throat loosen. "Who's there?" said Virginia, barely able to spit the words out.

The man didn't respond. She found she could move her legs again, and her instinct was to run, but she felt safety was in the other direction—toward the mansion, whose path was barred by this malefactor.

"I will have you know my employer is expecting me, and they are coming presently to escort me to the estate," Virginia bluffed.

The man moved toward Virginia.

"Stay back, or I'll scream," Virginia threatened.

"Please, please," said the man as he continued to walk toward her.

At that moment Virginia noticed the man was carrying something in his arms. He took a couple more steps forward, and she could see that he was holding a small child.

"Please, please, please," he kept repeating as he extended the child in his arms toward Virginia.

The fear began to drain from Virginia as she looked at the child. She thought the child looked unnaturally thin and saw no movement from it. She looked back at the man, and realized he was a hunchback and felt guilty about how monstrous she felt he appeared. When she looked at his face, she saw a pleading look in the man's eyes.

"Is the child sick?" asked Virginia as she put her hand on the child's forehead and felt the unmistakable heat of a fever.

"Please, please, please," repeated the man as he tried to hand the child to Virginia.

"Do you understand me? Do you speak English?" said Virginia, who placed her hands on the girl but didn't take her into her arms.

"Please, please, please," the man implored.

Virginia could see the desperation in the man's face and felt she had to help, as leaving the child out in the cold would mean certain death. As she took the child in her arms, tears streamed down the man's face as he tenderly ran his hand over the child's head.

As she held the child, Virginia could feel the fever emanating from the child's body and she started urgently walking to the mansion, when the man forcefully grabbed her arm. Startled and a little frightened again, Virginia turned to look at him.

"Lena, Lena, Lena," he said, pointing to the child.

"Lena," Virginia repeated, nodding toward the child.

"Lena." Ari nodded somberly.

Virginia felt him let go of her arm, but he kept his eyes on the child as he slowly backed his way off the path and faded into the dark forest. Virginia could still feel the heat of the child's body through her clothes, and she knew she had to get her to a doctor as soon as possible.

She took off her shawl and wrapped it around the child, then ran as fast as she could to the mansion.

60

Officers and Gentlemen

Entering the main area of the house, Virginia could hear voices coming from Myron's study. Under normal circumstances, she would never imagine interrupting Myron in his study, which was off limits to any servant other than Stetson, apart from times when she needed to clean it. But this wasn't a normal circumstance. With single-mindedness, she barged into the room to the shocked looks of the three men inside.

"Sir, I came across this child on the road to work. She's sick. She hasn't moved, and she needs a doctor," said Virginia to Stetson.

House protocol called for the staff to communicate with Stetson only, and if any conversation were needed with Myron, then Stetson would have those discussions. In the seven years that Virginia had worked at the estate, she couldn't recall a single conversation she'd had with Myron. But at that moment she didn't have the luxury for decorum; she knew that although she was addressing Stetson, she was talking to everyone inside the study.

Endicott and Myron both jumped from their chairs in response to the interruption. Stetson immediately stepped between the two men and Virginia and raised his palms in a reassuring manner.

"My apologies, gentlemen," Stetson said. "You must excuse me. I will tend to this matter." Stetson motioned for Virginia to follow him out of the study, and he led her to the servant quarters.

"What is the meaning of this?" Stetson asked her.

"Sir, I apologize, but this child is sick. She has a fever, and I fear if we don't get her help, she may die," Virginia said.

"Who is this child?"

"That I don't know; she was left abandoned on the road here. I found her as I was coming to work, and I couldn't leave her," said Virginia, knowing that Stetson had a particular dislike of men who abdicated their duties like this hunchback seemed to have done.

Stetson gave Virginia a suspicious glance and then put his hand on the child's forehead.

"Very well, lay her down and keep her warm," he said when he felt the heat coming off Lena. "I'll see if there's anything in the infirmary that will be of use. It is getting late, and you still must prepare tonight's dinner. In the morning if she is not better, I will see about finding the child a doctor. But I am cautioning you to be mindful of your place; I will not tolerate you disrupting Master Shackleton as you did just now," Stetson said.

"Please, sir, can we fetch a doctor now? I fear the child needs attention immediately. What of Dr. Dunbar? He comes here often to see Mr. Shackleton."

"Dr. Dunbar is Master Shackleton's personal physician and not a country doctor who is at our beck and call."

"Please, sir."

"You have my answer, now go lay the child down and start your duties."

Back in the study, Myron and Endicott tried to recover from the unexpected interruption.

"I apologize, dear Uncle. I assure you that outbursts like that are not tolerated in this house, and I will have Stetson speak to her," said Myron as he opened a humidor to offer Endicott a cigar.

Endicott seemed not to notice Myron's offer as he walked to the double door of the study.

"What of the child?" Endicott asked.

"I do not know who that child is and why she was brought here, but that is not our concern. You have been away too long. You don't deserve to have your evening thrown into such turmoil, and I will not stand for it. Stetson will do what needs to be done. I have learned that things aren't always what they seem. The child is most likely the progeny of some vagabond, whose thieving ways have brought about their own misfortune. Please do not let this interruption disquiet you at all."

"I would like to go check on the child personally."

"Dear Uncle, please do not feel like you have to. I am sure what needs to be done for the child is being done."

"To have to would imply coercion. In this matter, there is no such force at work. But still, I must. The life of a child is a far greater concern to me than the petty annoyances of a disrupted evening," said Endicott as he approached Myron and straightened his posture as he addressed his nephew. "You may be a wealthy man, with all the illusions of superiority that it brings, but don't forget who you really are. Your life is just as fragile as that child's, your destiny just as uncertain. I've seen kings fall and gods spat on. Don't fool yourself into believing you are different. You're a man—mortal and imperfect. But take pride in the breed of men you come from. Men who are marked by their compassion and known for their honor. A line of men from your father to his father, to his father before him. Men who may have conferred with generals but took to the battlefields and bled alongside soldiers. Men who understood that dining with a lord was not as noble as offering your table to the dispossessed. We are officers, sir! We are gentlemen, sir! And as such, we are bound by duty and obligation to do the right thing."

With that, the elder Shackleton turned and walked out of the study. Endicott was the closest thing to a parent that Myron had, and he found that even a powerful and wealthy man can feel the sting of disapproval. If he were to be honest, some of what his uncle said was true. He did feel, and he believed rightfully so, that he was elevated above certain things. There was a difference between a master and a servant. There was a necessary gap between the wealthy and the poor. There ought to be a chasm between the powerful and the disenfranchised. In his opinion, these were not beliefs in need of debate. They were simply as God intended them to be. But here was another powerful and wealthy man who had trampled on the very attitudes he had built his life on, and in a way that made him feel a measure of shame. Silently, he followed his uncle out of the study in search of the sick child. When they entered the servants' quarters, they saw Stetson talking with Virginia, who still cradled Lena in her arms.

"How is the child?" Endicott asked Stetson.

"Not well, sir. I believe she's in desperate need of a doctor," blurted out Virginia before Stetson could answer.

Endicott put his hand on Lena's forehead, and the concern was evident on his face.

"Quickly, bring me some wet towels and cold water. We must bring this fever down as quickly as possible," said Endicott as he took Lena from Virginia and laid her down on a sofa.

With everyone rushing to get towels and water, Endicott unwrapped the blanket around Lena. As he did, he saw a medal tumble onto the sofa. He picked it up to examine it and recognized it as a medal of prestige. Who was this child? And what secrets did she bring with her? His interest piqued, he surreptitiously put the medal in the pocket of his trousers and resumed removing more of the child's garments. He gently prodded the girl, trying to get some voluntary movement out of her.

"This child is unresponsive. Stetson, we must get a doctor here as soon as possible. Do you have someone we can call?"

"Only Master Shackleton's personal physician, Dr. Dunbar."

"Call him immediately and tell him we have an urgent matter and that he must come at once."

Stetson paused and looked over to Myron, who nodded his consent.

"As you wish, sir."

61

An Untold Tale

The following day, Ari remained lost in the forest. As he picked his way through the woods, the uniformity of the trees, bushes, and fallen branches made him feel as if he was in an endless maze. However, as he continued his trek, something incongruent caught his eye. He focused his attention on it until he recognized the unmistakable shape of a building.

It was a tiny cabin, hardly bigger than the shed he and his mother had lived in. It had all the telltale signs of being abandoned—rotted wood, a dilapidated roof, and overrun by weeds—but it beckoned to him. Like him, the cabin was unneeded and forgotten. It seemed a suitable place to bed down, and maybe an ideal place to call home.

Ari entered the cabin and saw a few old and dirty blankets, some empty jars and cans, and a wood-burning stove. He spent the next three days cleaning out the debris inside the cabin, reinforcing the roof with what branches he found, and collecting wood to make a fire in the cabin's stove. He used a stick to dig out a pit in front of the stove. He made the pit just big enough for him to lay in, filled it with leaves and covered it with the discarded blankets to make a bed. By the fourth day, it was as suitable a living space as he could make or need. He was able to snare a rabbit and found a stream half a mile away. As he prepared a fire to cook the rabbit, he finally had time to think.

He thought of Lena, and an intense feeling of failure and guilt came over him. He struggled to convince himself he had no other choice, so that he could drive those feelings away.

And as always, he thought of his mother. How he wished she was there to comfort him now. He might have been a man in age, but at his core, he remained a frightened boy. As a child, he imagined that when he grew older, he would be able to care for his mother and ease her burdens. Perhaps even build a modest home for her. But now he had to accept that when she needed him the most, he wasn't there for her—just as he wasn't there for Lena. If he could only speak to his mother one more time and tell her how sorry he was. Tell her how he wished she hadn't been cursed with such a useless and burdensome son. But that time had passed.

The fire from the stove warmed his face, and he thought of how similar this cold night was to all those he spent with his mother. It was nights like these that he and his mother would huddle around a fire—shielded from a cruel world—with his mother retelling another incredible tale. How he wished he could hear his mother's voice again and listen to another story. And then he remembered he could.

He reached into his pocket and took out the letter his mother had given him. Inside the still-sealed envelope there contained the last story Mariam would ever tell her son. He felt the time had come for him to hear this final tale.

He turned the envelope over and began to open it.

62

An Awakening

Upon receiving the urgent summons, Dr. Dunbar rushed to the Shackleton residence. When he saw the condition of the child, he immediately began working to reduce her fever. In this instance, being at the Shackleton estate was an advantage. The house had an infirmary and was stocked with medicine and equipment. Because of this, Dr. Dunbar had everything he would need to treat Lena. Even so, the look on the doctor's face was grim. After a few hours, despite lowering the child's fever, Lena still hadn't woken.

The doctor had the child placed in one of the guest bedrooms.

"Well, that's all I can do for her now," said Dr. Dunbar, addressing Myron and Endicott at the door to the bedroom. "Her fever is under control at the moment, but I'm afraid she's lapsed into a coma."

Endicott looked over to the bed, where Virginia was stroking the child's hand.

"Will she awaken from it?" asked Endicott.

"I believe this child has been sick for some time. I would like to give you a better prognosis, but it's possible that this child won't recover," Dr. Dunbar said.

"What are we to do with her?" asked Myron, whose question produced a piercing glance from his uncle.

"I would recommend we don't move her for now. We have everything we need to treat her here. I'll send a nurse in the morning who will take over her care. If she hasn't recovered after a few days, I'll have her transported to a hospital."

Endicott thanked the doctor, and he and Myron escorted him to the door. Before he left, the doctor turned to the two.

"We can only hope that this little girl has a fighting spirit. She will need one."

Unnoticed, Virginia had followed the men to the front door.

"Mr. Shackleton, would you allow me to stay the night and watch over the girl? I can be with her until the nurse arrives in the morning," she asked Myron.

"Very well," Myron said.

"Thank you, sir," said Virginia as she rushed back to the bedroom.

Myron and Endicott thanked the doctor and returned to the study. Instead of dining, they opted for drinking. Myron poured them each a glass of scotch.

"The child is to stay here," said Endicott, more as a directive to his nephew than a request.

"But, Uncle, wouldn't it be better if the child was taken to a hospital? And what of her parents, wouldn't they be looking for her?" Myron asked.

"What would they be looking for? A body to bury? If the child was abandoned in this condition, she was given over willingly to death. No, she is going to stay here. This child will be given a chance to fight for her life. She will not be abandoned again," said Endicott as he downed the scotch in one gulp and slammed the glass on the table.

The following day, word of the sick child spread throughout the estate. Each member of the staff stopped by the room to look in on the child. Those inclined toward religion prayed for her; others hoped the care she was receiving would result in a full recovery.

After a day, Lena was moved to one of the larger upper-floor bedrooms, just down the hall from the master suite. Virginia brought her baby blanket from home to cover the child. Martin, the stableman, hung a horseshoe over the child's bed. The housekeepers, Martha and Beatrice, were both devout Christians and placed a cross on the end table. Guy, the house chef, brought warm milk and chicken soup each day and put it on a table near the child in case she awoke. Henry, the maintenance man, built her a dollhouse and set it at the foot of her bed. And Plato, the groundskeeper, brought two vases of daisies and placed one on either side of the child's bed.

When someone asked what they should call the child, Virginia suggested the name Lena, and the staff immediately started referring to the sick girl by that name.

As the days passed, the word from Dr. Dunbar continued to be discouraging. He felt the longer the child stayed in the coma, the less likely she was ever to awaken, and he feared the child had probably already suffered permanent neurological damage. The news seemed to cast a shadow over the house. The staff went about its work as usual, but no one could deny the collective cloud of gloom that hung over their heads.

The only one detached from the child's plight seemed to be Myron. He found the child's presence in the house a disruption, and if he had it his way, would have had her removed, but his uncle forbade it. Endicott took a personal interest in the child, and he insisted that he and Myron would see this child through to her ultimate fate—whatever that may be.

"If you can spend time and fortune on colorful canvases to hang in empty rooms, then you can spare some resources for a child's life. You will find it far more rewarding. And if not, then you'll have to ascertain what evolutionary line you've descended from, because it would most certainly not be that of human," said Endicott, mincing no words to his nephew.

Four days after Lena's arrival, Myron was dressing for a business meeting when he heard a soft murmur come from the child's room. He peeked his head out of his bedroom but didn't see anyone else on the upper floor. He slowly made his way to Lena's bedroom and peered in.

"I'll be damned," he said.

Myron walked down the stairs and out to the back patio, where Stetson was serving Endicott tea. Plato was just off the patio cleaning up leaves, and Virginia was returning from the stables with some buckets of soil. It was Virginia who saw Myron first, and she dropped the buckets and let out a scream. Everyone swiveled toward Virginia, then followed her eyes to the back of the patio.

And there on the deck stood Myron, holding a wide-eyed little girl in his arms.

63

The Halls of Camelot

"Truly, it's a miracle. Besides being a little weak, which is to be expected, this child seems to be perfectly healthy," said Dr. Dunbar as he finished checking Lena's vitals.

"Good news indeed!" said Endicott. "Thank you for all you have done for her, Doctor. You have my deep gratitude."

"I think the credit should go to that little girl, who had more fight in her than any of us thought. And everyone here for taking such quick action," said Dr. Dunbar. "Have the authorities been notified?"

"They have, and we'll be meeting with them this afternoon," Endicott said.

"Very good. I'll be back to check on the girl over the next couple of weeks, but if there's anything you need, please contact my office," said Dr. Dunbar.

Later that day, the police arrived to meet with Myron, Endicott, and the entire staff. The purpose was to determine who this child was and from where she came. The most intense questioning was saved for Virginia, who was the only one with any tangible information. Since she had initially misrepresented the story of finding the child, she was too frightened to change her story now, so she stubbornly held to the version of finding the child alone and abandoned by the creek.

With no real leads, the only option the authorities had was to make the child a ward of the state. Endicott asked if the child could remain with them until the process was completed, a request that was granted no doubt due to the power and the influence of the Shackletons.

For her part, Lena seemed to adjust to her new environment nicely. After a week, her appetite returned, and Guy found himself with constant pots of soups and noodles on the stove. She was particularly drawn to Myron, whom she'd run to when she felt overwhelmed by the people around her. She'd crawl onto his lap and cling to him tightly like a baby panda. Perhaps it was because his was the first face she saw when she awoke, but for whatever reason, he seemed to be a source of security for her.

Myron wasn't certain how to respond to the child's attachment. After all, he was a man who had never been around children and who had never quite figured out the purpose for these little creatures. However, feeling his uncle would disapprove of anything other than a gentle interaction with the child, Myron would awkwardly comfort Lena until his uncle was no longer looking, at which point he would try to nudge her away.

It was just shy of a month since Lena arrived at the house when the state told Myron they would soon be ready to place her in an appropriate orphanage. He welcomed the news and looked forward to the house returning to its orderly structure. His uncle was also preparing to depart, this time to the Yucatan peninsula, to meet up with a renowned archaeologist and explore newly found Mayan ruins. On his last evening at the mansion, Endicott once again joined Myron in his study to share a drink.

"So that's it. Our little adventure seems to have come to an end. I'll be on my way in the morning. The child has her health back and will be taken away soon. And you will be able to once again dedicate your energies fully to business," Endicott said.

"It appears so. Everything is back to normal in its own way," Myron said.

"Yes, normal indeed," Endicott said. "But there is some appeal in abnormality. The laughter of a child and the patter of little feet have their pull."

"Perhaps to some."

"My dear boy, don't think that I'm so proud that I don't appreciate the differences in all of us. I know this past month wasn't easy for you. You're a lot like your father—blindly ambitious. Once he set his sights on a goal, all his energies were devoted to it until it was achieved. That's how he became a wealthy man. That's how he married your mother. I see that in you as well, and, like him, it's the reason for your success. And I know, only too well, that this type of single-mindedness does not have time for the whims of a child," Endicott said.

"Dear Uncle, I apologize if I ever seemed indifferent to the child. You were right, of course; our duty was to make sure the child recovered. Now I believe the best thing for her is to be placed in a suitable home," Myron interrupted.

"No, no, my boy, you misunderstand. I only mention this to let you know that your father loved you. I thought I knew my brother well. His every mood, his every nuance, his capacity to love and hate. But then I saw him when he first held you, and I realized I had much to learn about my brother—that I had much to learn about love. It was then that I saw the magic of a child. I never saw my brother more alive than at that moment. And for the only time in my life, I looked upon my brother with envy.

"I'm proud of you for seeing this child through. I'm sure she'll find a suitable home, but this home might suit her as well as any. She already knows its halls. And you've achieved so much in your life that I would hate for you to have reason to envy another. Good night, my dear boy."

Endicott walked out of the study to retire to his room, leaving Myron alone with his thoughts. Myron drank his last gulp of scotch and shook his head. It was clear to Myron why his uncle had devoted his life to unearthing man's more romantic past—his uncle was hopelessly quixotic. But to Myron, there was a reason these civilizations were relegated to antiquity, why their peoples were forgotten. It was due to this very belief in fanciful ideals, their foolish commitment to chivalry that left them weak and vulnerable. He knew the only thing that could sustain man was power and wealth. That was to be the business at hand. It was to be his life's work—cold, determined, and so beautifully unromantic.

———

Vartan eventually made it out of Turkey through the northern passages and settled in the Black Sea city of Sochi, Russia, alongside other Armenian refugees. He spent two years living and working as an independent groundskeeper and laborer—maintaining the vacation homes of Russia's ruling class.

Vartan cursed every second he wasn't searching for his daughter. Nothing else mattered to him anymore. His entire family, except for his daughter, had been wiped away. She was the only link he had to love; she was the only reason to go on living. He told himself he would find her one day, even if it meant knocking on every door in America.

He tried not to imagine her suffering. He convinced himself that Ari—someone he looked upon as a weak and incapable man—would somehow take care of his daughter long enough for him to arrive.

He saved as much money as he could, waiting for World War I to end so that he would be free to travel and he could begin his journey to America. Shortly after the end of the war, Vartan's patience and persistence paid off, and he was granted a working visa to France—putting him just an ocean away from his destination.

In his apprenticeship with Taniel, Vartan had learned to speak multiple languages because, as Taniel said, "Understanding builds trust, trust builds relationships, and relationships build business." Taniel would spend one entire day speaking to Vartan in a different foreign tongue. Mondays were Russian, Tuesdays French, Wednesdays German, Thursdays Spanish, and Fridays English. To make Vartan learn the languages faster, Taniel would refuse to answer any question unless Vartan asked it in the day's proper tongue. If he didn't know the right words, he would have to look them up in the various dictionaries Taniel had on hand. Although frustrating at the time, Vartan was now thankful for Taniel's stubbornness, because his grasp of so many languages had served him well, and it promised to make the search for his daughter easier.

Through his association with other Armenians in Paris, Vartan got a job as a concierge and operations manager for an exclusive Parisian hotel. His knowledge of so many languages immediately made him an asset to the hotel—allowing Vartan to respond to any issues or requests directly with the foreign guests.

It would take three years of working in France before he was finally able to secure the proper paperwork to emigrate to the United States. His big break would come from a man named Hershel Whitney, who was a wealthy land developer from America. Hershel vacationed in France once a year, and Vartan eventually got to know him.

Hershel appreciated Vartan's attention to detail and, when he learned that Vartan was interested in coming to America, offered to help him. Hershel offered to expedite Vartan's emigration to America if he would agree to accept his offer to be the chief groundskeeper for one of his properties in New England. Vartan asked him if New England was close to Boston.

"Yes, you could say that." Hershel laughed. "Very close, as a matter of fact."

64

A Fire from Within

Due to administrative issues, the state delayed the date to come and get Lena by two weeks. While the child remained in the house, Stetson gave Virginia primary responsibility for her. Stetson's only firm mandate was that she keep the child away from Myron so that "the child would cause the master no further inconvenience," as he put it.

Virginia was happy to watch Lena. She was a nurturing person by nature, but she felt an even deeper connection to, and responsibility for, this child. She was the only one who knew the truth—that she didn't accidently find Lena, but that the child had been entrusted to her hands. She didn't feel that she was the one who saved this child's life. That distinction went to the Shackletons and Dr. Dunbar. She was just thankful that she hadn't failed in what small role she played.

Lena was a far cry from the sick child who was brought to the mansion. She was now full of energy and nonstop motion. She wanted to explore every nook and cranny of the house, and it was all Virginia could do to keep up with her. Virginia's only reprieve was when she would lay Lena down for her midday nap.

One day, after laying the child down, Virginia made her way to the kitchen to help Guy. As she passed the study, she saw Myron poring over stacks of paperwork and Stetson escorting an unknown man into the study.

"They want how much!? Tell those sons of bitches we had agreed to a price, and I'm not paying one red penny more," Virginia heard Myron yell to the man.

Virginia couldn't help but smile. Myron bellowing with outrage was merely part of the natural sounds of the home, and in a way, it was comforting to hear it again.

Inside the office, the conversation continued.

"How the hell can they just change the terms like that? I was just going over the contract, and I was about to sign the damn thing," said Myron as he made his way to the liquor cabinet.

The man Myron was addressing was his chief negotiator, James Tellynson, and the topic of the day was finalizing a national transportation agreement with a major train company to ship product throughout the United States.

"They said the demands of their business have changed and can't hold firm on the price. In the end, if we don't use the railway, it'll cost us twice as much," said James as he followed Myron to the back of the study.

Myron grabbed a bottle of scotch but then thought better of it and instead opted for vodka. He poured himself a generous glass and drank it with one swallow.

"Look, I know how much it'll cost us if we don't use the railway, but an agreement is an agreement. What could have changed from now to when we talked to them?"

Myron's agitation continued to grow as he listened to James's reply, so much so that he poured himself another shot of vodka and quickly gulped that down, too. As he did, he caught something out of the corner of his eye. He looked across to the bookshelf on the other side of the room. To his surprise, he saw Lena climb onto a chair and pull his tattered teddy bear off the shelf.

An already aggravated Myron felt an even greater surge of anger as he marched over to the bookshelf. Myron approached Lena as she was sitting on the chair and smiling at the teddy bear she was holding.

"What do you think you're doing with that, you little vermin?" said Myron as he grabbed the bear to take it away from Lena.

To his surprise, the child gripped it tightly, refusing to let it go. Still holding on to half the bear, he looked down at Lena and saw her glowering back at him with stabbing eyes and clenched teeth.

"Why you little . . ." began Myron before ripping the bear out of the child's grasp.

Once he had it in his hands, he looked at the bear to see if the ragged doll had suffered any further insult to its appearance. As he was inspecting it, he didn't notice Lena had stood up on the chair. He felt something strike his shoulder. He turned his head slightly to see Lena, with the same angry look on her face, rear back and slap his shoulder again.

"Lena!" exclaimed Virginia as she burst into the room to witness the child in the middle of assaulting her employer. "I'm sorry, sir. I just lost track of her for a second. She didn't know any better."

Virginia, who was followed into the study by Stetson, wasted no time in grabbing Lena into her arms and away from Myron.

"I beg your pardon, sir. The child was not to disturb you. Virginia will remove her immediately," said Stetson, motioning to Virginia.

As Virginia carried Lena out, Myron noticed the child still glaring at him with a simmering fury.

"I will ensure the child doesn't disturb you again. My apologies," said Stetson.

"Yes, yes," replied Myron, who still had the image of the angry child in his head.

Myron looked down at the teddy bear and smoothed over its fur with his hand. He didn't realize how long he was looking at the stuffed animal until he heard James clear his throat.

"Is everything okay, sir?" James said.

"Yes, yes. Of course," replied Myron as he collected himself and put the teddy bear back on the shelf and turned toward James and Stetson.

"It's just that children mustn't just grab things," he said to his two companions. "One day it's a useless teddy bear, the next it'll be fine china. Nothing good will ever come of it. No matter how much they fuss."

"Should we get back to business?" James asked.

"I think we're finished with this business; I have some other work that I need to attend to. Tell the railroads we will only accept the terms that have been negotiated," said Myron as he sat at his desk.

He waited for James and Stetson to leave and then opened the bottom drawer of his desk and took out a skinny leather photo album. He opened the album to the first page. The page contained three photos, individual pictures of his father and mother and a picture of his parents on their wedding day. He noted how young his parents looked. He examined his father first and couldn't deny how much he resembled him. Then he looked at his mother and for the first time noticed how innocent his mother looked and how beautiful she was.

Myron turned the page and saw a picture of himself as a toddler sleeping in his mother's arms and his father sitting next to them. Both of his parents were looking at him in the picture with such joy that it took him aback for a second. He noticed he was snuggling his teddy bear as he slept. He couldn't help but feel that the picture looked so full, its two dimensions somehow filled with emotion, beauty, and peace.

He set the picture book back in the drawer and walked to the bookshelf and took down the teddy bear. He stared at it for a second and then squeezed it in his hands. He brought it to his nose, closed his eyes, and inhaled its familiar smell.

He walked out of the study with the teddy bear and ran into Virginia in the hallway.

"Virginia, where's the child?"

"Sir, my apologies again. She didn't know any better. I'll make sure she never disturbs you again. You can blame me. It was my fault and no one else's that she wandered into your study."

"I'm not upset with you, Virginia. I understand you're busy, and having to watch a child isn't easy and probably not fair to you."

"I don't mind, sir, truly. I'll just do better. You have my word."

"Of course, Virginia, I have no doubt of that. But where is the child now?" Myron asked.

"I laid her down for a nap, sir."

"Can you take me to her?"

"Sir?"

"Take me to the child. As you know, we have made arrangements for her to be placed in an orphanage and there will be people coming tomorrow to collect her. I would very much like to see her now."

"Ye-yes, sir," stammered out Virginia as she led Myron to Lena's bedroom.

The pair walked into the bedroom and over to Lena's crib. Myron looked in and saw a drowsy Lena sucking on a bottle of milk. He saw her looking up at him with sleepy, disinterested eyes.

"You can leave us, Virginia," said Myron, still looking at Lena.

"Are you sure, sir? I'll be happy to stay if you need me for anything," replied a confused Virginia.

"No, no. We'll be fine. Please leave us."

"Yes, sir," said Virginia.

Once Virginia walked out of the room and closed the door, Myron lifted the teddy bear to show it to Lena. The child's eyes grew wider, and she sat up and reached for the bear. Myron handed it to her and watched as she hugged it. She then lay back down, put her bottle back in her mouth, and slowly drifted off to sleep.

Myron continued to watch Lena sleeping with the teddy bear until he noticed how quiet the room had become. He looked around at the spacious bedroom, with its furniture removed and its walls stripped of their paintings. In fact, the only thing in the bedroom was the tiny crib that Myron was peering into.

But oddly, it felt so full.

65

Bacchus and His Pards

The next day, a pair from the state's adoptive services, Mary Standish and her young assistant Thomas, arrived at the Shackleton estate to pick up Lena. Virginia had packed what clothes and toys, including the teddy bear, the child had accumulated since she arrived at the house. Everyone on staff had come to see the child off. However, no one was more emotional than Virginia when she saw the pair pull up to the front of the house.

Before they could take the child, Mrs. Standish met with Myron to go over some paperwork. As Virginia knelt in front of Lena and helped her into her coat, Thomas looked on.

"You will be okay, darling. These nice people are going to find a good home for you. They will . . ." Virginia was unable to finish her sentence before emotions overtook her.

Virginia rose to her feet and stifled her cry as Thomas took Lena by the hand. For her part, the child seemed unsure and a little frightened.

Myron and Mrs. Standish emerged from the study. She handed Myron her contact information, along with some other miscellaneous paperwork. Myron heard Lena begin to fuss and watched as she tried to pull away from Thomas's grasp. Myron turned back toward the woman, even as Lena wailed louder.

"Geeena, Geeena," yelled Lena as she lunged toward Virginia.

"Could you not pull on the child so roughly? Can't you see it's hurting her?" said Myron to Thomas.

"Pardon me, sir. Of course. My apologies," said a flustered Thomas.

"Well, we should be getting on our way. Thank you for your time and all you have done for the child. We will take it from here," Mrs. Standish said.

Myron shook her hand and turned toward his study. Virginia found she couldn't bear to watch Lena as she cried and struggled to break free of Thomas's grip. Virginia excused herself and ran to the kitchen. Stetson remained calm and escorted Mrs. Standish, Thomas, and Lena to the door. When they walked outside, Stetson carefully closed the door and shut out the child's cries. As he walked past the study, Myron called out to him.

"Have they left?"

Stetson entered the room to find Myron nursing a glass of scotch.

"Yes, sir."

"Stetson, you have been a loyal friend to me. Do you mind if I ask your counsel?"

"Not at all, sir."

"Do you think I did the right thing?"

"Sir?"

"With the child? Do you think I did the right thing just now?"

"I do, sir."

"This house is no place for a child," Myron continued. "What do I know about raising a child? She would be unattended and uncared for. I did the child a service just now. She will have a home more suitable for her."

"Indeed, sir."

"Thank you, Stetson."

"Will there be anything else, sir?"

Myron finished his glass of scotch before answering.

"No, that is all. You're a good friend, Stetson."

Stetson tipped his head and exited the study. Myron stayed behind to finish his bottle of scotch. With the scotch gone, Myron opened a bottle of wine and wasted little time in finishing it up as well.

The Romans worshipped Bacchus as the god of winemaking, of libation, and perhaps not ironically, he was also the god of epiphany. Somewhere, while indulging in drink, a man is stripped to his very essence, and through the haze of the wine, clarity emerges.

Something began to tear at Myron, and he felt as if the wine was some cunning agent, bent on suppressing reason and rationality, designed to evoke useless emotion. In frustration, he threw the wine glass into the fireplace. He stumbled to the sofa, lay down, and forced himself to sleep off the haze. When he awoke hours later, night had fallen, and the haze of the wine was gone, but the clarity it brought wasn't.

He called for Stetson.

"Please fetch my car," Myron told his servant.

"Sir, it is late. If there is anything you need that cannot wait until the morning, I can have it sent for you," Stetson said.

"No, Stetson. This is something I must do myself."

"Very well. I will see if I can find a driver, sir."

"That won't be necessary. I'll drive myself."

"Sir?"

"Please, Stetson, no need to call anyone. I'm capable of driving my own automobile. Please just have it brought to the front."

"As you wish."

In minutes, a silver Pierce-Arrow was brought to the front of the house. Myron jumped into the car, checked the address on Mrs. Standish's card, and began driving. He reached the orphanage in just over an hour.

It was eleven o'clock at night and the three-story brown brick building was dark when he rapped on the door. Eventually an elderly man answered, identifying himself as Charles O'Sullivan—the director of the orphanage. Myron explained who he was and why he had come.

The man let him in and woke Mrs. Standish, who was staying at the orphanage while Lena got acclimated. After speaking with Myron, she told the director to take him to Lena's room. O'Sullivan led Myron upstairs and took him to a long room filled with twenty beds of sleeping children and an additional line of ten cribs at the end.

O'Sullivan guided Myron to one of the cribs. He looked in and saw Lena clutching the teddy bear with a look of fear in her eyes. Myron leaned into the crib, and Lena jumped up and hugged Myron around the neck. He could feel her trembling as she clung tightly to him—her soft cheek pressed against his. He hugged her back, even more firmly than she hugged him, as he lifted her from the crib.

"Come, Lena, it's time to go home," Myron whispered.

66

Immaculate

"Virginia, I understand that Martha has invited a preacher to come speak to the staff this afternoon," said Myron, who was finishing breakfast with a now seven-year-old Lena. "Even though I'm not personally inspired by these superstitions, I've been advised by some that being a good father should include exposing my daughter to religion. Could you see to it that Lena attends the sermon? Stetson and I will be out this afternoon."

"Of course, sir. It would be my pleasure. Would you care for anything else, miss?" said Virginia as she picked up the plate in front of Lena.

"No, thank you . . . miss," said Lena with an impish smile. "Father, I finished my breakfast. May I be excused?"

"Certainly, darling."

Lena got up and walked over to Myron, who was reading the newspaper, and gave him a hug. Myron smiled and kissed her forehead.

Lena scampered down the hallway and into the kitchen. Virginia was at the sink readying to clean the dishes, and Martha was stocking the refrigerator. Lena tugged on Virginia's dress.

"And what is it that you want, young lady?" asked Virginia, looking down at Lena.

"I wanted to see if I could help you."

"Now, now, run along, young lady, and mind yourself. What would your father say if he saw you cleaning in the kitchen?" Virginia said.

"Oh, let the child help you. It would do her some good," interjected Martha from across the kitchen. "My father would always say, 'No one ever died from work.' What you should be worrying about is idle hands."

"Yes, miss, let me help," said Lena.

"Are you sassing me, young lady?" Virginia said.

"You call me miss, so I can call you miss."

"I will give you miss all right. You are lucky you're so darn cute, otherwise I would give you what my mother gave me when I sassed her. A paddle on the bottom," said Virginia.

"Most certainly! Spare the rod, spoil the child, I always says," said Martha to Lena. "You will learn 'bout that when the preacher comes today, darling. He will have all sorts of stories about Moses, Jesus, and the Blessed Virgin Mary."

"Can I ask the preacher why they call her the Virgin Mary? Cause Plato said that Mary wasn't a virgin," said Lena.

"He said what!?" exclaimed Martha. "You never mind that treacherous sinner and his slithering words. He is fallen and in need of savin', although I'll wager even our ever-loving Lord might have washed His hands of him. Not a virgin indeed!"

Martha went back to stocking the refrigerator, while Virginia finished cleaning the last of the dishes.

"I'll finish tidying up the kitchen in a bit. Let's go see if we can find something pretty for you to wear for when the preacher arrives," Virginia said to Lena.

"Can I be as pretty as you?" Lena said.

"What did I tell you about sassing me? Just cause you're the lady of the house doesn't mean you don't have to mind your manners."

"But I want to be pretty like you," said Lena as she hugged Virginia around the waist.

Virginia took Lena by the hands and crouched down to look at her.

"Oh, honey, you're a lot prettier than I could ever hope to be. You have a beautiful chin, a beautiful nose, a beautiful smile, beautiful cheeks, and beautiful eyes," said Virginia, touching each feature as she counted it off. "But mostly because you have a beautiful heart. And that shines through every part of you."

"You have a beautiful heart too," said Lena as she pointed to Virginia's chest. "And I want to be just like you when I grow up."

"You're a silly, silly girl. And one day you will know just how silly you are." Virginia laughed as she gave Lena a hug.

67

The Magic Goblet

"Uncle Endicott!" screamed Lena when she spotted her great-uncle getting out of his car in the driveway.

Lena, now nine years old, ran to Endicott and jumped into his arms. He had been away for more than two years, sailing throughout the Mediterranean Sea and spending time off the coast of Portugal, following one lead after another, exploring every theory in search of the most tantalizing of all mysteries—Atlantis.

Before he left, he'd promised Lena that he would write to her every month. She would wait for his letters with the anticipation of a Christmas morning. When she would receive a letter, she would run to her father's study so she could read it to Myron. She stood in front of a two-foot-diameter globe as she read and looked for the places the letter described. The previous spring, as Lena was reading Endicott's latest exploits to Myron, the letter ended with:

My dear Lena, the world is far larger and more exciting than you can possibly imagine from the perspective of your Pennsylvania porch. I would like very much for you to join me this summer, so that I may share with you some of the majesty of God's creation that my humble eyes have beheld.

Lena jumped with excitement. She had never traveled anywhere other than Pennsylvania and New England, and the chance to join her great-uncle on an adventure was something that she always dreamed of doing.

"Father, could I please go?" she eagerly asked Myron.

"My dear, I'm not sure that's possible. I can't be away for the entire summer, and there is work here that will prevent me from leaving even for a few weeks. Perhaps some other time."

"Please, Father. I could go with Virginia."

"I don't know, dear. Virginia has duties here as well, and she has parents she has to care for."

"But if she will do it, will you let me go? Please, Father, I would very much like to go. Please."

Myron found it increasingly harder to say no to his daughter as she grew older and began exhibiting more independence. And even though he had reservations about his daughter traveling abroad without him, he still didn't want to disappoint her. After carefully considering it, he finally relented.

"Very well, if Virginia will accompany you, you may go, but only if she goes with you," Myron said.

Lena ran to her father and gave him a hug and kissed his cheek.

"Thank you, Father," said Lena as she turned and ran out of the study screaming, "Virginia, Virginia!"

Virginia and Lena spent the entire summer with Endicott, and just as her great-uncle promised, she saw breathtaking sights. From the stunning cliffs of North Africa to the blue harbors of the Greek Isles, nature put on a display throughout the summer that filled Lena with awe and wonder.

Before Lena headed home, Endicott promised that if he found any traces of a lost civilization, he would smuggle her home an artifact. It was a gift she hoped she would receive more for what it would mean to her uncle than anything else.

"Did you find Atlantis?" Lena asked Endicott as the two walked to the door.

"No dear, I'm afraid she remains as elusive as ever, but I did bring you something remarkable. Let's go inside, and I will show you."

Stetson arranged for Endicott's belongings to be brought to his room, and Endicott and Lena settled down on a sofa in the living room. Endicott put his satchel on his lap while Lena bounced with excitement.

Endicott reached into the satchel and brought out a decorative jade-green goblet. The chalice was encrusted with a depiction of a bearded man entwined in vines.

"What is it?" Lena asked.

"It's a goblet that is fifteen hundred years old. The figure on the goblet is King Lycurgus of Thrace, and the scene is depicting his madness. But what it really is, is magic! Come with me," said Endicott as he walked over to a window.

He put his back to the window and instructed Lena to stand in front of him. He slowly pivoted to let the light from the window hit the goblet, and when it did, the jade-green glass turned blood red.

"How did it do that?" Lena asked.

"We don't know."

"It's beautiful. Did you really bring that for me?"

"Of course I did. We discovered three of them in our excavations, and I was determined to keep one so I could give it to you. Do you like it?"

"Oh, I love it! Thank you, Uncle," said Lena as she hugged Endicott.

Endicott smiled as he handed the goblet over. He got as much joy from watching the wonder on her face as Lena did looking at the goblet. There was something special about holding an object no one else had or even knew about. He let her revel in the moment for a little longer, and then his mood became more serious.

"I have one other thing for you, my dear girl. It's something of yours that I have held on to for too long. I think it's time to give it back to you."

Endicott led Lena back to the sofa. He reached into the inside pocket of his jacket, pulled out a medal shaped like a star, and handed it to Lena.

"What's this?" asked Lena.

"That, my dear, is the Order of Osmanieh. It is a medal of honor given in Turkey," Endicott replied.

"Why did you say you had to give it back to me?" she asked in confusion.

"When you were brought here those many years ago, you were very sick, burning with heat. I did what little I could to get your fever down. You were wrapped in a blanket, and when I undid it, that fell out," said Endicott, pointing to the medal.

Lena stared at the medal. She had been told as much as her father knew about her past—that she was abandoned in the forest and that Virginia had fortuitously stumbled upon her and rushed her to the mansion.

Lena looked up at her uncle, unsure what to say.

"You should know that that medal is a prestigious honor," he said. "Whoever had it must have valued it greatly, and it was no accident that it was left with you."

Lena returned her gaze to the medal, expressionless. As she grew older, she noticed more and more how different she looked than her father and uncle. The men both had fair skin with lighter eyes, while she had glowing olive skin, deep raven locks, and sparkling brown eyes.

"My dear, what are you thinking?" asked Endicott cautiously.

"Does this mean I'm Turkish?"

"No, it means you're a Shackleton," Endicott said.

Lena walked to her room still under the spell of the mesmerizing goblet that her uncle had presented her. Without taking her eyes off the goblet, she walked into her bedroom and kicked the door closed behind her. As she walked to the window, she absently tossed the medal on her bed.

Lena spent the next hour opening and closing the curtains of her bedroom window, watching the goblet change from green to red. She most likely would have spent the entire day looking at the chalice and dreaming up its story, but a knock on her door reined her imagination back in.

"Come in," she said.

"Lena, time for dinner," Virginia said. "Please wash up and join your father and uncle in the dining room."

"Thank you. I'll be right down."

Virginia closed the door behind her, and Lena set the goblet on top of her dresser and gave it one last look. As she turned and walked past her bed, she caught sight of the medal resting on it. She picked up the medal, staring at it with the same expressionless look she had when Endicott first gave it to her.

She walked back to the dresser, opened the bottom drawer, set the medal inside, and covered it with scraps of paper.

68

The Guardian Devil

Heathcliff Coleridge, Myron's closest friend, was a classmate from Phillips Academy boarding school in Andover, Massachusetts.

The two became friends even though their personalities were polar opposites. Myron was a no-nonsense student who saw little reason for activities that weren't academically related. By contrast, Heathcliff didn't miss an opportunity to indulge in the less constructive aspects of adolescence. The two seemed to balance each other out. Heathcliff got Myron out of his social shell, and in return, Myron helped Heathcliff do enough schoolwork to keep expulsion at bay.

Heathcliff's carefree ways followed him into adulthood. He moved to San Francisco to oversee the western expansion of his family's banking business, and with the looks of a movie star and the wealth of a baron, he quickly earned the reputation of a playboy. Myron would be as likely to read about Heathcliff's romantic exploits on the scandal pages as he would be his banking successes in the business papers. Yet through it all, they remained close friends, and when Myron adopted Lena, he asked Heathcliff if he would be her godfather, and his old friend agreed.

Whenever he came back east, Heathcliff would carve out some time to drop in on his old classmate. It was one of those occasions, and Stetson was serving Myron, Heathcliff, and Lena lunch in the dining room.

Lena was fourteen years old, and she was growing into her beauty. Even though Lena had no way of knowing, she was a picture of her mother—especially her sparkling brown eyes that were set just above the cheekbones of a fashion model. She had grown to her full height of five feet, seven inches—long, thin, and naturally graceful. She was at an age where she felt she needed to put aside the frivolities of youth, despite their persistent pull, and become a lady.

The three dined amid stories of Myron and Heathcliff's time at Phillips Academy and the mischief they would get into. Myron had to cut lunch short to attend a business meeting he couldn't reschedule.

"Ah, the same old Shackleton, I see," said Heathcliff as he, Myron, and Lena were served lunch in the dining room by Stetson. "I thought having a daughter would soften you a bit, but you can't help yourself. I do believe it isn't the quest for more money that has you so driven, but rather the fact that you can't stomach seeing someone else getting rich on your watch," Heathcliff said.

"May I remind you that I was unable to reschedule the meeting," said Myron. "And I see you haven't changed as well. Always ready with a dig."

"It's what I do best. No matter, it'll give me some time to spend with my goddaughter."

After Myron had excused himself, Heathcliff asked Lena if she would like to take a walk.

"I have a better idea," Lena said. "What of a horse ride through the forest? It's a lovely ride. And the forest is so peaceful."

"That sounds perfect."

Stetson left the pair as they finished their tea, and he made his way to the kitchen, where Virginia was washing the dishes.

"Mr. Coleridge and Miss Lena would like to take the horses out for a ride. I would like you to accompany them," Stetson said.

"Did Lena request I go?"

"No, she did not. I am telling you to go."

"Sir?"

"I didn't realize I was being vague. While Mr. Coleridge is here, you are to accompany Miss Lena at all times. Am I clear?"

"Yes, sir."

Virginia stopped what she was doing and headed for the stables, just behind Heathcliff and Lena.

"Martin, could you be so kind as to ready two horses for my godfather and me?" Lena asked, addressing the burly stableman. "We would like to take a ride through the forest."

Martin nodded and turned to prepare the horses.

"Could you bring a third horse?" Virginia said to Martin and then turned to address a surprised Heathcliff. "I usually accompany Miss Lena when she rides off the property with the horses."

"Nonsense. She's in good hands. It'll give us an opportunity to catch up. I can assure you I won't take my eyes off her," said Heathcliff, smiling at Lena.

"It's all right, Virginia. We'll only be gone for a bit. I just want to show Uncle Heathcliff some of my favorite spots along the path," Lena said.

"Yes, dear, but I promised your father I would go with you when you were riding," Virginia said.

"Ah, that old croaker has always been a nervous nelly. There's nothing to worry about; we'll be back in no time," said Heathcliff, dismissing Virginia and helping Lena climb onto one of the horses Martin brought.

Fearing that she might offend their guest if she persisted, Virginia didn't push the matter any further.

Lena rode off in front, with Heathcliff following behind. They rode toward the forest and followed the riding trail in.

The sun had been hot, and the shade from the trees made for a comfortable ride, so Lena and Heathcliff let the horses prance along at a leisurely pace. It gave the two an opportunity to get reacquainted.

"How is San Francisco? I heard it's beautiful and extremely modern. Is that true?" Lena asked.

"Not as beautiful as you, my dear, but it is a lovely city just the same. You must come and visit me sometime," said Heathcliff, his eyes fixed on Lena.

Lena looked away from his glance, but she could still feel his eyes on her. After a generous pause, she looked over to him.

"I would like that very much. But father worries and is reluctant to let me travel much. I've been to Europe with Uncle Endicott, but I've traveled very little beyond that."

"Oh yes, Myron was always the type to see the danger in things rather than the excitement, but where is the fun in that?"

After riding on the path for an hour, the pair began heading back to the estate, with Lena in the lead. Just before they were to exit the forest, Heathcliff stopped his horse and dismounted in a circular clearing. Lena turned her horse around to see why Heathcliff wasn't following her.

"My dear, this is a perfect spot to take a little rest. Let's enjoy the cool air of the forest before riding back out in that torturous sun. Here, let me help you down," said Heathcliff as he offered Lena his hand.

Lena took his hand and slowly dismounted. They tied their horses, and Heathcliff led Lena to a fallen tree lying parallel to the path. Lena sat down first, and Heathcliff sat next to her, his leg pressing against hers.

Lena nervously looked away as she tried to slide along the trunk to create a little distance between the two.

"My dear girl, you have truly turned into a beautiful young woman. You'll have no shortage of suitors in the coming years if you don't have them already," said Heathcliff as he gently grabbed her chin and turned it to face him.

Something in the way he was looking at her unsettled Lena, and she wished she wasn't alone with Heathcliff.

"Thank you, I don't think boys fancy me much," stammered Lena, who placed a hand on her knee to keep it from shaking.

"Impossible. Every man appreciates beauty, especially one as rare as yours. You might have heard that I've been with many starlets, but I dare say that none compare to you," said Heathcliff as he pushed back Lena's hair and nuzzled her neck.

Lena had an impulse to scream, but for some reason couldn't bring herself to do it. She didn't understand Heathcliff's advances and no longer recognized the man. It was as if he had turned from a handsome man into a hideous one. She wanted to fight off his hands, which were aggressively grabbing her thighs and unbuttoning her top, but she was frozen.

"Please," she stammered again.

"Don't be frightened. It'll be a beautiful thing. I won't hurt you. And you'll enjoy it," said Heathcliff as he put a finger to Lena's lips.

Heathcliff began to kiss her exposed neck and ran his hand farther up the leg of Lena's riding trousers until he found the button. Lena trembled, and her eyes filled with tears. Heathcliff's kisses became more aggressive, and he started to unbutton her trousers, when Lena grabbed his hand with both of hers and tried to push it away.

"No, please don't," she said as a tear ran down her cheek.

Before Heathcliff could answer, Lena heard a yell and felt something push her off the tree trunk and onto the ground. When she gathered herself, she saw a short, bearded, hunchbacked man on top of Heathcliff. The hunchback had two handfuls of Heathcliff's perfectly groomed black hair and was desperately trying to hold down his much larger opponent. The hunchback gave Lena an urgent look.

"*Vazé!*" the hunchback yelled.

For a second, a strange feeling came over Lena. An odd sensation that was somehow familiar and comfortable—like a fleeting glimpse of some long-forgotten dream. But no sooner did the feeling come than it vanished.

She turned, leaving the two men struggling on the ground, and sprinted toward her home. This time, she found she could scream and started shouting for help.

———

Martin, Plato, Stetson, and Virginia were all in the stables waiting for the pair to return from their ride when they heard Lena's screams.

"Heathcliff . . . they're fighting . . . help!" said Lena through exhausted and panicked breaths.

"Martin, get the shotguns," ordered Plato as he and Stetson began running toward the forest. Martin fetched a pair of shotguns he kept in the stables and quickly caught up to his more senior colleagues.

Virginia held Lena, and the two cautiously followed the men into the woods.

The men arrived to see Heathcliff raining down blows on his attacker. Simply hitting his assailant wasn't enough. Heathcliff was so enraged that he grabbed the man by the throat and choked him—intent on strangling the life out of him.

"That's enough, Mr. Coleridge. We can take it from here," said Plato as he tried to pull Heathcliff off.

Heathcliff didn't seem to hear a word of it as he continued to choke his victim. Plato nodded to Martin.

The hulking stableman grabbed ahold of Heathcliff and hauled him off the man before assault graduated to homicide.

"I'll murder that filthy devil," screamed Heathcliff as he struggled to break free from Martin's grip so he could attack the barely moving hunchback again. "That animal attacked Lena and me, unprovoked. He must be dealt with."

"Mr. Coleridge, you don't have to dirty your hands any further. I assure you that we will deal with this matter," said Stetson as he stood in front of Heathcliff to calm him down.

Plato knelt in front of the hunchback, his shotgun slung over his shoulder. The man was barely conscious and was struggling to breathe. Plato sat the man upright, trying to help him get some air into his lungs. As he did, Virginia, who arrived with Lena, was able to see the man and gasped when she realized it was the same person who handed Lena to her those many years ago.

"Stetson, I want that monster shot!" Heathcliff screamed.

"Sir. This matter will be dealt with appropriately. I will see to it personally. Please let us return to the house so that we can have you cleaned up," Stetson replied.

Heathcliff calmed himself enough for Martin to let go of his hold. Heathcliff turned and walked out of the forest without looking at anyone. Stetson went over to Plato and whispered something in his ear as Martin stood watch over Ari.

Stetson approached Virginia and Lena and extended his arm to usher them out of the forest. Virginia couldn't take her eyes off the hunchback and found that she became flushed with guilt. She was the only one who knew the truth—that whatever reason the hunchback had to attack Heathcliff, it wasn't to harm Lena. She wanted to scream aloud and tell everyone who this hunchback was, but years of lies had built their prison, and truth would remain its captive.

Once they arrived at home, Virginia told Lena to go to her room and that she would come to check on her shortly. She waited for Stetson to approach, and when he did, she grabbed Stetson by the arm.

"Sir, the hunchback looked so harmless and frail, you won't have that man harmed, will you?" Virginia asked.

"That is not your concern. You should have had one concern," said Stetson, casting a glance toward Lena's room. "But apparently, I wasn't clear enough."

"Sir, I beg you, please do not harm that man," Virginia said.

"Again, that matter is of no concern to you. Plato and Martin will deal with it. Now go see to Miss Lena."

"Please, sir, what did you tell Plato to do with the man?" said Virginia, still holding Stetson's arm.

The look Stetson gave Virginia reflected his growing irritation. He pulled his arm away from Virginia.

"I told him to make sure that vagrant is never seen again."

A second later, Stetson's statement was punctuated with a shotgun blast from the forest.

———

Shortly after, Stetson walked into the study, where a still agitated Heathcliff was pacing with a glass of bourbon in his hand.

"What did you do with that creature? I hope you handled it as it needed to be," said Heathcliff when he saw Stetson enter.

"He was dealt with appropriately. I can assure you of that. You need not trouble yourself any further on the matter," Stetson replied.

"No punishment is bad enough for him. He surely had his sights on Lena, and had I not been there to protect her, who knows what the beast would have done."

"Indeed, sir."

"Look at me, I'm still trembling, and I'm filthy. Can you have the staff prepare a bath? I must wash the stench of that creature off me."

"That won't be necessary, Mr. Coleridge. I have an automobile ready for you at the front. Your things have been packed and are waiting for you at the front door."

Heathcliff stopped his pacing and blinked in stunned amazement.

"What's the meaning of this, Stetson?" he asked.

"Your stay here is ended, sir. I must ask you to leave," replied Stetson, calmly.

"You must ask me to leave? I don't know what Lena has told you, but she is probably still in shock."

"I haven't spoken to Miss Lena. I am sure she needs time to calm her nerves. She has had a fright. This encounter must have been very unpleasant for her. As I am sure would be your continued presence here," said Stetson, with a more direct tone. "So, let me be clear, sir. You will leave presently and not return. You will have no contact with Miss Lena. And if you need to speak or meet with Master Shackleton, then you will contact me first."

"What? Who do you think you are?" said Heathcliff, puffing out his chest in defiance.

Stetson walked up to Heathcliff until he was only an inch away from the latter's face and stared him dead in the eye.

"You know exactly who I am and what I am capable of," Stetson said.

Heathcliff tried to return Stetson's steely glare but found he couldn't. Heathcliff looked away, cast his eyes to the ground, and walked around Stetson and out of the front door and into a waiting car.

69

Confession

Just as Stetson had instructed, Virginia stayed with Lena until she felt Lena had gotten over the scare in the woods. Seizing the first opportunity, Virginia went looking for Plato. She found the groundskeeper inside the equipment house.

"Plato, I have to speak with you. I have to know what you did to the hunchback," Virginia said.

"The feller in the woods?" Plato asked.

"Yes, what did you and Martin do to him?"

"We did what Stetson told us to. Why are you so concerned about that feller, anyway?"

Virginia began pacing and wringing her hands.

"Plato, I've done something terrible. If I tell you what it is, would you promise not to speak a word of it to Stetson or Mr. Shackleton?" Virginia said.

"What's it that you did?"

"Please promise me that you won't say a word."

"Well, that's an awfully hard thing to promise, seein' as I don't know what it is that I ain't supposed to talk about. But as long as no harm will come by it, you have my word."

Virginia stopped pacing and slowed her breath to gather herself.

"I haven't been honest about everything. I lied about finding Lena," Virginia said.

"What!? Where did the child come from?"

"She was in the forest but not abandoned like I said she was. I was coming to work that evening, and just before I got to the grounds, I ran into a man on the path. He was holding Lena, she appeared to be sick, and the man seemed to be asking for help. I couldn't understand him, but he handed me the child, and then he ran off. The man was the hunchback fighting with Mr. Coleridge."

"You shoulda told the truth," said Plato as he turned away from Virginia, walked to the window, and looked out toward the forest.

"I know, but I was young and foolish. I didn't know what Stetson or Mr. Shackleton would do. I feared they wouldn't help her, and I tried to make the situation as desperate as I could so they would help. And once I lied, and saw that she was getting help, I was too afraid to tell the truth."

"I see," said Plato, rubbing his forehead.

"Plato, please know that I'm ridden with guilt, and I would blame myself if any harm came to the hunchback. So please tell me what you did with him," Virginia said.

"Something I ain't proud of," replied Plato.

70

A Father's Quest

In the spring, Vartan boarded an ocean liner in France heading to America. He began counting the years and realized his daughter would be fourteen—no longer the child he last saw sleeping in her crib, but rather a young lady whom he had no idea if he would recognize.

During the Atlantic voyage, Vartan shared a cabin with a young Serbian, Kočo Savich, who was traveling to Canada on a work visa. Kočo lived in Vratnica, a village in the foothills of the Šar mountain range in an area known then as Southern Serbia. The two men had a lot in common. They both had lived under Ottoman rule, both were traveling to an unfamiliar land, and both had a taste for Turkish coffee. However, the purpose for their journeys was different. Vartan was traveling largely on hope, praying that he would find his daughter, while Kočo's voyage was one of duty—leaving his family farm for a construction job in London, Ontario, to provide for the wife and two small children he'd left in Vratnica.

Both men spoke English and became traveling colleagues, sharing their stories and confiding their fears to one another over cups of Turkish coffee.

"Do you have any idea where your daughter is?" asked Kočo, as he handed Vartan a small porcelain cup of freshly brewed Turkish coffee just as the sun was setting on the horizon.

"Only that she was taken to Boston. I have a job in the area, and I know other Armenians have settled there. My hope is that once I arrive, I can get to know the other Armenians in the community. Then, if I explain who I'm looking for, they might help me find her. Boston can't be that big. What about you, how long do you plan to stay in Canada?" Vartan said.

"Maybe six months to a year. If I can make money and send it home, I'll stay longer. If there is no work, I'll return sooner."

"Do you plan to move your family to Canada if there is good work?"

"If there is enough money to make a living, then I'll bring them. My children are both young. My daughter, Mitana, is five years old, and my son, Jordan, isn't yet two. If everything goes well, and I can settle in, then I'll bring them when I'm sure we can build a life."

"As a friend, I would tell you that you should always keep your family close. Let my story be a lesson to you. You're a good man. I wouldn't want you to carry the pain I've had to," Vartan said.

"God will bless us both. You will find your daughter, and I will be with my family again," said Kočo as he raised his cup of coffee.

He would only be half right.

71

Embers of Madness

Vartan's first stop in Boston was the Garden of Hesperides Country Club, a botanical wonderland sitting on 150 acres just five miles outside of Boston. Hershel Whitney, whom Vartan met in Paris, owned and operated three country clubs—one in Chicago, another in Washington, DC, and his crown jewel, Garden of Hesperides, in the greater Boston area.

The club was situated on a stunning eight-thousand-acre lake and its grounds were speckled with maple and oak trees. On the shore of the lake, the country club was outfitted with a three-story lake house, three pools, and a private beach. The perfectly manicured lawns stretched as far as the eye could see. Shrub- and flower-lined walkways guided guests from one area to the next. Members had access to a pro-level, thirty-six-hole golf course, but the club's main attraction was its beautiful gardens and orchards. The gardens radiated with dahlias of all colors, poppies, delphinium, irises, among other native and imported species. The orchards contained rows of apple trees at the back of the property, which the club would use to make and market their own brand of cider.

The massive main clubhouse was built on a hill, outlined with five terraces of yellow daffodils. Members and guests could sit on the clubhouse's front porch, which spanned the entire length of the building, and take in the property's sprawling beauty.

Vartan had never seen such opulence and, if he didn't feel the urgency to start the search for his daughter, would have most likely walked the grounds in silent awe. When he arrived, he was directed to the supply and equipment building where he was greeted by the main groundskeeper, Aurelius Staples, whose job he was about to take over. The spry eighty-two-year-old had finally been talked into retiring by his eighty-year-old wife, and it was his duty to get Vartan up to speed in a short amount of time.

"There's an awful lot to learn, but I know Mr. Whitney, and if he didn't think you could do the job, you wouldn't be here. But don't worry none, we have a fine staff here. I trained them myself, I did. Only ever had to fire one fella in all the time I been here. So, you should do fine. What you really need to learn is who everyone is, and where to go to get things done," said Aurelius.

It took Vartan weeks of shadowing Aurelius to learn all the operations of the country club. He learned how to store and manage stock, how the groundskeepers were to maintain the grass on the courses, what the gardeners needed to keep the flowers in bloom, when it was time to harvest the apples, how to fulfill cider orders, and how to maintain the daily work schedule. He was provided lodging within the staff cabin, so he didn't have the added burden of finding a place to live.

He learned that there was an Armenian church, as well as a substantial Armenian community in the nearby city of Watertown. After settling into his job, Vartan took a bus to visit the church. He met with the priest, Father Vanko, and explained his desperate search for his daughter. He described Ari and had to admit he couldn't describe his daughter because he no longer knew how she looked.

"That doesn't sound like anyone in our congregation. Are you sure they came to Boston?" Father Vanko said.

"That's what I was told. Word was sent back that they reached America and were supposed to be taken to Boston with other Armenians," Vartan said.

"We will bring this matter before the congregation and ask for everyone's help. Rest assured, my son, if they are anywhere in Boston, we will find them."

"Thank you."

The following Sunday, Vartan returned to the church, and as the faithful gathered, Father Vanko addressed the congregation.

"We have a new member to our church. His name is Vartan Kasparian, and he needs our help. He has escaped unspeakable torture and suffering at the hands of the Ottomans. He is one of the fortunate ones; he has his life. Like too many, he has lost most of his family, but his daughter survived. She was rescued and brought to America, and he has come looking for her. She is the only family he has left. So, I ask that we all, in the name of our Lord and Savior, help reunite this man with his daughter," the priest said.

The message did not go unheeded. The entire Armenian community was mobilized, and finding Lena soon became the main talk and focus of the community. But no one knew of a hunchback in Watertown, so they expanded their search and inquiries to the greater Boston area, with no results.

After a few months, word started coming in that there was a hunchback and girl in Detroit. Multiple sources claimed that they saw the pair in a Detroit church. Filled with hope, Vartan began taking trips to Detroit whenever he could. He traveled back and forth over the next three years. Each trip appeared to bring him tantalizingly closer to finding his daughter. On one trip, he was told the hunchback and girl had been to the church the week before. Another time he was told that they were seen eating at the café down the street just an hour before Vartan arrived. He was even approached by teenage Armenian girls who said they went to school with Lena briefly, but that she said she would be leaving soon and then they never saw her again.

In the end, nothing came of the sightings but disappointment and heartbreak. The only thing Vartan knew with any certainty was that Ari and Lena made it to New York, so that soon became his place of focus. But that, too, didn't yield any results. Four years passed this way, and at the end, Vartan felt he was no closer to finding his daughter now than he was when sitting in an Ottoman cell.

Instead of time easing his pain, each year became more maddening than the last. He never thought anything could match the pain he felt knowing his daughter was half a world away.

He was wrong.

========

By Christmas 1933, America's roaring twenties, carefree and excessive, had given way to the whimpering thirties—downtrodden and uncertain. The Great Depression had dimmed the lights on the country's future. The American Dream, which had long been a peasant's currency, had devolved into the American Plague. It would be a decade that would punish those who dared to dream, casting out families from their homes and into tent cities, proving how thin the line between prosperity and poverty could be.

Like many ultra-wealthy families, the Shackletons were immune to the economic downturn. Myron had been diligent in diversifying his assets, making the stock market crash more of a financial speed bump than a life-altering event. While others were struggling to maintain their wealth, Endicott, with his ever-increasing archaeological cache, saw his personal portfolio increase in value.

Just as Myron had done, Lena went off to boarding school in Boston for high school, and Myron found it impossible to be away from his daughter. Myron decided to move to Boston to be closer to Lena. He bought a mansion in the city and asked his staff if they would move with him. They all agreed.

After graduating high school, Lena enrolled at Harvard. Inspired by her uncle, she had decided to study history, with a specialty in ancient civilizations. She was now twenty years old, a second-year college student on break for the holiday.

Christmas was always a special time for her and her father, but she was particularly excited to spend this holiday at home. For the first time in years, she would have her entire family home for Christmas. Endicott was scheduled to return from an archaeological dig in Egypt, and she couldn't wait to get caught up with her uncle.

Accompanying Endicott would be a new protégé, Jonathan Fillmore, a recent graduate of Cambridge. Two years prior, Endicott traveled to England for a three-day speaking engagement at Cambridge. It was Jonathan's final year, and he decided to attend the lectures to gather information for a paper he was writing. Jonathan was so enthralled by Endicott that he approached him and asked what it would take to become an archaeologist.

"Well, my boy, first you must ask yourself if you have a taste for backbreaking labor, foreign illnesses, all varieties of discomfort, and most importantly, disappointment. If you say you do, then you are clearly mad. No further clinical diagnosis is necessary. You must then determine whether your particular strain of madness includes the belief that myths are real. If it does, then, my boy, we just might make an archaeologist of you," Endicott said.

That conversation began a correspondence between the two. A correspondence that ended when Jonathan wrote: *"As hard as I have tried, and through all thoughtful and logical exercises, I cannot shake my belief that myths are indeed real. They're just waiting for man to dig them up."*

The reply to that letter was an airline ticket to Egypt.

Lena helped Virginia set the table and reminded her that they needed an extra place setting for Endicott's guest.

"Now, why don't you let me set the table? You're the lady of the house, you should be getting ready to meet your guests, not dirtying your hands helping me," Virginia said.

"You know I like helping you, this is the only time I get to talk to you. You're always busy with one thing or another and never have time for me," Lena said.

"Darling, you know that's not true. I only came to Boston because of you. The house was cold and drab without you."

"Shhhh, now don't tell Father, but I was the one who told him to move everyone here. I love my father, but I missed you the most. Sometimes, I feel like I don't belong with all these debutantes."

"Nonsense. First off, your father was beside himself when you left. Asking me every day if there was anything in the mail from you. We knew our days in Bethlehem were short. He was talking about moving every day," said Virginia as she grabbed Lena by the shoulders to look at her. "You are a wonderful girl and have a beautiful heart. Since my parents passed away, you and this house are all I have left. So, I'll be here for you, as long as you will have me."

The two hugged.

Lena had grown into a stunningly beautiful woman. She was tall and slender and her dark hair, piercing brown eyes, and soft skin gave her the look of an Egyptian goddess.

In the spirit of the season, she wore a red-and-white Raelene dress that outlined her figure, hugging the contours of her chest and hips and tapering around her slim waist.

As they finished setting the table, the doorbell rang.

"They're here!" said Lena.

When she got to the front door, she found Stetson had already welcomed in the two men. Lena rushed past Stetson and threw her arms around her uncle.

"Uncle Endicott, I've missed you!" she said as she gave her uncle a long hug and a shower of kisses.

"My dear, you have to be gentle. Your uncle isn't a young man any longer," said Endicott as he returned her embrace. "The truth of the matter is that I've missed you greatly as well, my dear. You bring warmth wherever you are, most especially to this drab house."

"Well then why is it that you come back so infrequently?" said Lena, breaking her hug to give her uncle a disapproving look.

"Stubbornness, of course. The kind that won't let you do what you know is good for you," Endicott said. "Oh, but where are my manners? I would like to introduce a young colleague of mine. Lena, this is Jonathan Fillmore. Jonathan, this is my great-niece, Lena Shackleton."

Lena looked over at the tall and handsome man beside her uncle. She was told Endicott would bring an archaeologist, but she assumed it would be a person of some vintage and not a young man around her age.

For his part, Jonathan had been so mesmerized by Lena's beauty that he didn't realize Endicott had just introduced them, and he remained silent and unmoving as he locked eyes with Lena. Lena rescued the awkward moment by extending her hand.

"Pleased to meet you, Mr. Fillmore," Lena said.

Jonathan gathered himself and shook Lena's hand.

"The pleasure is mine, Miss, Miss . . ." a suddenly cognitive Jonathan stammered.

"Miss Shackleton." Lena laughed. "But you may call me Lena."

"Yes, of course. Miss Shackleton . . . I mean, Lena. Please forgive me. Your uncle has shown me hundreds of wondrous treasures. But some you don't expect to be so breathtaking."

Lena gave a slight smile.

"You flatter me, Mr. Fillmore," she said.

"Please, it's Jonathan. And I'm not sure I could properly."

"Very well, Jonathan," said Lena as she linked one arm with her uncle and then offered her other arm to Jonathan. "Let's go have some tea. I can't wait to hear about all the secrets of Egypt that you and my uncle have uncovered."

As the three walked arm in arm, Endicott couldn't help but feel as if he had suddenly become an interloper.

And he smiled at the thought.

72

To Heed the Heart

Vartan established himself as a capable head groundskeeper at the Garden of Hesperides Country Club. He oversaw a staff of forty full-time employees and a pool of part-time workers. His position enabled him to hire several Armenians in need, and he rescued more than one family from destitution. When he couldn't hire Armenians directly, he would recommend them to other operational groups within the country club. As a result, the Armenian immigrants began to look upon him less with sympathy and more as a benefactor. He was now a leader and respected member of the community, never mind that he felt no different from that empty father who'd begged for everyone's help so many years before.

One of the Armenians he hired was Gusan Tumasyan. Like many during the Great Depression, Gusan lost his job, and, fearing that his family would be evicted from their home, he reached out to the church. The church asked if anyone could help, and Vartan offered the man a job. It was an act of kindness that Gusan vowed to repay someday. He began by quickly becoming Vartan's best worker—showing up early, leaving late, and doing whatever was asked of him. The two became fast friends. Over the years, Gusan saw the pain and anguish Vartan carried with him, and he wished his friend would give up on the idea of finding his daughter.

One day, Gusan approached Vartan and asked him if he could introduce Vartan to a cousin of his—a single mother. Her husband was killed in Turkey—leaving her to raise their son on her own.

"What can it hurt?" Gusan had said. "It's good to have someone. Someone who'll be there with you when you're old. She's an honest, hardworking woman. She would make a good wife."

Out of respect for his friend, Vartan agreed to meet the woman after church. The woman, Nare, worked in a bakery in Watertown. She was ten years Vartan's junior and lived with her son, Emin, in an apartment above the bakery. Nare was in her late thirties. Her hands and skin carried the marks of persistent work. However, she was still an attractive woman, with soft hazel eyes and a womanly figure.

Gusan introduced the pair one Sunday after church. Sensing her nervousness and feeling it would be easier to talk alone, Vartan asked if she would like to join him for coffee.

"I'm afraid I can't, I have my son, and we must be getting home," said Nare, pointing to an adolescent boy sitting in the pews.

Before Vartan could say anything, Gusan jumped in.

"Not to worry, he can come with us and get some ice cream. You go along with Vartan," said Gusan.

"Gusan, I don't think I can," Nare protested.

"Nonsense. It would do both of you some good to spend time with adults and away from children or employees who act like children," Gusan said.

"It would only be for coffee," added Vartan, sensing her apprehension.

Nare paused, either to try to devise a better excuse or to determine if her protestations had established the proper degree of virtue in Vartan's mind. Having not been able to come up with another excuse and feeling her chastity was no longer in question, she agreed.

They walked to a nearby café and shared a cup of coffee. As the conversation continued, Vartan began to feel as if they were kindred spirits—both coping with the loss of a spouse and struggling to fit into an unfamiliar world. Despite himself, he felt attracted to her in a deeper way than he would have thought possible.

"Gusan told me you work at a bakery. Do you like it?" Vartan asked.

"Yes, the owners are a nice older couple. They are Armenian as well. They let me and my son live in the apartment above their bakery. And we always have bread to eat, so we're fortunate," Nare said.

"How is your son coping?"

"I worry about him. He's a good boy, but he's shy and doesn't have many friends. He tries to hide it from me, but I see that he cries after school sometimes. I'm told other kids pick on him and make fun of him for being poor. But he won't talk to me about it. As the years go by, he seems less and less happy, and I don't know what to do," said Nare.

"How old is he?"

"He's nine."

"Did he know his father?"

"No, he was only a baby when my husband died. His father sacrificed himself so me and our son could escape and come here," said Nare, her eyes glistening. "I still have guilt about that."

"You shouldn't," said Vartan as he cast his eyes to the ground. "Your husband was a good man. Your son should be proud to have had a father like him. Not all fathers are that selfless. I know that better than anyone. You should tell your son that."

"Thank you for saying that."

They both took a sip of their coffee. They shared a moment of silence as Nare looked out of the window and Vartan looked down at his hands.

"How are you managing?" asked Nare, breaking the awkward silence. "I know you lost your wife and daughter . . ."

"I lost my wife!" Vartan exclaimed.

"Yes, of course. I'm sorry. I misspoke. I mean no offense. I know it's difficult for you. I can understand the pain you feel. It helps to have friends," said Nare as she placed her hand on Vartan's.

Vartan cast his eyes on Nare's hand resting softly on his, which caused Nare to quickly remove it. He looked back up to Nare.

"It does help to have friends. I had no right to snap at you like that just now. I'm sorry," he said.

"No, that's okay. It was my fault."

"I've never really been any good at this. But if it wouldn't be too much of an inconvenience for you, I'd like to see you again."

"Gusan thinks a lot of you. He told me how honest you are. How good you have been to him," said Nare. "But as you know, I do have a son and I'm not the type of woman who just sees men. If you're serious, then I would be happy for you to come with me and my son to church next week."

"I would like that."

Endicott and Jonathan spent two weeks at the Shackleton estate during that Christmas. In that time, Jonathan's flirtations slowly began to be reciprocated. Lena couldn't deny that Jonathan was a handsome man—standing just over six feet tall, with a runner's physique, wavy dark hair, and intense blue eyes. And despite his charm and outward confidence, Lena sensed there was a vulnerability to him that drew her in.

One night, after Myron and Endicott had retired for the evening, Lena walked to the back solaria to enjoy a coffee when she found Jonathan sitting on a recliner with a pad of paper and a pencil.

"Mr. Fillmore, what a surprise. I thought you had gone off to bed as well," Lena said.

"No need to be so formal, *Miss Shackleton*," said Jonathan, with emphasis. "Unfortunately, I'm somewhat of a night owl. Something that puts me at odds with your uncle as he wakes up torturously early. Please join me, I could use the company."

"Well then, I'm glad I came along. Why don't you come by the window? I love looking at the moon when it is in full bloom," said Lena, walking over to a semicircle of bay windows. Jonathan walked over and stood next to her, and they both stared up at the moon.

"It's a beautiful evening. I always enjoy ending the night in this room. I love the way the moon lights up the trees in the back. It helps me to clear my mind, and the moon makes me less afraid," said Lena.

"There really isn't anything to be frightened of," Jonathan replied. "Don't tell me you're still afraid of the dark."

"Maybe just from what you can't see."

"Ahh. *Omne ignotum pro magnifico.*"

"I didn't know you spoke Latin, Mr. Fillmore."

"It was a requirement in Cambridge. Do you know what the phrase means?" Jonathan asked.

"Yes, it means that we think of the unknown as being grandiose."

"Indeed, when usually it's simply mundane or a different variety of something we're already familiar with."

"Yes, of course. I'm just being silly. As you said, there's nothing to be afraid of," said Lena as she looked away from Jonathan slightly before turning back to him again. "So, you and my uncle will be leaving in a couple of days. I hope you enjoyed your stay. I know you must be eager to return to Egypt."

"Thank you, I enjoyed my stay very much. You and your father have been gracious hosts. I hope I can repay your hospitality one day."

Lena gave Jonathan a smile as the two locked eyes briefly before Lena broke the stalemate by pointing to Jonathan's pad.

"What do you have there?" asked Lena.

"Oh this. It's nothing. I've been trying to write a sonnet, but I don't think it's much good."

"A sonnet? Could I hear it?"

"Well, only if you don't mind bad poetry."

"Is there such a thing?"

"If there wasn't before, then I'm certainly its inventor."

"Well now I must hear it," teased Lena.

"Very well. I've never actually read my poetry to anyone before, but I'll read it to you if you insist. It's called "The Race." Here it goes," said Jonathan. He cleared his throat and began to read.

At odds, the heart and mind held a contest
A race to captain a young man's spirit

Would thought and reason put the clash to rest?
Or would hunger and passion show merit?
Pure, naked, and eager to win the day
The heart sped out in shameless vanity
With a determined march into the fray
The mind chased on with tempered sanity
Sirens sang for the heart to cast its chains
And leave order and penance in its wake
The sages urged the mind to take its pains
In mores and conscience to claim the stake
    Spent, desire's breathless pace proved too great
    Prudence prevailed and love would have to wait.

Jonathan looked up from his pad and saw Lena staring out the window thoughtfully.

"I told you it wasn't very good. And I can't get the meter right. I'm afraid I just don't have the ear for it. That's why I'm still tinkering with it," Jonathan said.

"No no, it's not that at all. I think it's lovely. What made you write something like that?"

"Well, I suppose I was trying to grasp the struggle we all have with ourselves."

"What struggle is that?"

"The struggle of having the courage to do what you want to do against the wisdom of doing what you should do," he said.

"And how is that, exactly?"

"Well, we can take this moment as an example. As a guest in your father's home, what I should do is respectfully bid you good evening and retire to my room," said Jonathan as he captured Lena's eyes. "But what I really want to do is kiss you."

"Is that so, Mr. Fillmore?" said Lena, looking up at him with an unbroken gaze. "And how will your race end?"

With the light of the moon shining on them through the windows like some celestial spotlight, Jonathan brushed Lena's cheek with the back of his palm. Lena closed her eyes and nuzzled his hand.

He pulled her close and kissed her.

73

All Things Fade Away

After courting for six months, Vartan and Nare's relationship developed enough that they started talking about marriage. It was decided that Nare would live with her son in their bakery apartment until Vartan found and purchased a suitable home, at which point the three of them would move and the couple could officially be wed.

One day, Nare and her son, Emin, came to see Vartan at the Garden of Hesperides Country Club after work. She prepared a picnic, and the three made it to the beach to enjoy the sunset on the lake.

"Thank you for coming to see me," said Vartan as he ate a slice of sausage.

"You always talked about how beautiful the sunset was here. I wanted to finally see it. This is such an amazing place. Do you ever get tired of it?" said Nare as she sat with one of her arms locked with Vartan's.

Vartan kissed her forehead. "It's work. We can all get tired of work. But it is beautiful, and even more beautiful now with you here," he said.

Emin was running on the beach, playing with his soccer ball. He looked at Vartan and his mother and kicked the ball at Vartan with a smile. Vartan caught the ball.

"Vartan, come play with me before it gets too dark," said Emin as he ran up to the couple.

"Go run along, Emin. Vartan just finished working, let him have a little peace and rest," his mother said.

"It's okay. I could use the exercise. Give me a few minutes, Emin, and I will be out there," said Vartan as he threw the ball down the beach.

Emin raced after the ball and started dribbling it.

"He really loves that ball. Thank you for buying it for him and for getting him to join the church team. It's like he's a different boy now. He's always outside playing and practicing, and it has helped him make friends. It warms my heart to see him so happy," Nare said.

"He's a good boy. A German taught me the game. He was a good friend, and he said sharing in sport was a gift. I never knew what he meant, until now. And Emin is very good. A lot better than I ever was," Vartan said.

"So, you didn't score many goals?" Nare laughed.

"No, but I did hit a girl in the face with the ball once."

"No you didn't!"

"I did," said Vartan with a nod of the head and a subtle laugh.

"Oh, she must have hated you."

"You would think so, but no, no she didn't."

As Vartan finished his meal, he stared down the nearly deserted beach. Only one other family was left, and he watched as the man—presumably the father—cast a fishing line into the water from one of the docks on the north end of the beach.

As the sun sank beneath the horizon, the man gathered up his gear, and he and what seemed to be his wife and young daughter prepared to leave. Vartan thought the girl looked about six years old. When the family neared Vartan and Nare, the father scooped his tired daughter off the sand. A long day in the sun had taken its toll on the young girl, and she rested her head on her father's shoulder and fell asleep.

Vartan watched as the child instinctively clung to her father as she slept. He noticed how securely the father held her as he treaded through the sand. Vartan kept his eyes on the girl as she and her family made their way up the beach and began to fade into the dusk.

"Vartan, are you coming?" yelled Emin from a distance.

"Yes, coming," said Vartan.

Before Vartan got up to join Emin, he looked back in the direction of the family, but there was no one there.

The child was gone.

=====

When Jonathan left for Egypt, he promised to write Lena. Even though the pair corresponded regularly, Jonathan now found it difficult to concentrate on his work, and after six months he had come to a crossroads, which he explained to Lena in a letter:

We are in the midst of a massive dig that promises to unearth treasures not seen for millennia, but I find that I can only think of you. It is as if I have been overcome by some mighty and irresistible force, and I find it harder to be apart from you more and more every day.

Having fallen into this state, I fear I am becoming less of an asset and more of a burden to your uncle. And I know I must commit to giving myself fully to either Egypt or to you. If not, I risk losing the confidence of a mentor and a friend, something that would cause me great distress.

I would like you to know that I have given my circumstance a great deal of thought and do not feel torn any longer. They say that Egypt is the great seducer of men. But I find her abrasive sands do not compare to your soft skin. Her mysteries not as alluring as your smile. Her monuments not as wondrous as your tender lips.

I now know where my treasure lies and where I must go to find it.

A month later, Jonathan arrived in America. Lena was there to greet him at the airport and rushed through a crowd to embrace him. She held him tight and refused to let him go.

"Please don't leave me again. I tried to put on a brave posture, but I couldn't stand not being with you. I love you like I have never loved anyone else. Promise me you will not abandon me again," Lena said.

"Neither God nor man could ever take me from your arms again. I promise you that," he said.

Jonathan enrolled in a post-graduate program at Harvard, where Lena was finishing her undergraduate work.

They both agreed that before getting married, they would travel. They spent the next two years journeying to China, India, Australia, South Africa, and South America. They returned home for Christmas of 1938, at which time Jonathan asked Myron for Lena's hand in marriage. An emotional father gave his consent.

Jonathan took Lena to the solaria in her father's house. And in front of the bay window where they shared their first kiss, he dropped to a knee and presented her with a ring.

"If there ever was a race, it has long been settled. There's no dispute between heart and mind. Both want you as my wife. Would you do me that honor?" Jonathan said.

"Yes!" Lena beamed.

The wedding was to take place the following Christmas. However, on September 1, 1939, Adolf Hitler and his Nazi army invaded Poland. Two days later, Britain declared war on Germany. Two weeks after that, Jonathan, a licensed pilot, received a telegram from his homeland. It read:

As an able-bodied citizen of Britain, you are hereby summoned by His Majesty to return home posthaste to be conscripted into His Majesty's Royal Air Force.

Europe had once again plunged into war, and weddings would have to wait.

74

The Battle of Britain

By the middle of 1940, the Nazi army had swept through western Europe, ultimately invading and then occupying France. The only thing between Hitler and near complete control of the continent was Great Britain. However, Britain posed a different problem for the Nazis. Whereas the German land-based blitzkrieg—with its armored tanks and motorized vehicles—took the European continent like a plague, Britain would have to be brought to her knees by sea or air. Hitler opted for the latter. Addressing the nation, British Prime Minister Winston Churchill was clear about what was at stake.

"What General Weygand has called the Battle of France is over. The Battle of Britain is about to begin," Churchill said.

In July of 1940, Germany initiated an air campaign against Britain, first targeting its ports and then its airfields. After nearly four months of fighting, the Royal Air Force thwarted the Nazi air fleet—known as the Luftwaffe—and forced them to give up their aerial assault. It would mark the first major defeat of the Germans in World War II.

Jonathan performed seven successful flights during the Battle of Britain and was credited with downing four enemy fighters. However, on his eighth mission as he was defending Portsmouth, his plane was struck, and the engine suffered damage. To avoid civilian casualties, Jonathan fought to control his plane and directed it to the rural areas north of the city. He was able to eject himself from the aircraft just before it crashed in a wheat field.

Two young brothers witnessed the crash and rushed in to take a closer look. By sheer chance, they stumbled upon Jonathan, who lay in the field bleeding and unconscious.

"Do you think he's dead?" asked the younger brother.

Before the older brother could answer, they saw Jonathan flick his eyes open and try to move before he fell unconscious again.

"He ain't dead. Let's get him out of here," the older brother said.

With that, the two boys began dragging Jonathan's limp body the two miles to their home. There, their mother cared for him until he was transported to a military hospital. Jonathan suffered broken ribs, a collapsed lung, a broken leg, and a skull fracture.

Despite his injuries, he was able to regain consciousness. Word reached Lena about Jonathan's condition, and she was finally able to write him while he was recovering in the military hospital.

Within a month, the doctors felt he would make a full recovery. Jonathan spent the next eight months getting his motor functions back and learning to walk again. He told Lena it was the thought of walking down the aisle with her that fueled his recovery.

When he was strong enough to leave, he asked to be taken to the home of the boys who'd saved his life. However, when they arrived at the house, it was no longer there. A German bomb had reduced it to rubble, killing everyone inside.

Although his injuries were severe enough for him to be discharged, he petitioned the Royal Air Force to reinstate him, which they ultimately did. He wrote to Lena to explain his decision.

> *It is not without great pain that I tell you our reunion must be delayed. I have recovered from my injuries, and His Majesty has determined that my wounds are ample payment to the kingdom, and he has relieved me of any further obligation to Britain. But I do not share his view. I have reenlisted, and I am determined to fight until Britain and the world are free from the threat facing them.*
>
> *I hope you believe me when I tell you there is nothing I want more than to look into your beautiful eyes, than to hear your soft voice, than to hold you once again in my arms. But I cannot do so if I am unworthy of your love. Would your eyes sparkle when looking upon a man who ran from battle? Would your words be as tender? Would you stay within the embrace of arms not willing to protect you? I would not ask that of you.*
>
> *I wish I could promise you that one day I will return to you. That the life we were planning can finally be lived. But in good conscience, I can offer no such guarantees. War does not accommodate love; she does not discriminate. Knowing this, I understand that in time you may have a decision of your own. To wait for something that may never come, or to go down a more certain path. I will respect any decision you make. And whatever you decide, and whenever you decide it, know that I will love you with my last breath—whenever that may be.*

Weeks later, as he boarded his fighter plane for his first mission since reenlisting, Jonathan was handed a letter from America. With a racing heart and trembling hands, he opened the envelope, and his eyes caught sight of the closing sentence of Lena's letter:

Jonathan, you silly, silly boy. I will wait for you until the end of my days!

75

Homecoming

In April 1945, the western and eastern European fronts of World War II converged on Berlin, squeezing the city like a vise. Germany, "the great conqueror," was reduced to fighting for her own survival, and on April 30, the Reichstag fell, effectively ending the war in Europe. A week later, Germany signed a total and unconditional surrender. Japan would surrender in August that same year.

It would be a year later when Jonathan was discharged from active duty. Jonathan, now thirty-five, hadn't seen Lena in seven years. As he sat on the commercial flight to New York, flicking a lighter on and off, he wondered what awaited him.

He saw the precarious duality of his own situation in the flame of the lighter. When lighted, the small flame burned with commanding intensity, drawing attention to it. But take his thumb off the igniter even slightly and that flame was easily extinguished, leaving an odorous, dark fume in its wake.

He remembered how close he had been to letting his own flame die. A night of drinking with his enlisted friends ended up at the flat of a young woman. He sat on the bed next to her, his hand under her skirt, caressing her thigh; she, kissing his neck. Her scent, like some wild berry, wafting in his nose. His mouth watering in anticipation. He recalled never wanting something so badly nor needing it so completely. But then he stopped. It was as if Lena's image came to him like a specter. He remembered the last time they talked before he left for war, and in his mind, he could hear the following conversation:

"You told me that you'd never leave me, but you lied," Lena said.

"I would never break my word to you. I go only because it's my duty. Every man, if he dares call himself one, understands obligation. But I will never leave you really, you will always be with me, in my heart and mind, until the day I can hold you in my arms again," Jonathan said.

"That's not the same thing. I don't want you to abandon and forget about me," she said.

"I would never. Why would you say that?"

"Because I know what it feels like to be abandoned. And it makes me afraid, because you can only abandon something that can't be loved."

"My darling. You're talking nonsense. Who couldn't love you? I see how your father dotes on you. I know your uncle well. I can tell you with certainty that he loves nothing like he loves you. Your uncle is a kind man, an honorable man, but emotions at times are nuisances to him, and he doesn't bother with them. Unless he is talking about you, and then he lights up like a child. No one would ever abandon you, least of all me," Jonathan said.

"I wish that were true, but I'm not who you think I am. I don't know who I am myself. I love my father, and I know he loves me, but I'm not his real daughter," Lena said.

"Darling, I know you're adopted, but that shouldn't matter. In the end, you are where you should be, with people who care about you."

"I know, but it isn't that easy for me. I'm grateful for my family, but we all come from someplace. I came from a ditch in the forest. Cast aside like trash. Left to die. Who would do that to a child? I want to think it was an evil person, a sick woman or deranged man. But sometimes I think, what if it was just me? What if I was tossed aside like garbage because that's what I am? What if I was abandoned because that's what I deserved?" she said.

"Lena, stop talking like that. You're being foolish."

"But what if it were true?"

"It's not."

"Then why are you leaving me too? What if I never see you again? What if you realize I never deserved your love?"

"My darling, no matter how long it takes, I'll be back for you. I'll die before I abandon you. And if you were ever to leave me, please know my love for you will never change."

"Promise you will come back to me."

"On my life."

After landing in New York, Jonathan took a train to Boston, where he hailed a cab to make his way to the Shackleton residence. The driver dropped him off at the front, and he walked his way to the door and knocked.

"Master Fillmore, my apologies, we were not expecting you," a surprised Stetson said when he saw Jonathan and his lone suitcase.

"Is she here?" Jonathan asked.

"She is, sir."

"May I see her?"

Stetson stepped out of the doorway and extended his arm so that Jonathan could enter. He then led Jonathan to the study, where Lena and Myron were playing a game of chess.

"Master, madam. Pardon me, but we have a guest," Stetson said.

Lena looked up and froze, staring without expression.

"Hello, Lena," Jonathan said.

It was reminiscent of the first day they met, only this time it was Lena who seemed spellbound. Suddenly, she jumped out of her chair and rushed into Jonathan's arms.

Neither said another word.

76

Preparations Soon Were Made

Even though seven years had passed, it was as if Lena and Jonathan had never been apart, and they immediately got to the business of planning a wedding.

Lena had always wanted a Christmas wedding, but with Christmas of 1946 quickly approaching, she knew it wouldn't give them enough time to plan the extravagance. However, she felt she had waited long enough and opted instead to have a wedding that upcoming spring. Jonathan agreed. The only thing that was left was to select a venue, and the planning could begin.

For that, the couple met with Myron's good friend, Hershel Whitney, who told them he had an ideal property for a wedding and invited the couple to tour the Garden of Hesperides.

Hershel told Vartan that a very important and wealthy couple were going to view the grounds as a potential venue for their upcoming wedding and he wanted everything to look exceptionally good. Vartan and a couple of his men were finishing up their work atop a ridge when he heard Hershel talking and approaching from the walkway below.

"Okay, let's get all the equipment out of here. We don't want it in the way of Mr. Whitney's guests when he's showing them around," Vartan said.

The men quickly collected all their rakes and spades and carted them off to the equipment house just as the trio were approaching. Vartan and the workers turned a corner and were out of sight before they could be observed by the guests.

"Of course, you could hold the ceremony inside," said Hershel. "We have a wedding chapel just down the way from our banquet hall. But if you want to take advantage of all our scenery, you should consider an outdoor ceremony. We can set up an altar on the deck overlooking the lake. It's a beautiful view anytime of the day, but in the afternoon, it is just breathtaking," said Hershel, as they all looked out over the lake.

"Oh, I love the view. Jonathan, an outdoor ceremony would be ideal. What do you think?" Lena asked.

"I think it's all lovely," Jonathan said.

"You won't regret it. There's far more energy and beauty outdoors. So, my dear, you've seen the banquet hall, we've toured the grounds, you've seen the view from the lake. We have one of the best chefs in New England, so there is no menu we can't accommodate. What do you think?" asked Hershel.

"It's perfect," Lena said.

<hr>

By early May, most of the arrangements for a June wedding were complete. Lena focused on her dress and other bridal trappings, while Stetson was left to oversee the food, music, and venue.

A week prior to the wedding, a nervous Myron insisted that he take a look at the venue one last time. He asked Plato to accompany him. Hershel was out of town, but he told them that his head groundskeeper would walk them through everything to ensure that it was to Myron's liking.

Vartan met the two in the lobby of the clubhouse.

"Hello, my name is Vartan Kasparian. May I offer my congratulations on your daughter's upcoming wedding," said Vartan as he extended his hand. "Mr. Whitney asked that I walk you through our preparations, discuss the logistics, and answer any questions you may have."

"Thank you. I'm Myron Shackleton, and this is Plato Williamson, he's an employee of mine," said Myron, shaking Vartan's hand. "He can help you in any way you and your staff need leading up to the wedding."

"Howdy, sir. You have an awfully nice place here," said Plato, shaking Vartan's hand as well.

"Thank you for the offer. We will try not to burden Mr. Williamson too much. This way, if you please," said Vartan as he gestured for the pair to follow him.

Vartan led the guests to the banquet hall. As Vartan talked through the layout for the reception, Myron took everything in with subtle head nods. After the tour of the reception hall was over and the trio were about to exit, Myron stopped.

"May I walk around the room again?" Myron said.

"Of course, sir. Is there anything specific you would like me to show you?" Vartan asked.

"No, no. I just want to walk around one more time alone and take a look at everything."

"Of course."

Vartan and Plato waited in the doorway and watched as Myron carefully walked through the room, inspecting every table, checking how sturdy the stage for the band was, looking up at each chandelier for any sign of dust.

After making his rounds, Myron returned to the two men.

"Do you have any questions Mr. Shackleton?" Vartan asked.

"No, no. Everything is lovely," he said.

Next Vartan walked them to the lake house where the ceremony would take place. The lake house was a three-story, twelve-hundred-square-foot structure made of gray-and-white marble. Its four corners were supported by fluted columns. Carved around the capitals of the columns were classical depictions of Atlas bearing the world on his shoulders. There were four of these carvings in each capital, giving the illusion that these miniature Atlases were supporting the vaulted roof.

The front of the lake house had a four-thousand-square-foot patio set in gleaming white marble. The patio was encircled by three-and-a-half-foot-high marble rails carved as fluted columns. At the two front corners of the patio stood two twelve-foot statues of the Goddess Hera. The pure white statues were both facing toward the patio, the head of each looking down to a golden apple that the goddess was cradling beneath her bosom. On the floor in the middle of the patio was a mosaic of the Golden Fleece, set in blue, gold, and gray stones.

Vartan first showed them the executive apartment on the top floor of the lake house.

"The apartment will be available to the bride for the weekend, so she can prepare at her convenience," said Vartan while leading the group from the apartment down to the second floor and then to the main staircase. "She will walk down these stairs, and if I understand it correctly, Mr. Shackleton, you will be waiting at the bottom of the stairs to escort the bride."

"Yes, yes. Or do you think I should wait at the door?" Myron asked.

"Either way works, sir. The guests won't be able to see the bride until she exits the door to the patio. But you will have the building to yourselves that day. The doors will be closed until the two of you are ready to walk down the aisle. I'm sure it will be a lovely sight when the doors swing open and the guests first see you and the bride," responded Vartan.

To make his point, Vartan swung open the double doors to the shining white marble deck where the ceremony would take place. The lake was shimmering from the afternoon sun as they stepped onto the deck and watched as a pair of workers were putting the finishing touches on the gazebo.

"Yes, that would be ideal. Making a proper entrance is important. Small details, I know, but those details are what's remembered," Myron said.

"There will be four ushers that day, two will be stationed on either side of the doorway and another two at either side of the seating area. They will be ready to address anything that may arise. Mr. Whitney wants to ensure that everything is perfect," Vartan said.

"Yes, yes. It all looks fine," said a fidgety Myron as he peered over the side of the deck toward the rolling landscape surrounding the lake house. "Do you always keep the grass at that length?"

"We just cut it this morning. We will have it cut the morning of the wedding as well. Is that acceptable?"

"It will do, I suppose. What about flowers?" Myron asked.

"We'll arrange any flowers any way you wish," Vartan said. "As you can see, we have an array of flowers, and we can display them in any manner that suits you and the bride."

"And what about those trees?" Myron continued.

"Sir?" Vartan said.

"Pardon me, Vartan, but could you excuse us for a moment? I would like to have a word with Mr. Shackleton," Plato said.

"Certainly."

Vartan walked to the other side of the deck to give his two guests some privacy.

"Sir, everything's beautiful, you're already working yourself up needlessly," Plato said.

"I know it. I can't help it. I just want everything to be perfect. And it's just . . . I want more color. You understand, don't you? Just more color."

"I understand, sir, but I'm afraid we might confuse these fellers more than anything. I'll be working with these fellers. Now don't fret none. It's going to be a beautiful weddin'. It's going to be a beautiful day."

77

Something Old

Lena had one reoccurring dream that kept coming at odd times. She first recalled having the dream when she traveled with Virginia to see her uncle in Europe. She had it again on the day they moved to Boston, and then multiple times when Jonathan left for war. Now as she prepared for her wedding day, the dream came back again.

It was always the same. She was a small girl—how old she never knew—and was being carried by an unknown man onto a ship. She rested her head on the man's shoulder yet couldn't see his face. She would feel relief as they stepped onto the ship, yet once on board, feared that the man would leave her, so she clung to him even tighter.

With his head bowed, the man set her down, turned, and began to walk away. Panicked, she found herself frantically trying to scream and move but was paralyzed. She thought if he could just look at her, he would see the pleading in her eyes and he wouldn't leave her. She saw him suddenly stop and begin to turn toward her. And just before the man's face came into view, she would wake up.

It was now the eve of the wedding, and Lena was in her bedroom trying on her wedding dress with Virginia's help. The formfitting, floor-length dress was elegant but short on extravagance, with no long train and no dominating headpiece. It featured a deep neckline, with sheer lace over the shoulders and midway down the arms. The lace pattern continued over the entire pure white dress. The small, modest veil covered only half her face. For the wedding, she decided to wear her hair pulled back in a bun.

"How do I look?" she asked Virginia, studying herself in the full-length mirror.

"Oh, Lena, you're beautiful," said Virginia.

"Do you think Jonathan will think so?"

"My darling, if he has any other opinion, then his judgment can't be trusted, and this entire matter must be reconsidered."

Lena smiled and turned back toward the mirror.

"Virginia, you know it means a lot to me that you're here. I might have never told you, but growing up, I always looked up to you. More than anyone, I didn't want to disappoint you. You knew how to make me feel special and loved when I needed it most. You always made time for me, even when I knew how hard it must have been on you, with your duties at the house and caring for your parents. You mean more to me than I can express. I hope you know that," said Lena.

Virginia put her hand to her mouth and turned away, lowering her head. Lena circled around Virginia, so she could look her in the face.

"Virginia, are you okay?"

"Yes, of course. To hear you say that means a lot. I only wanted what was best for you. I did all I could to do right by you, and if there was any way I failed you, I hope that I'll be forgiven," said Virginia as her eyes filled with tears.

"Don't be foolish, I wouldn't be the woman I am without you. I wouldn't be alive without you," said Lena as she hugged Virginia. "I love my father and my uncle, and the whole staff of our house. They are all family to me. But you were the one I loved the most. I was embarrassed to tell you, but sometimes I would imagine that you were my mother. I used to do it all the time when I couldn't sleep. I would imagine you were with me, holding me. It would give me so much comfort."

"Oh, hush child, you shouldn't say such things," said Virginia, fighting back tears.

"Why?"

"You're the lady of our house. I'm just a servant, that's all."

"No, you're more than that. You've always been more than that. You're my family, you are the person I've always wanted to be, and I love you," said Lena as she hugged Virginia tightly.

"Oh, look what you've done." Virginia laughed as she tried to compose herself. "I promised myself I wouldn't cry until tomorrow and here I'm crying like a baby. But we still have work to do. You can't be unprepared for your own wedding. How does the saying go? Something old, something new, something borrowed, and something blue. We both agree the dress is new."

"Yes, the dress is new, and I have something borrowed," said Lena as she walked over to her vanity and brought back a red suede box.

She opened the box to show Virginia a princess-cut solitaire diamond necklace on a silver chain.

"This is Jonathan's grandmother's necklace; his mother asked if I would wear it for the wedding," Lena said.

"Heavens, it's beautiful," replied Virginia.

"Do you think it could count for something borrowed and for old? You already tied a blue scarf and ribbon around my bouquet, so we have that accounted for, too." Lena asked.

"I think they should be different, but something old should be the easiest thing to find," Virginia said. "I have to run down to check on something, and I'll ask Martha and Beatrice if they have any ideas."

Virginia left the room, and Lena sat down in front of her vanity, closing the necklace's clasp around her neck. The sparkling heirloom looked striking against her olive skin, and she was grateful that Jonathan's family entrusted her with it. She unhooked the necklace, put it carefully back in its box, and opened the bottom drawer of her vanity, brushing aside a few scraps of paper. In doing so she caught sight of a green-and-red star-shaped medal.

She picked up the medal, stroking its enamel and running over the cut on its face with her thumb. She hadn't held it since she hid it away all those years ago. Back then, she didn't even want to look at it. She felt that whatever honor this medal once held had long since evaporated—until what was left was a gaudy, damaged trinket. One that had no significance, no value. One that could be discarded easily, just as she was. Looking at it now, she remembered her uncle's words when he gave it to her.

"It was not by accident that it was left with you," she recalled him saying.

She realized her uncle was right. Whatever this medal's story was, wherever it came from, whatever it meant, it was all a part of her.

"Dear, Martha gave me some wonderful ideas . . . What is that, dear?" said Virginia as she reentered the room and saw Lena holding the medal.

"Uncle Endicott gave this to me when I was a child. He told me this medal was in the blanket I was wrapped in when you brought me to the house. Have you ever seen it before?" Lena asked.

"No, dear, I haven't," said Virginia, suddenly subdued.

"Uncle Endicott told me it's an important medal and that it came from Turkey. Why do you suppose it was left with me?"

"I don't know, but there must have been a reason for it," said Virginia, wringing her hands.

"It's been in this junk drawer for years. I meant to throw it away, but I forgot that it was even there."

"No, dear, you shouldn't ever discard it," said Virginia as she walked over and knelt at the side of the chair Lena was sitting on. "Listen to me, dear. I'm not the real hero in your story. I was just fortunate enough to be there when a child needed help. Anyone would have done the same. The one who had to endure whatever trials needed to bring you there that day was the real hero. It could have been the farthest they could have brought you, and the only way they knew to help you. I didn't know about this medal, but it's important. I think it was their way of saying they'll still watch over you. Please promise me that you will always keep it."

Lena placed her palm on Virginia's face and kissed her cheek. For the first time, Lena felt that she was the one who needed to comfort Virginia.

"I promise," said Lena. "Do you think I could wear it for the wedding? Do you think that this could be something old? If you think it would work, I have an idea for it," Lena said.

"Oh, my darling, I think it would be perfect," said Virginia.

"Vartan, would ya mind if I had a brief word?" said Plato as he approached Vartan at the equipment house of the country club.

"No, of course not," Vartan said. "Is there anything wrong with the grounds?"

"No, no, everything's going just dandy. I think we should have everything to Mr. Shackleton's liking by morning. I just wanted to ask a favor of ya. A small favor."

"If it's within my power, I'll gladly do it."

"Much obliged, much obliged, but it's just a simple request. Would you be able to be here for the weddin' tomorrow? We just need you for the ceremony."

"Tomorrow? I would like to, but I had plans to travel to Concord. My son is playing in a soccer tournament. I could get one of my men to be here, and he could help you with whatever you needed."

"You have a dandy crew, no doubt there, but Mr. Shackleton requested you personally. It would only be for the ceremony. We should be done fairly early. We would just need you for the morning. If you could find a way to be here, it would go a long way in calming Mr. Shackleton's nerves. But I understand if you can't," Plato said.

Vartan considered the request. He had grown to respect Plato. The weathered gardener had a way of making him feel that they were old friends. Had it been anyone but Plato, he would have most likely begged out of it.

"Yes, of course. I'll be here in the morning. I could send my wife and son ahead and meet them there in time for his game," Vartan said.

"I do appreciate it. There's one more thing. Could you wear this?" said Plato as he handed Vartan a garment bag.

78

A Daughter at the Altar

"Howdy there, my friend, you look like you're the one fixin' to get hitched," said Plato when he saw Vartan outside the lake house. Plato wore the same white jacket and pants as Vartan, who was supervising the grounds crew as it completed its final touch-ups to the lawn and flowerbeds.

"How am I expected to do any work dressed like this?" Vartan asked.

"Oh, well you needn't fret, you ain't gonna do no work."

"Then why did you need me here today?"

"Well, Mr. Shackleton wanted two more people standing on either side of the staircase when Miss Shackleton comes down," said Plato. "So, he ordered two more suits. Turns out they got the measurements wrong, and I'm the only one that would fit into 'em. But as luck would have it, you look to be about my size. I would say just over six feet, 'bout hundred-ninety pounds or so."

"Around there," confirmed Vartan.

"Well looking at the rest of your crew, we felt you was the only one that could wear the other suit."

"So, all I have to do is just stand at the base of the stairs? That's it?"

"Yep, that's it. And I'll be standing right across from you on the other side."

"Not my place to question, of course. But seems odd."

"Oh no doubtin' that it is a sight better than odd, but once something gets into Mr. Shackleton's head, it becomes impervious to logic and reason. And we are left with making do the best we can with these idiosyncrasies. If not, then it would put Mr. Shackleton in a terrible state of discomfort," said Plato.

"Well, we wouldn't want that," said Vartan, with a smile.

"No, indeed we wouldn't," said Plato, smiling back.

Before going into the lake house, Vartan surveyed the grounds. He had worked at the country club for more than two decades, but he had never seen the landscaping look so beautiful. The blades of the lush lawn looked to be cut with the precision and care of a straight-edged razor. There wasn't a single flower that shrank from attention, but rather each lunged forward in a colorful display of shameless pride. No wayward branches extended beyond their mother tree's tolerance, but instead all reached out only as far as aesthetic allowed. Even the sun seemed to cast a purer light—one that shimmered off the water, giving the lake just the right amount of glistening accent.

The crew erected an altar on the patio of the lake house. Once the ceremony was over, the guests would take a meandering cobblestone path to the reception hall, while the bride and groom would be carried by a horse-drawn carriage.

"Well, we best get ready," said Plato to Vartan as the guests began to arrive. The two made their way to the lake house.

When they walked in, they could see a nervous Myron pacing in front of the grand staircase.

"Is everything okay, sir?" said Plato as they approached Myron.

"Yes, everything is fine. Just a little unnerving," said Myron.

Myron stayed directly in the middle of the staircase, with Plato at the right rail some ten feet away, and Vartan an equal distance away to Myron's left.

The bride appeared at the top of the grand staircase with Virginia at her side. Vartan watched as the veiled bride took one careful step after another as she descended to Myron to the sound of Ravel's *Boléro*. Vartan looked over to Myron and saw him fixated on the bride as she came closer to him; he saw Myron wipe a tear from his eyes with a trembling hand.

When the bride reached the bottom, she turned her back to Vartan and threw her arms around Myron's neck and held him tightly. Myron returned the embrace even more firmly.

Vartan thought it was a touching sight and felt guilty imposing on such a private moment. He went to turn his head so he wouldn't continue to intrude on father and daughter when something caught his eye. It was a brooch pinned to the back of the bride's hair, just under her bun. He focused his eyes on it and saw it clearly. It was a familiar item from days long forgotten. Something he'd once held in his hand. An object that had no place here. It was a green-and-red seven-pointed star with a gash in the middle. It was Ari's medal.

Vartan's heart began beating faster as he tried to make sense of what he was seeing. If the medal was here, then where was Ari? If he could find Ari, then he could find his daughter. He resisted the urge to rush toward the bride and beg her for information. Thoughts swirled in his head as he tried to think of a reasonable explanation.

Did Ari sell the medal to Myron? Was it lost or stolen? Did Ari work for this millionaire? And then a ridiculous thought came to his mind as Myron and the bride walked to the doors. The doors opened, and the sunlight cascaded through as Myron walked his daughter past the doorway and down the aisle with the guests standing in admiration. Vartan followed Plato and stood at the doorway.

Vartan locked in on the bride as Myron presented her to the groom. Myron lifted her veil and gave her a hug and a kiss. With her face uncovered, Vartan studied the bride's face. His knees began to shake when he saw how much this bride resembled the one he'd looked upon on his own wedding day. The more he studied her, the more he felt as if he were once again surveying the perfect face of the young girl he'd struck with the soccer ball. *Could it be, could it be?* Vartan thought. Vartan found himself struggling to breathe, and his legs went weak again, causing him to lose balance.

Plato saw Vartan stumble back and rushed over to steady him out of sight of the wedding party and guests.

"Are you okay, friend? You look a bit shaky. Is the heat gettin' to ya?" Plato asked.

"No, I just felt a little light-headed. I'm okay now."

"Are you sure? You still look a little unsteady there."

"No, thank you, I'm fine. I'm not a young man anymore. I'm ashamed to say my constitution isn't as strong as it once was."

"Well, just take 'er easy. Maybe we should go sit down. A feller dying has a way of puttin' a damper on a weddin'," said Plato.

"Thank you, but I'm feeling much better now. It's a beautiful wedding. I wouldn't want to take any attention away from it. Mr. Shackleton has been blessed with a beautiful daughter."

"Yes, Mr. Shackleton is a man that ain't short of blessin's, and I'd wager he'd tell you she is his greatest one."

Vartan paused to gather himself, his mind continuing to swirl. He was so overcome by thoughts and emotions that it was hard to speak. Yet he composed himself enough to ask a question he was both eager and afraid to have answered.

"Do you know the bride's name?"

"Miss Shackleton?"

"Yes, what is her christened name?"

"Her name is Lena."

79

The Hermit and the Child

Vartan would recall little of the ceremony, although it went flawlessly, with the sun shining down on the blissful lovers. His mind was still in a haze. Still standing by the door, he saw how much Lena's smile was like Anna's, how their eyes held the same sparkle, how Lena looked at her husband the same way Anna had looked at him.

Vartan was only shaken out of his daze when he heard the priest say, "It is my pleasure to present, for the first time, Mr. and Mrs. Jonathan Fillmore."

The crowd stood and erupted in applause as the bride and groom strolled down the aisle. The pair disappeared from Vartan's view once they started to walk down the stairs of the patio to the horse-drawn carriage.

"Well, then, that wasn't too bad, huh? 'Cept for the brief spell you had, I'd say it went off without a hitch," said Plato.

"Yes, my apologies. I don't know what came over me."

"Ahh, no worries, I think all the rich folk were too busy putting on airs to notice a couple of fellers like us. Well, that's all the work we needed you for, but you're welcome to stay and have something to eat. The good thing about working these sorts of things is that we get to eat before the other folks. 'Course it probably won't be as fine as the fare they'll be having inside, but it will be good vittles nonetheless."

"I would like that very much, thank you."

Vartan walked with Plato to the servant's area of the country club, where the staff had prepared a hearty meal for the grounds crew and staff. After filling their plates with chicken and potatoes, Vartan and Plato walked back outside to a small deck and found a table.

"Mr. Shackleton is certainly a man of detail. How long have you worked for him?" asked Vartan.

"I'd say going on close to forty years now."

"That's a long time. Since you've been working for him for so long, did he give any thought on inviting you as a guest to this wedding?"

"I don't think he gave it much thought at all. I was one of the first people he invited."

"Then why are you here with me and not with the other guests?"

"Oh, well, I'll go in eventually. Mr. Shackleton was working himself up with worry. Things had to be perfect, and he wudn't sure if yer fellers could do the job. No offense."

"None taken." Vartan paused. "Forgive me if I'm too inquisitive, but whatever became of Mrs. Shackleton?"

"Mrs. Shackleton? You mean Mr. Shackleton's wife?"

"Yes, what became of her?"

"Oh nothing, Mr. Shackleton has never been married. Been a bachelor his whole life."

"So how did Mr. Shackleton come to have a daughter if he was never married?"

"Oh, well, that's another story altogether. One of Mr. Shackleton's servants, Virginia, came home with the child one fall night. Poor little thing was close to death. She was out of consciousness on account of a fever. We fetched the doctor to come tend to her. Doctor came and said her fever was so bad that she would most likely not make it," said Plato, shaking his head at the thought. "But that little girl had some gumption in her, and after four days, she woke up. She's been living with us ever since. Not long after, Mr. Shackleton adopted her legally."

"And how did this servant, Virginia, come by the child?"

"Well, now there are two stories to that one. The story Virginia told Mr. Shackleton and the real one."

"And what would those be?"

"Well, for all the fine qualities Mr. Shackleton has and the good things he does, he never had much use for beggars. Especially young, healthy men. He feels a man should be able to tend to his earthly needs through hard work and perseverance. If he can't, then he is looking to make do off other folks' hard work. That never sat well with Mr. Shackleton. A beggar was not much better than a thief in his eyes. So, Virginia told him she found the child abandoned in a ditch as she was coming to work."

"And what's the truth?" Vartan asked.

"The truth is much sadder. Virginia was making her way to Mr. Shackleton's house through the woods one evening, and a hunch-back approached her, carrying a child in his arms. The feller didn't seem to speak English, but he went up to Virginia and tried to hand her the child. Apparently, all he kept saying was 'please,' as if it were the only word he knew. Virginia said she realized then that the child was sick, so she took her. When she did, the man grabbed her arm, pointed at the child, and kept saying 'Lena.' I guess the feller wanted to leave her with her name. Virginia said the poor feller was crying the whole time, so it was most likely her father or some other kin," said Plato as he looked over Vartan, whose fidgeting he took for agitation. "I hope you don't think too poorly of the feller. There are some decisions we can hope we never have to make. Hard to judge someone fairly unless you were in their shoes."

"You're right, of course. I didn't mean to seem judgmental in any way. I apologize if I did," said Vartan. "And what happened to the hunchback? Did you ever find out what became of him?"

"Well, we would see him about the estate from time to time. As you could imagine, he was an unsightly feller, and Stetson didn't want him around the house scaring folks, so he had us run him off. I was tryin' to tell him to leave, but he just kept looking at me oddly, so I shot my shotgun into the air, and he got the message and scampered off," said Plato, with downcast eyes. "I'll admit, I ain't too proud of that. That was before I learnt about who he was, of course. But I tell myself it was probably best for the child. Lena had much more of a chance in life as Mr. Shackleton's daughter than she did this other feller's."

"So do you know where this hunchback is now?"

"Most likely dead. Rumors were that he still lived in the forest that came up to Mr. Shackleton's old house. But we moved out going on twenty years now. But even still, I know folks back in Bethlehem and no one seen hide nor hair of him for years. Yep, if I was to guess, I would reckon he was dead by now."

"Did Miss Shackleton ever find out about the hunchback?"

"No. Virginia loves that girl like she's her own daughter. I don't think she could bear it if she found out she had lied to her all these years. I encouraged her to tell Lena, but she just doesn't have it in her. It would crush her if she lost Lena's trust. I might not agree with it, but it ain't my place to say."

80

Requiem of an Orphan

Vartan walked out shortly after Plato and followed the old groundskeeper as he made his way to the reception. He watched Plato take his seat with the rest of Myron's household staff at a table just in front of the bridal table. It was seating reserved for the bride's closest family. Vartan stayed at one of the banquet room's secondary doorways, at the far end of the room, which was used primarily by the staff.

The ten-foot wooden double doors swung open, and Jonathan and Lena proudly strolled in, arms locked together. The pair walked to the center of the dance floor and turned to face each other. The orchestra began to play Tchaikovsky's "Waltz of the Flowers," and husband and wife had their first dance.

The entire room fell silent, with all eyes locked on the couple, most of all Vartan's. He peered carefully through the doorway, so as not to be noticed by anyone inside. He felt as if a warm wave had washed over his body, leaving him soaked in numbing peace. The only thing left was to speak with Lena and tell her the truth. He imagined the joy on her face. He imagined her embracing him as tightly as he would embrace her. He could picture her smiling with happiness. And then an epiphany woke him rudely from delusion when he realized he *was* already seeing her smiling with happiness.

Vartan looked around and began taking in more details from the room. The beautiful centerpieces on the tables were sure to exceed an honest man's wages. The fine china and silver utensils would be treasures to him. He looked at Lena, but this time he didn't focus on her face. Instead, he saw the jewels that sparkled from her neck, wrists, and ears. Her dress seemed more like some work of art to be appreciated at a distance than a garment to be exposed to the eroding process of wear. He looked back at her face where he saw the same look of happiness as she danced with the man she loved.

He stayed rooted in the doorway as husband and wife finished their dance and through the obligatory toasts. He watched as Myron stood to address his guests just before they began their dinner.

"I would like to thank everyone for your attendance today. It's a great honor that each of you is here to celebrate this day with me," began Myron. "I've always been a private man, and some here may be surprised to learn that I was an orphan. But I was the rarest of orphans—an orphan who did not arouse sympathy. You see, I was an orphan of privilege. While other children were raised on scarcity and want, I was reared on excess and indulgence. My parents died in a fire when I was two years old. In place of this loss, I was given wealth and, like a desperate castaway, I clung to it. After all, what hungry void is there that couldn't be filled with the finest of foods and the sweetest of wines? What loss is suffered that cannot be overcome by the gain of capital? How could a home be empty when it was teeming with treasures?

"I often thought of what it means to be an orphan. I know now that it's not the loss of parents, but the absence of love. Lore, as old as time, tells us love is a treasure sought by prince and pauper alike. But love was too fragile, too uncertain, for a man of business to pursue. Love was best left to the innocent and the poet.

"So, for all I had acquired in my life, for everything I was given, everything I owned, everything I earned and collected, I could never count love among my assets. Not the love a mother has for her child, as beautifully naive as it is. Not the love a father has for his son, in all its inconvenient honesty. Providence had found it fitting to deny me that love, and I thought it just as well. After all, when we scrape away love's shiny veneer, don't we find its true qualities—cruelly hidden and quietly lurking—to be nothing more than disappointment and pain? Or at least so I had myself believe.

"But then one November evening a child was delivered to me. She did not arrive from the warmth of the womb to the tenderness of a parent's arms, but from the bitterness of autumn to the chill of a reluctant heart. There we were—two orphans—both lost, both scared. And then something in this child began to shine. With every smile, every hug, every look of affection, she shed light on a darkened resolve and kindled an ember in a home that had grown accustomed to its cold emptiness. And as that ember rose to a flame and its light spread, I was able to see that I finally held love—not in my hand, but in my heart. The most wonderful love of all—the unbounded love a parent has for their child. And at that moment, I was an orphan no more. It is the greatest gift I've ever received. I will always love you, my dear child."

Vartan stood in numb silence and looked around the room at women wiping their eyes with handkerchiefs and men clearing knots in their throats. He looked back and saw Lena rush to Myron and embrace him. The two held each other tightly, neither seeming to want to let go, both openly weeping. The emotion was not lost on Vartan, who continued to watch from the doorway.

Vartan felt it was no mere coincidence that he'd found his daughter on her wedding day. No, chance cannot occur with such ironic beauty on its own accord. This day had the fingerprints of a higher power. It had unfolded like a fairy tale, following a divine plan.

But what part had God authored for him in this fairy tale, if not that of the thief come to rob the princess of her enchantment?

81

The Princess Bride

"Plato, may I have a word with you?" Vartan called out as he saw Plato in the lobby.

"Vartan. Yes, of course. I thought ya had gone," said Plato.

"I had some things I had to tend to before the morning, and I thought it best to do it before I left for the evening. By the way, you said that Mr. Shackleton used to live in Pennsylvania?"

"Yes, indeed. Bethlehem, Pennsylvania, as a matter of fact."

"I never been to Bethlehem, but I heard it's a lovely place."

"It was home to me for a while, so it has a fond place in my heart."

"Plato, I don't mean to take you away from the reception, but could you grant me a favor?"

"Absolutely, what's it ya need?"

"In my custom it's considered bad luck if you see a bride on her wedding day and don't wish her good fortune. Would you allow me to approach the bride and give her my blessings?"

"I don't see why that would be a problem. I would just have to talk to Stetson and see what I can do," said Plato.

"I would be forever grateful," replied Vartan.

Plato excused himself and made his way to Stetson. The butler was too busy surveying the room to make sure everything was in order and on schedule to notice Plato approaching.

"'Cuse me, Stetson. I had a request from a gent that I hoped you'd consider," Plato said.

"And what would that be?"

"Well, that feller over there is one of the groundskeepers that helped us set up, and he wanted to pass good tidings to Lena on her weddin'," said Plato, motioning over to Vartan. "It's a custom of his, and apparently it means a lot to him."

"Although it is a fine gesture, I am sure he will understand that Miss Shackleton, uh I mean Mrs. Fillmore, has responsibilities to her guests first. It would be considered bad taste if she didn't spend some time with each guest, and the cake still hasn't been cut. Even a small interruption at this time would be unmanageable."

"I understand, but he is a fine feller. Ain't there a way you can make an exception?"

"Please do not take this the wrong way, I am certain that he is a decent man, but I am not sure if Master Shackleton would consider it an intrusion."

"I would consider what an intrusion?" asked a booming voice from behind.

Stetson and Plato turned and saw Endicott standing behind them.

"My apologies, sir. I did not see you standing there, but we were speaking of your nephew," said Stetson.

"Oh, were you now? And out of curiosity, what is it that the honorable Myron Shackleton would consider an intrusion on this day of all days?" Endicott asked.

Without giving Stetson a chance to explain, Plato interjected and told Endicott of Vartan's request in the hope that the uncle could serve as a more influential liaison.

"And why is it your belief that Myron would frown on such a harmless request?" Endicott asked.

"There are still many things yet to do, and it would be a challenge to disrupt the schedule any further. Mr. Shackleton has arranged for the cake-cutting ceremony at nine o'clock, and we are fast approaching that time," Stetson said.

"Poppycock!" exclaimed Endicott. "A man wishing to pass along graces should not be denied. We have too little of it in this day and age as it is. I'll take this gentleman to Lena myself, and if my nephew has any issues, he can deal with me."

And with that, Endicott followed Plato to Vartan, leaving Stetson behind to bite his tongue and clench his fists.

Plato introduced Endicott to Vartan. Upon learning that Vartan was Armenian, Endicott recounted the brief time he'd once spent among the Armenians during one of his many explorations. Endicott had seen some of the atrocities against the Armenians firsthand, and he had kept up with the Armenian plight through news reports.

"It was a messy situation. A messy situation," said Endicott, shaking his head.

After their brief conversation, during which Vartan talked about childhood in Van, Endicott asked Vartan to follow him. As he got closer to Lena, the emotions within Vartan intensified and drowned out everything Endicott was saying. A few yards away from Lena, Vartan saw Endicott give him a blank stare.

"Yes, thank you," replied Vartan, hoping that would be an appropriate answer to whatever Endicott had asked.

"Well, good," Endicott said.

Vartan's emotions raged against his effort to suppress them and manifested as sweat on his brow and trembles in his limbs. He wiped his brow with a handkerchief and wrung his hands to try to disguise his limbs' unsanctioned actions. He took a deep breath.

Endicott and Vartan approached the bride and groom just as they finished chatting up a pair of guests.

"Jonathan and Lena, if you have a moment, I would like to introduce you to one of the staff members here. His name is Vartan, and he is one of the groundskeepers who helped coax nature into the picture of beauty it was for your wedding today."

"It is a pleasure to meet you. Everything looked so beauti—" said Lena as she was transfixed by Vartan's translucent blue eyes that were intensely staring back at her.

"Yes, thank you indeed, for helping make this day so special," Jonathan echoed.

"Well, my friend here is Armenian," said Endicott. "A people you can trace back to our earliest historical days. And he told me it would be a sin if he didn't pass his blessings to the bride on her wedding day. So, if you could spare a few moments for this fine man, my dear, I would like to commandeer your husband for a brief word. I understand he has some interest in exploring the Himalayas and I have a Sherpa that I can recommend."

After Endicott left with Jonathan, Lena turned back to Vartan, who was still looking at her intently. Despite trying not to be, she found she was drawn to his odd eyes. A few more seconds of awkward silence passed before Lena decided to speak first.

"I'm sorry. I don't mean to stare, but I don't think I've ever seen eyes like yours before," said Lena, even though somehow, she felt that wasn't true.

"I've been told that. They've always been different," Vartan replied. "People tell me they always change, sometimes they are lighter, sometimes darker. My mother said that her brother had the same eyes. I don't know if that's true, I never met him. But my mother said that she could tell if her brother was happy, sad, scared, or angry by the color of his eyes. But she was never sure with me. She said they always were the same when she would look at me. I don't know why."

"They seem so striking. They might be the prettiest eyes I've ever seen," Lena said.

"I've seen more beautiful ones. They were brown, like yours," said Vartan.

Lena smiled and looked away before turning back to him again.

"So, my uncle mentioned that you were Armenian. How long have you been in America?" Lena asked.

"It's been many years now. When you've been away from your homeland as long as I have, you only remember customs and traditions. But otherwise, this is my home now, I'm really an American."

"Oh, so is your family here as well, then?"

This time it was Vartan's turn to look away. His eyes dropped to the floor; he shuffled his feet and noticed that his black shoes were scuffed and dirty. He looked back up at Lena.

"No, no. I had a wife, but she passed during the war," said Vartan, who paused before adding, "I had a daughter, too."

"I'm truly sorry to hear that," Lena said.

"Thank you. My wife I know is in a better place, as is my daughter.

God rewards the just and looks after the innocent. I believe that now. He has plans for us all, and with His love, we will all be reunited one day."

"I admire you for your faith. I know that it can be a great source of strength."

"And of hope. I have remarried here. I found a wonderful woman, and I'm helping raise a son. I hope to be a good father for him," said Vartan. "As part of tradition, I wanted to give you my blessing on your marriage before I left. I hope the greatest joys you have known pale to the joys that await you."

"Thank you, that is very kind of you."

"I've always felt there's no sight as beautiful as the happiness of a bride on her wedding day. It infuses all with hope for the future."

"That's a lovely thing to say. I consider myself blessed to have so much love around me. I'm truly grateful for all that I've been given and for the friends I've known."

"A daughter's happiness is all a father can ask. Your father is a fortunate man, and he gave a beautiful speech. I don't mean to be personal, but was what he said true? Were you an orphan?"

"No need to apologize, sir. Yes, as he said we were both orphans. A little ironic when you think about it," said Lena with a slight laugh and shake of her head.

"Yes, yes indeed," said Vartan. "But as he said, you're only an orphan if you feel like one. With the love around you, I hope you never felt like one."

"I suppose your mind always wonders when you're young and know nothing of your past. But the odd thing is that I never felt alone, even when I was by myself. I always felt someone was watching over me. Is that silly?" Lena answered.

"No, no it's not," said Vartan with a slight smile and nod of his head. "I know I have taken up a lot of your time, so I should go. But before I leave, will you accept a small gift?"

"Oh, sir, that's not necessary. Please don't feel as if you need to give me anything."

"I understand, but it would be a great honor to me if you would accept it."

"Well then, yes. You seem like a kind man. It would be my privilege," she said.

Vartan took out a gold necklace with a crucifix attached. It was the one his father had given him on his deathbed.

"This may be just a simple necklace, but it's a treasure to me, nonetheless. It was given to me by my father. It was a gift from him that I was supposed to give to his only granddaughter, but I never got the chance. It would mean a great deal to me if you would have it," said Vartan as he took Lena's hand and placed the necklace in it.

"Oh, sir, I can't accept this. It obviously means a lot to you. It should stay with you."

"I'm an old man, and there would be no sadder thing than if it were to be buried with me. My father gave it to me just before he died so that I would pass it on. I've held on to it for too long. There's no more fitting place for it than in the hands of a bride. It is what he would want. Please take it and remember to always have faith. And if you do, all things are possible."

Vartan clasped down on Lena's hand as she held the necklace. He remembered the last time he'd held her hand. It was when she was still a toddler, and he left her to see his dying father. He had never forgiven himself for letting go of her hand then, and he found himself struggling to let go now.

His emotions started to get the better of him again, and he could feel his eyes glisten with tears.

"Thank you, I'll always cherish it," said Lena.

Just then Stetson approached the pair and cleared his throat.

"Pardon me. Mrs. Fillmore is needed at the cake-cutting ceremony. I hope you understand, sir," said Stetson to Vartan.

"Yes, yes of course," responded Vartan as he slowly let go of Lena's hand. "I didn't mean to take up so much of your time, Mrs. Fillmore. May God bless you."

Vartan gave Stetson a nod of acknowledgment, then turned to walk away. He could feel Lena's eyes still on him with every step he took. He made it out of the room, then walked out of the building.

Once outside, he noticed the sun was setting, and dusk was upon him. He started breathing heavily and began to run through the rolling hills of the grounds until he came to a sycamore tree. As if possessed by some wild animal, he began to climb it. He reached so high that the tapering branches began swaying from his weight. When he could climb no higher, he held on to a branch with one hand and with the other reaching toward the heavens he gave out a primordial scream.

"Why me? Why this worthless soul?" he yelled. "I damned you for forsaking me, but you didn't! I've sinned. I gave in to weakness. I was broken and lost, and you were there to show me mercy! Lord, how can I ever be worthy again? Take what you will from me! Ask for anything and I will give it! What is it that you need of me? Tell me! Oh Lord, I beg you, tell me!"

He stopped to catch his breath and listen, but there was only silence. The sun set and darkness engulfed him.

82

Atonement

A week after the wedding, Vartan told Nare that he had to leave for Pennsylvania to see a friend. She offered to go with him, but he said he didn't know how long he would be gone, and she needed to stay and take care of Emin.

Vartan made arrangements at work for an extended absence and packed up some belongings and set out.

He took a train to Bethlehem, Pennsylvania, where he found an old mansion with a front yard encircled by a stone wall and a gate adorned with a large star. It was the former home of Myron Shackleton. With a knapsack slung over his shoulder, Vartan walked around the property to the back, and just as the old groundskeeper had described, he saw the trail that meandered its way into the woods. He walked toward the path slowly and deliberately, carefully taking in the view of the property. When he reached the entrance to the forest, he looked back at the house and closed his eyes, and he began to imagine his daughter running through its spacious halls and playing in its yard. The house was quiet now, but he hoped that those halls and that garden had grown familiar with his daughter's laughter through the years. Before he turned away, he took a deep breath and filled his lungs with fresh air, as if he were somehow breathing the same air as her.

Vartan lingered for a few minutes longer, then walked toward the trail that led into the forest. He followed the trail in, scanning every inch of the old, dense forest for man or structure. As he continued deeper into the forest, he would occasionally go off the trail on either side to look over a hill or around a thick overgrowth. He searched the forest that way all day but saw no living creature bigger than a squirrel. He searched the next day with the same result. Day three brought more of the same, but Vartan wasn't deterred. He had resolved that this forest would be his deliverance or his grave, and he marshaled on, only leaving to renew his supplies.

On the fourth day of his search, Vartan sat down in a clearing to prepare his evening meal, when something in the distance caught his eye. He stood to get a better look and saw a white doe staring at him from atop a knoll. A gust of wind swept through the forest, and Vartan could see the grasses and leaves around the doe moving with the wind, but the deer seemed untouched. Vartan began walking up the knoll to get a closer look at the doe, but it turned and sprinted away. When Vartan got to the top of the hill, he could see the doe through the trees; it was still again and looking back at him. He began chasing after it but could never get close to it.

After following the doe for half an hour, he noticed that it once again stopped. But this time as Vartan got closer, it didn't move. His heart beating from exhaustion, he made his way closer to the animal. He was now two feet away from it, as it stayed motionless. Vartan reached his hand out and ran it down its neck and noticed it staring back at him, calmly. Then without warning, it bolted away. An exhausted Vartan tried to follow it with his eyes but quickly lost sight of it. His shoulders sank with disappointment. He turned back to where the doe had stood and noticed, for the first time, that there was a tiny cabin in front of him. It was barely seven feet tall, and the door was so short that a grown man would have to bend to enter.

Heart still pounding from exhaustion, he walked to the cabin, cracked opened the door, and peered in. The cabin had only one room, and it looked empty at first, but as his eyes adjusted to the darkness, he could make out what looked like a pile of blankets in the corner. As he approached the pile, he thought he saw it move and began to hear labored breathing.

"Hello, is there anyone there?" he asked softly in English.

There was no sound or movement.

Vartan walked closer to the pile and peeled back the blanket to reveal a man huddled in the corner. The man kept his head down to hide his face, but Vartan could see the protruding hump on the man's back.

"Ari?" Vartan asked. But the man remained curled up, his head in his knees.

"Ari, it's Vartan from Van. A friend from home," said Vartan in Armenian.

Unlike before, these words had an effect, and the man weakly looked up.

Vartan knelt before him, instantly recognizing Ari's misshapen but soft brown eyes. Despite the familiar deformities, Ari looked nothing like the child he'd known in his youth. Like him, Ari was an old man now. The smooth, youthful face he remembered as a boy had been overrun by the creases and folds of age. His gray hair was long, dirty, and unkempt, his beard patchy. He looked sick, feeble, and afraid. Ari stared back at Vartan but didn't say a word.

"Ari, it's me, Vartan. I've come looking for you. Ari, do you understand me?"

Ari's eyes blinked in recognition. "Var . . . Var . . . Vartan."

"Yes, it's me, Vartan."

"Vartan! You've come! You've come for Lena," Ari cried out as he clutched Vartan's leg. "Vartan, Vartan, I don't have her. Oh Lord, what have I done? What have I done? You have come for your daughter like I knew you would, and I don't have her. I gave her away. I couldn't take care of her, Vartan. She was sick, and I couldn't help her. I abandoned her like I abandoned my mother. I don't know where she is; she's gone. I tried to watch her, I tried to keep her for you, but I couldn't. I was scared. She was so young, Vartan, I didn't know what to do."

"Shhh, shhh. Ari, it is okay. Ari, she is grown and healthy," Vartan said.

"Please forgive me. Please forgive me," Ari said, nearly inconsolable. "You've come for Lena, and I don't have her. I lost her. Oh Lord, what have I done? She was entrusted to these hands, and I could do nothing for her," said Ari, tears in his eyes as he held up the twisted fingers of his hands.

Vartan grabbed hold of Ari's face with both hands, so that he could look straight into his eyes.

"It's okay. It's okay, Ari. I found her. She's safe. She's well."

"You—you've seen her? Did she . . . ?" a tearful Ari caught himself. "How is she?"

"She's beautiful," said Vartan as his voice cracked and he fought back his own tears.

"Such a beautiful child . . . always so beautiful, Vartan. They say she has her mother's eyes because they are dark, but she doesn't. They are magic eyes, like yours. I've seen them, Vartan, it's true. And she's strong like you, so much stronger than me. Vartan, I was going to tell her all about you when she grew older. I was going to tell her about Van and the man you were, so she could be proud. But she got sick, and I had to find help before . . . before . . . I'm sorry, Vartan, I'm so sorry," said Ari, weeping with guilt.

"Ari, no one on God's Earth has less cause to apologize to another than you. And I least of all deserve your apology," Vartan said. "On this day, the only person who should ask for forgiveness is me, as undeserving as that forgiveness would be."

A fit of coughing gripped Ari. Vartan could hear Ari's breathing become more labored, so he moved to sit next to him and cradled Ari in his arms.

"Are you okay, Ari?"

"Yes," said Ari as his coughing subsided and his eyes still glistened with tears. "I'm happy now. You've brought me a gift. I'm happy, I'm truly happy. But you should leave me now. Please go to Lena. You should be with your daughter."

"Lena is fine, Ari. I've come looking for you. I've come to help you. I've come to take you with me," Vartan said.

Ari looked away with a distant stare.

"No, no," Ari finally said, shaking his head slowly and deliberately. "This is my home now, and just as you found your daughter, it will soon be time for me to join my mother. I'm not afraid, Vartan, I'll go there happily now. But please, go to Lena. She doesn't know what it means to have a father. I know that feeling too, I never knew my father. I know how empty her heart must be, how she has longed to have you by her side. Can you imagine how happy she'll be now, to finally have a father?"

"No, Ari, you're wrong. She's always had a father. A man who had the strength to sacrifice everything for her," Vartan said. "Someone brave and selfless. Someone strong enough to watch over her and keep her safe. She has grown into a beautiful woman and has a beautiful life now, not like we had. She knows nothing of the suffering we knew. She's had a father since the moment you lifted her in your arms. You've always been with her. You'll always be her father."

Ari reached up and touched Vartan's face, turning his chin slightly.

"Can I look at you, Vartan? I must see your eyes. They've always spoken for you," said Ari as he searched Vartan's eyes. "It's true, Vartan. Your eyes tell me that I did good. Vartan, what a gift you've brought me. What a gift."

Vartan's eyes glistened with tears, and he turned his face away, squeezing Ari tighter as he held him.

"What gift could I give you, Ari? What gift could ever take away all that you have suffered? I saw you hungry and alone as a child, and I did nothing. I saw pleading in your eyes, and I looked away. I'm ashamed."

"No, Vartan. Don't pity me. On this day of all days. Please just take my hand and share in my joy," said Ari, his trembling fingers searching for Vartan's hand. "Lena, that beautiful child is well, and you have found her. Oh, my beautiful child. Bless you, Vartan, for giving me this moment. Bless you."

Vartan could feel Ari's body trembling. Fighting back tears, he began rocking Ari as the two fell silent. He could hear the wind outside whistling as it began to blow, and the door of the cabin flew open. Vartan looked at the darkened doorway, and it was empty. He saw the leaves swirling in a six-foot vortex just outside the door. The dust devil began losing its energy and the leaves settled on the ground, until all was still, and there was only silence.

"Yes, sir, yes, sir. I'm coming. I'm ready now. I'm ready," said Ari, staring at the empty doorway.

Vartan could see that Ari's eyes suddenly had fresh life to them. But when Ari turned his eyes back to him, they looked feeble once more.

"Vartan, remember when we were in school, and we were sitting next to each other?" asked Ari.

"Yes, I remember," said Vartan, even though he had only a faint memory of Ari attending school.

"Do you remember when those boys wanted to race us? Do you think we would've beaten them? I think we would have, Vartan. I know we would have. You and me, we would've won," said Ari, his voice getting weaker and his words trailing off.

"Yes, Ari, we would've won," said Vartan as he wiped tears from his eyes.

"They couldn't beat us, Vartan. I know we would've won. I know we would have . . ."

Ari's lips curled in a faint smile and his eyes closed. Vartan felt Ari's body turn cold and saw his face ashen.

Vartan stopped fighting the tears and wept over his body—as only a friend could.

Epilogue

Vartan took what little money he had saved and bought a cemetery plot not far from the old Shackleton mansion. The burial ceremony was simple and solitary. The only ones in attendance were Vartan, the priest delivering last rites, a pair of gravediggers, and a curious white dove that seemed to take everything in from a nearby oak tree. Vartan bought Ari a black suit and was careful to bury him with all his personal effects except for one. Among Ari's few possessions was a mysterious letter inside of a crumpled, yellowed envelope. On the front was written: *To my son Ari.* To Vartan's surprise, the envelope was still sealed.

As the priest prayed over Ari's body, Vartan placed the envelope in one of the pockets of his trousers. He was intrigued by the letter but had decided to wait until after the ceremony to read it. Maybe it contained something that would help him understand Ari better. Maybe there was something about his daughter. At the very least, he thought, it would give Ari's mother a voice after so many years.

The priest finished his prayers, and Vartan laid a single rose on Ari's body. As he turned to walk away, he was surprised to notice that he was holding the envelope in his hand. His eyes locked in on the words on the front of the envelope.

To my son Ari. Four simple words, one simple message.

Vartan turned back, held the envelope in both hands and approached the casket. He placed the letter inside of Ari's jacket—over his heart. Vartan stepped away and the gravediggers sealed the casket, lowered it into the ground, and filled the grave with dirt.

Vartan had the grave marked with a simple tombstone shaped like a cross with an inscription that read:

ARI HOVHANNISYAN
1884–1947
"A NOBLE FATHER"

About the Author

Boban Jovanovski is a Detroit-based writer and business professional. A graduate of Wayne State University's school of journalism, Boban has experience writing in a variety of styles and fields, including news reporting, corporate communications, advertising copy, and public relations. A father and husband, Boban loves to learn and explore new cultures and enjoys sports, reading, traveling with his family, and sharing new adventures with his wife, Val.

Boban's lifelong love of history led him to discover and understand the tragic events of the Armenian Genocide. He was struck by how the trauma from an event that unfolded over a century ago was still prevalent in the Armenian community today. It inspired him to tell a story of struggle, sacrifice, and salvation within this historical setting. Boban hopes Ari's story not only commemorates the Armenian tragedy but also celebrates the moral models that guide each of us on our own journeys. They are our teachers, our judges, and our protectors. In the end, it's their example that we strive to live up to.